THE
SHADOW
KING

THE
SHADOW
KING

HARRY SIDEBOTTOM

ZAFFRE

First published in the UK in 2023
This edition published in 2024 by
ZAFFRE
An imprint of Zaffre Publishing Group
A Bonnier Books UK company
4th Floor, Victoria House, Bloomsbury Square, London WC1B 4DA
Owned by Bonnier Books
Sveavägen 56, Stockholm, Sweden

A CIP catalogue record for this book is
available from the British Library.

ISBN: 978-1-83877-799-9

Also available as an ebook

1 3 5 7 9 10 8 6 4 2

Typeset by IDSUK (Data Connection) Ltd
Printed and bound in Great Britain by Clays Ltd, Elcograf S.p.A.

Zaffre is an imprint of Zaffre Publishing Group
A Bonnier Books UK company
www.bonnierbooks.co.uk

Harry Sidebottom was brought up in racing stables in Newmarket where his father was a trainer. He took his Doctorate in Ancient History at Oxford University and has taught at various universities including Oxford. His career as a novelist began with his *Warrior of Rome series*.

Fiction
(The Warrior of Rome series)
Fire in the East
King of Kings
Lion of the Sun
The Caspian Gates
The Wolves of the North
The Amber Road
The Last Hour
The Burning Road
Falling Sky

(The Throne of the Caesars trilogy)
Iron & Rust
Blood & Steel
Fire & Sword

The Lost Ten
The Return

Non-fiction
Ancient Warfare: A Very Short Introduction
The Encyclopedia of Ancient Battles
(With Michael Whitby)
The Mad Emperor

To Lynne and Ernie Moss

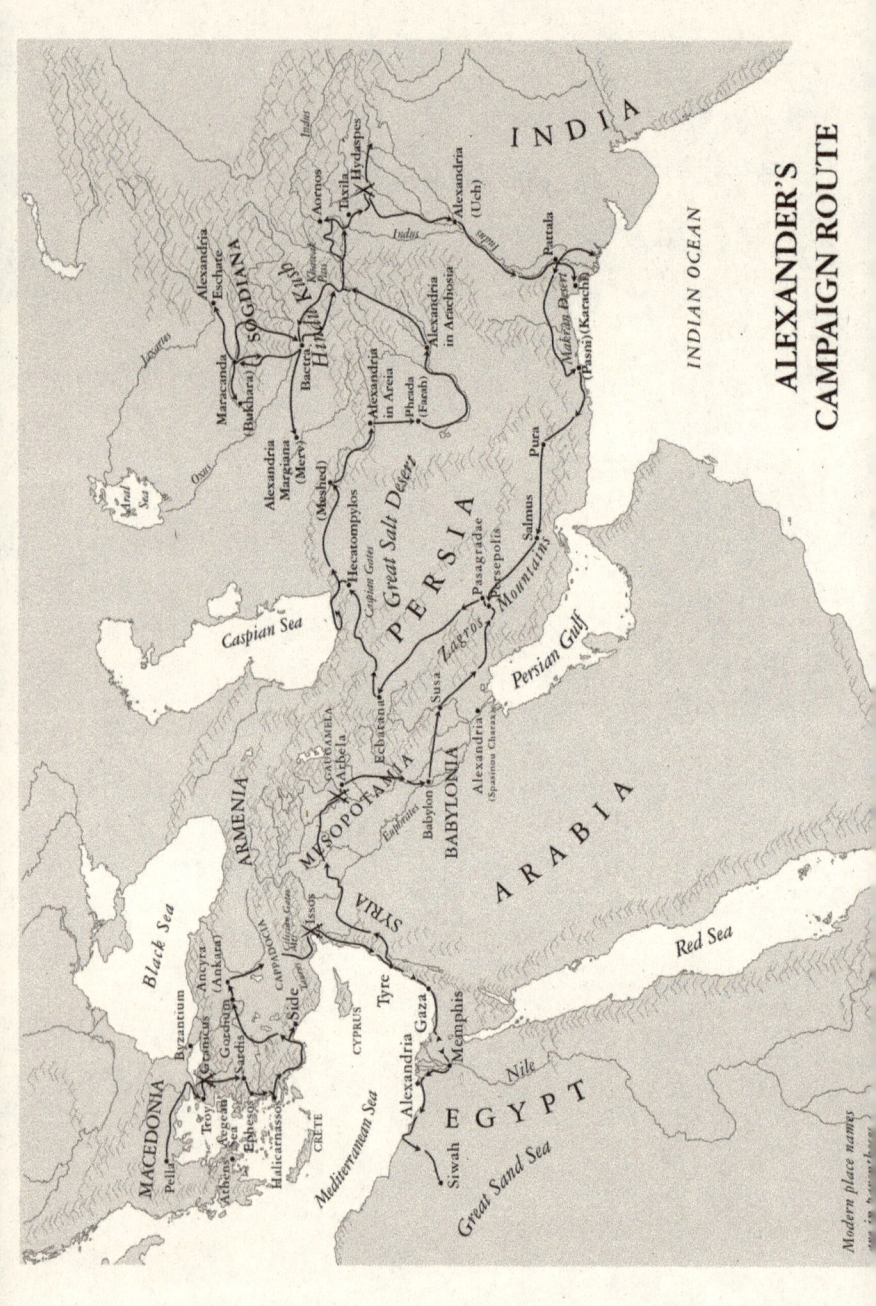

ALEXANDER'S
CAMPAIGN ROUTE

MACEDON

PAIONIA
ILLYRIA
Pelagonia
THRACE
R. Nestus
R. Stymon
Amphipolis
R. Axius
LYNCESTIS
Bottaia
Pella
Mieza
Eordaia
Aegae
ORESTIS
Chalkidike
Pydna
Elimeia
Pieria
Thermaic Gulf
Dion
EPIRUS
Tymphaia
THESSALY

A LIST OF MAIN CHARACTERS

Those in italics are fictional

Aeropus – Lord of Lyncestis, head of the Bacchiad house, father of Arrhabaeus, Heromenes, and Alexander Lyncestes, given to drink and flute-girls

Agathion – Tyrian slave-boy bought, and named ('Good-fellow'), by Alexander Lyncestes

Alexander of Lyncestis – youngest son of Aeropus, 'Xander to his family, Lyncestes to Alexander son of Philip, and to various Macedonians, Greeks and Persians he is *The Shadow King*

Alexander of Macedon – son of Philip II and Olympias, known to history as Alexander the Great

Amyntas (1) – son of Arrhabaeus, twin brother of Neoptolemus, pious nephew of Alexander of Lyncestis

Amyntas (2) – son of King Perdiccas III, nephew of Philip II, who set him aside to take the throne

Antigone – Macedonian slave girl, mistress of Philotas

Antigonus the one-eyed – senior Macedonian officer, commands the Greek allies at Gordion

Antipater – general of Philip and Alexander, father of Cassander, Iolaus, *Electra*, father-in-law of Alexander Lyncestes

Aristander – seer to Philip and Alexander

Aristotle – philosopher, and tutor to Alexander the Great and his foster-brothers at Mieza

Arrhabaeus (1) – taciturn son of Aeropus, brother of Heromenes and Alexander Lyncestes, father of the twins Neoptolemus and Amyntas

Arrhabaeus (2) – son of Alexander Lyncestes and *Electra*

Arrhidaeus – son of Philip II and Philine of Larissa, his mental deficiency rumoured to have been caused by poison administered by Olympias

Atarrhias – Macedonian veteran from Lyncestis in charge of camp servants

Attalus – Macedonian nobleman, uncle and adoptive father of Cleopatra (2), father-in-law of Philip II

Batis – Babylonian eunuch commanding city of Gaza for the Persians

Bessus – Persian kinsman of Darius III

Calas – Macedonian officer from former royal house of Elimea

Callisthenes – Greek court historian to Alexander the Great

Caranus – infant son of Philip II and Cleopatra (his reality is often doubted)

Cassander – sickly son of Antipater, detests Alexander the Great

Cleitus the Black – older Macedonian officer of traditional cast of mind

Cleopatra (1) – daughter of Philip II and Olympias

Cleopatra (2) – niece and adopted daughter of Attalus, wife of Philip II

Coenus – phalanx commander from Elimea, son-in-law of Parmenion, defender of Macedonian traditions

Copreus – Macedonian gaoler (perhaps of Thracian ancestry)

Craterus – from the former royal house of Orestis, dislikes Philotas, hates Hephaestion

Cynnane – daughter of Philip II and Audata the Illyrian

Darius III – Persian King of Kings

Demaratus of Corinth – old friend and envoy of Philip II

Demosthenes – Athenian orator, inveterate enemy of Philip II

Electra – daughter of Antipater, wife of Alexander Lyncestes (her real name is unknown)

Eumenes – Greek secretary to Alexander the Great

Eumaeus – Lyncestian veteran, serves Alexander of Lyncestis

Euphraeus – philosopher, pupil of Plato, once court philosopher in Macedon

Europa – infant daughter of Philip II and Cleopatra

Eurydice – mother of Philip II, from the Bacchiad house of Lyncestis

Harpalus – member of the former royal house of Elimea, lame and hunchbacked

Hector – son of Parmenion, a Royal Page

Hephaestion – foster-brother and lover of Alexander the Great, hates Craterus and Alexander Lyncestes

Heromenes – embittered son of Aeropus of Lyncestis, brother of Alexander Lyncestes, who calls him Horse-face

Iolaus – youngest son of Antipater, a Royal Page, lover of Medius of Thessaly

Leonnatus – kinsman and older friend of Alexander of Lyncestis

Leucippe – Tyrian slave-girl bought by Alexander Lyncestes

Machatas – head of the former royal house of Elimea, father of Harpalus

Medius of Thessaly – foster-brother of Alexander the Great, lover of Iolaus, son of Antipater, fond of a party

Memnon – ambitious Macedonian officer, who wants to be *Strategos* of Thrace

Memnon of Rhodes – Greek mercenary commander fighting for the Persians

Nearchus the Cretan – foster-brother of Alexander the Great

Neoptolemus – twin brother of Amyntas, the wilder nephew of Alexander of Lyncestis

Nicanor – son of Parmenion, brother of Philotas, commander of the *Hypaspists*

Olympias – wife of Philip II, mother of Alexander the Great, worshipper of Dionysus, said to be a witch, schemes against Alexander Lyncestes

Parmenion – general of Philip and Alexander, father of Philotas, Nicanor, and Hector

Pausanias – from Orestis, Royal Page, and sometime lover of Philip II

Pausanias *Kalos* – Royal Page, and lover of Philip II

Perdiccas – phalanx commander, member of former royal house of Orestis

Peucestas of Mieza – young Macedonian officer, who speaks Persian

Philip (1) – Philip II, Argead King of Macedon, father of Alexander, Arrhidaeus, Cleopatra, Cynnane, Thessalonice, *Caranus* and Europa

Philip (2) – son of Amyntas, phalanx commander from lowland Pieria

Philip (3) – son of Menelaus, Macedonian officer, takes over Thessalian cavalry at Gordion

Philip (4) – Greek doctor to Alexander the Great

Philotas – son of Parmenion, held to be arrogant, dislikes Craterus

Ptolemy – young Macedonian noble, rumoured to be an illegitimate son of Philip II

Rhascus – Thracian kinsman of Sitalkes

Roxane – daughter of a Bactrian chief, wife of Alexander the Great

Seuthes – Thracian, elder brother of Sitalkes

Sisines – Persian nobleman, suspected of being a spy

Sitalkes – Thracian, son of King Cersobleptes of the Odrysians

Timocleia – a Greek woman from Thebes

Zopyrion – ambitious Macedonian officer in Thrace

PROLOGUE

Summer 323 BC

I, ALEXANDER OF LYNCESTIS, WILL die in the morning. Far from home, under a pitiless sun, in the gaze of Alexander the King and of all the Macedonians, my friends and companions will kill me.

Do I deserve this fate? Am I a traitor? Those are questions for you to answer. I have tried to do the right thing, to remain true to the ways of my ancestors, to show courage. Once, when I was young, I prayed: *If I must die, let me first do some great thing, that men hereafter shall remember me.* I have done some extraordinary things, not all of them good, but that prayer, too, is now in your hands.

It is late, and my kinsman Leonnatus is waiting. I will finish now, and give him these rolls of papyri. He will keep his side of our pact, and find some safe place to preserve my story.

I will keep my side of the pact when I die in the morning. Unless . . . When Pandora opened the jar, and all the evils in the world flew out to torment mankind, Hope remained. Despite everything, even in this darkest of nights, Hope remains to torment me.

CHAPTER ONE

Winter 343 to 342 BC

TRACKS IN THE SNOW.

Winter comes early in Upper Macedonia, and it comes first to the mountains of Lyncestis. A blind man could have followed the trail of the raiders. The snow was spattered with dung, pockmarked with the prints of boots and the hooves of sheep, trodden to slush in the centre of the path. They were heading west, to the pass up at Crystal Spring, and beyond to the safety of their tribal lands in Illyria.

Leonnatus halted the column, got down from his horse, and went ahead on foot with old Eumaeus to study the tracks. The rest of us dismounted to take the weight from the horses. Forty riders, swaddled in heavy cloaks, breath pluming in the cold air. It was an unimpressive gathering. No more than a dozen men of fighting age. The remainder were greybeards, *doves* as they are called, or mere youths, no older than me. Almost all the warriors were away in the lowlands serving in the army of King Philip.

I looked at the twins, my nephews. Amyntas, piety sharpened by fear, was mouthing a prayer to Heracles the Ancestor. Perhaps he was unaware that he was speaking aloud. Even his brother, Neoptolemus, usually so wild and carefree, looked tense as he fussed with the bridle of his mount. By an accident of birth, I was no older than the two of them. This was our fourteenth winter. Sometimes my father called me the runt of the litter. Not because I am short, but because I was so late born. My brothers were already grown men. In his cups my father had a cruel tongue.

Leonnatus returned. My father, the head of the Bacchiad House, the Lord of Lyncestis, should have been leading, but he too was away at the court of Philip. Had my mother not been too old she would have taken command. Leonnatus was only a couple of years my senior. Yet he was a close kinsman, from a collateral branch of the house, despite his inexperience, the men would follow him.

'The droppings are fresh.' Leonnatus drew himself up, and tipped his head to one side. Somehow I knew the posture was copied from someone else. 'Eumaeus tells me there are no more than twenty Illyrians, none of them mounted. They are less than an hour ahead. We will catch them well before Crystal Spring. The approach to the pass is wide, at least a hundred and fifty paces across. The snow is not yet deep, the going there good. Ideal country for cavalry. We will outflank them, ride them down as they run.'

'So much for Bilip conquering the Illyrians,' one of the greybeards muttered in the thick Macedonian dialect that pronounced *Ph* as *B*.

Leonnatus swung round angrily. Broad shouldered and thickset, he was more impressive when he dropped the artificial pose and moved naturally. 'This is nothing. Before Philip defeated their chieftains thousands of tribesmen would have been burning your homesteads, raping your wives and daughters, not a handful of outlaws rustling a flock of sheep.' Although a scion of the Lyncestian dynasty, Leonnatus, had been a Royal Page for two years, and had recently been named as a foster-brother of

Philip's son, my namesake Alexander. It was unwise to forget that he was devoted to the Argead King of the lowlands in distant Pella.

Free speech is the birth right of every Macedonian. The lowest swineherd can speak openly to a king. Now, nobody contradicted Leonnatus. The truth of what he said was undeniable.

We remounted in silence. Vaulting onto the back of my horse – never easy in war-gear – I was careful that the heavy scabbard did not tangle my jump. A sword does not hang properly from a rope belt. In Lyncestis we kept the old ways. Instead of a sword-belt a man must wear a halter, like a horse, until he has killed an enemy.

The road followed a stream. The water slid past, glossy and black. The way curved between folded slopes of ridges, most timbered in beech and oak, some bare. Where the view opened the peaks of the mountains were dark, sharp and black against the sky. Clouds were beginning to build over the summits. Soon it would snow again. It was only *Audounaios*, the first month of winter, but within days the pass would be blocked.

Above the headwaters of the stream, where the deciduous trees had given way to pine and juniper, was the tiny plateau of Three Ways. The main track ran west towards the pass. Another headed south to the Macedonian canton of Orestis. The Illyrians knew we were coming. They had taken the narrow goat path north, which clambered over the great, humped rock to Lake Lyke. That was the end of the hope of an easy victory, of riding them down in the open. But our honour would not let us turn back.

Leonnatus left five of the *doves*, the oldest and most infirm, with the horses. We formed up on foot into a rough column five wide. As befitted my status – a member of the House of

Lyncestis should always be among the *promachoi*, the front-fighters – I went to stand beside Leonnatus. But he called eight of the men of fighting age to his side. You do not argue with the war leader in the field, but sensing my hurt pride, he put a hand on my shoulder.

'Alexander, in close country an ambush falls as often on the tail as the head. They are the places of greatest danger. Take your nephews, and the other four men in their prime, and command the rearguard.'

Swelling with pride, I stationed myself at the right of the final rank, the unshielded side.

Before we moved out, Leonnatus sent Eumaeus ahead as a scout. Although well past the strength of his youth, Eumaeus had been a mighty warrior, and no one was a finer hunter or woodsman.

We had gone no distance when the slopes closed in, and my pride deserted me. Ahead I could see nothing but the nodding horsehair plumes of helmets. On either side the trunks of huge, ancient pines blocked the view. The clatter of our gear echoed back. The air smelt of new sweat and old leather and the sickly resin of the trees. Any number of barbarians could be hiding a few paces away. Fear rose in my chest, like a sharp shard of stone.

I had waited all my life for this; the blood rite to manhood. Now it was approaching, with the inevitability of dusk, I wished I was somewhere else. Even back with the children in the Hall at Lebaea, watching my mother oversee her women at the looms, warm and safe.

As we trudged up the path, I could not take my eyes off the slope to the right. There was little undergrowth, and the snow had not yet penetrated the foliage. But the pines were massive. Two grown men could not link their arms round their trunks. Vision was limited to a stone's throw. Nothing moved. No wind sighed through the trees. There were no birds. I clenched my jaws to stop my teeth chattering. It was not the cold. Sweat was running down between my shoulder blades. Not all youths pass the test. There were *doves* in the party who still wore the rope halter.

A glimpse of movement. Too quick to identify. Some thirty paces upslope. I did not cry out. It would be shameful to yell if it was no more than a deer or rabbit. There it was again. Pale tan, camouflaged against the bare earth, moving parallel to the column. Leonnatus called a halt to catch our breath. The men talked quietly to each other, their voices tight. It started to snow. The first flakes small, twisting, but falling straight down.

The lynx padded out from behind the gnarled bole of a tree. It was a mature adult, full bearded. Its dappled body was some four feet long, with powerful shoulders and haunches. Its ears swept back in magnificent black tufts. The beast stopped, and looked at me. Its pale green eyes, luminous in the shade, regarded me. The murmuring of the men faded. No one else had noticed the visitation. Then, without haste, the lynx continued on its way, and was gone.

'Alexander!' The voice of Neoptolemus snapped me back. The men were hefting spears and shields, the column preparing to get underway.

The old women say that if you look into the eyes of a lynx it will steal your sight, and you will live out your life as a blind man, begging for crusts. It was a story for nurses to frighten children, to keep them out of the woods. Lyncestis is the land of the lynx. It is the sigil of our house. Some deity had sent the sign to remind me of my duty. The words of Homer came into my mind: *Indeed, these are no ignoble men, these kings of ours, who feed upon the fat sheep, and drink the exquisite sweet wine, since there is strength of valour in them, since they fight in the forefront.*

My chest was still tight, but the rank fear had gone. My senses were heightened, as if I could count every spinning flake of snow, hear each one fall. The air smelt different, rich with the lanolin scent of sheep, and sharp with the sour tang of the long unwashed bodies of men.

It is our duty in the forefront to take our stand, and bear our part of the blazing of battle.

'They are round the next corner, at the top of a rise.' Eumaeus was back. 'The gradient is steep, but the path is wider; enough for eight men abreast in open order.'

Leonnatus told the men where to take their places. Twenty-four would make the assault in three ranks. Leonnatus would lead, the rest of the dozen men of fighting age with him in the vanguard. The remaining eleven in the party – my nephews and myself, along with the other youngsters and the very aged – would form the reserve, under the leadership of Eumaeus.

I swallowed the slight, shamefully relieved not to have the responsibility. We took off our heavy winter cloaks, and left them by the side of the track. I looked at the older men, and wondered which of the poor old bastards would not need them later. Any thought of my own mortality had gone.

There was no uniformity to our armour. Men wore their own, or items taken from the storeroom or off the walls of the Great Hall at Lebaea. There were open, fluted helmets, favoured by cavalrymen, and those with cheekpieces, both the ones called Phrygian with tall metal peaks like the bow of a ship, and the plainer ones often used by the chiefs of the Illyrians. The cuirasses were of metal, leather, or linen. A few men were snapping on bronze greaves to protect their shins, but the rest of us remained in our riding boots. All the shields – which we would have left with our cloaks if we had been fighting on horseback, as we had expected – bore different devices painted in every colour of the rainbow. Most were the circular Macedonian type without a rim, although a handful of men carried the wider and heavier shields of the Hellenes in the south, and a couple had brought light Thracian *peltae* fashioned like a crescent moon.

My fingers were clumsy as I retied the laces of my Phrygian helmet. I had chosen it hoping its comb would make me look taller when Eumaeüs was training me. Now its metal cheekpieces, reaching down to my chin, offered a certain reassurance. Likewise my linen corselet was familiar from long hours on the training ground. It fitted perfectly, as my mother and her women had altered it to my physique. It was dyed a brilliant white. Once, when practising fighting with staves, Neoptolemus had caught me a blow which gashed my head. The blood had splashed bright onto the white linen. The memory was ill-omened, and I pushed it away.

While our defensive equipment was ill-matched, at least there was some consistency in our weaponry. None of us had the *sarissa*, the national weapon of Macedon, the long pike wielded with both hands. Only an elite mounted unit can use the *sarissa*, which calls for much training, and this thrown-together posse was far from that. Instead we had each brought a *xyston*, the standard shorter cavalry spear, as useful on foot as on horseback. Its cornel wood shaft was tough, and if the head was hacked off, there was another blade at the other end. The butt-spike, the *lizard-killer*, was razor sharp. If that failed, every man had a sword.

'It is time to step onto the dancing floor of Ares, ladies.' The joke was ancient, almost habitual, but most of us managed to grin at Leonnatus' words.

Rounding the corner, and shuffling into formation, we saw the ground and the enemy. The path was indeed steep for fighting, perhaps one in five, and the heavily timbered sides of the gully steeper yet. The Illyrians waited on the skyline. Eight across, but impossible to say how many deep. In their all-enveloping black felt cloaks, they resembled a close packed encampment of tents, yet there was a terrible menace in their silent immobility. Glancing to my side, I saw Amyntas and Neoptolemus were white faced with apprehension. Like me, they would be steeling themselves for the fight.

Supposing you and I, escaping this battle,
Would be able to live on forever, ageless, immortal,
So neither would I myself go on fighting in the foremost
Nor would I urge you into the fighting where men earn glory.

The sky had the yellow tinge of a coming storm, and already the snow was falling more heavily.

Leonnatus stepped out from the ranks, then turned to address the men.

'We are down here, they are up there. We are Macedonians, they are Illyrians. We grit our teeth, and stand close to the steel. They see no dishonour in flight. We are armoured, they are not.

We are freemen, many of them are slaves. We need to be up there. Our ancestors saw off the Spartans. One charge and these Illyrians will take to their heels.'

A low growl of approval met his words. Its bluff enumeration of our advantages made up for any lack of rhetorical elaboration.

'Raise the war cry, advance at a walk, charge when I do.'

Leonnatus walked back. Now, almost as if they had been waiting for him to finish, the Illyrians stirred. They cast off their dark cloaks, and stood almost bare to the elements in their striped sleeveless tunics.

Al-al-al-al-ai! Our chant raised the hairs on my neck. As it built, the men began to rhythmically beat the shafts of their spears on their shields. The noise echoed back from the slopes, filled the air. Then it faltered.

Two Illyrian warriors led a small boy out of their ranks. From his dress he was a Macedonian, probably a shepherd boy captured with his flock. One of the Illyrians spread his hands wide, palms down to the ground. His breath steamed in the frigid air as he intoned some prayer. The other caught the boy by the hair, dragged his head back, and cut his throat. They both stepped back to observe the death throes of the child.

The barbaric sacrifice was too much for Leonnatus' men. With a roar, they set off up the path, all order vanished. I saw Leonnatus shouting and gesturing. When he realised he could not hold them back, he joined the stampede.

Even the youths and greybeards of the reserve started to be drawn after them. My nephews and I shuffling forward with the rest. Eumaeus, sprightly for his age, leapt out in front. He turned, faced us, held his spear horizontal across the path.

'We are stationed here, and here we will stay!'

Shamefaced at our lack of discipline, we halted.

'Dress your lines behind me! Two ranks of five.'

We did as we were ordered. In the confusion I had become the right-hand man in the second rank, Neoptolemus to my front, Amyntas on my left.

We watched as the vanguard streamed up the hill. It was about a hundred paces to the top. The Illyrians were capering, brandishing their weapons, and screaming like disturbed gulls.

When our men had almost reached the little corpse, were no more than twenty paces away, the Illyrians hurled their javelins. Some found their mark. Three or four Macedonians went down. But the charge was not checked. Leonnatus' men crashed shield on shield into the barbarians. The din of the impact rolled down the slope like the sound of a great wave crashing onto a cliff.

We stood, rooted to the spot, deafened by the cacophony. We were lost in the drama of the combat, oblivious to anything else, like women in the rites of Dionysus. I sniffed the air. My sense of smell had always been keen, but a god put this in my mind. Perhaps Herakles the Ancestor. A stench of unclean humanity. Illyrians only wash three times: birth, marriage, and death.

Dragging my eyes from the fighting, I saw them coming down the side of the gully, ten or twelve of them. Each had a conical shield and a couple of spears, but they were as agile as goats, using the trees to brake their descent. Fear held my tongue. My mortality pressed hard upon me. *If I must die, let me first do some great thing, that men hereafter shall remember me.* And I shouted.

'On the right, Illyrians! Form line to the right!'

The men looked round, stupid and slow with surprise. I grabbed Amyntas, dragged him forward to stand at my right shoulder.

A tribesman cast a spear. It streaked towards my face. I leapt sideways, felt the wind of the missile slicing past my head. Clumsily, I collided with Neoptolemus. He staggered. Scrambling to regain my balance, I pushed my shield out in front, wielded my spear overhand in my right. The Illyrian lunged. Somehow I got my shield in the way. There was a loud crack. The impact jarred up my arm into my shoulder. The shield was split in half, useless. I threw the thing away, backed off, gripped the shaft of my spear two handed, underarm.

The warrior gathered himself, spear point weaving like a snake, seeking an opening. He was bearded, and wore a round hat, like an upside down bird's nest. From a baldric over his shoulder hung a curved sword with its hilt carved in the shape of an eagle. He wore no belt, and his loose tunic billowed about him.

When the Illyrian feinted to my right, I covered the movement with my spear. Too late I realised my mistake. He was past the blade of my spear, and thrusting at my chest. The training ground and Eumaeus saved me. Memory took over. My left foot went back, my spear came up vertical, my body twisted, and the shaft of my spear pushed his strike wide. Using the weight of my weapon as a pendulum, I brought the butt-spike up into his midriff. He grunted with pain. No time to reverse my spear, I drove forward. The Illyrian went back. His feet slipped, and he went down. I was over him. With all my weight, I pushed the lizard-killer into his stomach. A slight resistance, then it was as easy as driving a stake into wet ground. He gasped out his life, fingers grasping at the smooth shaft of cornel wood.

'Alexander!'

Another Illyrian was coming at me from the left. The lizard-killer was stuck in the ribs of my victim. I grabbed for my sword.

The wretched halter had shifted. The hilt was behind my back, hard to draw. It was all too late. A foot of sharp steel was almost in my teeth. Then the wicked spear point jerked aside. The warrior crumpled to his knees. Behind him Eumaeus wheeled away like a big mountain cat. Neoptolemus punched the tip of his spear between the shoulder blades of the Illyrian.

'They are running!'

Amyntas was beside me, panting, leaning on his spear like an old man. The blade was covered in gore, blood running down over his fingers.

The Illyrians were scrambling up the hillside. Pale in the gloom under the trees, they looked like white fish swimming up a dark river.

There were Macedonians cheering up the track at the crest. It was snowing hard. The fight was over.

CHAPTER TWO

Winter 343 to 342 BC

HIGH ON A SPUR of the mountains, Lebaea has been a refuge forever. The outer walls were the work of the Giants before the time of men. The Great Hall was built by Bromerus the Founder, the other buildings by my more recent ancestors. There was only one practical approach for an army, the track up from the east. Lebaea had been the cornerstone of the power of the Kings of Lyncestis. It had never fallen to an assault. Just one surrender had broken our independence.

Riding up from the Plain of Lyncestis, the limestone fortress gleamed white against the pine-clad slopes in the clear winter sunshine. A great plume of smoke, as if from some hecatomb to the gods, rose above the stronghold. We had been three days out. After the battle we had rounded up the sheep, penned them at Three Ways, and lit a huge fire. We roasted two of the animals. The owners would not begrudge the tithe after the return of the rest. Although there was little wine, some of the warriors had danced in armour, the metal and their eyes flashing in the firelight. The second day, we had driven the flock down to its winter pasture. Now we were heading home.

The battle had been hard fought. Three of our men were dead, seven others carried wounds more serious than a scratch. The Illyrian numbers had been greater than twenty. It was generally accepted that there had been another party waiting in the hills to cover the retreat of the raiders. Leonnatus and Eumaeus had not misread the tracks. No one made the point that Leonnatus had led us into a trap, from which we had been saved only by our prowess and the sacrifice of our comrades.

The Illyrians had left a dozen men on the field. As we held the ground, we finished off their wounded, and stripped the corpses. Unlike the Hellenes, it is not a custom of the Macedonians to build a trophy. Although the Illyrians were barbarians we placed a coin from the meagre plunder in the mouth of each, and sprinkled a little dust on their heads. If the rite was not observed, if they could not pay the ferryman, their shades would walk, and might seek vengeance. After that, we left them for the birds. Our own dead we had strapped across their horses to give them back to their families. For some our return would be a thing of tragedy.

A trumpet sounded from the battlements as we neared the gate. Rattling under the arch, we saw the courtyard was bustling with servants and horses. It could only mean one thing, and my spirits sank. The groom who took my horse confirmed my fears. My father was visiting from the lowlands, and with him my brother Heromenes. There would be a feast in the Great Hall.

Water had been heated for baths in the private quarters for the four members of the dynasty in our party. Leonnatus had already gone to report to my father when I announced that I would wash at the well in the courtyard. Neoptolemus said he would join me. Amyntas said we were as pig-headed as each other.

The old ways are hard. A new-born baby is placed on its back on a hard floor to toughen and flatten the back of its head. Only after childbirth should a Macedonian woman bathe in warm water, a man never.

Even now doubtless servants in Lebaea will talk of us breaking the ice. The water was cold, terribly cold, but there was no ice. We stood naked, sluicing ourselves down, roaring with the cold. Out of sight, I could hear women wailing, mourning the dead.

Dripping, we raced to our quarters. Two servant girls towelled us dry, rubbed us with sweet-scented oil. Our Lyncestian forebears might have looked askance at such luxury, especially when Neoptolemus retired for some privacy with his serving girl, but I knew the point had been made, and that news would reach my father. Dismissing my girl, I dressed in a white tunic, dragged back my still damp long hair with my fingers, and put on a pair of sandals. Finally, I hung the eagle-headed sword that I had taken from the Illyrian from the rope halter round my waist.

When Neoptolemus returned, I waited while he dressed, then we set off for the feast.

It was late afternoon, and the torches were lit in the hall. The couches and chairs were arranged along both sides. Most were already occupied; men to our left, women to the right. Through the smoke rising from the central hearth, at the far end could be seen two thrones. They were both the same size, the dark wood elaborately carved with lynxes and other fierce beasts, their eyes inlaid with jade and precious stones. My mother sat next to my father. Macedonian women, especially in the highlands, are very little like those of the veiled and secluded Athenian elite. Many of the females of the five great houses of Upper Macedonia are trained in arms. Time after time over the centuries it has proved its worth, when the warlords were away, and the Illyrians came raiding. Someone had to lead the levy protecting the flocks and the strongholds.

I greeted my mother in Macedonian style: right hand raised, palm towards her. It was a gesture of benediction, and also showed the arrival had no weapon in hand. My mother stood, and I went and kissed her cheek.

'Xander,' she said. Only my family called me that. My mother smelt of jasmine. Her face, framed by ringlets of gold wire plaited into her hair, was unmoving and regal. But her eyes shone with pride and affection.

Turning to my father, I made the same gesture. Aeropus, Lord of Lyncestis, made a cursory wave of the hand. He did not rise, and I had to stoop to kiss his cheek. Close to, his eyes were slightly glazed. There was already a smell of wine about him.

The formalities perfunctorily concluded, Aeropus motioned to his steward. The old retainer came forward holding a white cloth sash and a sword-belt of white leather. I took the bird-headed sword from the rope halter, untied the latter, and let it drop to the floor. Still my father remained seated. The steward tied the sash of manhood round my waist, slung the sword-belt over my right shoulder. Finally, I attached the scabbard of the Illyrian blade to the belt.

'The Late Born has become a man early.' My father spoke to my mother in a tone almost of surprise. 'You always said there were big paws on the puppy.'

'Alexander is born from a line of mighty warriors.' Her voice left no doubt that she referred to her own bloodline. The Lords of Orestis had ruled in the uplands even longer than us Bacchiads. Orestes, in the generation after the fall of Troy, had founded their kingdom while in exile from Mycenae.

I stepped back, seething with anger, and watched while my father showed the same lack of respect as he let his retainer fit the sword-belts and sashes of Amyntas and Neoptolemus. The latter was given a baldric of bright scarlet, tooled leather, which pricked my envy.

When my nephews were standing beside me, Leonnatus came forth, and presented Aeropus with the plumed helmet that he had stripped from the Illyrian chieftain. In days gone by it would have been the head itself. My father examined the thing, like a child would a new toy, then handed Neoptolemus a golden cup. Among his many vices, meanness was not one. If anything, Aeropus was widely considered a spendthrift.

The ceremony concluded, my father bade the trumpeter sound the note for the feast.

My nephews and I were shown to our places. We did not recline, but sat upon upright chairs, as we had yet to kill a wild boar unaided and without nets. We were halfway down the men's side of the hall. Although neither showed it, I knew my nephews felt we were not shown enough honour.

My father reclined at the head of the room. By rights he should have shared the couch with his victorious kinsman Leonnatus, or his adult son Heromenes. Instead, he lounged with Damasippus, a lowland drinking companion from the army. Damasippus had a reputation for coarse buffoonery and prodigious drinking. Even before the food, both men were draining their cups. Aeropus was quaffing from the Cup of Heracles. The flagon was an heirloom that held a suitably heroic amount.

On the second couch, Leonnatus was putting himself out to be amiable. It had little effect on Heromenes. Both my brothers were taciturn. As a child I thought that they resented me; always I was our mother's favourite. Over the years I had realised that they were the same with everyone. The silence of Arrhabaeus came from shyness. The father of the twins was diffident, never putting himself forward, easily led. With Heromenes it was something else. There was a sour bitterness about Heromenes, as if life had done him a bad turn. The impression was not ameliorated by his looks. The rest of the Bacchiads are handsome; tall, well built, with the blue eyes of our Hellenic forebears in Corinth. Heromenes' head was too long, and his teeth prominent and too large. Privately, Neoptolemus and I knew him as Horse-face.

The tables were brought in. Mine was shared with Amyntas. Although I cared for my nephew, he was seldom light-hearted company, nearly as dour as his father and uncle. Dutiful and pious were the words most often used of Amyntas. And now he was sulking, having correctly interpreted my washing in the cold water of the well as a thing designed to irritate my luxury-loving father.

The food was plentiful, great platters of roast meat. Although my mind was elsewhere, I ate with the appetite of youth. I have no great stomach for wine, but several times I called for my cup to be refilled. We Macedonians drink our wine unmixed with water, unlike the effete Hellenes of the south.

As Amyntas was not inclined to talk, I gazed at the hearth in the middle of the hall. Our house is old. Not as ancient as that of Orestis, but still old; twelve generations in Lyncestis. We were here when the ancestors of King Philip arrived. The very hearth in this hall had been our undoing. There had been three brothers, for some crime outlawed from Argos in the Peloponnese. In the kindness and simplicity of his heart, Bromerus the Founder had taken them on as labourers. The youngest, Perdiccas, was set to watch the goats. But the youth was a thief. Every day he stole twice his allowance of bread. When banished, they had the temerity to ask for their wages. Bromerus pointed to the sunlight coming down through the smoke hole: *There are your wages.*

With typical Argead guile, young Perdiccas took his dagger, three times he drew it round the outline of the sunlight coming down from the smoke hole and shining around the hearth, three times he mimed gathering the sunlight into the folds of his tunic. When they had left, the companions of the King explained the magic to Bromerus. The Founder sent men on horseback after them. The fugitives had just forded the Beres River, when they were sighted by the mounted men. Some malign deity, or some Argead witchcraft, suddenly raised the river in spate. The Lyncestians could not cross, the brothers made their escape, and Perdiccas founded the kingdom in the lowlands.

Although from the start the Argeads flaunted the sunburst on their standards and shields, it took centuries for the magic to claim our hearth. Time after time Philip's ancestors marched against us, time after time we sent them homeward. Even when they enlisted the Spartans, under their great general Brasidas, we drove them back into the lowlands. Three years before I was born, Perdiccas III, the elder brother of Philip, marched into the highlands, and made camp beside the Beres. This time the river did not betray Lyncestis. By its banks my grandfather, Arrhabaeus III, with his own hands cut down the Argead King. Four thousand lowlanders died with Perdiccas. The river ran red, and the warriors in the Great Hall of Lebaea thought the magic was broken, and our hearth would remain free forever.

They were mistaken. Philip came the following summer. He was only Regent then, before he set aside Amyntas, his brother's son, and took the throne. Argeads can never be trusted, especially by their closest relatives. Philip came with his new army forged as his brother's governor in the east in many battles against the wild Thracians. Out on the plains, at the Hyacinth Meadow, his cavalry outnumbered ours. When our horsemen had been driven off, Arrhabaeus rallied our foot, and those of his ally Bardylis of Illyria, and formed them into a square. Assailed from all sides, they held out through the heat of the day, until, near dusk, both Arrhabaeus and Bardylis were killed fighting in the front rank. It is said seven thousand were left dead on the field when the square broke.

After the disaster my father made the ritual submission, offered earth and water, and swore the oath of allegiance to Philip. To save his life, for the first time a Bacchiad surrendered the stronghold of Lebaea. And that was the end of our freedom. Finally, we had been conquered by Argead cunning.

'A toast with you, madam,' Aeropus called across to my mother.

Such a thing would have been unthinkable at the court of Philip, where they aped the manners of the Hellenes. With a shudder of distaste, they would have accused us of behaving like Illyrians or some other barbarians. Yet, of course, we were holding to the ancestral Macedonian customs, which they were abandoning.

My mother returned the toast. The cup from which she drank was small. Public drunkenness is shameful in a woman. Traditional freedoms are one thing, licence another.

The servants were removing the remains of the meat, bringing in a dessert of nuts and fruit and pastries. Damasippus whispered to my father. Despite their grey hair, they both giggled like immature youths.

'We have brought sophisticated entertainment, three skilled flute-girls, all the way from Corinth,' my father said.

'Then I and the women will leave you.' The look my mother gave her husband was not fond. Marriages for love were best left to the poets I read with my tutor. They cause nothing but grief. In Macedonia, among the peasantry as much as the elite, betrothals were family affairs, made for land, influence, or some other mutual advantage. Love might develop over time, but mutual respect was the best that might be expected. Sometimes, as in the marriage of my parents, even the latter failed to appear.

My mother stood, and led the women out. One or two pudding-faced farmers' daughters quickly stuffed into their mouths a handful of sweet delicacies. They were still chewing as they trailed after my mother.

Impatient, before all the respectable females had left, my father rang a bell. The noise jangled my nerves. A bell is only fit for sheep or goats not a servant. I took another swig of the dark wine.

Three figures emerged from the door to my father's private rooms. They were veiled and wrapped in voluminous robes that betrayed nothing of their figures. I thought of my namesake Alexander, the Macedonian King long ago. When ambassadors from Persia had been behaving disgracefully at a feast, demanding reputable Macedonian women for their entertainment, he had thus disguised some young warriors. Under their robes they had carried daggers. The bodies of the easterners were buried secretly. The King of Kings never discovered their fate. There was no Persian revenge. Sometimes Argead duplicity was to be admired.

The three figures stood motionless in the centre of the hall. It was so quiet, you could hear the logs ticking in the fire. The anticipation was palpable, it caught in your throat.

At a gesture from my father, the robes slid to the floor. There was a low intake of breath from the watching men, released as a collective sigh of lust. Underneath the girls wore nothing but tunics so sheer and clinging the material might have been soaked. Somehow it was more revealing than if they had been naked.

Two were olive skinned, had tumbling black hair. The third was blonde. She was the dancer. As the others played, she began to move. Languorously, she swayed. She was tall, her breasts round and firm. Her nipples were clear through the diaphanous material. She moved faster. The men started to beat out the rhythm with their cups upon the tables. Lascivious beyond measure, her hands ran over her own body. Faster and faster, as if coming to the end of the act of love.

Then it was over. She collapsed, panting, to the floor. The men cheered, clapped, called out witticisms and compliments. I looked across at my father and Damasippos. They were the only men not looking at the girl. Doubtless they had enjoyed her before. Instead, they were measuring the reaction of the other diners. They might as well have shouted we have had her and you never will. A petty act of power, unworthy of their position.

The germ of an idea formed in my mind. I wondered if Neoptolemus was thinking something similar. Then I crushed the idea. It would lead to nothing but trouble. An argument over a slave girl had brought terrible suffering to the Achaeans in the *Iliad*.

My father waved the blonde to come to the couch he shared with Damasippos. Smiling, she got up from the floor. She had a beautiful smile – no matter how insincere – it was wasted on those old goats. Both men pawed her as she wriggled up between them.

Aeropus gave her the Cup of Heracles. As she struggled to sip from the heavy thing, he laughed, and recited some lines of Homer.

I for the sake of the girl Chryseis would not take
The shining ransom; and indeed I wish greatly to have her
In my own house; since I like her better than Klytaimnestra
My own wife, for in truth she is no way inferior,
Neither in build nor stature nor wit . . .

This was going too far. My father caught my eye. His face, already flushed with wine, darkened. He snatched the ceremonial cup back from the girl, brusquely told his steward to fill it to the brim, and drained it in one pull. Then pointed at me.

'A toast with you, my late-born son.'

Standing, I took the cup in both hands. The red wine looked fathomless. Everyone was staring at me. There was nothing for it. I would not be faced down by this man. Steadying myself, I began to drink. There was no end to it. Once, I paused to get my breath, and heard a mocking laugh. Again I tipped the vessel. Finally it was empty.

There was a roar of approbation from the men. My father was regarding me with disfavour.

Already my head was buzzing. I gestured the steward to fill the thing again.

'Another toast with you, my father.'

Aeropus laughed. 'Big paws on the puppy.' Again he drained it in one practised motion.

The cup was back in my hands. My stomach was bloated and queasy, my head clouded by wine fumes. *To Hades with him.* I started to drink. This time I had drunk no more than a quarter when I felt my gorge rise. Stopping, gasping like a landed fish, I closed my ears to the noises round me. The humiliation would be the result of my own pride. No, I would not face his scorn. Lifting the cup, I opened my throat, let the choking liquid pour into my guts. Some splashed down onto my tunic. It was like drowning, torture. And then it was empty.

Then men thundered their approval.

My father looked like a spoilt infant robbed of some treat.

Carefully, I handed the cup to the steward. My head was reeling, my innards fighting to rebel. What was going to happen was inevitable. But not yet, not in front of him.

'I give you joy of your return, Father.' I enunciated every word as if it was something precious. 'Now it has been a long day on the road, and I will take my leave.'

Walking the length of the hall was a trial. Everything in me was urging me to run. But I kept to a walk. Every step placed with extreme care. *Do not stagger. Don't give him that satisfaction.* The wine was welling up at the back of my throat. *Not yet, just a little time longer.* Breathing in through my nose, and out from my mouth. Deaf to those who spoke to me. Trying to ignore the hideous smell of stale food and drink. A servant opened the great doors. I turned on the threshold, saluted the company.

Out of the bright rectangle of light, I tried to run. It was more of a lurching stumble. In the darkness at the corner of the hall, I could go no further. Doubling up, grabbing the wall, I threw up convulsively. Once started, it was impossible to stop. The vomit burnt the back of my throat, clogged my nostrils. I could not draw breath, but still my body voided the stinking wine and half-digested food.

'Here, rinse your mouth with this.'

Leonnatus handed me a goblet. I sluiced the clean water round my teeth and spat.

'You did well,' Leonnatus said.

Shoving the goblet back to him, I was sick again.

'It will soon pass. Drink some of the water.'

I did as I was told. The nausea receded a little.

'I have news that will revive your spirits.' Leonnatus was rubbing my back, as you would that of an ailing horse. 'There was a letter waiting for me. You, and your nephews, are summoned to Aegae. The three of you will have the honour of being appointed Royal Pages to King Philip.'

A fresh wave of nausea spared me from making any answer.

CHAPTER THREE

Spring 342 BC

THE AIR WAS FILLED with the tinkling of bells and the bleating of sheep. The flock blocked the road. Leonnatus pulled our small party to the side. We were in no hurry, and the weather was beautiful. It was early in *Xandicos* the first month of spring. The shepherds whistled their fierce dogs to heel, and hailed us affably as they passed. They rode with their legs dangling from one side of their mules, their long crooks slanted across their thighs like spears.

An age-old scene. For centuries sheep had bound Macedonia together. It had always been a land of two parts. In the summer the flocks grazed in Upper Macedonia; a world of mountains, small enclosed plains and alpine meadows, of villages built for defence on wooden piles in highland lakes, and drystone refuges in remote fastnesses. Its wooded slopes were the haunt of lynx, wolf, bear, and lion. For centuries it had been the wild domain of the five upland kingdoms: Pelagonia, Lyncestis, Orestis, Elimeia, and Tymphaia. There had been a sixth, Eordaia, but long ago it had been conquered and overrun by subjects of the Argead kings. Sometimes the remaining highland lords had acknowledged the suzerainty of the distant Argead monarch, quite often they had not. In the autumn the majority of the vast flocks were driven down to pasture in the wide flat plains and marshy fens around the Gulf of Therma. The lowland was a tame place of industrious small farmers and big estates, of navigable rivers running to the sea, of commerce and cities, like the Argead capitals of Pella and Aegae. Every spring the shepherds left that ordered and affluent land and returned home to their rough uplands with their animals.

Nothing can change the old ways. Every year the sheep will make their two long migrations: down in the autumn, up in the spring. Some things are eternal. But Philip had forged new chains to bind Macedonia together. After his victory at the Hyacinth Meadow, he had acted with surprising magnanimity. The surviving rulers of the uplands, along with many of their mounted companions, were granted generous estates in the lowlands. My father was given lands in the east along the Strymon River, close to Amphipolis, in the territories recently won from savage Thracian tribesmen. But while Philip gave with one hand, he took with the other. The highland lords were no longer to be styled kings. The best of their peasants were drafted into Philip's phalanx, their mounted *hetairoi* into his own Companion cavalry. The lords themselves were to serve as courtiers and officers in his army, their sons as Royal Pages. More damaging to any future dream of independence, broad swathes of their realms were confiscated and handed over to lowland colonists in newly founded cities. Philip's city of Heracleia now watched over the north of Lyncestis. Its inhabitants had no ties to the old Bacchiad lords in Lebaea. Worst of all, justice in the uplands was no longer administered by the ancient dynasties, but by judges appointed by Philip.

The flock shambled up into the foothills leaving the road clear. We rode out onto the green plain of Lyncestis. There was a huge sky, radiantly blue with little rafts of white clouds. Some ten miles ahead, the foothills of the Burnous mountains lay in a low line across the eastern horizon.

Leaving this morning had not been easy. My mother had been austere, saying no soft endearments. Instead, she warned me to always be on my guard, and watch what I said in the lowlands. Never let wine loosen my tongue. The court was riven by factions. The Companions of Philip often tried to bring down their rivals by denouncing each other to the King. All the wives of King Philip would be suspicious of my Argead blood. Especial care should be taken around Olympias of Epirus. The woman was a witch. The King's mother, however, could be trusted. Eurydice was descended from the house of Lyncestis. Finally, my mother had searched my baggage, in case any of the house servants had hidden any treats. Despite this show of sternness, there had been tears in her eyes as she gave me a final embrace. Taking leave of my father had been less of a trial. Although I had to admit that since the night in the hall he had seldom called me 'the late-born', and not once 'the runt of the litter'. It made me glad that I had not attempted to seduce his Corinthian flute-girl. If Neoptolemus had shown the same restraint I was uncertain.

Trivial thoughts about slave girls would not have been in my mind, and the leaving would have been much harder, had I known that I would never see either my home or my mother again. The young not only see themselves as immortal, they transfer that quality to those they love. It is good that the gods do not give us foresight.

It was a small party that had clattered under the gate. There were just eight riders – Leonnatus, my nephews and myself – each of us accompanied by one retainer. Old Eumaeus was with me. Eight riders, but sixteen horses. Open-handedly, my father had equipped the four members of his family with four mounts apiece. In his opinion an officer on campaign should have at least ten horses, but at court a mere four might suffice. He would not have the dignity of the house of Lyncestis disparaged. Leonnatus, of course, already had his own string in the lowlands.

We forded the Beres at noon, and went by easy stages. The ground began to lift and gently roll as we approached the southern end of the plain. We rode through Grande and Cellae, populous villages expanding to the size of market towns. Old Eumaeus said that before Philip imposed peace, they were miserable and desolate hamlets. He looked shifty when I caught his eye, but I did not reprove him. A Macedonian is entitled to express his opinions. Unlike me, Eumaeus admired the Argead King. He and his brother had served in Philip's phalanx. On discharge, Eumaeus had returned to Lebaea, but his brother, the only family Eumaeus possessed, had married a woman from the lowlands, and been granted a farm down by the coast.

At sunset the sky was full of rooks returning home to roost. We camped in the shelter of the Pass of Brasidas. Here, at the last gasp, the Spartans had stormed one of the heights, and escaped utter destruction at the hands of my ancestor Arrhabaeus I. When the blood has cooled, it is right to honour the courage of one's enemies. The nights were still chilled, and we built a large fire. We all pitched in to gather the firewood. No Macedonian warrior should stand on ceremony, or think manual labour beneath him. There was flatbread fresh from this morning, and sausages, cheese, onions, and wine. After we had eaten, we passed round an amphora and talked. The darkness was fragrant with woodsmoke and the stars wheeled overhead.

'It is a tough life as Royal Page,' Leonnatus said. 'Hard work, long hot marches, when your throat is so parched you would kill for a drink, tough discipline, exhausting watches through the night. But it is the best training for war, and, if you do not disgrace yourself, it leads to advancement.'

'It is demeaning,' I said.

'Philip is a fair man. You will not be beaten except for disobeying an order, and no one but the King himself will dare lay a hand on you.' Leonnatus paused, considering his next words. 'It might be best to avoid affairs with other Pages or older men. Of course, there is nothing wrong with such arrangements. Philip himself has a favourite among the Pages, a youth called Pausanias, but our family history warns how such affairs can lead to disaster.'

Our house descends from the Bacchiad rulers of Corinth, and through them from Heracles, and thus from Zeus himself, the King of the Olympian gods. The intemperate love of a boy by one of the Bacchiads had led to the expulsion of the whole clan from Corinth. It was just one of the lessons of their past that the dynasty of Lyncestis had taken to heart.

Neoptolemus spoke. 'Alexander is right. The Argeads should be our servants. Everyone knows that Philip's grandfather was illegitimate, and his father was the son of a slave owned by the Lyncestrian King Aeropus.'

'There is no truth in those old wives' tales.'

Leonnatus sounded tetchy, as if he would like the subject changed, but Neoptolemus was not deterred. Macedonian free speech can lead to trouble, especially when wine has been taken.

'Aeropus, our ancestral kinsman, was King of all Macedonia, and his son Pausanias after him.'

'They were troubled times. The succession was uncertain.' Leonnatus made a dismissive gesture. 'Anyway, they did not hold the throne for long, and the army only acclaimed them in the first place because they had Argead blood. As does every member of our house, but it is not something to boast about, or even dwell on. No king, certainly not Philip, looks kindly on a potential rival.'

I took a draught of wine. Since that night in the hall, my capacity had increased, and I had become bolder. 'If my grandfather had not lost at the Hyacinth Meadow, if my father had not surrendered after the defeat . . .'

'You understand nothing.' Leonnatus now sounded genuinely annoyed. 'Lyncestis was a grain of corn ground between Illyria and the Argeads. Your grandfather may have struck the blow that killed Perdiccas, but it was the warriors of Bardylis the Illyrian that defeated the lowland army. Just as it was the forces of Bardylis that were then vanquished by Philip. Your grandfather had no choice but to fight for the Illyrian. We exchanged a barbarian master for one of our own people. Afterwards, your father had no more choice than your grandfather. All our best fighters were dead, the other upland kings had made their peace. By the rights of blood feud, Philip could have killed our entire line.'

There was silence. Leonnatus took a drink, sighed, then went on more equitably.

'You must think beyond just our family. Philip found the people of the uplands scratching a living in the mountains, dressed in skins, cowering in refuges, unable to protect their herds from the Illyrians. He brought them down from the hills, brought them peace and the security to work the land. He gave them laws and well-defended cities, equipped them with good weapons of war. Before Philip, Macedonia was not at the mercy of only the Illyrians. From the north the Paeonians, the east the Thracians, the south the Hellenes; all of them plundered and enslaved our people at will. Now many of them pay tribute, and they all do our bidding, or fear the consequences of refusing. There has never been a king like Philip. Europe has never produced such a man. And then there is his son . . .'

Leonnatus left the sentence unfinished. For a moment he was lost in a reverie, like a man in love, then he grinned. 'One word of caution, when you meet Philip, just do not stare at his right eye.'

The next day, we mounted in the grey half-light, well before sunrise. Leonnatus wanted to make better time. After descending the pass, the road almost doubled back on itself, going north-east along the low hills overlooking the shores of Lake Begorritus. The air smelt of sedge and still held the chill of the night. As the sun came up, there were geese on the water and ducks flighting above.

I rode in silence, thinking on Leonnatus' words. It was easy for him to be reconciled to Philip's new order. From a collateral branch of the family, he would never have become king of an independent Lyncestis. But, in the natural run of things, as the third son of Aeropus, I would not have taken the throne either. If anyone, Arrhabaeus the eldest should be resentful. Yet – as far as one could tell, he was always reserved – he seemed sanguine enough. Heromenes was the one with a black bitterness in his heart. My horse-faced brother was no example to follow. There was no joy in his life. A man's fate, his *moira*, is set at birth. Railing against it brings only misery. Should I want to achieve any great thing before going down to Hades, it might be that I too, like Leonnatus and Arrhabaeus, must set aside my ancestral pride. Such were my thoughts. For I was young then, as I rode in the sunshine by the lake, and wanted above anything for men to remember me.

Towards the end of morning the road turned east. It snaked down through shadowed, timbered foothills that blocked the view. All too often for Leonnatus' liking, came the sound of bells, and we had to pull our horses to the side, and let the flocks pass. Sometimes the sheepdogs appeared first, huge shaggy beasts, themselves savage as wolves to strangers. The trick was to throw a scatter of small stones. When the dogs stopped to look at them, hurl a bigger stone. The one you hit would run off yelping, the others would follow.

It was well after midday when we reached the city of Edessa. Never having been to the lowlands, it was the largest settlement I had ever encountered. Left to myself, I would have explored its sights. But Leonnatus was determined to press on, and we stopped only to water the horses, and buy fresh bread.

Not long after we had left the town, we crested a rise, and there, spread out before us, was Bottaia, the heart of Macedonia. The plain stretched like a great emerald cloak, with threads of white roads stitching it together. In the distance was the deeper green of the marshes around Lake Loudias, and further still – forty miles away, fifty? – the sun glinted on the Gulf of Therma. It was my first glimpse of the sea, but I knew the rule of the King ran on beyond the horizon. It ran to the east across the gulf, to Chalcidice and Thrace and the Hellespont; to the north, to Paeonia and all the way to the Danube; to the south, to Thessaly and many of the other lands of the Hellenes. The view brought home to me the reality of the immense power of Philip. And I thought, if he was such a man as Leonnatus claimed, perhaps it would not hurt my honour, the honour of a descendant of kings, to serve such a mighty King as Philip. In his battles I could win glory that would prove I was a worthy son of the House of Lyncestis, would show my father and brothers that I was no mere *runt of the litter*.

After a couple of miles, we turned south off the main road to Pella. Philip was at the ancient capital of Aegae. In the spring the King returned to perform the traditional religious ceremonies there and at the sanctuary in nearby Dion at the foot of Mount Olympus. The soil here was lighter than in Lyncestis; yellow and sandy looking. But it was fertile and well worked. Everywhere farmers were sowing spring wheat and pruning vines. This was the original Garden of Midas, and the sides of the road were enamelled with flowers; scarlet poppies, pink silene, and blue lupins. To our right were the forested lower slopes of the range of Mount Bermion. It was into them we rode to make camp at the approach of evening.

Each of us rubbed down, fed and watered two of the horses, and tethered them for the night, before tending to ourselves. Animals must be seen to before the needs of men. We built a fire and ate almost in silence, not constrained by any ill feeling, but tired from the long day. Neoptolemus drew the first watch. No country is so peaceful that there are no thieves or brigands in the hills. Wrapped in my cloak, as soon as my head touched the rolled blanket serving as a pillow, I fell fast asleep.

Someone loomed over me. I sensed the presence even through the deepest slumber. Heart leaping in my chest, I snatched for the dagger under my pillow.

'Shh.' Neoptolemus put a hand on my arm.

Everything was quiet. Nothing to see except the glow of the embers. The rest of the party were sleeping.

'What?'

'Look.' Neoptolemus pointed up to Mount Bermion. There were lights moving up in the hills. One of the horses stamped and ruckled softly down its nostrils. Then I thought I half heard from far up the slopes a woman's cry and a snatch of song. As realisation dawned, my spirits quailed. When the maenads roam in the wild places no man should look on the mysteries of Dionysus.

'Come on,' Neoptolemus whispered, 'let's go and see "the women like mating birds in the bushes, snuggling together in the joyous nets of love".'

'Are you mad?' Amyntas, next to us, was awake. 'You quote Euripides, but forget the fate of Pentheus, torn apart by his mother.'

Neoptolemus smiled. His teeth showed white in the ambient light. 'It is just a play. If Euripides had known anything of fate, he would not have come to Macedonia to meet our ancestors' hunting dogs.'

At the mention of that ghastly death, I clenched my right thumb between the first two fingers of my hand to make the sign to avert evil. Blood guilt can reach down the generations.

'Come on, Alexander.'

'I don't know.'

'Amyntas can take my watch. We will be back before anyone knows we have gone. You are not scared, are you, Alexander?'

There is a wildness in the blood of our family. Sometimes it makes us deaf to the gods. Apollo at Delphi gave an oracle of a millstone that would crush the rulers of Corinth. The Bacchiads failed to heed the warning, and were driven out of the city.

'No, I am not scared.'

The night was milder than in the highlands, and both of us left our cloaks. Taking a sighting on the lights, and a bearing on the moon, we slipped out of the encampment. The lower slopes were clothed in beech, oak and chestnut. There was little undergrowth, and the inclines were not steep, but they were cut with many gullies. Scrambling in and out of the obstructions, the scabbard hanging from my sword-belt kept catching on projecting roots and getting in my way. Soon we had lost sight of both our campfire and the torches of the maenads. It was not just the exertion that was catching at my breath.

'We are lost. We should go back.'

Before Neoptolemus could answer from all too close burst music and a wild chorus echoed through the trees: '*Evoe, Evoe.*'

'Over there!' Neoptolemus laughed, as if the god had robbed him of his wits. 'Follow me!'

We flitted from one tree to another. Neoptolemus leading, me reluctantly following. We reached another gully. On the far side were the lights and the women. Crouching in the shadow of a tall pine, well back from the brink, we watched.

They danced in the clearing. Clad in dappled fawn skins, flashes of white tufts of wool at the hems, their arms and legs were bare. Their faces were obscured by wreaths of ivy, and sprigs of oak and fir. Each brandished a thyrsus, like a long spear. Flutes and drums beat an incessant rhythm. They circled a tall mixing bowl, drinking as they passed. I could smell the wine, the resin of the pine torches, the hot scent of the women's bodies. It was intoxicating and terrifying. In the light of the streaming torches, the thyrsi seemed to writhe with a life of their own.

Neoptolemus started to crawl forward. I grabbed his belt.

'What are you doing?'

'Blessed is the man who has the good fortune to know the mysteries of the gods.'

'There is no cover. They will see you.'

He shook off my hand. Eager to see what should remain secret, he slithered towards the lip. Heart thudding in my chest, I slunk back against the trunk of the tree. Lost in their revelry, the maenads remained oblivious to the approach of Neoptolemus.

Drawn like a moth to a flame, Neoptolemus must have made a false move. Without warning, the edge gave way beneath him. With an involuntary shout, and a crash of falling earth, he tumbled into the gully. At once, on the other side, all was consternation. The music died. The women were not dancing. They hugged each other. Some screamed in outrage or fear.

Without thinking, I rushed to help Neoptolemus. The gully was not deep, but sheer sided, like a ravine. Neoptolemus was trying to claw his way back up. Lying prone, I reached over. Catching his extended hand, I hauled him to the top. He was grazed and battered, covered in dirt. I helped him to his feet.

A lone maenad stood on the other side of the void. She was tall and stately, her face hidden by the shadow of the ivy wreath in her hair. She pointed her thyrsus at us like a weapon. Suddenly I was very conscious of my sword-belt gleaming white in the gloom.

'Let Justice come for all to see, let her come sword in hand, stabbing through the throat to his death the godless, the lawless, the unjust . . .'

Her words put ice in my blood. And then I saw the snakes. They coiled round the thyrsus, slithered round her arms and neck. Neoptolemus tugged at my arm, and we turned and ran.

My memories of our flight are confused. Running and sliding, swerving round trees, falling, scrambling to our feet, panic stricken, lost, but always tearing downhill. Terrified of our profaning the mysteries, terrified of what retribution – human or supernatural – might be on our heels. At the end, the surge of relief when I heard a horse calling, smelt woodsmoke.

Amyntas said nothing when we crept back into the camp. Knowing I could not sleep, I took the next watch. In the morning, despite our scrapes and bruises, we were not questioned. Perhaps the others thought even to mention our nocturnal wandering might bring some pollution. Neoptolemus, for all his boldness, never spoke of that night again.

CHAPTER FOUR

Spring 342 BC

THE CITY OF AEGAE can be seen from far out on the Macedonian plain. Clouds piled up high above the town where the northern foothills of Mount Olympus turned back the winds. We rode in through innumerable burial mounds. The tumuli were peaceful in the sun, vibrant and fragrant with spring grass and flowers. Surely they would bring joy to the shades of the departed, should any awareness remain in the afterlife.

We dismounted and waited at the gate. It was mid-morning, and the gateway was still thronged with the carts and pack animals of farmers bringing in produce. The walls were built of smooth, dressed limestone. Towers projected out at intervals of less than a bowshot. Ballistae could be seen behind the battlements. These outer works were not just designed to impress. Looking above the town, there was an acropolis halfway up the mountain. Aegae would be a hard place to take.

When our turn came, a few words from Leonnatus to the guards secured our entry. Inside, the street was steep. We led our string of horses on foot through a district of public buildings. There was a gymnasium to the right. Leonnatus stopped and watched through the entrance a wrestling match between two youths. His passion for the sport was only matched by his love of hunting. Over the winter he had taught me some new holds and throws. Useful on the battlefield, so he said. Now he grunted appreciatively as one of the youths went down heavily.

'Philotas will not concede. He is proud, the son of the general Parmenion, but he is outmatched by Craterus.' Leonnatus grinned. 'They do not care much for each other, but you will get to know them both. They are Royal Pages.'

The street climbed past the agora and its temples, then turned left by the theatre, before ascending to the palace. Like my nephews, I stood speechless, gawping like a rustic. It was far the biggest building I had ever seen. You could have lost the whole of Lebaea in one of its wings. The palace faced east, like a sanctuary of the gods, and like a temple it was fronted by columns. There were dozens of columns, and they were on two levels, reaching up to the impossibly high roof. But most astounding of all, the building was open. People came and went freely between the columns. Lebaea, like any Macedonian dwelling, presented a closed face to the world; just one, at most two, doors for security. The palace was an eloquent statement of the confidence and accessibility of King Philip.

We left the horses with Eumaeus and the other retainers. It was just one step up to the palace. There was another portico behind the first. There were benches for people to wait. Many groups sat chatting. Most were Macedonians or Hellenes. But some were more outlandish: Persians, and other easterners, in flowing robes, with kohl-lined eyes; tattooed Thracians in fox-skin hats; even Celts in checked trousers and cloaks.

'Leonnatus, son of Anteas, greetings.' My kinsman returned the greeting, but I caught only the Persian's name, not that of his father.

When we had passed on, I asked Leonnatus the identity of the easterner.

'Sisines is an exile from Persia. There are rumours he is a spy, but he seems an honourable man to me.' Leonnatus was evidently pleased that the older man knew him. It reminded me that my relative was only a couple of years my senior.

We came to a doorway. The guards, in tunics, cloaks, and round *kausia* local hats, were not equipped for war. But each wore his sword-belt, and had a long *sarissa* in his hand. Their shields, painted with the emblems of their units, hung on pegs on the wall. There was no other doorway, at least not on this side of the palace. The assurance of the Argeads, I thought, only went so far.

Leonnatus explained our business to the officer, and a soldier led us through.

Inside was a colonnaded courtyard. It was paved and enormous. An army could have mustered in that space; three thousand or more men.

The soldier took us along the northern shaded walkway. We halted outside a great hall open to the courtyard. Through the pillars was a crowd. They had their backs to us. All were facing the throne at the rear of the room. The man on the throne was illuminated by shafts of sunshine from windows on the upper level. He was bearded, in middle age, wearing a simple white tunic. Even from this distance I could see the white scar of his ruined right eye.

Philip was holding court. An elderly man, with strange, almost blue-black hair and beard, stood before the King. In the hush, Philip's words were audible outside.

'The Macedonians are rough and rustic. They call a spade a spade. Some say we still reek of goat. The Macedonians will not respect a judge who dyes his hair and beard. Mine are shot with grey. You are dismissed from your post until yours also show your true colour.'

Leonnatus whispered in my ear, 'Antipater will not be pleased. That judge was appointed on the recommendation of the general.'

This was a reminder of my mother's warning. The royal court was divided into factions, like hostile tribes.

After the disgraced judge had left, a functionary came out.

'Health and great joy, Leonnatus.' He spoke with no trace of a Macedonian accent.

'And to you, Eumenes.'

So this was Eumenes of Cardia, the trusted Hellene secretary of Philip.

'And you have brought . . . ' He consulted a roll of papyrus.

'Alexander, son of Aeropus, and Neoptolemus and Amyntas, sons of Arrhabaeus.'

'Excellent. Philip will receive them now.'

Do not stare at his eye. To not look at the puckered, pale skin in an otherwise tanned and handsome face, I studied the others around the throne. Half a dozen guards were ranged along the rear wall, four Royal Pages in front of them. Closer to Philip were two of his Companions, and another Page; a handsome youth with an ivory chariot design inlaid on the hilt of his sword, obviously some favourite.

'You are ready to swear before me and the eternal gods to defend me by word and the work of your hands?'

The question returned my attention to the King. Focusing on his undamaged eye, I invoked terrible curses on myself if I should fail to serve: 'No man, so long as I am alive and see the light of day, shall lay the weight of his hands on you or your descendants.'

After Neoptolemus and Amyntas had also taken the oath, a woman entered by a door to the left which previously I had not noticed. She was imposing and dressed respectably in a plain dress and shawl. She wore a veil, over her hair, like a scarf, and not covering her face. Philip had five wives. Unlike the Bacchiads, and the rest of the great houses of Macedonia, the Argeads were polygamous. It gave benefits in diplomatic dealings, but created endless problems of succession. As any man with Argead blood could become King if acclaimed by the army there was always a ready supply of pretenders.

A strong emotion, unreadable to me, flickered across Philip's face as he turned to her.

'These Pages have come from nearly as far out of the west as you.'

One of his wives, Audata, was Illyrian.

'Olympias—' Philip spoke carefully, as if his words might be unwelcome '—the youngest son and the grandsons of Aeropus of Lyncestis have taken the oath of allegiance.'

So this was Olympias – the notorious Epirote princess and witch. There was a story that Philip had met her at the mysteries on the island of Samothrace, and fallen in love with her on sight. Even if true, the marriage had brought political advantages; an alliance with the kingdom of Epirus on the shores of the Adriatic, and the birth of a son, Alexander. Yet there were whispers of darker things. Philip had already got a son by the Thessalian Philinna. The boy was full of promise; intelligent and active. Olympias was thought to have poisoned him, by spells or philtres. Arrhidaeus had survived, but now his mind would remain that of a child forever.

'It is easy to catch a hedgehog, but hard to keep hold of it,' Olympias said.

Hearing her voice, I knew we had met before; in the dark woods, on the slopes of Mount Bermion. Olympias was looking directly at me. Not at my face, but my white sword-belt. And I knew the recognition was mutual.

The words of her curse rang in my mind, like stones dropped in a well: *Let justice come for all to see, let her come sword in hand, stabbing through the throat to his death the godless, the lawless, the unjust.*

* * *

We were late setting out to return to Aegae. Philip had gone to sacrifice at Dion. Before midday, when we were leaving the sanctuary, an old peasant woman had presented Philip with a petition. He had said that he had no time. The crone had replied, 'Then stop being King.' Philip had turned back, dismounted, and affably heard her out.

Afterwards the King and his Companions had ridden ahead, leaving the Pages to make their way on foot.

Attending the King at sacrifice was one of our duties. There were some eighty Pages, nine or ten on duty at any time. We served Philip at table, saw to his arms and armour, brought out his horse, and helped him mount. At night we guarded his quarters, brought in his concubines. We accompanied him if he went to hunt, or rode to war. When not on duty, we were educated by orators and philosophers from Hellas, the best the treasury of Macedonia could hire.

The institution was old, but vastly expanded by the conquests of Philip. We were drawn from all the noble families of Upper and Lower Macedonia. A few Pages were even Hellenes from

Thessaly and beyond. Although most Hellenes regarded our duties as fit only for slaves. Of course we were hostages for the fealty of our kinsmen, but our service was also intended to instil in us unswerving loyalty to the King. The loyalty, however, was not certain. Archelaus the Argead King had been killed by his Pages; two of them his slighted lovers.

In the heat of the afternoon, we trudged north. At first we talked and laughed and drank. After a couple of hours we were silent and our flasks empty. The day was still and cloudless. We changed the order of march frequently. A fine dust gritted the eyes, and worked itself into the noses and mouths of those at the rear. The shade of the wooded lower slopes of Mount Titarion on our left, and the waters of the Gulf of Therma on our right, tempted us with visions of coolness. Pausanias, the older youth, leading us, kept to a relentless fast march.

Before we reached the town of Pydna, we took a cart track that branched off north-west towards Aegae over the shoulders of the foothills. By now, my tongue was parched and thick, sticking to the roof of my mouth. Another boy suggested sucking a smooth stone. It did little good.

As the sun was grading down towards the western peaks we came upon a wayside inn. It was a dilapidated small building with some rough benches outside under a vine trellis. To us it had the allure of a Persian paradise.

'A drink to set us up for the last stage,' Neoptolemus said.

'Philip ordered us not to step off the road,' Pausanias said.

'He will never know.'

Pausanias fiddled with the ivory-inlaid chariot on his hilt. 'We carry on.'

'Go fuck *yourself* for a change.' Neoptolemus, like many of the Pages, resented Pausanias' intimacy with the King. 'Amyntas, you coming?'

'Pausanias is right,' his brother said. 'We have our orders.'

'Alexander?'

'A quick drink will do no harm.' Taking orders from Pausanias did not sit easily with me. The youth was from Orestis, but not from its ruling house.

The rest continued on their way as I followed Neoptolemus to the inn.

There was no breeze, so we did not sit under the trellis, but went inside. It was dark and cool with an agreeable smell of sawdust and old wine. Four farmers sat in a corner, and two serving girls and the innkeeper were at the bar. The latter, seeing our red-bordered white cloaks, the mark of Royal Pages, greeted us fulsomely.

We ordered a drink, and took a table. One of the girls, dark haired and not unattractive, brought the wine and some roasted broad beans. Neoptolemus flirted with her. Soon, with false reluctance, she was on his lap.

'We really have no time,' I said.

'There is always time for Aphrodite,' Neoptolemus said. 'It is impious to deny the goddess.'

The girl, all coyness cast aside, led him to the stairs at the back of the bar. There would be rooms above. The innkeeper stopped Neoptolemus at the foot of the stairs, and held out his hand. A brief discussion, and Neoptolemus paid him.

After they had gone upstairs, the other girl came over. 'Another time,' I said. 'To rush such a pleasure would be a crime.'

She pouted, pretending to be disappointed, then grinned and walked away. The sweetness of her smile almost made me call her back.

It was fully dark, late in the first watch, by the time we reached Aegae. After Neoptolemus had returned, we had drunk another jug.

Torches burnt in cressets at the south-east gate. Flanked by curved towers, it was a monumental entrance. This was the way embassies from the Hellenes of the south would enter the city. The architecture said something about diplomatic priorities of Philip.

The officer of the guard was brusque. 'The King is in the western courtyard. He wants to see you.'

The western courtyard was entered via a long corridor off the southern walkway of the main palace. Tucked away out of sight, it was the service area and stables. Philip was sitting on a mounting block. Olympias was standing next to him. Bucephalus, the phenomenally expensive Thessalian horse of their son, was being led away. Husband and wife seemed to be arguing.

The other Pages moved back as we approached, distancing themselves from the royal displeasure. Amyntas looked at Pausanias. The latter appeared uncomfortable.

Philip got up. 'You disobeyed my orders.'

'It was my fault,' Neoptolemus said. 'I take full responsibility.'

'That is honest,' Philip said. 'Your punishment will be no more severe than that of your kinsman.'

Olympias spoke, her voice chilling. 'The house of Lyncestis has always been over-proud subjects. This latest disloyalty demands exemplary punishment. They must both be sent into exile.'

'And make two more enemies to wander the world, talking ill of me, and taking service with my foes?'

'Then the punishment must be death.'

Suddenly sober, I felt like a man walking carelessly in the hills, who has stumbled to the edge of a precipice.

Olympias continued remorselessly, 'You executed the Royal Page, Archedamus, for flouting your commands.'

'His was a far worse offence in wartime. I had ordered no one to plunder until I gave the signal. Driven by greed, he put aside his weapons, and endangered his comrades.'

Another woman walked out into the stable yard. She was very old, walking with a stick, yet still regal.

'Mother.' Philip got up, and kissed her.

This was my first sight of Eurydice. There were many lurid tales of the Queen Mother: how she had cuckolded her husband with her son-in-law, tried to poison her spouse, and yet somehow been pardoned; how, after the death of her husband, she had contrived the assassination of her eldest son, and then betrayed her next son. The fondness of the greeting by Philip, her youngest son, gave the lie to such stories.

Philip owed his life and his throne to Eurydice, as had his elder brothers. When they were young, the kingdom had been seized by a pretender. Their mother, risking everything, had spurned marriage to the usurper. Instead, fleeing with her sons, she had braved the long and dangerous journey through barbaric Thrace to the distant Hellespont. There, as a suppliant, she had thrown herself at the mercy of Iphicrates, the Athenian general. Before his death, her husband had adopted Iphicrates. Now, passing over any claim of his own, the Athenian had restored his adoptive brothers to Macedonia.

'You have come to plead for the lives of your kinsfolk,' Olympias snapped. 'What else – disloyalty is your Lyncestian heritage. But the King has no need of the prejudiced advice of a senile crone.'

Eurydice fixed her daughter-in-law with old, yet bright eyes. 'Better than that of an Epirote witch. You forget – a king has many wives, but only one mother.'

Philip laughed.

Olympias, knowing she had lost, turned and stalked off, her back rigid with fury.

Philip looked relieved.

'No more than youthful high spirits,' Eurydice said. 'Let them take their beating.'

Philip nodded, relieved to have her advice to follow. But, when he turned to us, his voice was sharp. 'Twelve strokes. Strip!'

Macedonians, like Hellenes, exercise naked. Persians and other easterners are reluctant to expose their soft and pale, slug-like bodies. For us there is no embarrassment or shame in nudity. Shedding my clothes in public did not disconcert me. But removing my sword-belt for a beating was to revert to childhood.

Philip indicated the mounting block. Someone had brought him a whip.

Leaning over, I clenched my teeth. A Lyncestian warrior does not give his enemies the pleasure of showing any pain.

The first stroke – a line of fire across my shoulders – nearly made me gasp. That little catamite Pausanias would suffer for informing against us.

By the third, I could feel blood trickling hot down my back. My anger turned to another target. So much for it being honourable to serve Philip. Silently, I listed the Argead Kings who had suffered the vengeance of Lyncestis: Orestes, Amyntas the Little, Perdiccas III. All dead at the hands of my ancestors. I repeated their names like a religious litany. As the blows sliced in, I added another name: King Philip.

CHAPTER FIVE

Summer 342 BC

A WILD BOAR WAS TERRORISING the farmers around Lake Loudias. It was huge, they said, four or five feet tall, with vicious curved tusks. A veritable monster, like something out of myth, it had a long white scar on its left shoulder. Philip decided it was a worthy quarry for a king.

When the monarch goes hunting normally it is a great occasion. Many courtiers and any visiting embassies, Hellene or barbarian, go along to admire his prowess, and hope to have his ear in the informality of the field. This time Philip was taking only his two most trusted generals; Antipater and Parmenion. Of course a king goes nowhere without Royal Pages. Our group, led by Pausanias, was on duty. Since the beating, I had treated Pausanias with a cold formality. Neoptolemus was less restrained. Although not insulting him to his face, my nephew made frequent jibes in his hearing about the general untrustworthiness of catamites. Two of the older boys had left to join the Companion Cavalry. They had been replaced by a couple of lowlanders. One of the new youngsters, also called Pausanias, was exceptionally good looking. As leader, Pausanias tried to have his namesake known as Pausanias the Little. It did not catch on. Instead Neoptolemus had dubbed him Kalos – Beautiful – Pausanias. To annoy the King's favourite, like the rest, I usually called the newcomer just Kalos.

A breeze from the sea cooled the morning as we rode down from Aegae. The Pages were mounted, not to slow down the party. Amyntas was in charge of the hounds. The mixed pack, Laconian and Molossian, happy to be out, ran ahead, their tails waving like standards. Baggage horses brought up the rear, loaded with provisions, purse nets, stakes, javelins and boar-spears.

Swallows darted and banked above us, flaring gold in the sunshine. The plain was green and scented with thyme. Despite the day, my thoughts were dark. The hunting field is full of danger, not just from the quarry. Were I Pausanias, I would take care not to get between the boar and Neoptolemus or myself. A miscast javelin could bring anyone down. King Archelaus had died out hunting. His killer might have passed it off as an accident had he not tried to seize the throne. Like his predecessor and kinsman, Philip himself was only mortal.

When the sun was directly overhead, we came to a hamlet on the edge of the cultivated land north of Aloros. Two locals were waiting to guide us through the marsh to the beast's lair. Philip said we would take our midday meal before proceeding.

As ever Pausanias was cupbearer to Philip. I served Antipater, and Neoptolemus poured wine for Parmenion. In an oriental court we would have tasted the wine for poison. But it was not a Macedonian custom. The three men sprawled on the grass, perfectly at ease with one another. Philip, the youngest, often said he could sleep soundly if either of the others was awake. In some ways these men were much alike; bearded, tough and tanned. In others they were very different. With his broad, ruddy cheeks and plain, white tunic, Antipater gave the impression of a moderately well-to-do smallholder.

Parmenion, on the other hand, resplendent in purple, looked more regal than Philip. The King, like Antipater, was clad in white; now travel stained and dusty.

There was fresh wheat bread baked before dawn in the kitchens of the palace. The rest of the food was army rations: salt pork, cheese, onions, and wine. On campaign, Philip lived like an ordinary soldier.

'Sit and eat, boys. We can help ourselves to more.' Philip gestured to the pair of rustics. 'You too.' A Macedonian king must be amiable and accessible to his subjects. We seated ourselves round the great men. The hounds, too well trained to beg, crouched on their haunches and waited for scraps in an outer circle. I was glad of the food. After our early start, my stomach was growling.

'You boys look as hungry as Menecrates at dinner last night,' Parmenion said.

Menecrates was a famous doctor, who styled himself the King of Medicine. Not content with that, he had taken to referring to himself as Zeus, and even dressing as the god, because in his own estimation he had the power of life and death. Taking him at his word, when the food was brought in the night before, Philip had ordered only incense burnt before Menecrates.

'Are you sure Aristotle is the right tutor for your son?' Parmenion asked. 'You were responsible for the destruction of his hometown.'

'His father was doctor to mine.' Philip's good eye was shrewd. 'No doubt he hopes good service might be rewarded with the refounding of Stagira.'

'Philosophers are trouble at court,' Parmenion continued, 'remember Euphraeus.'

A pupil of Plato, Euphraeus had held great influence over Philip's brother Perdiccas. He had tried to insist that no one could share in the royal feasts unless he knew how to practise geometry or philosophy. It had been much resented by the hard-drinking Macedonian barons. When Perdiccas was dead, Euphraeus had fled home to the island of Euboea.

'That is why Aristotle will educate Alexander and the others in the countryside at Mieza.'

'That, and it gets Alexander away from the influence of his mother,' Antipater said.

Philip laughed. Were it not for his ruined eye, he was a handsome man. 'And that too.'

'Well, I did not like the look of Aristotle,' Parmenion said. 'Too pleased with himself, always has that superior smile on his face. The pack of philosophers teach the young to question the gods.'

'No, Aristotle does not doubt the gods,' Antipater said.

'I had forgotten, Antipater, that you are now quite the man of letters.' Parmenion's tone was mocking, but not unkind. '*The Deeds of Perdiccas in Illyria*, an odd subject for a history considering how it ends.'

Philip answered before Antipater could speak. 'Not odd at all. My brother met his fate at the hands of a great warrior.' The King raised his cup, first to me, then to each of my nephews. 'It is all the more to our credit that the gods eventually granted us victory.'

The graceful compliment left me cold.

'How is your work going?' the King asked.

Antipater pulled a face like a farmer asked why the harvest was late. 'It would go quicker if you did not keep finding other tasks for me.'

'On that line, there are things we must discuss.'

Both the generals laughed, Parmenion somewhat ruefully. He fished out a gold coin from the wallet on his belt, and tossed it over to Antipater.

'Parmenion bet me you wanted nothing but the pleasure of our company.' Antipater tucked the coin away.

'The walls of the palace have too many ears,' Philip said.

Parmenion waved his hand in a circular motion. 'And the countryside does not?'

'If I do not trust my Royal Pages,' Philip said, 'how will they learn to trust me?'

More fool, you, I thought.

'For now the west is settled. The Illyrians are peaceful.'

Tell that to the Lyncestians who died last year on the path to Lake Lyke, I thought.

'We have placed Olympias' brother on the throne of Epirus.'

Antipater chuckled. 'Of course he is well accustomed to *serving* you.'

Pausanias flushed and looked furious. The youth was jealous. So it was true – Philip had taken the Epirote prince as lover as well as hostage.

Philip ignored the interruption. 'It is time we turned east and dealt with the tribes of Thrace. Next month I will open the campaign against the Odrysians ruled by Cersobleptes. His kingdom must be conquered.'

'What about the Getae up towards the Danube?' Parmenion asked.

'Their King Cothelas has a daughter of marriageable age. Oaths and a wedding and some mules with panniers full of gold – it is more pleasurable to make an alliance in the marriage bed than on the battlefield.'

Antipater nodded. 'The smaller tribes will come over to you. The Odrysians and the Getae are their neighbours. They fear them more than distant Macedonia.'

'What about the Hellenes in the south?' Parmenion said. 'Athens depends on grain from the Black Sea. The nearer you get to the Hellespont, the greater the danger the Athenians will break the treaty.'

'Some of their orators claim we were behind the failed attempt to burn their fleet in port,' Antipater said.

'They have no proof,' Philip said. All three men smiled. An unvoiced admission of complicity. 'I have written offering to give the island of Halonnesus to Athens, and proposing to extend our treaty with the Athenians to a common peace among all Hellenes.'

'They will not be won over by one tiny island, and a peace that might benefit other cities,' Parmenion said. 'And there is the civil strife on Euboea. It is right on the doorstep of Athens.'

'We must be allowed to aid those on Euboea who ask for our protection. It is just in the eyes of the gods.' Philip beamed at his companion. 'And that is why you, Parmenion, will go there with sufficient force. You will take mercenaries – all Hellenes, no barbarians, and no Macedonian troops. It might help allay Athenian fears.'

'When do I go?'

'As soon as we return from the hunt. You will take ship from Pydna. The mercenaries are already gathered there.'

'And me?' Antipater said.

Philip took off his ring, and handed it to the older man. 'You will remain as Regent in Macedonia. Keep an eye on all the Hellenes. In the autumn go to Delphi, and preside over the Pythian Games in my name. Men gather from all Hellas, tongues are loose at a festival; nothing remains secret.'

They all took a drink, and turned to practicalities: logistics, the division of forces, and the need for light infantry in the wild ranges of Thrace. So the fate of kingdoms and cities, of many tens of thousands, was decided by three men over lunch.

Philip made offerings to Heracles the Hunter and Artemis, goddess of the chase, before we set off. Somehow I knew his piety was not feigned. For all his deep cunning, this was a man who respected the gods.

The locals took us through small fields moated by ditches. Aspens were growing up along the ditches, but this flat landscape obviously had recently been reclaimed from the marsh. Gulls screamed overhead. Someone said they came inland before a storm out in the gulf. So far the sky remained cloudless.

After a time we came to an open sward, backed by a thick bank of reeds, and our guides said we must proceed on foot. The hunting gear was unloaded, and the horses tethered. Kalos and the other new boy were left to look after them. With the hounds leashed, we walked into the untamed marshland.

The path was muddy and sucked at our boots as we laboured along burdened by all the unwieldy impedimenta needed for the chase. The tall reeds shut out the view. It was hot and close, without a breath of wind. Clouds of gnats hung round our heads, whining into our eyes and ears. A fetid stench of decay filled the air.

The locals said we were close to the lair, and Philip slipped his favourite Laconian bitch. She quartered the ground, nose down, tail erect. When she picked up the scent, she made no sound, but looked back. At a word, she trotted ahead, and we followed in single file.

Soon there were signs of the boar: hoof prints in the soft ground, broken branches in the undergrowth. Where there were trees, often the bark was scarred by its tusks. The damage was ominously high on the trunks. Weighed down by a bulky roll of netting, and unarmed except for the sword in its scabbard, at every step I expected the beast to burst through the reeds. The runt of the litter, my father had called me. I would prove myself a true son of Lyncestis, a better man than him. Fear would not master me.

Following the line, the hound came to a wooded hillock. Boars make their dens in such places; shaded and well watered, warm in the winter, cool in the summer. The bitch stopped and barked, just once, not to provoke the boar. Philip tied her with the others, and told us to get everything ready. There is an art to setting nets. The belly of the net must be set forward, the supporting stakes well placed, so the beast can see through and not see the trap when it charges. We fixed the outside cords to trees. A boar can easily uproot thorn bushes or scrub. Beyond the nets, we blocked the open ground with brushwood, so the beast would not run out to the sides.

'Philip, you wait here, Parmenion and I will flush it out,' Antipater said.

'And have my Pages think that I would send my two oldest Companions into the most danger, while I look to my own safety? No, you two stay behind the nets. You can compete for the honour of the kill.'

'The King can never hunt with just boys.' Antipater was firm. 'It is against our customs. At least one Companion must always go with him. It will be me.'

Accepting this, Philip told Amyntas and another Page, and both the guides, to attend Parmenion. The hounds were put on slip leashes, and the weapons passed out. I took a boar-spear, and the leads of a pair of big Molossian dogs.

Philip addressed those who would accompany him. 'Antipater and I will lead. You boys keep well spaced. If he turns, and we are too close together, someone will get gored. Release the hounds on my command, and raise a shout. Should he double back, and get past your spear, throw yourself flat, grip the earth with your fingers. His tusks curve up, to savage you he needs to get them under your body. You will not be much hurt if he only tramples you. If anyone goes down, the nearest must go to his aid, draw the beast towards himself. Are you ready?'

We skirted the base of the knoll. It was slow going, splashing through stagnant pools, and stumbling over fallen boughs. Keeping my feet took all my attention, leaving no room to dwell on the proximity of a ferocious, man-killing animal. Eventually, satisfied that we had put the lair between us and Parmenion, Philip gave the order to spread out in a line, facing back the way we had come.

I found myself near the centre. Philip was on my left, Antipater beyond him. Neoptolemus was to my right.

'Slip the hounds!'

They went bounding up and vanished into the timber.

'*Alalalalai*!' We yelled the war cry.

As we went up the slope, the trees were bigger, more widely spaced. The day had turned overcast, almost gloomy.

A furious burst of barking somewhere up ahead.

Lame from an old war wound, Philip was slow. Neoptolemus to my right was drawing slightly ahead.

The cornel wood shaft of my spear was smoothed by the sweat of previous hunters. The long iron spearhead and projecting wings, all razor sharp, gave a certain reassurance. I kept pace with Philip, moving carefully, half turned, spear in both hands, left leading.

The barking was louder. Then something large crashed through the undergrowth, and a hound howled in pain.

'*Alalalalai!*' We bellowed at the top of our voices.

Suddenly the boar emerged from a tangle of briars. The hounds jumbled out after, yapping and darting, just out of its reach.

The boar stood, tail twitching. Its head swinging this way and that, snout dipping, tearing up clods of earth and roots in its fury. Perhaps, long schooled in the hunt, it had learnt that the entangling nets waited if it fled away from the hounds and the noise of the beaters.

A Molossian rushed at its flank. The boar, nimble for all its bulk, swung round. A toss of its head, and the dog went tumbling, a hideous red gash in its side. The other hounds retreated.

And then the boar saw the line of puny men. Without hesitation, the hounds forgotten, it charged the nearest. Accelerating quickly, it thundered down the slope straight at Philip.

The King crouched, braced himself, spear poised. Frozen, I watched the muscles flexing in the smooth flank of the boar. Men were shouting. Antipater was running to his friend. Then it was over. A terrible impact and Philip staggered back a couple of paces. Somehow the King kept his feet as the beast ran itself onto the wicked point. Two or three massive convulsions, and the boar collapsed. Blood was surging from where Philip's spear was lodged deep in its chest.

Men were cheering. Antipater had cast aside his weapon to hug Philip. Up in the wood a few of the hounds were still barking.

Dead, it looked no bigger than other boars. Not the gigantic creature of myth. Its tusks were short. Its left shoulder was unmarked. Not a boar, but a sow.

Everyone was moving to congratulate the King. A movement upslope, at the edge of my vision. Those hounds still giving tongue in the wood. Turning, I saw the new threat.

Massive, slope-shouldered, with a bristling ridge down its back, it pushed half out of its cover. A jagged, white scar showed on its dark flank. Here was the primeval beast that had put terror in the hearts of the villagers.

Its piggy little eyes, shone with malevolence, as it regarded the two unarmed men standing over the body of its mate. In the beat of a heart, it had made its bestial calculations. No thought of flight, it wanted revenge.

Antipater was nothing to me, and Philip had beaten me like a child.

The boar pawed the ground, gathering itself.

But I had sworn an oath: *so long as I am alive, and see the light of day.*

The beast hurled itself forward.

With a wordless cry of warning, I ran into the path of the boar.

The ground trembled under its onset. Hefting the spear, I tried to get into the correct stance – trying to remember everything Eumaeus had taught me – left foot in front, left hand over it, right hand and foot together, legs bent, no further apart than wrestling. The boar was on me before I was set. At the last moment, it jinked its head to one side. Instinctively, my left hand, guiding the spear, started to follow. Somehow I dragged it back. The beast straightened. It was not a clean strike. The spearhead punched in below the throat, but at a glancing angle. The impetus drove me backwards, boots slipping. The boar's jaws were snapping at the shaft. And then the spear snapped. As I went down, I felt a terrible pain in my thigh. Then a crushing weight as the beast landed on top of me.

It was impossible to breathe. The boar was thrashing. Hot blood was stinging my eyes, running into my mouth. As if from a great distance men were shouting. The beast tried to rise, a foot hit me hard in the ribs. Then the awful weight descended again, and was still.

'Is he alive?'

They heaved the corpse off me. I gulped the air, but it felt as if someone had driven a dagger into my chest. Then that was nothing to the agony in my thigh. I pressed my hands to the wound.

'Let me look.'

As my hands were pulled away from the wound, for a moment there was nothing to see except a thin, white line. Then the line gapped into a hideous red tear.

'Give me the wine.'

A searing pain as the cut was washed. I bit back a cry.

'Nasty, but, when clean and dry, we can stitch it,' Philip said. 'If it does not go bad, you will live. Something to show with pride.'

'From now he can recline with the men at dinner,' Antipater said. 'Killed his man, killed his boar, not fitting he remains a Page, but too young for the army.'

'You are right,' Philip's one eye gazed down into my face. 'We owe you our thanks. In recognition, I declare you a foster-brother of my son, Alexander. You will be educated with him at Mieza.'

CHAPTER SIX

Summer 342 BC to Spring 340 BC

THE THREE YOUTHS WERE naked, panting, covered in dust. They were arranged like a sculpture group; *The Ball-players*. By the way they were standing the one in the middle was Alexander. He was half a head shorter than the other two. Philotas, on the right, I already knew from Aegae. The one on the left, his hand resting casually, but proprietorially, on Alexander's shoulder had to be the prince's lover Hephaestion.

'Alexander, son of Aeropus.' I introduced myself formally. 'King Philip has sent me to be educated with you.'

Hephaestion regarded me with disdain. 'Another uplander, as if we did not already have to put up with that oaf Craterus, and the cripple from Elimeia, Harpalus.'

I had known Harpalus from childhood. He was a member of the royal family of Elimeia. It was not his fault that he had been born with a hunched back and a withered leg.

Hephaestion was not finished. 'The closest the house of Lyncestis has ever come to culture was slipping hunting dogs on Euripides.'

'It was fate.' I spoke reasonably, keeping my rising anger out of my voice. 'There was bad blood – Euripides had demanded a gold cup from the King that was owed to my ancestor for courage in battle – but the hand of a god caused the death.'

Hephaestion snorted. 'You rework the story. The King said, "You have a right to ask, but Euripides has a right to receive the cup even though he did not ask." With Lyncestian manners, your kinsman threw his drink at the King.'

Hephaestion would have said more, but Alexander silenced him with a gesture. 'And the King forgave him with the words "He did not throw the drink on me, but the man he thought me to be."'

Alexander smiled. 'Raking up old tragedies is no welcome to our brotherhood.' His face and chest were flushed from exercise. His eyes were the colour of hyacinths, one oddly darker than the other. Alexander stood very erect, his head slightly tipped to one side. That was where my kinsman Leonnatus had copied the stance.

'You are welcome as my foster-brother.' Alexander dragged his dirt-matted hair back from his forehead. 'Two Alexanders will cause confusion. Would it be acceptable if we call you Lyncestes?'

I smiled at Alexander, then looked at Hephaestion. 'It would be an honour.'

'Will you join the game,' Philotas said. He was one of the oldest of the foster-brothers, perhaps eighteen, or even nineteen.

It was not yet a month since the boar had gored my leg. The wound was barely healed and still tender. But my pride would not let me use that as an excuse.

'With pleasure.' Old Eumaeus had accompanied me to Mieza. I stripped, and handed him my clothes.

When I too was naked, the scar showed pink against the tanned flesh.

'Far from being rewarded,' Hephaestion said, 'Pages have been flogged for getting between the King and his quarry.'

'My father's spear was lodged in the first beast,' Alexander said. 'Lyncestes showed true Macedonian courage.'

As the others turned back to the game, Alexander bent and studied the wound on my thigh. 'Are you recovered enough to play?'

Despite the sweat and grime, there was a scent, almost like incense, from his body.

'Yes.'

Alexander looked dubious. 'There is no dishonour in an injured man sitting out a contest.'

'I will play.'

'If you are sure, join my team.'

The court was marked out in the sand: the two base lines, and the halfway line. Harpalus was among the handful of spectators. The rest appeared to be retainers or servants, apart from one middle-aged man, dressed in flashy clothes, and leaning on a stick. My heart went out to Harpalus. Alone of the foster-brothers, he was unable to join the game.

There were only eight on the team of Hephaestion, nine now on that of Alexander. Normally there would be at least a dozen a side. It would leave space on the wings, and create gaps in the centre. A fast game on an open field could not be worse for a player carrying a leg injury. I took a post in the centre, where strength should matter more than speed or agility. Philotas lined up opposite. He had an advantage in age and size. I felt a tightness in my chest, almost as it had been before the fight on the mountain trail towards Lake Lyke.

Alexander had the ball. He beat the first defender with a feigned pass and a neat body swerve. But it left him off-balance.

Hephaestion's tackle smashed him to the ground, and dislodged the ball. Alexander just laughed as his friend helped him up.

Craterus was first to the ball. He threw a long pass. I had left Philotas too much room. He gathered the ball, and had time to accelerate towards me. I was back on my heels, crouched, waiting to see if he would try and get past on my right or left. Instead, he dropped his right shoulder, and drove full speed into my chest. As I reeled back, somehow I grabbed one of his arms. Then, falling, I caught hold of a leg, and dragged him down on top of me. His weight knocked the breath from my chest.

'Not bad,' Philotas said, as he got up. He did not offer me a hand.

When I got the ball, I went to make a break. Trying to sidestep Craterus, my left leg let me down, and I took another hard tackle to the sand. By now my thigh was throbbing, and I was worried about the scar opening.

Alexander slipped me the ball. I knew a teammate was free outside, and shipped the ball straight through my hands without looking. The ball was well gone when someone hit me from behind. Unprepared, I went down awkwardly. My head thumped onto the ground.

Groggily sitting up, I saw Hephaestion jogging away. I took my time, waiting for my head to clear.

'That is enough,' Alexander called.

'The game is not finished,' Hephaestion shouted.

'We need to bathe before eating.' No one else questioned Alexander's decision.

I was still gathering my strength when a hand fell on my shoulder. A fragrance like myrrh told me it was Alexander.

'How is the leg?'

I pulled a rueful face.

'You showed spirit.' He helped me to my feet. The hyacinth eyes looked into mine. 'I know the history of our families has not been good, but I hope we can be friends.'

'I hope so too.'

Over Alexander's shoulder I could see Hephaestion watching us. Not half an hour in Mieza, and already I had made an enemy.

* * *

Mieza was tucked into the foothills of Mount Bermion. The sanctuary of the Temple of the Nymphs, where we lived, was some miles from the town. The country here was green and well watered, the slopes studded with caves. In the autumn and winter it never seemed to stop raining. Yet in many ways it was idyllic.

The woods were full of game, and we spent many of our free days hunting. Harpalus showed me a trout stream in the hills, and taught me to fish. We played ball and wrestled and raced on foot. Alexander spurned athletics. Very much the heir to the throne, he said he would only participate if his competitors were also kings. Hephaestion, and a few others, aped Alexander's disdain. I did not share their sycophancy, but waited for my leg to fully heal. Each of us was allowed to keep two horses, and we hacked them down to the plain to race. King Bilip – although a couple of the brotherhood were Hellenes, among ourselves we tended to slip into Macedonian dialect – had sent Bucephalus to Alexander. Grooms on foot had had to lead *Ox-head* all the way from Aegae. Alexander had broken him in, by turning him towards the sun, so he was not frightened by his own shadow.

Since then the great, black Thessalian stallion would let no one else ride him. Bucephalus was fast, but Alexander did not always win. Alexander took it well, saying speed was less important for a warhorse than courage in battle.

The King sent officers from the army to improve our training. Often the instructor was Cleitus, the brother of Alexander's old nurse. His nephew, Proteas, was one of the brotherhood. Cleitus was a typical Macedonian warrior: tall and strong, outspoken and independent. The back of his head was very flat, and he sported a fine dark beard. From the latter he was known as Cleitus the Black, to distinguish him from another officer, Cleitus the White, who had pale golden hair.

We were well fed and, as young Macedonian noblemen, were given plenty to drink. There were always girls in the town happy, for a present or two, to go with a Royal Page. Thinking to please Alexander, late one night Philotas and Harpalus brought back a girl for him. When he asked why she came at such an hour, she replied, 'I had to wait for my husband to go to bed.' Alexander sent her home, and rebuked his friends for almost making him an adulterer. He was always abstemious about such matters. It could have been Alexander thought to admit to physical needs was a weakness. Hephaestion, possibly, was sufficient. There was little overt about their relationship. As the son of the King, Alexander had his own room, and more privacy than the rest of us.

There were two clouds in my life at Mieza. One, obviously, was Hephaestion. The son of a petty landowner at Pella, he had been a childhood friend of Alexander. Hephaestion was very aware, as were we all, that it was the only reason he was part of our brotherhood. It made him touchy, and jealous of anyone who might get close to Alexander. He never missed a chance to make jibes in my hearing about uncouth youths from the uplands. Yet most of his vitriol was aimed at another highlander, Craterus of Orestis. The two loathed each other. Once Alexander had to separate them when they came to blows.

The other cloud was Aristotle. The philosopher's temperament was not ideally suited to teaching high-spirited Macedonian youths. Once I heard him say something like, 'A young man is not a proper audience for political science; he has no experience of life, and because he still follows his emotions, he will listen to no purpose, uselessly'. Discipline was often a problem. As he liked to comment, 'The young do not keep quiet of their own accord, education serves as a rattle to distract them'. He spoke with a lisp, which did not help. Nor did his looks. He had small eyes and spindly legs, had his hair elaborately curled, and wore too many rings.

The intention of Aristotle seemed to be to teach us every subject known to man. Endlessly, we walked up and down the portico of the Nymphaeum as Aristotle held forth on politics and ethics, literature and history, astrology and medicine, botany and zoology. The best way to distract him, and stop him asking us questions, was to present him with any strange plants or bugs and beetles we found out hunting. At least I learnt that hedgehogs mate standing up.

Although Mieza was remote, and far from events, Cleitus the Black and the other instructors brought us news from the army. Philotas was insufferably proud that his father Parmenion, with a force of mere mercenaries, had installed rulers loyal to Macedonia in most of the cities on the island of Euboea. Aristotle was less enthusiastic that Parmenion had captured and executed Euphraeus, the previous holder of his position of philosopher at the Argead court. The summer after Parmenion had left, however, almost all the Euboean cities had expelled these rulers.

Of far greater interest to the rest of us was Philip's campaign against the tribes in Thrace. It had been long and hard fought. Antipater had needed to send reinforcements, and the fighting had continued into the first winter. Eventually, a mixture of force and diplomacy had proved successful. The Odrysian kingdom of Cersobleptes had been annexed. As Philip had predicted at the boar hunt, he had won over Cothelas of the Getae, and taken his daughter Meda as his sixth wife. Parmenion's warning that the extension of Macedonian power towards the shores of the Hellespont would lead to war with Athens looked certain to be proved correct. It was rumoured that this year Philip would besiege the cities of Byzantium and Perinthus, allies of the Athenians.

'My father will leave nothing for me to do,' Alexander said.

We were waiting in the portico for Aristotle. A spring shower had left the air clean and sweet.

'It will take time to bring all the Hellenes under our sway,' Hephaestion said.

'Only a few years.'

'There is always Persia.' Hephaestion always wanted to soothe Alexander.

'My father has time. He is only forty.'

'Even if the Hellenes marched with us, it would be too few,' I said. 'The King of Kings can put a million men in the field. When Xerxes invaded, his army drank the Echeidorus dry.'

'And he has the wealth to hire all the mercenaries in the world,' Harpalus said.

'You are both wrong.' Alexander was adamant. 'Persia is rotten at the core. All their myriads of warriors, all their gold and silver, could not stop Xenophon and ten thousand Hellene mercenaries marching from the heart of their empire to the Black Sea. Victory goes not to the side with the greater numbers, but the greater courage.'

'You are right, Alexander.' Aristotle had an unsettling habit of suddenly appearing. 'Persians and other barbarians are naturally servile, unlike Hellenes. It is better for barbarians to have a master.'

'Treat barbarians as plants or animals,' Hephaestion parroted one of his sayings back to Aristotle.

This was one of the philosopher's theories with which we could all agree. My only doubt was where Macedonians fitted in Aristotle's scheme.

'Today we will discuss again the nature of politics.'

One or two of the foster-brothers groaned.

'The roots of education are bitter, but the fruit is sweet.' Aristotle started walking, and we followed. Up and down, up and down, while the sun glistened silver on the green foliage outside.

'Lyncestes!'

I had been thinking of Persia, of spices and harems, of sheer silk on smooth flesh.

'Lyncestes, sum up our conclusions so far on the nature of monarchy.'

Luckily, this was far from the first time we had been herded down this path.

'Monarchy is dominion by one man. If he follows the path of virtue, and rules for the benefit of his subjects, he is a true *basileus*, a king. But if he turns to vice, and uses power for his own pleasure, he becomes a tyrant. A king is loved and protected both by his subjects and the gods. A tyrant is hated by everyone, and should be killed.'

'Quite good, as far as it goes.' Aristotle had that condescending smile on his face. 'Kingship, as we have already observed, may be classified in the nature of aristocracy. Like aristocracy it is based on merit.'

A man in a travel-stained military cloak came into the portico.

'The merit on which it is based may consist in personal, or family qualities.'

We all turned to see. Cleitus the Black was walking so fast he was almost running.

'It may consist in benefits rendered; it may consist in a combination . . . ' Aristotle, realising that he had lost his audience, stopped talking.

Ignoring the philosopher, Cleitus saluted Alexander. 'Your father has summoned you home. When he marches against Byzantium and Perinthus, you will act as his Regent in Macedonia. Your foster-brothers will accompany you.'

For a moment we all looked at each other incredulously, then we raised a cheer. Once we had started, it was impossible to stop. We hugged, whooped, slapped each other on the back. As he walked away, everyone thronged around Cleitus, as if he had brought a pardon from prison.

Glancing back, I saw Aristotle; left alone, leaning on his stick. For once he was not smiling.

CHAPTER SEVEN

Summer 340 BC

U<small>P ON THE HIGH</small> ground bonfires blazed in every direction. Snatches of wild songs and barbarian shouts echoed through the night. We were surrounded in this remote and nameless mountain valley. It was only three months since Cleitus had brought our release from Mieza. Now I was sure that I was not the only one who secretly wished he was back enduring the safe drudgery of Aristotle's sardonic tongue.

'No, I don't think they will attack tonight,' Antipater said.

By the light of the campfire not all the council looked convinced. Worryingly, they were the older, more experienced officers. One of them had said that the Thracian tribes were notorious for night attacks. Still, we had pickets out, the men had been told to keep their weapons to hand, and a Macedonian was worth any number of tribesmen.

Philip was away, far in the east besieging the Greek city of Perinthus on the Propontis, when the news arrived. A hill tribe called the Maedi had risen, killing the officers sent to collect their tribute. As Regent, Alexander had been left with the great seal of Macedon. As an untried youth he had also been left with Antipater and Parmenion as councillors. They had both advised a cautious campaign: march east through Macedonian territory to Amphipolis, then advance north up the Strymon River, scouting for ambushes, driving the Maedi before us, taking their settlements one by one, until we reached their final refuge at Mount Dounax; if they were rash enough to risk open battle, so much the better. Most likely they would sue for peace after a few strongholds had fallen. Such caution had not appealed to Alexander, who had overruled his father's generals. Instead, leaving Parmenion in Macedon, he and Antipater led a flying column north up the valley of the Axios River. His plan was to cross the southern outcrops of the Messapion mountains to the headwaters of the Doberros, then strike due east into the heartland of the rebels before they knew he was coming.

Except the Maedi had known we were coming. We had not reached the Doberros, were not clear of the high country, when they had brought the war to us. As we pitched camp this evening they appeared, thousands of them lining the ridges.

Antipater was sitting on a log by the campfire. His pale face and white tunic shone in the light.

'In the morning we need to storm the ridge we came over,' he said.

'It is shameful to run from these savages,' Neoptolemus said.

Everyone turned to look at Neoptolemus. I shot him a warning look. Macedonian free speech did not extent to youths criticising their elders. As young noblemen we had been included in the war council as a courtesy; to learn, rather than contribute.

Antipater betrayed no irritation. 'We retreat to regroup and return, like a ram to butt harder.'

Several of the older officers smiled. Antipater was quoting Philip after a defeat in Greece. They trusted Antipater, and it did the old general no harm to remind them that the King trusted him.

Alexander had been pacing. Now he stopped. 'If we could tempt them down from the heights . . . ' The sentence trailed off.

He gazed at the burning logs, lost in thought. No one had said that this was his fault, but I knew the thought oppressed him.

'If we retreat is there a danger that other Thracian tribes will join the Maedi?' This time Neoptolemus tactfully phrased it as a question. My nephew was headstrong, but no fool. It was a good point.

'A matter of a few days,' Antipater said, 'they will not have time.'

As ever, Hephaestion hovered close to Alexander. 'They are a rabble. One charge of our horsemen will clear them from our path, and chase them all the way to Mount Dounax.'

'No,' Alexander said. 'They would just give ground, draw us deeper into their territory, then turn on us when we were completely cut off.' He smiled at Hephaestion to soften the blow. 'Antipater is right. We will withdraw. But perhaps there is a way yet we can turn this in our favour.'

* * *

The sun would soon rise. Above the dark sides of the valley the sky was regal in scarlet and purple.

Aristander the seer led forward the goat. This was one ceremony he would not perform. Long ago a herd of goats had led Perdiccas to the foothills of the Pierian mountains, where an oracle told him to found Aegae as the capital of his new kingdom of Macedon. At dawn every day since the King or the Regent had sacrificed a goat in front of the army standards to Heracles the Ancestor.

The animal suddenly stopped. There was a terrible silence. The sacrificial beast should approach the altar willingly. Aristander gently tugged its lead, and the goat moved again. An audible sigh of relief came from the men. Everyone knew the gods were never closer than on the day of battle. They were drawn, like ghosts to blood, by the one emotion they did not share with men – the fear of death.

At the portable altar Alexander purified his hands with lustral water. Taking a handful of barley grain, he sprinkled it over the victim's back. The goat stood quietly. Alexander took the vessel with the water, and poured some on the beast's head. It nodded its assent. With a sharp knife Alexander cut a hunk of hair from the goat, and threw it into the altar fire. Intoning a simple prayer for *Victory*, he pulled back the victim's head, and slit its throat. As it should, the blood splashed onto the altar.

Ignoring the stolen sunbursts on the standards, I joined in the prayer. Heracles was as much ancestor to the house of Lyncestis as that of the Argeads.

Overhead the sky had turned a clear blue, the few clouds underlit with gold. The sun had risen.

Last night in the council Antipater had suggested we attack in the dead hour before dawn. The Thracians were habitual drunkards. They had no discipline, and would be sleeping off their excesses. Alexander had said that would be to steal half a victory, when we could win a crushing one by daylight. Then he had outlined his plan.

The sacrifice over, a Page led up Bucephalus. It was time Alexander toured the troops, spoke words of encouragement. He vaulted onto the great Thessalian warhorse, and cantered off alone.

The men cheered as he approached; a wave rippling down the column. The Argeads, descended from the gods, had always been popular with the rank and file. Losing some ancient battle they had placed the cradle of infant King Aeropus I among the warriors. His mewling presence inspired them to turn the tide.

Every few yards Alexander reined in and talked to the soldiers. He had inherited from his father the gifts of remembering names and knowing the right words; a joke here, a serious exhortation there. They laughed or nodded with easy familiarity, as if he, like them, was a veteran of many battles, not a callow youth untested in the field.

Even with his frequent halts, Alexander was soon returning. Ours was a small force. There were just two battalions of the phalanx, fifteen hundred heavy infantrymen in each, and one company of two hundred of the Companion Cavalry. The Macedonians were supported by no more than a couple of hundred archers on foot. These were mercenaries from Crete. They fought for money, not honour, but were famed for their skill. Their loyalty would not be suspect today. If this went wrong, they could expect more mercy than the rest of us. The Thracian tribes were known for their inventive tortures.

I could not help looking up at our enemies. Yesterday evening, in the twilight, they had been dark shapes under the trees on the slopes, or black silhouettes on the bare ridges. Now, they capered and danced in the sunshine. The Maedi were a backward tribe. They still wore fox-skin caps and cloaks bright with geometric patterns, brandishing little shields like crescent moons, painted with eyes or leering faces. Their standards were bleached skulls on poles; most animal, some human. There was no point in counting the standards. They came to war by clans, not regular units. Anyway, it was obvious they outnumbered us many times.

The tribesmen were howling and chanting. There were thousands of them. This was no skirmish like the sheep raid at Lake Lyke. This was my first battle. Dozens of drums were thundering. The sounds filtered down through the trees, echoed from the sides of the valley. They were drinking from huge vessels made from the horns of cattle. Fear enters through both the eyes and the ears. Part of me wished we could wait until they became befuddled and clumsy with drink. Part of me just wanted to get this over.

Alexander was back. His odd hyacinth-coloured eyes shone with pleasure, as if we were going to a feast, not to face thousands of tribesmen who wanted to eat our livers raw.

'Mount up,' Alexander said.

Old Eumaeus led up Borysthenes, the chestnut my father had given me. I smoothed the saddlecloth, ran my hand over his crupper with the brand of the lynx. When I checked his curb bit, he tried to bite me. At least he was spirited. For all his faults, the Lord of Lyncestis had seen me well mounted.

Beside me Neoptolemus leapt onto his grey. I let Eumaeus give me a leg up. My heart felt very small, with no more courage than a deer. Once I had sorted the reins, retied the laces of my helmet, and was settled, Eumaeus passed me my spear. He smiled and, without any words, turned to make his way to the baggage train. I watched him go, envious of his place of comparative safety, then glanced at my nephew. Neoptolemus looked tense.

Supposing you and I, escaping this battle, would be able to live on forever . . . No, there was no escaping this battle. This was our duty – to take our stand in the forefront, where men earn glory. Today I would prove my father wrong, give the lie to the disdain of my brothers. I was no weakling, no runt of the litter. Before the sun went down I would show that I was a warrior, a true son of the House of Lyncestis. But fear was hard on me – fear of pain and death, fear of disgrace. Surely the long years of training – old Eumaeus at Lebaea, Cleitus and the others at Mieza – would see me through. All my life had been shaped towards this moment. This was my fate.

The Companions jostled into order; a line fifty wide and four deep. We were stationed at the rear of the army. Today it was the place of greatest danger. Alexander took his post in the middle of our front rank, flanked by Hephaestion and Parmenion's son Philotas. I was immediately behind Alexander, with Neoptolemus on my right shoulder, Cassander, son of Antipater, on my left.

Unnoticed by me, Alexander must have given the order. A trumpet rang out. The call was repeated from unit to unit. Peering round the crest of Alexander's helmet, I watched the army move off. The Cretans went first. The loose swarm of men in red tunics jogged back the way we had come, towards the narrow pass out of this trap. They were followed at a steady pace by Antipater with the two battalions of the phalanx. The uplanders from Elimea led by Coenus, a kinsman of their lord, were on the right, the lowlanders from Pieria commanded by the veteran Philip, son of Amyntas, on the left. Here on the valley floor each battalion was arrayed in a hundred and fifty files each ten deep. The dense mass of their long *sarissas* swayed above their heads like tall reeds in a breeze.

Between the phalanx and us was the baggage. It was a small train, just over five hundred men, perhaps seven hundred animals. The regulations of Alexander's father decreed only one servant and mule for each Companion cavalryman, the same for each ten man tent of infantry. Of course none of the Companions would dream of going to war without at least one spare horse. But there were no wagons, and no women. Unlike those who followed barbarians – hordes of innumerable slaves, concubines and dependants, even children – the Macedonians who led the mules and horses were far from helpless. Either they were old warriors, like Eumaeus, or youths waiting to join the army.

The baggage was in motion, and we walked after. The whole army advanced in silence; just the tramp of boots and hooves, the creak of armour, the occasional command of a junior officer to dress the lines. Up above, the Maedi continued to shout and sing. Although there was no heat in the day yet, sweat was running down my sides under my linen corselet.

The Cretans had reached the foot of the incline up to the pass. It ran for some three hundred paces, broad at the bottom, narrowing to little more than twenty paces across at the top. Up there the Maedi had made a rough barricade of rocks and logs. The pass was overlooked by rugged heights on both sides. Barricade and heights were thick with tribesmen. The Macedonian vanguard would have a hard time.

The phalanx halted behind the bowmen, the baggage behind them. Finally, we Companions drew up in place. Up on the crests, the Maedi yelled louder than ever. A trumpet call, and the two units of the phalanx realigned like well-oiled doors. A few moments later, without noise or confusion, they stood in two columns, side by side. Each column was ten men wide, and one hundred and fifty deep. The screeching of the Thracians faltered. Even the most drunken savage must have realised these were no mean opponents they had trapped.

The Cretans set off walking up the incline. There was no trumpet. From now, all Antipater's orders to the infantry would be word of mouth. Although out of range, some of the Maedi archers started shooting straightaway. When the arrows began to fall among them, the Cretans broke into a run, swerving and jinking into the gathering storm. About a hundred paces from the barricade – well within effective bowshot, but beyond any thrown missile – they stopped, opened their quivers, and shot back.

We sat on our horses and watched the unequal contest. The Cretans were outnumbered, their opponents uphill and mainly in cover. If the Maedi had had the discipline to loose in volleys, they would have swept our men from the bare slope. As it was, the widely spaced Cretans managed to dodge most of the arrows, or fend them off with the small round shields strapped to their arms. Yet here and there, a man went down. It was impossible to gauge the effect of their own shooting.

The Cretans endured for a time. Then, as one, turned and ran downhill. Most sprinted for their lives. Some, professional in adversity, were slower, helping their wounded. Only a dozen or so unmoving figures in red tunics were left sprawled on the track.

From all sides came the exultant shouts of the tribesmen. I glanced up at the heights on our left. They were leaping with joy, barely able to contain themselves.

When the Cretans were returned, the phalanx moved forward at a steady march; silent, weighty, seemingly implacable. A hundred and fifty paces out, they shifted from open to close order. Shields overlapping, each man occupying a frontage of no more than a foot and a half, they shuffled into the hail of missiles. Muffled from within the carapace of shields, came the

Macedonian war cry: *Al-al-al-al-ai!*. It was almost lost in the cries of the tribesmen.

A deadly hail of arrows streaked in. Some were deflected by the upraised shafts of the *sarissas*, others ricocheted off helmets, or embedded themselves in shields. Yet a number would be getting through. The noise and the fear would make the phalanx a terrible place. Most exposed was the extreme right-hand file. There the Elimiot veterans of Coenus had somehow hung their shields from their straps to cover their right. That was a trick worth learning.

When the phalanx was perhaps fifty paces from the barricade the chant of *Al-al-al-al-ai!* faded. Imperceptibly, the advance ground to a halt. The maelstrom of missiles increased. Stationary, unable to hit back, the Macedonians hunkered down.

Again I gazed up at the rim of the valley to our left. Worked into a frenzy, tribesmen were beginning to scramble down the steep slope to get at us. So far they came – slipping and sliding, clutching at boulders and the trunks of trees – in ones and twos: the bravest, the most maddened. A quick look to the right confirmed it was the same there. It would be worse behind us. There they had a broad path to our exposed backs. The Maedi had stopped the feared Macedonian phalanx. They sensed victory was within their grasp.

A deafening clamour from the front. Tribesmen were clambering over the barricade, tumbling down the overhanging rocks that flanked the pass. The phalanx was edging backwards. Slowly, one step at a time, still in order, the Macedonian infantry were retreating.

Looking wildly to either side, my heart shrank when I saw the barbarians coming down the sides of the valley. Now they came not as individuals or isolated handfuls, but in great groups. To our rear those holding the other pass had a clear run to our defenceless backs. Anxious voices were calling from those Companions who could see.

'Eyes front! Silence in the ranks!' Alexander roared.

The prince himself was looking back. Everything depended on his timing. He was unnaturally calm, as if in a trance, or possessed by some god. If he delayed a moment too long, it would all be over. They would catch us at a stand, our advantage gone. They would swarm our flanks and rear, drag us down from our mounts.

'Counter-march!'

Alexander and all the front riders wheeled to the right, walked back through the unit. With the second rank, I did the same. Within a few heartbeats, we were all facing the other way.

The enemy filled the valley floor, thousands of them. A dense horde of men on foot racing towards us, gaudy cloaks streaming, the faces on their shields shifting like snakes about to strike. Above them, long blades flashed in the sunshine. The terrible, two-handed *rhomphaias*, which could sheer through armour, cleave the skull of a horse.

'Each troop form wedge!'

The Thracians were only a couple of hundred paces away, closing fast. We shoved our horses into position. Now we faced them in four arrowheads of fifty riders. Alexander was at the apex of ours. I was still behind him, with Neoptolemus on my right, but Hephaestion to my left.

'Charge!'

We dug in our heels. The chestnut was eager. He leapt forward, almost unseating me. Desperately, I wrestled with the suddenly ungainly length of the spear in my hand as I regained my seat. Hephaestion swore at me to mind my weapon.

No time to build up speed, we booted our mounts straight to a gallop.

A knot of mounted warriors advanced behind the Maedi tribesmen. Alexander angled our wedge slightly towards them. I concentrated on the barbarians in front. The cornel wood of the *xyston* was slick in my hand, my breath tight in my chest.

No warhorse, no matter how fierce and well trained, will run into a solid object like a line of men on foot. The Maedi had no formed line. They had been dashing to join a massacre, not face a cavalry charge. They shied away from the tip of our wedge. It opened a gap into which we rode.

Alexander speared one, Hephaestion another, and we were in the midst of them. Our close order was gone, but we were moving through them. A fierce face, blue tattooed and bearded, mouth open as he swung the *rhomphaia* at Alexander's head. My overhand thrust caught him square in the chest. The spear-point stuck in his ribs. The momentum pulled the shaft from my grip. My fingers closed on the eagle-headed hilt of my sword, dragged it free of its scabbard.

'Keep moving!' Alexander was shouting. 'On me! Aim for the horsemen!'

With my thighs I urged Borysthenes forward.

The other three wedges were almost motionless, stabbing and hacking their way through the mass of footmen. Inspired by Alexander, we were nearly free. A Thracian cut at Borysthenes' neck. I blocked the *rhomphaia* with my blade. One of the rear rank riders stabbed him in the back. And then we were out the other side.

An open sward of meadow. The Maedi chieftain and his noble warriors, helmets and arms gleaming at the far end. These were not men who would run.

'*Al-al-al-al-ai!*' We were screaming. The Thracians howling back their cry. Both sides charged.

The ground seemed to shake under the pounding hoofs. The horses ate up the distance. There, in that remote glen, the war god Ares brought us together.

Alexander unhorsed their lead rider, and was gone into their midst.

A curved sword hacked at my face from the right. Although I ducked, the blow clanged off the side of my helmet. I thrust my straight Illyrian sword at his midriff, felt the point turned by his cuirass, before our mounts took us past each other.

'Xander, your left!' Neoptolemus' voice.

I twisted to face the threat. A Thracian spear thrusting at my body. Somehow I deflected it with my blade. Now the warrior and I were face to face, too close to wield our weapons. With our spare hands we clawed at each other's faces. Behind him, Hephaestion, watching, did nothing to help. The Thracian's nails scratched across my cheeks, seeking my eyes. I clutched his beard, hauled him backwards, off balance. Then his body jerked, and he grunted in shock. Slowly, he toppled off his horse. Neoptolemus was there, blood on his blade.

'They are running! It's over!' someone yelled.

It was true. The Thracians were streaming away.

We chased them the length of the valley, not sparing any. Our arms getting tired with the killing. When we reached the pass, we saw their camp below us: tents, wagons, women and children.

'Come on,' Neoptolemus shouted. 'They are ours for the taking.'

'Not until we are sure we have won.' My voice was hoarse after the fight.

As other Companions gathered, we gazed back. Sure enough, Macedonian standards flew over the other pass. Once we had charged, the phalanx had reversed its feigned retreat, and stormed the barricade. Alexander's stratagem had worked. Rather than just fight our way out, we had lured the Thracians down, and defeated them conclusively.

'Now we can plunder,' Neoptolemus said.

'No.' Alexander had appeared, armour scratched and dented, covered in gore. 'The infantry can have the camp. The Companions will chase the tribesmen until dusk, make sure they cannot re-form.'

Neoptolemus was not the only horseman who looked mutinous.

Alexander laughed. 'Do not look so sad. I will reward each of you, when we are back in Macedon.'

CHAPTER EIGHT

Summer 339 BC

'LYNCESTES, READ THIS LETTER from my father,' Alexander said.

Hephaestion, already leaning over Alexander's shoulder, gave me a venomous look.

> *My son, what on earth gave you the deluded hope that you would make faithful friends out of those whose affections you had bought?*

'What is he talking about?'

'You,' Alexander laughed. 'Well, not just you. It is the gifts I gave the Companions in Thrace.'

'Naming a city after yourself might have been unwise.' I had said at the time that presuming on the prerogatives of the King was bound to anger Philip. The gifts were just a pretext.

Once we had defeated the Maedi, we had marched through their lands. Most settlements had surrendered. Those that did not we had stormed and enslaved the population. The rebels had made their final stand at their stronghold on Mount Dounax. When we had got over the walls, no one was left alive. At least no men of fighting age. Alexander had brought in settlers: landless Macedonians, Thracians from loyal tribes, and some Hellenes from the south. He had called the refounded town Alexandropolis.

'It is not that,' Alexander said. 'Philip saw the advantages of a garrison in the upper Strymon.'

'He is jealous.' Hephaestion was always ready to flatter Alexander. 'Your campaign was a triumph. Last year he failed to capture either Perinthus or Byzantium. The sieges achieved nothing but entangle us in a war with Athens. Now, marching home through Thrace, he has been defeated by another tribe. They say his men fled from the Treballi, abandoning all the baggage. Philip was lucky to escape with his life.'

'A bad wound – a spear went through his thigh, killed his horse.' Alexander looked thoughtful. If his father had died, his own accession was not assured. There were other men – older men than me – with Argead blood. Before being acclaimed King by the army, Philip had been Regent for Amyntas, the son of his elder brother. Amyntas was some ten years Alexander's senior. More often than not the death of a Macedonian king caused a vicious struggle for the throne.

'The troops are calling Philip their *general*, but you their *King*,' Hephaestion said.

Alexander snapped out of his reverie. 'Some things are best not repeated. The injury will not have improved my father's temper. Although perhaps it was timely. Unbroken good fortune tempts the gods. Anyway he defeated the Scythians at the mouths of the Ister. All he lost was the plunder he had taken.'

Cassander, the eldest son of Antipater, walked into the room. Alexander glowered. Although Cassander was one of his foster-brothers, there was bad blood between them. There was some story of a fight before I had arrived at Mieza. Although Alexander was not tall, it would have been an unequal contest. Cassander was a thin and sickly youth.

Sketching a faint salute to Alexander – no more than a wave of his hand – Cassander turned to me.

'My father wants to see you.'

'I should wash and change.' We had been exercising the horses, and I was filthy.

'He told me to bring you straightaway.'

From the steps of the palace at Pella the whole city lay spread out on the plain below. A neat grid of paved streets ran down to the port, beyond which the saltwaters of Lake Loudias glittered in the sun.

'What does your father want?'

'That is for him to say.' My friendship with Alexander meant that Cassander was never comfortable in my presence.

We walked down towards the harbour. Despite his wealth, Antipater maintained a modest house well away from the palace. Its proximity to the sanctuary of Darron, the local Macedonian god of healing, seemed intended to show that the great general was not estranged from his humble origins in the small traditional village of Paliura.

Cassander left me at the gate, and walked away with the air of someone who had accomplished a distasteful task. The porter led me down the corridor and across a peristyle to a reception room.

Antipater was waiting, a letter in one hand, a plain wooden cup in the other. Seated next to him was his eldest daughter Electra. I had seen her at various festivals.

'Health and long life.'

After the greetings there was a silence. The room was painted with the abduction of Helen. She was depicted walking up the gangplank of a ship. There was little sense of reluctance. Looking back, she raised a hand; more in farewell than horror.

'Why do you have no beard, and wear your hair so long?'

Electra's questions set me back. She might as well have openly accused me of effeminacy. Antipater spoke before I could answer.

'It is the fashion among the foster-brothers of Alexander.'

'Why?'

Antipater appeared to be suppressing a smile.

'The heroes in Homer wear their hair long,' I said, 'and an enemy can catch hold of your beard in a fight.'

Electra regarded me with her light grey eyes. There was a resemblance to her father, but her features were fine, with a small, straight nose and high cheekbones.

'Being clean shaven served me well in the battle with the Maedi.'

Her eyes dropped to my sword-belt. The white leather was dirty, and I was very conscious that I was sweat stained and stank of horse.

She looked at her father. 'He will do. At least he is not as unprepossessing as the others.'

Now Antipater laughed out loud.

I waited, uncertain what this was about.

Antipater waved the letter. 'Philip has decided to bind Lyncestis closer to the lowlands. One of the Bacchid house is to marry my daughter. Electra has chosen you not your brothers.'

* * *

The wedding feast was in the palace. Philip was there, but Antipater was the host. There were twenty men in the great room, which was decorated with scenes of hunting. Each wore a wreath of gold, but not all were full of goodwill. Of my brothers,

Heromenes was the more put out. This was yet more evidence for Horse-face of life playing him a bad turn. The demeanour of Arrhabaeus was sullen, but resigned. Hephaestion had a superior look on his face, and had already made a comment about up-country peasants reeking of goat. Cassander – sitting on an upright chair, like a child, as he had not yet killed his boar – looked ill, consumed with antipathy to his sister marrying a friend of Alexander.

'The bride and the women!'

We got to our feet. My father somewhat unsteadily. Aeropus had been drinking before the ceremony.

Veiled and demure, Electra led in the women. There were twenty; one to dine with each man. Among them was Olympias, tall and beautiful, radiating disapproval. As Philip had found, not all marriages are easy. Now that Eurydice, the King's mother, was dead, no one doubted that Olympias held the first place among the women at court. None of Philip's other wives were at the ceremony.

Electra stopped before the couch which I would share with her father. From the threshold, a chorus of young girls and boys sang a hymn. Then her mother removed her veil. It brought a raucous cheer from the men.

Electra kept her eyes down, as a bride should. Yet she seemed composed, older than her sixteen years. I stepped forward, took her hand, and led her to the chair by my side of the couch. When she was seated, the other men escorted the other women to their places.

A young boy carrying a winnowing basket entered and spoke the ritual words: 'I escaped the bad, I found the better.' What they meant, no one knew.

From the basket he produced a loaf of bread, which he placed on the table in front of Antipater and me. I drew my sword with its eagle hilt. Antipater placed his scarred old hands on mine, and together we cut the loaf. In Macedonian custom Electra and I were now husband and wife.

Olympias stood to propose a toast. It was as well there were no Hellenes present, apart from Alexander's foster-brother Medius of Thessaly. The freedom of our women was one of the many things they found barbaric about Macedonians.

'The giver of the bride, the bridegroom, and the bride.' She spoke the line of poetry as if it were a curse. Nevertheless, everyone drank. I struggled to remember where it was from.

Suddenly I realised that Electra was getting to her feet. Her face was set, like a mask, as she faced Olympias, and raised her cup.

'You are a clever woman, no stranger to dark knowledge.'

It was Euripides – Creon's words ordering the witch Medea into exile. Olympias looked as if she would hurl her cup in Electra's face. Violence was not uncommon at Macedonian feasts. Usually it was among the men.

'Ladies, this is a wedding, not a battlefield.' Philip's good eye gazed at each of the two in turn. Then he raised his cup. 'He that drinks most will have least sorrow.'

At a sign from Antipater, a trumpet sounded for the first course. Great platters of roast fowls – duck, goose, chicken – were brought round. We helped ourselves, and gave the rest to the servants. As I ate, I looked at Electra, and wondered that she would dare confront Olympias. On our few chaperoned meetings she had given no hint of such resolve. What sort of bride had I married?

There were two more courses – oysters, scallops and fish, then a whole roast boar, stuffed with thrushes and warblers – and finally fruit, nuts and cheese. There were conjurers, sword-dancers, and fire-breathers; flute girls and singers, sambuca players from Rhodes. The wine was Thasian, Mendean, Lesbian, served unmixed with water. The noise rose as the guests drank. Throughout, I kept looking at Electra, thinking about her fierce display, and what was to come.

At long last the feast was over. I took Electra's hand, and we led the procession to the small house I had bought down by the lake. Alexander walked with us as my best friend. I would have chosen Neoptolemus as my *parochos*, but his twin Amyntas would have been put out. Antipater and Electra's mother headed the rest of the guests, carrying torches and calling out words of good omen. Not everyone from the feast followed. Philip's right thigh was still too lame from his recent wound. My father probably too drunk. Olympias had other reasons for her absence.

In the house we stood by the hearth and the others tossed nuts and dried fruits and sweetmeats over our heads. The women took Electra to the bridal chamber, and I drank with the men until it was time. Then they took me to the door, laughing and joking, making lewd suggestions. They pushed me inside, and shut the door.

Electra was on the bed. In the light of a lamp, her face was tense, as if going into battle. From outside came the sound of an old bawdy song.

She held her arms out towards me. Unbuckling my belt, stripping off my tunic, I went to her. She was wearing just a thin shift. The material clinging to her body was more arousing than had she been naked. My experience was with farmers' daughters or prostitutes, not sheltered virgins. I tried to be gentle, tried to take my time, make sure she was ready. Evidently, I was too slow. Her shift rucked up round her waist, she spread her legs, and reached down to guide me. When I entered her, she cried out loudly in pain. But when I started to draw back, she clasped my hips, pulled me back into her. Again she cried out.

'There has to be blood on the sheets, or there will be rumours that I am not a virgin.' Her breath was hot in my ear. 'Besides you want your friends to think you are a man.'

Again I wondered just what sort of girl I had married, before all my thoughts vanished in the pleasure of the moment.

CHAPTER NINE

Summer 338 BC

O LD EUMAEUS WOKE ME well before dawn. I had slept badly, and was tired. Alexander had returned in the middle of the night from a war council with Philip. Only the most senior commanders had been invited. Alexander had looked excited, bursting with news, but was reticent when asked what had been discussed. Now he was asleep in the tent pitched under a huge oak.

The camp of the Companion Cavalry was by a river, so I went down to wash in the cool of the early morning. Big white-blue irises glowed in the ambient light. Their flowers scented the air like violets. Other Companions were already bathing. It was safe enough. Sentries were posted both on the far bank and downstream. The enemy had not exhibited any activity in the previous nights.

We had come south into Hellas at the request of the Amphictyonic Council which controlled the oracle at Delphi. The council had declared a Sacred War against the city of Amphissa, which had been farming lands dedicated to the gods. We had punished the sacrilege, but it was common knowledge that Amphissa was no more than a pretext. Our expedition was intended to finish the war with Athens. Philip had hoped to persuade Thebes, the most powerful city in central Greece, either to join us, or, at least, remain neutral and allow us free passage through its territories. After all Thebes was our ally, and had many differences with

Athens. An Athenian orator called Demosthenes, an inveterate enemy of Philip, had put paid to those hopes. For the last two days we had faced the combined armies of Athens and Thebes, as well as some of their allies, on the plain in front of the small town of Chaeronea.

When I came back from the river the army was stirring. Thousands of men – as ever Philip had banned all female camp followers – were rolling out of blankets, stiffly getting to their feet. As the camp fires, banked up for the night, were kicked into life, a myriad of lights sparked across the dark plain. The soldiers were talking and joking. Some of the voices were tight with anxiety, some of the laughter a little too loud. Under the boughs of the oak tree, Hephaestion and some others were hanging about. Alexander was still sleeping. That showed strong nerves – better than mine – given what was to come.

This was the battle that would decide the fate of both Hellas and Macedon. If we won, we would be masters of the Greeks, and Philip would be free to pursue the often discussed campaign into Asia against the Persian King of Kings. If we lost, the Thracians would rise up, the Athenians strike at our possessions across the north Aegean, and the Paeonians and Illyrians would pour over the borders. From the walls of Lebaea, once again my mother would see the smoke rising from burning farms on the plain of Lyncestis, once again have to ready the defences with old men and boys as the barbarian warriors came up the track to the stronghold.

The sky was beginning to lighten – a hint of azure above the eastern heights. Eumaeus gave me some food and drink, and went off to see to my mount. The salt pork was cold and greasy, revolting on an already queasy stomach. The hardtack was too dry and tough to chew. I tried dipping it in watered wine, but still found it difficult to swallow. After a time I gave up.

Parmenion and his son rode up through the gloom. After dismounting, he threw his reins to Hephaestion, and told Philotas to get off his horse and go in and wake Alexander. I was delighted that Hephaestion looked furious at being treated like a groom. Two years had passed, but I had not forgotten that he had left me to my fate in the fight against the Maedi.

It was time to arm. I pulled on my soft leather cavalry boots. Then, like heroes in Homer, Neoptolemus and I helped each other buckle together the breast and back plates of our corselets. My white linen armour had been altered as I had grown, and still felt comfortable. We tied our sashes round our waists, slipped the sword-belts over our shoulders, and finally put on our helmets. I tied and retied the laces of my helmet several times, until I was satisfied it was secure, but not so tight it would be a distraction.

Eumaeus led up Cynagos. The black stallion was spirited, sometimes too bold in the hunting field. I would have preferred to ride Borysthenes in battle, but he had gone lame on the march. I checked the girth and curb bit, inspected his feet. When the trumpet sounded, Eumaeus gave me a leg up, and handed me my spear.

'Let us be men,' Neoptolemus said. The encouragement had been old when Agamemnon had been High King of Mycenae. Together we went at a walk to form up in our squadron.

Sunrise revealed the plain; less than two miles across, and ringed with hills. Chaeronea straggled up the foothills to the west. The buildings of its acropolis were already bathed in the first yellow light. To our left, still in shade, the Cephissus River meandered at the base of a smooth grey slope of rock. Further south its banks gave way to a broad marsh.

The enemy were about four hundred paces away, drawn up diagonally across the plain from below Chaeronea to where the swamp swelled out from the river. A solid phalanx of hoplites, at least eight deep. Over the preceding days we had come to know their contingents. The Thebans were opposite us by the marsh, the allies from the smaller cities in the centre, and the Athenians on their left overlooked by Chaeronea. Their cavalry were stationed behind the phalanx, and their light infantry could be seen climbing goat tracks to extend their line to the town.

To win the Thebans over, the Athenians had not only agreed to bear the majority of the cost of the war, but had ceded command of the army. The Theban generals had chosen a good defensive position. Resting on the river and the hills, it could not be outflanked. A notch in the hills behind them was the Kerata Pass through which they could retreat if they were losing. As they were set well back, and at an angle across the plain, we must advance between the river and the western hills. Should they prevail in the centre, our left might well find itself trapped with its back to the Cephissus.

When Alexander appeared, the pikemen in front of the Companion Cavalry cheered. Coenus' battalion from Elimea banged their *sarissas* on their shields, then fell silent to hear what Alexander would say. He would ride along the left wing of our forces, stopping to speak to each battalion under his command. Philip would be doing the same on the right.

Alexander was alone, bare headed and mounted on Bucephalus. He gestured at the enemy.

'Count them. More than thirty thousand. More than us.' He pointed at the Thebans opposite. 'Now count the number of trained soldiers – just the three hundred of the Sacred Band. All the rest of that vast array are farmers or potters or merchants; among the Athenians there will be any number of orators and philosophers.'

He spoke in Macedonian dialect, and the men laughed.

'We train all year round, campaign in the cold of winter and the heat of summer. We are thirty thousand veterans. The odds in our favour: a hundred Macedonians to one Greek!'

Again the uplanders cheered as he rode off. The Athenians had hired a couple of thousand mercenaries, but what Alexander said made sense. I wondered if he would say the same to each battalion. Knowing Alexander he would find new words fitting each audience. It was easy to see why the men loved him.

Resting my spear across my thighs, I slid my sword part-way out of its scabbard. The eagle hilt was somehow reassuring in my hand. I had been through this before; in the pass above Lebaea, in the unnamed valley of the Maedi. I had not disgraced myself then, and would not do so today.

I looked at the riders around me. Pausanias and his namesake that we called *Kalos*; both recently promoted from Royal Pages to Companions. They loathed each other. Neither was a friend of mine. There was Hephaestion, always my enemy. At least my kinsmen Neoptolemus and Leonnatus were here. I was of the house of Lyncestis. *These are no ignoble men, these kings of ours.* If I had not the courage to emulate Achilles, at least I would not play Thersites, the most worthless of the warriors before Troy.

Alexander cantered back to take his place at the head of the royal squadron of the Companions. There were three other squadrons of Macedonians, in all just under a thousand riders. They were matched by a thousand Thessalian cavalry, led by Parmenion, on our right. The Thessalians were armed and equipped like us. Noblemen from the wide pastures of northern Greece, they were natural horsemen. It was said they were the second best cavalry in the world, after the Macedonian Companions.

From far off to the right a trumpet rang out. It was repeated down the whole line. We watched our phalanx move off. Philip was on the extreme right with the *hypaspists*, the three thousand elite shield bearers. Next to them were the fifteen hundred pikemen from Lyncestis and Orestis commanded by my father. For all his feckless drinking, Aeropus was trusted by Philip to fight; probably because the Lyncestians fought better under their natural lord. Twelve more battalions of Foot Companions stretched from the *taxis* of my father to that of Coenus on the extreme left; the entire front line infantry of Macedonia.

They went at a slow walk, *sarissas* erect. Twenty-four thousand men, ten deep, moving as one in perfect silence. No gaps opened in the line, not even when those on the right splashed through a stream running down from the hills. It was impossible to see what the cavalry on either side could do until one phalanx or the other broke. If defeated, we would screen the retreat, if victorious brush their cavalry aside – southern Hellenes are poor horsemen – then ride down fleeing men. The thought was comforting as we walked our horses over the grass trampled by the phalanx. I had no wish to die on this distant plain in Hellas. Much of me wished to be back in Pella with Electra. Unlike that of Philip and Olympias my marriage was not a battlefield.

On the slopes to our right the light infantry of our allies – mainly men from Thessaly – was engaged with that of the Hellenes. In the distance the tiny figures of bowmen and slingers took shots from a hundred paces or more. Diminutive javelin men – mere dots on the hillside – dodged out from behind rocks at closer range, hastily threw, and ducked back again. It was like watching insects fight. Unless one side drove the other completely off the hills, and could turn on the flanks of the heavy infantry, it would have no effect on the outcome of the battle.

The dust raised by Coenus' men was making it hard to see the enemy. There was a smell of thyme and other wild herbs bruised by their feet. I thought of Electra; her perfume distilled from narcissi and roses.

A gust of wind parted the clouds of dust. There were the Thebans, less than two hundred paces ahead of Coenus' men. Along their front rank, identical round shields each painted with the club of Herakles, the symbol of Thebes. This was the Sacred Band, a hundred and fifty pairs of male lovers, trained to war. Their predecessors had humbled the Spartans at Leuctra and Nemea. They would rather die than be dishonoured in the sight of their beloved. The Sacred Band had never known defeat.

Again a trumpet signal from Philip was passed from unit to unit. A hundred paces from the enemy the Macedonian phalanx halted, except for the right wing. The *hypaspists* with Philip and the Aeropus' battalion moved to the attack. Their *sarissas* of the front ranks came down to the horizontal, the rest angled forward over their heads, like some mythical creature flexing its spikes. They raised the war cry – *Al-al-al-al-ai!*; the Athenians sang their *Paean*.

It made good sense this echeloned assault, let the best troops hit one flank, then turn inwards, and roll up the enemy line. Philip was skilled in generalship.

We heard the clash, but were too far away to witness individuals fighting: the Macedonians jabbing underhand, trying to get the heads of their *sarissas* between or under shields, aiming for the groin; the Athenians using their big shields to force apart the hedge of pikes, get inside, and strike their shorter spears downwards at the face. It did not matter we could not see. This was seasoned professionals against amateurs and some men fighting for pay. There could only be one result.

The sun was hot on our faces. A blustering wind had got up, blowing down from the north. It too was hot, bringing little relief. I watched a bird flying over the Theban ranks. Not an omen, just a gull. It dipped and soared on the gusts.

'Look,' Neoptolemus said, 'we are falling back!'

He was right. There was no doubt. Philip and my father's men were giving ground. They were not running, but step by step they were retreating. Huddled behind their spearpoints, crouched under their shields, they were being driven back on the rest of the army. My heart shrank. This was going to be a terrible day.

A tremor ran through the rest of the Athenians and the allies next to them. 'Chase them back to Macedon!' The shout came from the Athenian ranks. Philip was retreating. They sensed victory was within their grasp. With a roar, the Athenians, followed by their allies in the centre, surged forward. Soon some were running, others walking, their close order falling into disarray. The battalions of the Macedonian phalanx, so far uncommitted, swung down their pikes, and set off to meet them with perfect discipline. Over on the right trumpets blared. Philip had rallied and returned to the attack.

'He has drawn them out!' Neoptolemus was grinning. 'The old fox!'

'And his cub,' Alexander said over his shoulder. 'But wait, there should be more.'

The gaze of all of us cavalry was fixed on the Thebans. If they joined the impromptu assault of the rest of the Greeks, launched themselves up the plain, their right would no longer be screened by the marsh. There would be room for us to ride between them and the river, crash into their unshielded side.

The Thebans did not move. The discipline of the Sacred Band in their front rank held them in place. A groan of disappointment went up from the Companion Cavalry.

'Patience, men.' Alexander did not look in the least downhearted. 'There is more than one way to skin a cat.'

Of course! A gap was opening between the advancing allied Greeks in the centre and the backs of Coenus and the other Macedonians heading for stationary Thebans on the enemy right. Twenty paces, forty, soon a hundred paces yawned open like a gate.

'Follow me!' Alexander had drawn his sword. The sunburst standard pointed the way. We booted our horses, and in one great wedge, an arrowhead tipped by Alexander, the Companions angled into the opening. Led by Parmenion the Thessalians followed in our wake.

'With me!' Alexander turned to face the Greek horse behind their phalanx.

Looking back, I saw the Thessalians swerving to the right, aiming for the flank and rear of the enemy centre. Old Parmenion had seized the opportunity.

'Charge!' Alexander yelled.

The enemy cavalry were caught by surprise. One moment they had been safe, watching the backs of their seemingly victorious hoplites, now, as if sprung from the earth, the most feared horse-men in the world were bearing down on them. They did not wait. Sawing at their reins, they yanked round their horses' heads, and bolted. The Greeks scattered across the plain, every man seeking to save himself. Most galloped south, some raced towards the Kerata Pass.

Many veterans will tell you that cavalry are like a slingshot; once released they cannot be recalled. It is not true. Not of the best trained horsemen. Reining back to a canter, Alexander led us in a wide semicircle so we were facing the rear of the Theban infantry.

You had to admire those Theban hoplites. Threatened from the rear almost any phalanx will fall apart. Although the pike-men of Coenus and the others were about to crash into their front, the last four ranks of the Thebans turned to face us.

'Charge!' Alexander kicked on into a gallop. Without hesita-tion we followed.

A cavalry charge is a gamble. It can only prevail through fear. No horse will run into a solid block of men on foot, let alone one tipped with sharp steel and bronze. If infantry stand firm, maintain an unbroken line, they are safe. The horses will pull up; refusing they will throw many of their riders to the ground. In an instant the horsemen will be reduced to impotent confusion.

But it is a hard thing to stand against a mounted charge. The terrible noise, the ground trembling beneath thousands of hoofs, the very air seeming to shake, the size and speed of the men on horses. Fear enters by the eyes and the ears.

The Thebans were brave, but the ordeal was too much. A crack opened in the Theban frontage. Just a handful of hoplites shuf-fled slightly away from Alexander and the point of impact. And that was enough – we were among them, spears jabbing down, the weight of our mounts barrelling men aside.

The world narrowed to the reach of a weapon. The tip of my spear caught in a Theban shield. The shaft splintered. Urging Cynagos on, I dragged my sword from its scabbard. Another hoplite – eyes wild above the rim of his shield – thrust at my thigh. I turned the blow with my blade, recovered, and slashed backhanded. The heavy edge of steel sheered away his face from eyes to chin like cutting an apple.

Al-al-al-al-ai! Macedonian voices raised in triumph. The Thebans were broken. No, not all of them. The Sacred Band fought on. Back to back – the older man and his younger beloved, those that were still alive – stubbornly defied us.

'Finish them!' Alexander was by my side. Together, we launched the final charge.

The Theban who faced me was young – smooth cheeks, long hair – but resolute. He crouched, wielding his spear in two hands. The point took Cynagos full in the chest. Falling, the mortally injured horse smashed the youth aside. I hurled myself sideways, desperate not to be crushed by Cynagos. Landing awkwardly on my back, I felt a stab of white hot agony in my chest. Unable to draw breath, I lay helpless. My sword was gone. An older Theban towered over me. The butt-spike of his spear poised to punch down into my torso. Then a sword sliced into his shoulder, buckling his armour. He staggered. The sword cut down into his neck, and he toppled away.

There were boots on either side of me. Still unable to breath, panic stricken, I tried to get up.

'Stay down, you are just winded.' From nowhere, Leonnatus covered me with a Theban shield.

Painfully drawing air into my lungs, I watched the last Thebans die.

When it was over, my kinsman helped me to my feet. All around us were scenes of butchery. Macedonians hacking at the ankles and shins of dead Thebans, severing their feet. These ghosts would not walk, never seek vengeance.

* * *

We were reeling, heroically drunk. Unlike the Hellenes, we do not build a trophy after a victory. Once, long ago, a Macedonian called Caranus had piled up the weapons of another lord he had defeated. A god sent a lion down from the mountains. The beast scattered the trophy. Caranus understood the god. A lasting memorial creates lasting enmity. Instead of a trophy, we devote ourselves to drinking.

After the battle, we gathered our dead – they would be cremated tomorrow with sacrifices, games, and all honours. That grim task accomplished, we stripped off our armour, dressed our wounds, and washed. Then we feasted. There were roast oxen, and sweet dark wine. Alexander played the lyre – there were no flute-girls in the camp. Some warriors danced. Philip joined them, then cursed his lameness. Alexander told him to rejoice in the injury; every step recalled his valour. Father and son were happy. We were all happy. Even my father and my sour brother Heromenes seemed joyful. We were the masters of Hellas.

Philip called for a *komos*. The line of revellers snaked out from our camp towards the pens where the servants guarded the prisoners. Not all the Athenians had reached the Kerata Pass. Many had fled into a nearer gap in the hills. It was a dead end. Their panic had added two thousand prisoners to their thousand dead. The allies in the centre, and the Thebans on the right, surrounded by our cavalry, had suffered worse.

As we approached the Athenians, Philip began to sing.

Demosthenes, son of Demosthenes,
Paeanian, thus proposes . . .

The rest of the *komos* took it up. The wine had dulled the pain in my ribs, but not enough to sing.

Demosthenes, son of Demosthenes,
Paeanian, thus proposes . . .

Over and over, the opening of the decree which led to the war. Demosthenes was not among the prisoners. It was said that as he had fled through the Kerata Pass, his cloak snagged on a bramble, without looking round, he had begged, 'Take me alive!'

A man got up from the huddled prisoners.

'King Philip, Fortune has cast you as Agamemnon, are you not ashamed to play Thersites?'

There was a shocked silence. Philip's rages were notorious.

Philip reached up, removed the garland of flowers from his head, and threw it away.

'Who are you?'

'Demades, the orator.'

Now Philip appeared entirely sober. 'You are a brave man, Demades. I need an orator with the courage to speak the truth.' He gestured for the guards to free Demades.

'You will be my envoy to negotiate peace with Athens.' Philip raised his voice to address all the prisoners. 'I have no enmity towards the Athenians. You were misled by Demosthenes and a few other demagogues. All of you will be released without ransom.'

There was a ragged cheer from the prisoners. Not building a trophy is not the only way to win over the defeated. Had Philip ever been drunk? Had he planned this scene?

We went on across the battlefield, quietly talking about the events of the day.

When we reached marsh, by which the Sacred Band had fallen, it was like a charnel house in the light of our torches. The bodies of the lovers were naked and mutilated, many had had their feet hacked off.

Philip put his arm round young Kalos. Tears streamed from Philip's good eye. With his free hand he pointed to the corpses of the Sacred Band.

'A curse on those who imagine that these men ever did or suffered anything shameful!'

Philip kissed Kalos on the lips.

At the edge of the torchlight, Pausanius, the King's slighted lover, stood rigid with fury.

* * *

'Wake up!'

Neoptolemus was shaking me. It hurt my ribs.

'Wake up, now!'

My head hurt from the wine. 'Let me sleep.'

'No.'

A sharp pain, like a knife in my chest, when I tried to rise. The ribs were cracked, not broken. Last night old Eumaeus had placed one open hand on my back, the other on my chest, then suddenly squeezed. I had grunted with pain. He said if they had been broken, I would have screamed.

'What time is it?'

'Philip has exiled your father.'

'What?' The fumes of the wine clouded my thoughts. 'But Aeropus fought well.'

'After the *komos*, he and Damasippus brought a flute-girl from a local inn to their tent.'

My father and his friend had disobeyed a direct order: no women in the camp.

'Who has taken command of his battalion; Arrhabaeus or Heromenes?'

'Perdiccas of Orestis.'

That would make my brothers, especially Horse-face, even more bitter. But Perdiccas was the son of Orontes, the Lord of Orestis, and half the men were from their lands.

'I had better say farewell to my father.'

'They have already left.'

I said nothing.

'You do not seem upset.'

'You know we were not close.'

Neoptolemus nodded. 'Where do you think they will go?'

'The King of Kings welcomes anyone at odds with Philip. It could be we will meet again in Persia – on opposite sides of the battlefield.'

CHAPTER TEN

Summer 337 BC

'LOVE! WHAT HAS LOVE got to do with a wedding!'

We were walking up to the Palace at Aegae.

'You did not love me,' Electra said. 'And I married you because my father told me to choose one of the sons of Aeropus.'

'But we are happy now.'

'Stop looking so sulky.' Electra squeezed my hand. 'We are fortunate, but we did not marry for love. Philip must be nearly fifty. It is madness for him to say he is besotted with this girl, and must have her as his wife.'

'I cannot see it matters,' I said. 'Philip has had six wives, why worry about a seventh.'

Electra raised her eyes to the heavens. 'Perhaps I should have chosen one of your brothers. Either Horse-face or the silent one would have had more sense. None of Philip's other wives have been Macedonian.'

'Phila was from Elimea.'

'She bore no children. This Cleopatra is the niece and adopted daughter of Attalus, one of the great Macedonian noblemen of the plains. Olympias is a witch from Epirus. There have always been whispers of adultery, that Philip was not Alexander's father.'

I stopped, turned to face her. 'They are nothing but lies spread by Alexander's enemies at court.'

'No man knows what she does with the maenads in the hills.'

I said nothing.

'And her maids say sometimes she makes dark hints about a god visiting her bed. They say he comes in the form of a serpent.'

'That will just be the house-snake. Many households keep one to catch mice. This is all nonsense, idle gossip from the women's quarters.'

'Perhaps, but if Cleopatra gives Philip a son, he will be a threat to Alexander as heir.'

That was ridiculous, and I laughed. 'Alexander is almost twenty, has been Regent of Macedon, and won the battle of Chaeronea. The army would never acclaim a child of Cleopatra unless Alexander was dead.'

We walked on, but Electra still looked serious. 'Yes, that is exactly what Olympias will think.'

The wedding feast was in a room decorated with the home-coming of Agamemnon. I shared a couch with Leonnatus halfway down one side. Throughout the first course I was dis-tracted, my eyes turning to the mural: the King trapped in his bath, Clytemnestra urging her lover to plunge the sword into her husband. Not altogether auspicious.

The slurs about Alexander's paternity were nothing, but Electra might be right about this wedding. Philip could be introducing needless conflict into his court. Everything else was going well. After Chaeronea Philip had kept his word and treated Athens leniently. Alexander and Antipater had been his envoys. They had returned the prisoners and the ashes of the dead without ransom. Things had been different for the Thebans. They had broken their oath of alliance. The Thebans had to pay for the return of their dead, and their prisoners were sold as slaves. A Macedonian garrison was installed in their acropolis, the Cadmea, and their government was given to an oligarchy of three hundred men loyal to Philip.

My ribs had been slow to heal. I was sent back to Macedon with the wounded, and did not accompany the army south into the Peloponnese. Philip had summoned the Greeks of the mainland to Corinth. All had come, except the Spartans. The Hellenes had sworn to keep a common peace, and elected Philip their leader. A campaign was to be launched against the Persians; to free the Greeks under their rule, and to exact revenge for their burning of Athens long ago. Every *polis* would contribute troops. As *Hegemon*, Philip was to command the combined forces. After a brief campaign against some Illyrian tribes, Philip had returned to Macedon and begun to prepare the army to cross to Asia.

Everything was going so well, and now Philip was marrying this girl.

'He likes the grapes when they are green,' Leonnatus said.

I realised I had been staring at Cleopatra.

'Boys or girls, he likes them young.' Leonnatus took a drink. 'It might not have happened if Kalos had not played the hero and got himself killed in Illyria. Pausanias goaded him to his death; always questioning his manhood, calling him a catamite.'

I looked round the room.

'Pausanias was not invited. Attalus was fond of young Kalos.' Leonnatus leant closer with a confiding air. 'Attalus told her to hold out, not to spread her legs until after the wedding; marriage or nothing. Have you heard the other news about Attalus?'

Sometimes bluff Leonnatus liked to act the court insider to his younger relatives, especially to me. 'That he wants to marry Parmenion's eldest daughter?' I kept a straight face.

Behind me, I heard Electra laugh. Of course she had told me this gossip.

Leonnatus looked vaguely put out. 'Father-in-law of the King, married into the family of the great general – wants watching does Attalus.'

The words of Leonnatus were prophetic, far sooner than anyone could have imagined.

The trouble came, as so often, in Macedon, when the food was over, and the serious drinking started. If I were King, I would forbid men to carry arms at feasts. Better if there were no weapons on the walls, and the guards were outside. Too many feuds are started, too many brave men die.

Attalus got to his feet, flushed with wine and good fortune. Next to him Philip also looked worse for wear. The King had been pledging his guests. Each time he drained the Cup of Nestor. The gods alone knew how much that Argead heirloom held.

'A toast!' Attalus swayed as he raised his cup. 'To the bride and groom!'

We all drank.

Attalus had not finished. 'Now surely there will be bred for us true-born kings!'

A terrible silence followed his words.

Alexander was on his feet, face white with anger. 'What of me, you wretch? Do you take me for a bastard?' His arm went back, and he threw the cup in his hand full at Attalus' face.

The older man ducked. But he was slow, befuddled with drink. The heavy gold flagon caught him a glancing blow to the back of his head, red wine splattered his white tunic. Straightening, mouthing an obscenity, Attalus went to hurl his own cup at

Alexander. But now Philip was off his couch, rushing at his son, dragging his sword from its scabbard.

The King's lame leg gave way. He went sprawling.

Alexander pointed at his father. 'Look now, men. The one who was preparing to cross from Europe to Asia, and he cannot get from one couch to another!'

With no time for thought, I was up, and grabbed Alexander's left arm. Hephaestion had his right.

'We must leave,' I said

Philip was roaring, fingers scrabbling across the floor for the hilt of his sword.

'Lyncestes is right,' Hephaestion said, 'we must go.'

Philip was back on his feet, but Antipater and Parmenion held him back. The King bellowed like a trussed bull.

Together Hephaestion and I manhandled Alexander from the room.

Out in the moonlit courtyard the three of us stood, unsure what to do. Thankfully, Alexander had not drawn his blade, had offered no violence to the King. All might be forgiven in the sober morning.

A tall shadow from the open door. Hephaestion and I moved to shield Alexander. He pushed us away.

Olympias was alone. From inside we could hear Philip shouting. Another, slighter figure slipped out after Alexander's mother.

'We must leave Macedon.' Unveiled, Olympias' face was set.

'Never,' Alexander said. 'I will not run from that drunkard.'

'He is the King,' Olympias said. 'You have made him look a fool. You know his nature. He must have revenge.'

'I will have his head, and that of Attalus.'

His mother put her hands on his shoulders. She was taller than Alexander. 'One day you will be King. But now look around you: one woman and two companions. We will leave Aegae tonight, ride west, take refuge with my brother in Epirus. He will not betray his blood.'

Alexander stood undecided.

'Philip will not be restrained long. We have to go now,' she said.

Alexander nodded, and let his mother and Hephaestion lead him off towards the stable block.

'You must go with them.'

I had not noticed Electra approach.

'But . . .'

'Philip will remember that you were with Alexander. He will take out his anger on you.'

'But I don't want to leave you.'

'I am Antipater's daughter. I will come to no harm. Your nephews and your brothers are here.'

'Olympias and Hephaestion hate me.'

'But Alexander loves you.' She stood on tiptoes and kissed me. 'And I love you. But you have to go now.'

We rode through the night, south-west through the deep gorges of the Bermion range. In Aegae, as we hurriedly tacked up the horses, four more of Alexander's foster-brothers had surreptitiously joined our flight: Nearchus the Cretan, Medius of Thessaly, Harpalus, and Ptolemy, who rumour held was the natural son of Philip. It was a measure of our weakness – two foreigners, a cripple, and a bastard.

We reached Elimea in the morning. Its Lord Machatas was less surprised to see his son Harpalus than he was Olympias and Alexander. Harpalus concocted a story about Olympias rushing to the bedside of her brother the King of Epirus who had been taken ill. Our lack of servants undermined the credibility of the tale – when did the royal family travel without any? – but Machatas said nothing direct. Instead, while we were eating, he told an anecdote of being summoned to appear in a court case judged by the King. Philip had been drunk, and had fallen asleep. When he woke he found against Machatas and imposed a fine. Machatas said he was going to appeal. 'To whom?' Philip had shouted, losing his temper. Machatas had deftly replied, 'From Philip drunk to Philip sober.' Later, when the drink had died out of him, Philip had not reversed his decision, but had paid the fine himself. Often it was safest to offer oblique advice. There were informers in every noble household. The message was clear. What Philip did in anger he would later make right, as long as it did not impinge his majesty. From their demeanour neither Olympias or Alexander accepted the moral.

We had to set out again in the afternoon. If horsemen arrived from Aegae with orders for our arrest, should Machatas not comply he would be guilty of treason. His brother had been executed a few years previously on that charge. Although to be fair, Derdas had taken up arms against Philip.

The Lord of Elimea provided us with spare horses, provisions, and local guides. The latter led us by remote paths through the Macedonian canton of Tymphaia, and on into Epirus. Their fathers would have used these tracks for cattle raids. They still knew the way well. Most likely the custom was not entirely dead.

It was several days tough travel through the mountains. It was hard on Harpalus, with his bent spine, but he did not complain. It would have been hard on most women. Olympias, however, rode astride like a man, and showed no weakness. Much of the time she kept her mount next to that of Alexander, and talked in a low and vehement tone. Should any of us approach within earshot, she sent us away with a sharp word. Ptolemy and me she regarded with especial suspicion. No doubt our Argead blood – much diluted in me, and unacknowledged in Ptolemy – was reason enough to assume we were spies.

As we plodded onwards, spelling the horses, eating hard tack and cheese, I wondered if Electra had been right. I had taken an oath to Philip not Alexander. Had I broken my word? A man's honour was nothing if he was forsworn. The oath did include Philip's descendants. Could that ease my conscience, or was it a mere sophistry? Philip had been generous to me, but Alexander was my friend and foster-brother. Electra had spoken of love. But she was Antipater's daughter. The safety of her family and mine had been in her mind. If the royal house was divided, should it come to civil war, both families were safer having a foot in each camp.

Alexander the King of Epirus was holding court at the oracle at Dodona. Again we had outrun the news of our coming. For two days Alexander was secluded with his mother and her brother, windows shuttered, guards outside the doors. The rest of us kicked our heels. Some of the others consulted the oracle under the great oak trees. It seemed unwise for me to join them. The gods punish the impious who enter their sanctuaries. My broken oath to Philip did not hold me back as much as the curse Olympias had uttered on the slopes of Mount Bermion: *Let Justice come for all to see, let her come*

sword in hand, stabbing through the throat to his death the
godless, the lawless, the unjust . . .

On the third day, Alexander announced we were leaving.
Olympias would remain with her brother, while we travelled
north to the various Kings of the Illyrians. A weight was lifted
from my heart. The witch would be left behind. In our party now
my only enemy was Hephaestion.

Again we went without servants. The King of Epirus could
not be seen to give us too much help. Philip had put him on
the throne, and might seek to cast him down again. Offering
sanctuary to Olympias was enough of a risk.

On the road north, Alexander swore us to secrecy. He took a
ring carved with a cameo from his finger. Each of us kissed it;
sealing our lips, as you would seal a document. Then he told us
what had been decided.

The King of Epirus would send an army to put Alexander on
the throne, but only if we could rally sufficient support from the
Illyrians.

'Why not rouse the Greeks?' Harpalus asked. 'They resent the
overlordship of Philip. Offer them their freedom.'

'They are crushed after Chaeronea,' Alexander replied.

'Offer them money. They will do anything for gold.'

'Where would I find that gold?'

'Persia,' Harpalus said. 'The Great King would be happy to
shower wealth on anyone who could prevent Philip taking an
army to Asia.'

'No!' Alexander was adamant. 'My father may disinherit me,
but he is right about Persia. The Great King is the enemy of
Macedon. I will not seek help from a man I will fight when I
come to the throne.'

'And the Illyrians are not our enemies?'

Alexander did not answer.

Like all Macedonians, Harpalus was entitled to free speech.

* * *

Through the months of *Hyperbetaios* and *Dios*, as summer turned to autumn, and the winds from the Adriatic stripped the leaves from the trees, we sojourned among the Illyrians. We feasted in the hall of one uncouth chief after another. None gave us a straight answer. They were torn between their desire to plunder the rich pastures of Macedon and their fear of Philip. In the month of *Apellaios*, when it was already cold enough to flay the hide off an ox, our luck ran out.

Twenty horsemen escorting an envoy from Philip clattered up the path to the stronghold of Pleurias of the Autariatae. The envoy was old Demaratus of Corinth. In his youth the Greek had won great renown fighting in Sicily. In recent years he had acquired a more sinister reputation as a confidential agent of the King of Macedonia. Demaratus and Pleurias were talking in the hall.

'If the packs on their horses are stuffed with gold,' Harpalus said, 'the Illyrian will not hesitate to sell us to your father.'

'If Philip is my father.'

None of us spoke. Never before had Alexander deigned to mention the rumours about his mother. All the time with Olympias after the shock of exile must have turned his mind. None of us dared to look at each other.

Eventually it was Harpalus who spoke. 'Alexander, you are Philip's heir.'

Alexander nodded. 'For how much longer?'

We had barred the doors of the room we had been assigned, and were waiting. Alexander had sent Ptolemy and Medius down to the stables to ready the horses on the pretence of going hunting. We had our swords and boar-spears, but not war-gear; no helmets, shields, or armour.

'We will fight our way to the horses,' Alexander said, 'then cut our way out.'

'A hunchback with one good leg is of little use,' Harpalus said.

'We will not leave you.' Alexander embraced Harpalus and kissed him. Then he did the same to Nearchus, me, and Hephaestion. 'If fate decrees it, I could not meet my end with better men.'

At that moment I loved him more than anyone, even Electra. My tastes do not run that way – the Bacchiads never forget our expulsion from Corinth – but I almost understood the physical desire of Hephaestion.

There was a hammering on the door.

We looked at each other, fingering the hilts of our swords.

'Open it,' Alexander said.

I pulled back the bar, swung the door back.

Demaratus was on his own.

'Take your hands from your swords, young men.'

There was no one in the corridor behind Demaratus. If it was a trick, the old man would be dead before anyone else reached the room. I let go of the eagle-headed hilt, rubbed my palm on my tunic. It was wet with sweat.

'Alexander, your father would be reconciled with you,' Demaratus said. 'He has sent me to bring you home.'

'But I am not reconciled to him.' Alexander's eyes were blazing. 'He let his new father-in-law call me a bastard; raised his sword to his own son.'

'Your father is magnanimous.'

Alexander said nothing.

'You cannot outmanoeuvre Philip.' Demaratus spoke gently, but without condescension. 'All your plans have come to nothing. Alexander of Epirus is to marry your sister. You will get no help there. These Illyrians have been paid.'

'Can my companions return?'

'Yes.'

'And my mother?'

Demaratus reached out his hands, as if in supplication. 'Philip believes she poisons you against him.'

'I will not return without Olympias.'

'That is up to Philip. Talk to him.'

Alexander relapsed into silence.

'It is time to reclaim your place,' Demaratus said, then added quietly 'while you can.'

'While I can?' Again Alexander flared up. 'Has the old goat already got Attalus' daughter pregnant?'

'Not that I know, but Philip has taken measures to ensure that Macedon has a king, should he fall in battle, and you remain away.'

'Who?'

'Philip has given Cynnane, his daughter by Audata, to your cousin Amyntas.'

'Amyntas! He could never be King, never hold Macedon.'

Demaratus shrugged. 'Amyntas is not a strong man, but as a child he was King, and your father was his Regent.'

Alexander scowled, but looked irresolute.

Demaratus smiled. 'Your father gave me a message for you: "If you have competitors for the kingdom, prove yourself honourable and good, so that you may obtain the kingdom not because of me, but because of yourself."'

CHAPTER ELEVEN

Spring 336 BC

'NOTHING COULD HAVE BEEN better calculated to make Alexander return than an appeal to his honour and ambition.'

It was mid-afternoon and we were in bed in the house in Pella. The shutters were open, and the sunshine on the water reflected ever shifting patterns on the ceiling. We had made love. Apparently there were many things an Athenian wife would not do in the bedroom. I was glad Electra was Macedonian.

'Exile has made you pompous,' she said, 'but I am pleased you are back.'

'So am I. The women in Illyria never wash.'

She pinched my arm. 'You are not the only one with needs. All the best doctors say it is very bad for a woman's health not to have sex.'

I moved my hand to her breast. But she took my hand in hers, and sat up.

'Many things have changed while you were away.' It never ceased to surprise me how Electra could turn from uninhibited physical pleasure to calculated pragmatism in a heartbeat. 'Attalus has become insufferable. You remember Kalos?'

'We were Pages together.' I yawned and stretched, my mind elsewhere.

'Attalus never forgave Pausanias for hounding Kalos to his death. He invited Pausanias to dinner. Why Pausanias went I have no idea.'

'Pausanias is ambitious and weak,' I answered absently, not altogether interested, 'perhaps he hoped for some reconciliation.'

'Attalus plied Pausanias with wine. When he was insensible, Attalus and his friends took turns to rape him. When they were done, they threw him in the stables for the muleteers.'

Now she had my attention. 'There will be blood.' I raised myself on an elbow to look at her. 'Pausanias is from Orestis. The old ways still run deep in the uplands. After such an outrage, he has no choice but to kill Attalus.'

'Pausanias complained to Philip.'

I snorted with derision.

'Philip tried to make light of it.'

'The humiliation . . .'

'Philip was reluctant to punish his new father-in-law, so he tried to mollify Pausanias by making him one of the seven royal bodyguards.'

'Pausanias accepted?'

'Yes.'

'Then he is beneath contempt.'

'No doubt, but you are missing the point. Attalus believes he can do what he likes. His daughter is near her confinement. If she gives Philip a son, Attalus will be yet worse. And now he leads an army.'

An advance force had crossed to Asia to establish a bridge-head and see if it could bring some of the Greek cities over from Persian control.

'Parmenion is the senior officer in Asia,' I said.

'Attalus is married to Parmenion's daughter.'

'Even if Philip has another son, a newborn is no threat to Alexander. Anyway, Attalus' daughter is here in Pella.'

'But Alexander's cousin Amyntas is with the army in Asia. He was King before Philip, he could be acclaimed again.'

'Amyntas was a child then, now he is an adult he has no desire for the throne.' I knew the prince from court; a few years older than me, a quiet and studious man.

'Amyntas is married to Philip's daughter Cynnane. They say she killed an Illyrian queen in battle. She has her father's nature – his ferocity and desire for power.'

'None of them would dare revolt against Philip.'

'But they would all conspire against Alexander. As his foster-brother you are in danger.'

The Macedonian court had never been safe. Many Kings, and more nobles, had died by the sword – out hunting, dancing at a festival, when drinking with men they thought their friends.

'I will talk to Alexander,' I said. 'He is worried that when Philip takes the main army to Asia he will be left behind here, and this time your father will be Regent, not him.'

'The arrangement is prudent. What would happen to Macedon if both Philip and Alexander fell fighting the Persians? If Amyntas died in Asia as well, there would be no obvious heir. The Macedonians would look to others, including you. There would be civil war. All Philip's gains would be lost; the Hellenes, the Thracians, the Illyrians.'

I laughed, kept the conversation on Alexander, not the dangerous subject of my royal heritage. 'Prudence is not one of Alexander's virtues. If he is left in Macedon, he is thinking about a campaign north of the Danube against the Scythians, or into the far west.'

Electra looked concerned. 'My father will not agree. Philip has given Antipater strict instructions to maintain the borders, above all watch the Greeks.'

'Alexander is not easily dissuaded.'

'You will have to try. Persuade him to give himself over to pleasure. He needs to take a wife, breed an heir.' Electra looked mischievous. 'Is it true he has no interest in women?'

'No, but I think he prefers boys. Now I should take your advice myself.'

I reached for her, but she pushed me away. 'There is no time. You need to bathe, get dressed, and go to dine with your brothers.'

I pulled a face.

'You may not care for them, but they are your kin. It is natural they should welcome you back.'

Reluctantly, I got up.

Electra lay naked on the bed. 'Don't get too drunk. There is always later.'

* * *

It proved impossible to follow Electra's instruction about sobriety.

Heromenes and Arrhabaeus greeted me with huge flagons of unmixed wine to toast my return. We were half drunk before any food arrived.

There were just the three of us, which was a surprise. Neoptolemus was with the advance force, but my other nephew

Amyntas was in Pella. Although I found my brothers uncongenial, and usually tried to avoid their company, I assumed even they must have friends.

The food was good: fried fish and salad, then suckling pig and black pudding with artichoke hearts. We talked of the things that interest Macedonian noblemen: hunting dogs and horses, drinking and sex, the barbarity of Illyrians, and the iniquities of Greeks. It was undemanding, and not totally unenjoyable. The lights cast a soft glow, and my head was light with the wine.

Arrhabaeus was more talkative than usual. He assured us the cleverer a Greek, the worse his character. Look at Euripides. In Macedon at the court of Archelaus the playwright had shown his true nature: greedy and vicious, a menace to all well-brought-up youths and girls. It was divine justice when our ancestor's hounds tore him to pieces. A good hunting dog was worth any number of plays like *The Bacchae*.

When the servants brought in the nuts and apples, Heromenes dismissed them for the night.

Arrhabaeus was not finished with Euripides. When the Greek had tried to assault a Royal Page, the boy had merely said he had bad breath. The King had handed Decamnichus over to Euripides to flog. It was a typical Argead outrage to Macedonian customs. Even a boy was allowed to speak his mind, and everyone knew that no one was allowed to punish a Royal Page except the King. Archelaus had got what he had deserved when Decamnichus joined the plot that killed him.

Heromenes got up, looked outside into the dark corridor, then bolted the door and pulled a heavy curtain across the entrance.

'We have heard from our father,' he said.

My head was still reeling, but my heart sank.

'He is in Persia. The Great King has honoured him, given him the revenues of three villages, and appointed him to command a force of mercenaries.'

It was not unexpected – where else would Aeropus have gone? – but I was horrified. 'Then he will fight against us in the summer.'

'Philip exiled our father for a trivial offence.'

'Aeropus disobeyed a direct order.'

'The flute-girl was an excuse to get rid of him.' Heromenes grinned without humour, showing his long, equine teeth. 'Philip has treated the House of Lyncestis shamefully: abolished our kingdom, conscripted our men, confiscated our lands.'

'Philip has made Macedon great,' I said. 'Before we cowered behind the walls of Lebaea when the Illyrians crossed the border, now the whole world fears our arms. Philip has given us all commands in the army, granted us estates in the lowlands. We have to forget the past. We must be Macedonians first, Lyncestians second.'

Arrhabaeus shook his head. 'We need another Decamnichus.'

'Are you both mad!' I exclaimed. 'The Macedonian army would never acclaim a King from Lyncestis.'

'They have in the past,' Heromenes said, 'and why do you think Olympias so hates and fears you? Anyway there are others who would welcome the death of Philip, your friend Alexander among them.'

'Never!' My anger was rising. 'Alexander's honour would not let him stoop to patricide.'

Heromenes and Arrhabaeus looked at each other. I wondered if I would leave this room alive. We all wore swords, but were there armed men outside waiting for a signal?

'In the name of Bromerus the Founder,' I said, 'you must forget this insane idea. You will destroy us all. Never breathe a word of this to anyone again.'

'Our father was right,' Heromenes said. 'The late-born is weak, no true son of Lyncestis.'

Arrhabaeus looked uncertainly at Heromenes. He had always been easily led. 'Perhaps our brother is right.'

Heromenes scowled at me. 'Best you leave.'

I got up warily and moved towards the door, not turning my back on them.

'Do not go running to Philip,' Heromenes said. 'You hold our lives in your hands, but we have friends – don't think your little wife would survive our execution.'

CHAPTER TWELVE

Summer 336 BC

*W*REATHED IS THE BULL. *All is done. There is also the one who will smite him.*

Philip had asked the Delphic Oracle a simple question: Would he conquer the Persian King? As a member of the Amphictyonic Council that administered the shrine, he had expected a positive response, but this was beyond his hopes. Usually oracles were ambiguous, but this was clear. He did not need Aristander the seer to interpret: the Persian King was the bull, and Philip himself the one who would smite him. Apollo and the gods were on his side.

Abroad things could not be better. In Asia, Parmenion and the advance force had liberated Greek cities as far south as Ephesus. Several Aegean islands had come over, including Chios and Lesbos. Reports from Persia explained the lack of resistance. In the way of oriental courts, a eunuch had assassinated the Great King and placed an obscure relative of the royal family on the throne as Darius III. The new King had promptly forced the eunuch to drink poison. At home, Philip had gathered the main expeditionary force at Aegae. It would march east, then sail after the Etesian Winds had died in mid-September and before the sailing season closed in early November. A winter campaign, when the Persian fleet could not enter the Aegean, should see the Macedonians as far south as Caria, with all the Greek cities of Asia united behind them. The next year the decisive land battle would be fought deep in the territory of the Great King. Then Philip would smite the Persian bull.

There was more good news at home. Attalus' daughter had been delivered of twins. Philip had named the boy Caranus, the Macedonian for 'lord', and the girl Europa. Yesterday he had given Cleopatra in marriage to Alexander of Epirus. Olympias, who had returned for the wedding, had had to watch in impotent fury as all her schemes came to nothing with the wedding of her daughter by Philip to her brother. The Kingdoms of Macedon and Epirus were bound closer together.

The wedding feast had been lavish. Greeks had been invited from all over the mainland. They had presented Philip with crowns of gold. A famous actor had recited verses of Aeschylus as if they foretold the fall of the Persian King.

Your thoughts reach higher than the air . . .
But there is one who goes his way obscured in gloom,
And, sudden, unseen, overtakes
And robs us of our distant hopes –
Death, the source of mortals' many woes.

The drinking had gone on late. Eumaeus woke me long before dawn. My head hurt, and my stomach was bilious. There were stale wine fumes on my breath.

'Call yourself a man?' Eumaeus was unsympathetic.

'You are like aged Nestor, "from whose lips the streams of words ran sweeter than honey".'

Eumaeus grunted. 'Yes, "and in my time I have dealt with better men than you".'

'And you are always ready with a line of Homer.'

Eumaeus smiled sourly. 'In my day a Macedonian could handle his drink, not whine like some effeminate Athenian.'

'Maybe that was why we used to lose so many battles?'

Before he could reply, I had to grab a bowl and throw up. When the retching stopped, he gave me a cup of water.

I had not told anyone about my conversation with my brothers; not even Eumaeus or Electra, the two people I could trust with my life. The next day Arrhabaeus had sought me out. It was just drink talking, he had said. Heromenes was bitter because he had been passed over for command. He believed the battalion of the phalanx from Lyncestis and Orestis should have gone to him not young Perdiccas. What Heromenes said when drunk, he regretted when sober.

When I had washed and eaten a morsel of bread, I felt a little better.

Outside it was still dark, but the streets were full of people making their way to the theatre. The day was given over to musical and athletic competitions. I walked up past the theatre to the palace, where the procession was assembling.

'Herakles' hairy arse, you look rough.' Perdiccas was standing with Leonnatus. They both laughed.

'You don't look very well yourself.'

'Well, I have felt better.'

'You should eat cabbage,' Leonnatus said, 'very good for hangovers.'

'Fried with bacon,' Perdiccas agreed. 'Cleanses the bowels too, Aristotle used to say.'

'I am glad you got something out of his teaching, but can you both stop talking now?'

A pale strip of yellow light low in the east announced the coming day.

Philip arrived, looking spruce and fresh, impressive at his age, given he had set the pace of the drinking.

'That man is indestructible,' Leonnatus said. 'He must be nearly fifty.'

The procession, timed to arrive in the theatre at sunrise, set off. At its head were gilded statues of the twelve Olympia gods. With them was carried another statue, no different in scale and magnificence, depicting Philip. That should prove the talking point of the day. His supporters would point to the statue of Philip placed in the Temple of Artemis by the citizens of Ephesus: the power of the King could only be compared with that of the gods. His enemies – and there were many among the outwardly friendly Greeks – would see it as overweening pride: had he not already infringed on the gods by commissioning a building to himself and his family in the sanctuary at Olympia?

We halted at the eastern entrance to the theatre. The sun rose over the horizon, shafts of golden light struck the theatre. A choir sang and the effigies of the gods and that of Philip made their entrance. From outside we heard the applause. Had it faltered for a moment as the spectators caught sight of the image of Philip? Certainly it then picked up to a crescendo. Was that typical Greek sycophancy? I doubted many Macedonians joined. We prefer our King as a first among equals, not some elevated theocratic figure.

Philip spoke to his seven bodyguards. 'Wait here until I have taken my seat. I will show these Greeks that I am protected by the goodwill of my subjects, not armed men.' The King then turned to us. 'My friends, please precede me. I will enter alone and unarmed.'

I went in with Leonnatus and Perdiccas. Our seats were on the far side, near the other entrance.

The statues of the gods, with that of Philip in their midst, were ranged along the back of the orchestra. There was a buzz of expectation from the crowd. Sourly, through my hangover, I thought the Greeks would be hoping for some largess. Harpalus was right – there was nothing Greek that money could not buy. At some point they had lost the honour of their ancestors who fought on the windy plain before Troy.

Philip walked out into the empty, sunlit space. He wore a plain white tunic and cloak, a golden wreath on his head.

The crowd rose as one, shaking back their cloaks, they applauded. This was what it meant to be a king.

Philip held out his hands in a gesture of welcome, even benediction.

The cheering rose like a wave driven by a storm.

A figure emerged from the tunnel through which Philip had come. One of the seven bodyguards. They needed no permission to approach the King. It better be important, I thought, Philip would not want to share this moment.

It was Pausanias. The King had not seen him. From under his cloak Pausanias drew his sword. Now Philip turned. Too late. Pausanias ran the last few steps, and drove the blade deep into Philip's chest.

The King staggered back a couple of paces. His fingers clutched at the hilt with its inlaid chariot. Then he fell.

Suddenly there was silence. I could hear the stamp of Pausanias' boots as he ran towards the western entrance.

Pausanias was gone. There was uproar. People rushing to Philip. Others jabbering and clutching each other in the stands.

'After him!'

Perdiccas and I barrelled after Leonnatus.

It was dark in the corridor. Then we came out into an almost painful brightness. A squad of *hypaspists* stood outside, looking confused.

'Where did he go?' Leonnatus was good in a crisis.

One of the soldiers pointed down the street running west. 'What has happened?'

'Give me your javelin.'

Perdiccas and I took Leonnatus' example, and grabbed weapons.

'Follow me!'

Pausanias had a head start. He was out of sight. We pounded along the paved street.

'He must be making for the south-west gate,' I panted.

The others pulled ahead. My legs were like lead, the effects of last night's indulgence. We turned left then right and came to where the buildings ended.

There was Pausanias! The gate was no more than a hundred paces away. Riders were waiting with a spare horse. Pausanias was almost halfway there.

The street had given way to a country track; packed earth lined with trees and vines. Pausanias stubbed his boot on a root, and went sprawling.

Leonnatus cocked back his arm.

'Don't kill him!' I yelled.

Leonnatus' arm snapped forward. As Pausanias pushed himself up the javelin caught him between the shoulder blades. Perdiccas rushed forward to finish him.

Under the arch of the gate the horsemen turned to leave. One wore a hood. The face of the other was partly obscured by a broad-brimmed travelling hat. But I saw the big, animal teeth.

Back at the theatre a crowd, headed by Antipater, was waiting.

'The King?' Perdiccas asked.

Antipater shook his head. 'Pausanias?'

'Dead,' Leonnatus said. 'His accomplices got away.'

We went to enter the theatre. Antipater took my arm, led me aside.

'Who were they?' Antipater whispered.

This was the fork in my path. I did not hesitate. 'My brothers.'

'You are certain?'

'Heromenes, yes; Arrhabaeus no.'

'No matter, custom dictates the whole family dies.' The broad bucolic face of Antipater gave nothing away as he thought. Finally, he spoke. 'You might still save your life; that of my daughter too.' Then he told me what to do.

Inside, the throng parted for Antipater.

Alexander cradled the head of his father. There was bright blood on Philip's snow-white cloak. The golden crown had fallen in the dust.

I stepped out from behind Antipater, and raised my right hand in the traditional Macedonian greeting.

'King Alexander lives and reigns!'

Alexander looked up, as if uncomprehending.

King Alexander lives and reigns! The crowd took up my words.

Gently, Alexander laid his father's head on the ground, and got to his feet.

'Alexander.'

The odd coloured eyes of my foster-brother focused on me.

'We must go to the palace, wash and arm ourselves, then put you before the army for acclamation.'

Antipater was at my shoulder. 'Lyncestes is right. I will summon the men to the plain.'

Now, Alexander was surrounded by his friends – Hephaestion, Ptolemy, Perdiccas, Harpalus – all the Macedonians from Mieza. The Greeks like Nearchus and Medius hung back. They had no role in electing a King of Macedon.

As we left the theatre, I glanced over my shoulder. Philip remained where he had fallen. The servants had not yet appeared to take up his body. The greatest man Europe had produced lay in the dust. Up in the stands Olympias looked down on her dead husband.

CHAPTER THIRTEEN

Autumn 336 BC

WE WERE BACK ON the plain below Aegae. It seemed an eternity, but it was only a couple of months since we had been here; first to acclaim Alexander, then to cremate his father. There had been so much blood shed since then. There was more to come today, for me the most painful of all.

In the opening anxious days of the new reign everything had hung on Parmenion. The old general commanded the army in Asia; more than ten thousand veteran Macedonians and mercenaries. His son-in-law was with him, and Attalus was unlikely to accept Alexander as King. It was not the Macedonian way for either Attalus or Alexander to ever forget, let alone forgive, the insults they had exchanged at Philip's wedding. Parmenion, however, was unlikely to declare for Caranus, the new-born son of Philip, who was Attalus' grandson. Caranus was in Aegae, and such a move would be his death sentence. But another candidate was to hand. Amyntas, son of King Perdiccas III, was with the advance force. As a child, Amyntas had briefly been hailed King, before his place had been taken by his Regent and uncle, Philip. Should Parmenion acclaim Amyntas there would be civil war. If Parmenion offered the Greeks their freedom, they would rise in arms. Those of us with Alexander would have to fight on two fronts; more if the Thracians and Illyrians and Paeonians also shrugged off Macedonian rule.

Alexander had sent men east. They had ridden their horses into the ground, requisitioned more when they floundered. They had outrun the news of Philip's death. The riders were headed by Hecataeus of Cardia. The Greek was an old companion of Parmenion. Philip had employed the Cardian on many delicate or clandestine missions, although perhaps never on one of this importance. The orders of Hecataeus were simple – Parmenion must be persuaded to arrest Attalus and Amyntas. To this end, Alexander had sent Philotas, his foster-brother, with Hecataeus. Convinced, either by his old friend or his son, Parmenion had abandoned both his son-in-law and the harmless sometime King. Attalus and Amyntas had been killed.

The Greeks had risen anyway. The Thessalians refused to recognise Alexander as their *Archon* in succession to his father, and sent troops to block the Vale of Tempe. Further south the Thebans had expelled both the Macedonian garrison from the citadel of the Cadmea and the oligarchy which Philip had installed in the city. It was reported that Demosthenes was urging the Athenians to declare war. The Greeks, amateurs at war, will never understand just how fast a Macedonian army can march, or the obstacles it can overcome. We moved down the coast, then cut steps into the face of Mount Ossa to clamber over and bring us down into Thessaly in the rear of their forces. There had been no fighting. The Thessalians had elected Alexander as their *Archon* for life. When we reached Thebes the citizens rushed to capitulate with all the usual excuses: it was not their fault, they had been misled by a few individuals, they had always been loyal in their hearts. Alexander had left me in command of the re-established garrison as he moved on to accept the renewed allegiance of Athens and the other cities. At Corinth he was elected *Hegemon* of the Hellenes to continue the campaign against Persia. When Alexander came north again, I handed over the Cadmea to my nephew Amyntas and re-joined the army.

Our return to Macedon was like walking on stage into a Greek tragedy. The main actor had not worn a mask. While we were away, Olympias had shown her real nature. It was not true she had ordered Philip's children, Caranus and Europa, roasted to death over an open fire in front of their mother. But she had commanded their throats be cut while their mother was forced to watch. Then she had handed the young woman a rope, and gloated as she hanged herself. Alexander was furious, deaf to his mother's entreaties that she had done it for him – Caranus was a rival for the throne, and custom demanded that all the family of a traitor should be killed. Yet there was nothing to be done. The dead cannot be brought back from Hades.

Now, as the chill winds fretted at our cloaks, we were back on the plain below Aegae to witness further horror. There was a huge mound of fresh red earth over the last resting place of Philip of Macedon. At its summit stood a cross on which hung the mouldering corpse of his assassin Pausanias.

While we were away someone had briefly placed a gold crown on the putrid head of Pausanias. It was widely thought to have been Olympias. Some claimed she had encouraged the assassin. Other names were implicated as behind the killing: Demosthenes of Athens, and Darius of Persia. Electra told me that a few – never in my hearing – even detected the hand of Alexander. That at least I could not believe. Alexander would have never committed patricide. It might have been different if Olympias had persuaded him that Philip was not his father. But Alexander's words in Illyria had been prompted merely by the bitterness of that moment. Alexander was a lion, not a fox. I could never credit my friend would stoop to something so underhand.

Two other crosses lay on the ground next to that of Pausanias. I wished I was with Amyntas in Thebes, or anywhere but here. Yet I was a Lyncestian, from the land of the Lynx, and would show no weakness.

Every Macedonian nobleman is entitled to a public trial before the Macedonian army. As Heromenes and Arrhabaeus had escaped, they were tried in their absence. On the rack their slaves had confirmed my testimony against my brothers. They had been waiting with horses at the gate to help Pausanias get away, because they had conspired with him to kill the King. The Macedonians had found them guilty of treason. The punishment was death. If they had been present, the troops would have stoned them or run them through with javelins there and then.

Heromenes and Arrhabaeus had been caught in Elimea. Its Lord Machatas had arrested them, as once he might have detained Alexander. My brothers had been heading south. The direction of their flight argued against the involvement of Attalus in the assassination of the King. Perhaps they had hoped to stir up rebellion among the Greek cities, or, more likely, they intended to cross the Aegean to reach our father in his Persian exile. Perhaps their route gave credence to the involvement of Demosthenes and Darius in the killing. Once taken Heromenes and Arrhabaeus were loaded with chains, confined in a cart, and brought back under heavy guard to Macedon. In Aegae, they were thrown in a dungeon. No one was allowed to see them, although no one had made such a foolish request.

A trumpet blared. It disturbed a crow perched on the remains of Pausanias. The black bird of ill omen rose, cawing into the dark sky.

Two shambling figures were led out onto the mound. Bent and filthy, with matted hair and scabs on their limbs, they had aged far beyond their years. Evidently they had been tortured. A stab of guilt and fear struck deep in my bowels. Either they had not revealed their treasonous conversation with me at dinner, or they had not been believed. Had Alexander been present as the pincers tore their flesh and the cellar reeked of flesh burnt by the hot irons? It made little difference, every word wrenched from them would have been reported.

A herald read out the charges and the sentence. His words were snatched away by the wind. I could not look at silent, ineffectual Arrhabaeus, but kept my eyes on Heromenes. All my life I had had nothing but ill will from him; he had dragged Arrhabaeus to this awful place. He was a bitter, hateful man. Yet he was still my brother, and I had denounced him. Of course I had taken an oath to Philip and his descendants, but that did nothing to ease my conscience. I refused to think about our mother.

The broken men were manhandled down onto the crosses. Heromenes tried to shout something – defiance or an entreaty; perhaps a curse, on Alexander or me; maybe he railed against the gods themselves? – but at the base of the mound it was inaudible. Then they screamed as the iron nails were hammered through the flesh and tendons of their wrists and ankles. That carried only too clearly. It was a slow process. I looked away at the still open dark mouth of Philip's tomb.

The crosses began to jerk upright, men straining and hauling on ropes, then were packed home. Against my will, I looked up at them hanging there. Arrhabaeus seemed unconscious. Heromenes was still mouthing something.

'That is enough,' Leonnatus said. 'We have done our duty, and should go now.'

The crowd parted as if the kinsmen of the traitors were polluted with their guilt. We walked slowly, and I tried to catch no one's eye. Then I realised we were not alone. Perdiccas, lame Harpalus, Ptolemy; all those from Mieza were walking with us.

A hand took my arm. It was Alexander.

'I am sorry,' he said. 'It was hard for you to witness that. You have lost your brothers, but we are all your foster-brothers. As your friend, I thank you for your loyalty.'

I could not speak, and merely nodded.

Inside, I was in turmoil. Alexander would not thank me if he knew what I had done. It was nothing to do with not informing on the treasonous talk at the dinner. Electra had been persuasive. My nephew Amyntas and I had made our peace with Alexander, and been pardoned. Olympias hated us, but we were safe for now. Neoptolemus, however, was with the advance force in Asia. Tainted by association with Attalus and Amyntas, he was suspect and in danger. He must get away. Anyway, Electra had argued, who could tell what would happen in the coming war? For the good of the family, it was better to have men of influence on either side, and my father was nothing, a drunkard of no account. So I had sent Eumaeus east, across the Hellespont, to urge Neoptolemus to seek refuge with Darius the King of Persia.

CHAPTER FOURTEEN

Spring to Autumn 335 BC

'YOU NEED A WAR,' Leonnatus said. 'Nothing like getting into the field to stop a man brooding.'

'I am not brooding.'

Electra laughed at me. 'Yes, you are.'

We were eating cake, half drunk at the end of the meal. There were just the three of us. Eumaeus, who had returned safely, was serving.

'They were your brothers, but they never cared for you.' With his bristling beard Leonnatus was the epitome of a bluff upcountry Macedonian nobleman. Sometimes it was very irritating.

After they had been taken down from the crosses, Heromenes and Arrhabaeus had been interred in the mound over Philip's tomb. It was strange to think they would lie there for eternity with the man they had betrayed. My mother had written to me. One of the few women in Lyncestis who could read and write, she had learnt to help with the running of Lebaea. There had been no word of reproach, but she had issued a stern reminder that, with my father an exile, I was now the head of the Bacchiad House, and should see to producing an heir. The advice had been unnecessary. For all our lovemaking, Electra had not become pregnant. Although we did not talk of it, I knew it preyed on her mind also.

'Anyway, you did the right thing.' Leonnatus was warming to his subject. 'Fighting the Triballi will take your mind off it.'

'"Some Thracian now takes pride in my shield . . . let it go, I will get another."'

'Is that poetry?' Leonnatus sounded suspicious.

'Archilochus.'

'You read too much. Everyone knows it robs a man of his courage.'

Electra laughed, now at Leonnatus not me, which was better.

'Alexander will enjoy taking revenge for the Triballi defeating Philip.' Leonnatus appeared unaware of the gentle mockery. 'You remember how he always used to say his father would leave him nothing to achieve.'

The Triballi lived north of the Haemus Mountains in Thrace, up towards the Danube. Now they were pressing south, threatening the Thracians loyal to us and the city of Philippopolis founded by the King.

'A very savage people – sacrifice their own fathers, and people say they can cast the evil eye.' Leonnatus shook his head at such barbarity.

'Old women say that,' Electra said.

Leonnatus changed tack. 'Quite right – nothing a stout ash wood spear can't settle. A quick, bracing campaign, then we can think about Persia.'

'It might prove rather more taxing,' Electra said, 'since the death of Meda.'

She had been the daughter of King Cothelas of the Getae. Philip had taken her as a wife to secure an alliance. She had fallen sick and died in the winter. For once no one talked of Olympias and poison, but Philip had had no children with Meda. Alexander had ordered her to be buried in an antechamber of Philip's tomb. That honour might not be enough to prevent her people joining the neighbouring Triballi. The Getae were said to be numerous and fierce.

'Our western flank will be secure,' I said, 'now we have the Agrianes as allies.' Langarus their King had come with a thousand picked warriors to fight at our side. Alexander had betrothed his half-sister Cynanne to him. The wedding would be here in Pella after the campaign.

'Poor girl,' Leonnatus said. 'First her husband Amyntas is executed, now she will have to live in a hut up a hillside surrounded by natives in sheepskins.'

'Her mother was Illyrian,' I said, 'she will soon get used to it.'

'And no Macedonian woman has much say in who she marries.' Electra's tone was bitter.

'Thank you,' I said.

She smiled. 'Some might think me luckier than others. Another drink?'

* * *

The Haemus Pass was not a narrow defile that could be defended by a handful of men. Instead it was a wide and bald saddle at the highest point of the crossing. The enemy were massed at the top behind a barricade of wagons.

We had marched east from Macedon, keeping Mount Orbelus on our left and Mount Pangaeum with its gold mines to our right. Having forded the Nestus River, and skirted the southern ranges of the Rhodope Mountains, we reached the Hebrus, and followed its waters upstream until we arrived at the entrance to the pass. In the foothills lay Seuthopolis, the capital of the client King of the Odrysians. The whole journey had taken no more than seven days.

Seuthopolis was a large town with stone-built walls like a Greek *polis*. There we were joined by Sitalkes, one of the sons of Cersobleptes the King of the Odrysians. Sitalkes would accompany us with a thousand picked peltasts. These javelin men and their leader were partly reinforcements, partly hostages. After a day of rest, it took another two days to ascend the winding track to the pass.

'How many of them are up there?' Alexander asked.

'Not as many as might be thought.' Sitalkes had fiery hair, and a gap in his teeth. He spoke good Greek, and from his appearance could have been taken for a Macedonian, except for a discreet tattoo of a double-headed axe on his neck; the mark of his royal birth.

'The King is not with them,' Sitalkes continued, 'they are a local levy, at the most ten thousand fighting men. They appear more because they have brought their women and children.'

'Why not send them into the mountains for safety?' Philotas asked.

'Men fight better under the eyes of their loved ones.'

Philotas made a noise that somehow expressed both his contempt for such barbarous practices and a certain lust. 'They will be a reward for our men.' Philotas was a great one for women.

'What are they loading into the wagons?' I could see men working methodically.

'Stones to weigh down the light mountain carts,' Sitalkes said.

Alexander turned to the whole group of commanders. 'How would you arrange a barricade of carts?'

'Nose to tail, tied together to form a solid barrier,' Craterus said.

'Yes,' Alexander said, 'but there are spaces between them, and their wheels are facing us.'

Philotas slapped his hand on his thigh. 'They are going to roll them down the slope into us.'

Craterus looked as if he wished he had realised that first. The rivalry between him and Philotas was strong. I remembered them wrestling on the day I first entered Aegae.

Alexander studied the slope, head on one side, thinking.

'They will cause havoc in our phalanx,' Craterus said. 'There is no way to avoid them. When our line is disordered, the tribesmen will charge, get into the gaps. Once beyond the hedge of pikes the curved blades of their *rhomphaias* will outreach the swords of our men.'

'Actually,' Alexander said, 'there might be a way to deal with the carts. We will put our archers as a screen out in front. The bowmen can dodge out of the way as individuals, then come together to shoot down the warriors charging in their wake. If we only use three battalions of the phalanx in open order – six feet for every file – each formation should have room to open lines to let the carts pass through. If that is not possible, form close order – a foot and a half for each man – lie down, and lock their shields together over their heads like a roof. If the carts are light enough, they should run over them like a ramp.'

No one seemed very excited about the idea of lying down in front of the carts. They might be light, but we could see them being piled with stones.

'We only have five hundred archers,' Craterus said, 'not enough to cover the whole front.'

Alexander was untroubled. 'Coenus your battalion from Elimea will take the right. Perdiccas, you and the men from

Orestis and Lyncestis the centre. The archers can screen both of you. I will lead the *hypaspists* on the left. We will take our chance.'

Both Sitalkes and Langarus said it would be an honour for their javelin men to cover Alexander.

'No, your men are from the mountains. They will be needed to lead the pursuit, otherwise almost all the Triballi will get away. They know the trails, and my Macedonians are weighed down with armour.'

Craterus still looked dubious. 'If you only send three battalions, they will be outnumbered by more than two to one, and the tribesmen will get into the gaps between them, and get at their flanks.'

'When their stratagem with the carts fails, they will lose heart,' Alexander said. 'If not, we are trained soldiers, and they are herdsmen. We have to trust ourselves.'

After Aristander the seer had pronounced the entrails of the sacrifice were propitious, we set off. I was in the front rank of the *hypaspists*, along with those of Alexander's foster-brothers who did not hold independent commands. The place of a King of Macedon was among the fore-fighters, and it was our duty to be with him.

We advanced in silence. The fourteen foot *sarissa* with its iron head and bronze lizard-killer was well balanced, but heavy. Its haft of ash, gripped in two hands, was slick in my sweaty palms. The round shield was slung by a strap over my shoulder, and the fingers of my leading left hand clutched the handle inside the rim, but the awkward thing still banged and clattered.

I was so lost in keeping my place on the steep incline, and managing my ungainly equipment, that I took no notice of the enemy until someone shouted, 'Here come the carts!'

The first few were already running free, gathering speed. Men were shoving the others. The crest was perhaps a hundred paces away.

I saw one wagon off to the right hit a rock and turn over. It tumbled, wheels spinning in the air, and smashed itself to kindling. But now there was a wall of them stretching across the slope and descending fast. Here on the left, bordered by a steep, wooded ravine, there was no room to make lanes to let them pass.

'Close ranks!' Alexander yelled.

We shuffled together, bumping shields and shoulders, but not panicking. These were Alexander's Companions leading the Royal Guard, pride if nothing else would keep us together.

'Lie down! Form shields!'

I dropped my *sarissa*, and hurled myself full length. The carts would be on us in a moment. If we were not ready, it would be carnage. Digging the rim of my shield into the short grass, I angled it back over my head to rest on my shoulders. The shields of Leonnatus and Ptolemy on either side overlapped mine. I felt those of the next rank slam down onto mine.

The earth trembled and roared as if with the fury of earth-shaking Poseidon. Close by someone was praying to Herakles the Ancestor, another was swearing monotonously. My nostrils were filled with the smell of sweat and leather and the earth. I had to force myself to breathe.

A blow, like a hammer onto an anvil, drove the shield down into my shoulder blades, crushed my face into the dirt. I gasped with shock and pain, then another pile driving impact smashed me down again. There was a heartbeat of silence before a terrible, rending crash from behind. Wood and rocks hitting metal and leather, crushing and rending muscle and bones. Men were screaming in agony.

'Up! Form ranks!'

Groggily, I clambered to my feet. My shoulders hurt, and my helmet was knocked down over my brow. I pushed the helmet up out of my eyes, stooped clumsily to retrieve my shield, slung its strap, then fumbled to get a grip on my *sarissa*.

The slope was filled with tribesmen. They tore down howling their hatred. In front of Perdiccas' battalion our archers were shooting as fast as they could. There was nothing between us and the descending Triballi.

'Prepare to receive a charge!'

The *sarissas* of the first four ranks came down horizontal, their wicked iron points projecting from our line. Those of the rear ranks sloped over our heads.

The Triballi were backwoods Thracians: bearded, blue with tattoos. A huge warrior brought his curved blade two-handed down, lopping the head off my pike. He forced the next spearhead away, pressed towards me. Desperately, I let go of the shaft of my now useless *sarissa*, and dragged my sword from its scabbard. I saw the *rhomphaia* raised above me, about to chop down, cleaving my helmet and head. Then a pike from behind took him clean in the chest. He fell but another was in his place, screaming some outlandish war cry. Again the glint of curved steel over my head. Stepping forward, I punched the tip of my straight sword deep into his groin. We were locked together, his fingers clawing at my face, as if oblivious to his death wound.

When I managed to push the Thracian away, he curled and fell. With the savagery of fear, I brought the edge of my blade down onto his exposed skull again and again.

Al-al-al-al-ai! The chant rang out across the slope.

The warriors in front were running. They were all running.

'After them!' Alexander's voice carried through the din. 'Don't let them rally!'

With little order we surged up the incline.

A small knot of Triballi nobles – with helmets and armour, their faces swirled with inked patterns – made a stand. Like a river in flood, the Macedonians flowed over them. The rest threw away their shields and weapons the better to run.

A high wailing of women and children came from those wagons that had not been pushed down the hill.

A trumpet sounded – the prearranged signal for Sitalces and Langarus to unleash the pursuit.

The fighting was over, only the pillaging remained.

Philotas, beaming, recited a line of Homer: "'Let no man be urgent to take his way homeward until he has lain in bed with the wife of a Trojan.'"

Alexander, known for his abstinence in such matters, just laughed. 'Your desire for women will be the death of you.'

As the men streamed into the encampment, Alexander turned to me. 'Have Craterus bring up his battalion and post guards. It is unlikely the enemy will rally, but the rest will soon be drunk.'

I started to leave, but he took my arm. 'When the army is beyond the Haemus, I need someone I can trust to oversee the southern tribes. You will remain and be my *strategos* in Thrace.'

* * *

Sitalkes and I rode down from the hills, his Thracian servant and Eumaeus following. Artemis, Mistress of Animals, had been kind. We had taken a great stag with a fine spread of antlers. The beast was slung over one of the packhorses.

Like me, Sitalkes was the younger son of a king defeated by Philip, who had offered earth and water. Like me, he had been educated by a Greek man of letters. Our tutors had not been the sort who made a reputation in Athens, or received large sums to make the journey to Pella. Necessity had driven them to the frozen north to warm their chapped hands at the fires of obscure client rulers. Sitalkes' elder brother, Seuthes, reminded me of Heromenes; the same black bitterness at fortune. But Sitalkes, with his broad, gap-toothed smile, was open and amiable. We had become friends. Although nothing had been said, I knew Sitalkes had arranged the hunt to take my mind off my concerns.

Initially, after the battle at the pass, the war in the north had gone well. As expected, the Getae had joined the Triballi. Alexander had crossed the Danube and defeated the Getae, whereupon the Triballi had surrendered. But then, while Alexander was breaking his journey back to Pella with Langarus, three Illyrian tribes had risen. One of them were the Autariatae with whom we had taken refuge in our exile. Langarus had said his Agrianes would deal with them. However the Dardani had invaded Upper Macedon, plundering their way through Pelagonia and Lyncestis. Alexander had given chase. When they moved west, back into Illyrian territory, he had besieged them in a settlement called Pelium. The latest reports said that the warriors of the third tribe, the Taulantii, had seized the surrounding heights, trapping Alexander and the Macedonians.

My worry was not the position of Alexander; already he had an air of invincibility. Somehow you knew he would not just extricate himself, but crush any foolhardy enough to stand against him. No, my fear was for my mother and my home. Once again across the plain of Lyncestis, the farms would have been reduced to charred timber, people and cattle slaughtered. Once again, those who had escaped would be huddled behind the walls of Lebaea. I had told myself a hundred times that Lebaea had never fallen; my father had opened the gates to Philip, but the Illyrians had never breached them. There was no reason to think things would be different this time. Yet a worm of doubt kept crawling into my thoughts – all the fighting men of Lyncestis were with Alexander or the armies in the lowlands.

Lyncestis was not the only thing oppressing my spirits. As *strategos* of Thrace my time was consumed with endless disputes. They concerned boundaries and water rights, stolen women and livestock. Most stretched back generations, and involved blood feuds. None of the speakers told the truth. Although it tried my patience, I listened for hours, attempted to be equitable, but, obviously, many left dissatisfied. Those who courted my favour were happy to relay, and embellish, the complaints: I was too young for such responsibility, and had only been promoted as a favourite of Alexander. Sometimes I thought they were right; perhaps it was as well that fate had not made me King of an independent Lyncestis, let alone of all Macedon.

We crested a rise and there below us was Seuthopolis, its walls bathed in autumn sunlight.

'Horsemen!' Sitalkes said.

There were half a dozen of them, riding hard up the trail towards us. They carried no spears, and wore hats not helmets. Even so Eumaeus and Sitalkes' Thracian closed up on either side, all of us with hands on the hilts of our swords. No country was so pacified that fast moving horsemen did not mean danger.

'It is Memnon.' Sitalkes had sharp eyes.

My deputy as *strategos*, Memnon was very conscious of his dignity, and never went anywhere without an escort. His hasty advent was not something to welcome. Memnon resented both my closeness to Alexander and, what he termed, my good fortune. Unlike him, I had fought at Chaeronea. Above all he was resentful that he was not *strategos* of Thrace.

We relaxed a little. If Memnon wanted to encompass my death, he would have done it out in the hills, not within sight of Seuthopolis.

The horsemen reined to a halt. Memnon, dispensing with the salute due to a superior officer, blurted out: 'People are saying that Alexander is dead.'

'People say all sorts of things.' To give myself time I kept talking. 'It would take more than some Illyrians to kill him. What people are spreading this story?'

'In Athens Demosthenes brought an eyewitness before the assembly.'

'A Greek will say anything.'

'The Thebans believe he is dead. The city has revolted. Our garrison is blockaded in the Cadmea.'

Dread gripped my heart. 'My nephew?'

'Dead,' Memnon said. 'The Thebans caught him and a man called Timolaus outside the defences.'

Sitalkes put his hand on my arm. 'May the earth lie lightly on him.'

I nodded my thanks. This was no time to grieve. Alive or dead, Alexander was in the far west with the field army. The garrison left with Antipater in Macedon was inadequate. The Greek revolt would spread. If there was no immediate response Thessaly would cast off its allegiance. That would open the way to Aegae, and on to Pella. In all of Thrace there were only two units of Macedonians: a battalion of the phalanx under Zopyrion, and Memnon's squadron of Companion Cavalry. They had to remain to keep the tribes loyal.

'Sitalkes, how many men can you have ready to march in two days?'

He considered for a few moments, counting on his fingers. 'From around Seuthopolis two thousand *peltasts* and perhaps five hundred horsemen. But if I send out messengers the Odrysians and the other tribes could have ten thousand waiting for us on the lower Hebrus, and another couple of thousand mustered this side of Mount Pangaeum.'

Less than fifteen thousand warriors. Perhaps Antipater could spare some troops as we passed through Macedon. If not, speed would have to make up for numbers. 'As soon as we reach the town,' I told Sitalkes, 'send out the couriers.'

'What are you going to do?' Memnon was full of suspicion.

'I am going to Thebes.'

'You are going to take a barbarian army to fight the Greeks?'

'Yes,' I said, 'and you are going to remain here with the Macedonians as *strategos* of Thrace.'

Memnon almost smiled, a look of calculation in his eyes.

If Alexander was dead what would happen? There was no obvious heir. His cousin Amyntas had been executed, Olympias had murdered one of his half-brothers, the infant Ceranus, and her witchcraft or poison had left the other, Arrhidaeus, a man with the mind of a child. The only remaining legitimate

Argead blood ran in the veins of distant relatives. They were all from the old upland Houses: Perdiccas and Craterus of Orestis, Machatas and his sons of Elimea. And then there was the House of Lyncestis – Leonnatus and myself.

CHAPTER FIFTEEN

Autumn 335 BC

ALEXANDER WAS NOT DEAD. Far from it, Antipater assured me. Alexander had defeated the Illyrians, and was force-marching the field army south. Even now he would be approaching Thebes.

Leaving my Thracians on the road round the head of the Gulf of Therma, I had ridden to Pella to confer with Antipater. As Regent, Antipater decided that my force should continue into Greece. Alexander had more than enough troops – over thirty thousand – to deal with Thebes. But several cities in the Peloponnese had voted to support the rebellion, and Athens, as ever whipped up by Demosthenes, was wavering. Should the Peloponnesians cross the Isthmus, and if the Athenians decided on war, another fifteen thousand Thracian warriors would be a useful addition to Alexander's army.

As I left, Antipater added enigmatically that fighting in the streets of a city was dangerous, anything could happen, a roof tile can hit anyone. It would be good if I was at Thebes with men at my back should some disaster strike. He gripped my shoulder, like some honest farmer settling a deal at market, and said that as my father-in-law he would support whatever decision I made.

After a night with Electra, I was on horseback again. I caught up with the Thracians at Pydna. The gates were shut, as they had been at every town since we crossed into Macedon. A squadron of Companion Cavalry from Amphipolis *escorted* the Thracians. It is always difficult to stop troops plundering on the march, and Thracians had a well-earned reputation for violent depredations. The irony was not lost on Sitalkes or his warriors that the Macedonians they were coming to aid did not trust them, and regarded them as no more than savage barbarians.

Eight days hard marching – down the Vale of Tempe, across the plains of Thessaly, through the narrows of Thermopylae, over the hills of Phocis – brought us into Boeotia and the territory of Thebes. Despite the punishing pace, very few warriors were left behind. The Thracians were aliens in a hostile land. They could have had few illusions of the fate of any stragglers.

Sitalkes and a kinsman called Rhascus oversaw the column. It left me all too much time to grieve my nephew Amyntas, and, almost worse, to ponder the oblique words of Antipater. If Alexander fell in the chaos of the storm of Thebes there was no clear Argead heir to the throne. An outsider might stake a claim. To strengthen their position, pretenders in the past had married into the royal house. Alexander of Epirus already had Alexander's sister Cleopatra as his wife. More likely the Macedonians under arms, always suspicious of foreign rulers, would exercise their right to acclaim one of their own there and then. The troops had long followed Parmenion. He had a proven record as a war leader. Either of Alexander's half-sisters – Cynnane who was promised to the King of the Agrianes, or young and unwed Thessalonice – might find themselves with a new and unexpected husband.

Or the Macedonians might demand a king with Argead blood, no matter how thin it ran in his veins. That meant the houses of the lords of the uplands. Machatas of Elimea was too old, and his son Harpalus a cripple. Harpalus had two brothers with the army, but they were still youths and untested. Much more obvious were two men from the house of Orestis: my friend Perdiccas and his kinsman Craterus. They would both be at Thebes, and commanded battalions of the phalanx. Finally there were the last survivors of the house of Lyncestis left in Macedon: Leonnatus and myself. If Alexander died, I would face a terrible choice.

Another day on the road and we reached Thebes. Alexander was encamped to the south-east of the city, opposite the gates to Eleutherae and Athens.

'You are here at last,' Alexander said.

The others in his big tent were laughing.

This was unfair. 'I came as quickly as I could.'

Alexander embraced me. 'It is a joke. When we arrived the Thebans were so convinced I was dead they believed you were in command of the army.'

I hoped my face did not betray any of the thoughts that had haunted my journey.

Sensing something was wrong, Alexander stepped back. Then a look of compassion dawned in his eyes. 'Forgive me, I had forgotten.' He hugged me again. 'I am very sorry about Amyntas. I know you were fond of your nephew.'

'Thank you.'

The rest greeted me. Most did so with warmth, Leonnatus with beaming pleasure, but Philotas was distant, and Hephaestion made scant effort to conceal his loathing.

I needed to know how things stood. 'They have not surrendered?'

This provoked another bout of general mirth.

'We offered generous terms, just hand over a couple of ringleaders.' Craterus found it so funny he found it hard to get the next words out. 'And they demanded we give them Antipater and Philotas.'

Interesting the Thebans had singled out Philotas among the younger men. He did not seem to find it amusing. Nor did Alexander.

'They have broken their oath again.' Alexander's face was set. Everyone else stopped chuckling to hear him talk. 'An example has to be made, or all the Greeks will betray us as soon as we cross to Asia. We storm the walls tomorrow.'

On the way through the camp I had seen no siege towers or rams, precious few scaling ladders. An ill-prepared assault would be costly, might even end in a bloody repulse.

'How many men do they have?' I asked.

'Deserters tell us fifteen thousand or more. They have freed their able-bodied slaves and enlisted resident aliens.'

Odds of two to one, even if many of the defenders were not trained soldiers, were not enough against a prepared position. With my Thracians the odds were three to one – perhaps still not enough.

Alexander smiled at the look on my face. 'It's not as bad as you think. Come outside, and I will show you.'

The walls of Thebes were old. In places were hastily patched repairs. But the circuit was still formidable.

'The Theban hoplites man the walls facing us, but see there.' Alexander pointed. 'The southern walls of the Cadmea are the defence of the town. So outside them they have constructed two lines of palisades and ditches. The inner is to bottle up the Macedonian garrison, the outer to keep us out. That is where the slaves are stationed. Perdiccas noticed their discipline is lax at dawn. His battalion goes in at first light tomorrow. Once he has taken the outer palisade, the battalion of Amyntas, son of Andromenes, will follow. When they have drawn some of the Thebans away from us, we attack the gates here.'

I gazed up at the Cadmea, thinking about my serious young nephew.

'The gods have foretold the doom of Thebes.' It was Aristander the seer. 'The statues in the marketplace were seen to sweat. A ripple of blood ran along the waters at the Spring of Dirce. The marsh at Onchestus bellowed like a bull.'

We all listened attentively. The gods come close in time of war.

'A spider spun a huge web in the Temple of Demeter. Their oracle of Zeus Ammon told the Thebans: "The woven web to one a bane, to one a boon."'

The gods are not to be mocked, but that was suitably ambiguous.

'Where are my Thracians to be stationed?'

'To the left of the palisades, facing the south-western gate.' Alexander gestured. 'The walls there are high, but guarded by youths and old men. Have your men prepare axes and ladders today as soon as they camp. Tomorrow do not advance until I send a messenger.'

* * *

It was quiet in the long watches of the night. The Thracians were exhausted after the hard march. They knew nothing of the assault. None of the soldiers had been told, only the senior officers. It is one of the oddities of war that a few men will always desert into a beleaguered town, no matter how dire its position. Every army contains brutal men whose fear of punishment for their crimes will drive them to change sides. Some cowards will do anything to postpone death.

Unable to sleep, I strapped on my armour, wrapped myself in a cloak against the chill of the autumn night, and went to tour our pickets. Several were fast asleep. It has always been a weakness of Thracians. At Troy, Odysseus and Diomedes stole into their camp as they slumbered. I woke them, using the smattering of Thracian that Sitalkes had taught me, and threatened no punishments. I knew it would be easy to murder an officer in the solitude of the night. But they had to be alert. There was the ever-present danger of the besieged making a sortie.

The torches of the watchmen moved along the walls of Thebes. Away to the north the fires of our outposts pricked the blackness. They were tended by Phocians and other Greeks from nearby cities with a deep hatred of Thebes, nurtured by long oppression. When my eyes were accustomed to the dark, and I had orientated myself, inside Thebes I could make out the lights of the Macedonian garrison on the low rise of the Cadmea. I wondered if Amyntas had been given a sprinkle of earth and a coin for the ferryman. It was unlikely as he had been murdered down in the city away from his men. When Thebes fell I would seek out his remains. It pained me that he had died almost alone. It was worse that his shade might be wandering unable to cross the Styx. In a sacked city, it would be no simple task to find his remains.

Looking at the lights of the trapped garrison, I thought it should be possible to devise a system of signalling even complex messages by torches. But my mind balked at the effort. It kept slipping back to the dangers of the succession should Alexander fall. Either I would have to make a bid for the throne, or back someone else. There was no way to stand aloof. Even if I chose the winner, and did so with alacrity, it might not guarantee my life. The new King would always see me as a potential rival. While Alexander was King I was safe. And Alexander was my friend. I found myself praying to Heracles the Ancestor that he survived.

The darkness was no longer absolute. There was a thin line of amber over the barren hills to the east. The torches of the Theban watchmen flared slightly less bright. I could make out the shape of the gatehouse opposite, although the small postern just along the wall was still invisible. A sharp scent of morning hung in the air. It was fresh and good after the stale smoke and sweat and faeces of night in an armed camp.

I sensed, rather than saw, movement down to the south where the shelters of Perdiccas' men were pitched. There was no sound, nothing yet to warn the defenders. Perdiccas was a good commander, his soldiers well trained. Rousing the nearest of my sentries, I sent them to tell Sitalkes and Rhascus to begin to wake the Thracians.

The light was gathering. Now I could just detect movement. A black shape, like a great earth-born beast from myth, shifting towards the outer palisade. Perhaps a hundred paces to go, Perdiccas' battalion was advancing as one in silence.

Behind me, loud Thracian voices; some giving harsh orders, more raised in sleepy complaint. Sitalkes appeared at my side, a few moments later to be joined by his kinsman Rhascus. The latter handed me a hunk of bread.

A shout from the palisade. A Theban with sharper wits than his companions had seen the danger. A trumpet sounded. It was answered from below by the full-throated cry of Macedon: *Al-al-al-al-ai!*.

There was consternation behind the palisade. Defenders ran here and there, seemingly without orders. Everyone was shouting at once. What else would you expect from newly liberated slaves?

The outer trench was no more than five feet deep, the berm behind it perhaps a couple of feet high, the stakes of the palisade less than the height of a man. The leading Macedonians jabbed overarm with their *sarissas* to clear the defenders, while others ducked under the shafts to tear the stakes free with crowbars. In no time there was a breach over a hundred paces wide into which the men of Perdiccas vanished.

The sky had turned rose and yellow, vaulting up from the eastern horizon. Now it was light enough to see clearly.

The roar of combat drifted from the space where men struggled between the two palisades. Coming up in support the battalion of Amyntas, son of Andromenes, moved into the breach. Perdiccas had reached the inner fortification. Recovered from their surprise, the defenders were making a stand. I glimpsed a figure in a gleaming yellow cloak fringed with purple – the mark of a Companion – vault onto the stockade. Then it was gone, and a great howl of fury came from fifteen hundred throats. Perdiccas' battalion was stymied, unable to sweep away this last line of defence.

Sitalkes grunted through a mouthful of bread and pointed. Alexander was sending in more reserves. He could orchestrate a battle like the master of a chorus. The Agrianes and archers jogged forward towards the gap in the outer stockade. Their missiles could harass the defenders while Amyntas' men moved through those of Perdiccas to launch a fresh attack.

A small group emerged back from the breach. They carried a motionless figure in a yellow and purple cloak. That explained the setback. Perdiccas had fallen. If it was fatal, it was a good death for a warrior from Orestis.

A yell of triumph brought my attention back to the fighting. The Macedonians were over the inner fortification. They were driving the enemy down a sunken lane towards the Temple of Heracles.

'This will soon be over,' Rhascus said in heavily accented Greek, 'soon time to plunder.'

'Not yet.' Sitalkes pointed. 'They are bringing up reinforcements.'

Not far from the Temple of Heracles was an open sanctuary dedicated to the hero Amphiaraus. A solid body of men with big round shields and spears was getting into position. More men waited with horses.

'Those are Theban citizens,' I said. 'They fought well at Chaeronea. This is not over.'

Sure enough the Macedonians, tired and disordered by combat, began to give way before this new assault. At first it was step by step, all facing the foe. But soon the pace increased, and the first faint hearts were slipping away to run back out of the outer palisade.

Out on the plain, Alexander had drawn up the other battalions of the phalanx. There was no point in sending any of them into the breach, there was no room between the palisades. At least our defeated men could rally behind them.

From the town, voices were raised in a triumphal paean. From all across the city, down the streets and along the battlements, more and more Thebans were coming to join the pursuit. Our soldiers were pouring out of the defences. The Thebans were close on their heels, only pausing to stab those who lagged behind or tripped.

'Look! Look!' Sitalkes grabbed my arm. 'The fools think they have won.'

Some god must have possessed the Thebans. Their troops were rushing out after our men. They were coming not only from the breach in the palisade, but from the gates in the wall beyond. All jumbled together, keeping no order, in their mad enthusiasm they were surging towards Alexander's disciplined ranks. The Thebans were turning a victory into a defeat. Aristander had interpreted the words of Zeus Ammon correctly.

There is a fascination in watching from perfect safety other men fight and die. This was like a tragedy, where *hubris* leads to catastrophe. No one was heading towards us. The wall facing us was nearly bare of troops. Looking more closely, I saw the postern gate was completely unmanned.

Now it was my turn to grab Sitalkes. 'Get the axes!'

He just stared, unmoving. In my excitement I had spoken in Macedonian. I repeated myself in Greek, then bad Thracian. 'Your best men with us, the rest wait opposite the main gate.'

Alexander had told me to wait for his messenger, but this was an opportunity not to be missed.

As we lumbered towards the little door it dawned on me that I had forgotten to tell anyone to get my helmet or shield. I muttered a prayer to Heracles, offering a dozen rams if my stupidity went unpunished.

The postern was just round the south-west corner of the circuit, out of sight of the battle. At every step I expected the alarm to be raised up on the battlements. It never came. The remaining guards must have had all their attention on the fighting south of the city.

The Thracians wielded their axes in an ecstasy of destruction. Splinters flew, and the timber boomed and groaned. From above, finally I heard a shout of alarm, followed by trumpet calls. It was too late. The door gave way, and we entered the city.

Once inside, I turned right and sprinted to the rear of the main gate. As Alexander had said, it was guarded by the very young and old. They saw us coming and ran. Most got away, but a few of the greybeards were chopped down. We hauled the gate open.

As soon as the Thracians were inside all control disappeared. Howling with joy, they vanished into the alleyways in search of plunder and rape and other bestial pleasures. Soon only Sitalkes and those bound to him by blood oaths remained; at most two hundred warriors.

'What now?' Sitalkes asked.

'To the Cadmea.' It seemed best to me to reach our beleaguered garrison. From up there we could get a view of the battlefield. And if everything went wrong, we would be safe behind its walls, for a certain amount of time.

The Cadmea is not as high as many an acropolis, but every now and then we caught sight of the roofs of its temples. Rounding yet another corner, we ran straight into a barricade manned with Thebans. They took one look and fled.

As the Thracians tore down the obstruction, helmeted heads peered down from a gatehouse on the citadel.

'Wait!' This time I remembered to speak in Thracian. 'They may mistake us for the enemy.'

There would be archers up there, men with javelins. It would be a hideous irony to be shot down by the men we had come to rescue. There was a way the defenders might realise our identity.

'Stay here, until I say.'

It took an effort to force myself to walk out beyond the barricade. I was very conscious of lacking a shield, of having nothing protecting my head. Sheathing my sword – I had no memory of drawing it – I took the corners of my cloak in both hands, and held it high above my head. The newly risen sun shone on its yellow material, picked out the purple border.

'Who is in command?' I shouted in Macedonian.

'I am,' a familiar voice said.

'But you are dead!' I said stupidly. 'You were killed with Timolaus.'

Amyntas laughed. 'No, that was another Theban called Anemoitas. You and those Thracians had better come in.'

There was no time for much of a reunion. From the southern battlements of the Cadmea the scene was spread out like a painting. The whole Macedonian army was inside the walls, pressing up from the south. The majority of the Thebans, fighting men and civilians alike, were fleeing through the streets, seeking asylum in the temples. The Phocians and our other Greek allies were joining the Thracians in an orgy of destruction and killing. A few hundred Thebans still resisted in the open space of the sanctuary of Amphiaraus.

'Lend me half your garrison.'

My nephew, ever dutiful, looked uncertain. 'My orders were to hold the citadel. Nothing more.'

'Circumstances change.' At times Amyntas could be infuriating. 'We can finish this now.'

Reluctantly, Amyntas agreed.

It went as I hoped. As soon as they saw some seven hundred Macedonian pikemen bearing down on their rear the Theban last stand collapsed. Their cavalry managed to get clear by an unblocked street to the north-east. Less fortunate, their infantry dropped their weapons and appealed for a clemency they did not find.

After a time, sickened by the slaughter, I made my way alone back up to the Cadmea.

* * *

There were no corpses on the Cadmea, but the ghastly stench of burnt flesh drifted up from the town. It was the afternoon after the sack. The order had gone out to stop the looting and killing: six thousand Thebans were thought dead. The fires were under control, and most of the troops back with the standards, although many of my Thracians were still absent. Alexander had summoned the Companions to the Temple of Zeus Ammon, who had foretold our victory. Some of the Macedonians looked worse for wear, myself included. I had drunk late with my nephew. It was good Amyntas was alive.

'The Greek allies will vote to destroy Thebes.' Alexander looked fresh and rested. His capacity for recovery from a debauch was high, even by Macedonian standards.

The vote was no surprise. In the past the Thebans had passed the same savage verdict on the cities of Plataea and Thespiae and Orchomenos. Few Macedonians would object. We had suffered heavy losses: five hundred dead, including Eurybotas the commander of the archers, more than twice that number wounded, among their number Perdiccas. The Orestid was tough, and likely to live.

'They want every building levelled and all the captives sold into slavery.'

That was within the laws of war.

'As *Hegemon* of the Hellenes, I will propose a certain clemency. The temples, sanctuaries, and the house of Pindar are to be spared.'

Alexander always honoured the gods, and his respect for culture was wider than just his beloved Homer. Long ago, Pindar had written an ode praising the King's ancestor and namesake Alexander I.

'Similarly, those Thebans who are priests, guest-friends of Macedonians, or descendants of Pindar will be set free without ransom.'

Philotas took off his helmet, the age-old custom when a Macedonian wanted to speak in council or assembly. 'Will some of the Greeks accuse us of barbarism? Easy to imagine one of their orators fulminating that we have *plucked out one of the eyes of Hellas*.'

Alexander was unmoved. 'Twice the Thebans have broken the oaths they took at Corinth, not only to us, but to the other Greeks. It will be the Greeks who pass sentence on them.'

'Thebes is useful as a counterweight to Athens,' Parmenion said.

'The destruction of Thebes will serve as a warning. Athens and the cities of the Peloponnese will come to heel. As soon as they get news they will all despatch embassies begging forgiveness, which we will grant.'

'The Athenians will need watching.' Parmenion stuck to his theme. 'They will be looking for a chance to stab us in the back while we are campaigning against Persia.'

'Antipater will be left with enough troops as Regent. Many Greeks still remember and fear Athenian ambitions. Anyway

Sparta has stood aloof from the League of Corinth, and remains as a check on Athens.'

Craterus put up his hand; he had a cut on his forehead, and was not wearing a helmet. 'We think there are about thirty thousand captives. As the other Boeotians hate them, they will all want a Theban slave. That should keep the prices high.' He counted on his fingers. 'So maybe about forty talents of silver. You know how Harpalus is always moaning there is no money in the war chest.'

There was a commotion outside. One of the Royal Pages appeared, saluted Alexander, but spoke to me.

'There are some Thracians outside with a prisoner. They want to talk to you.'

I glanced at Alexander, who nodded, and told the boy to bring them in.

It was Sitalkes and two of his Thracians who led a woman by the rope that bound her hands. Although her dress and hair were dishevelled, the woman walked proudly, her eyes looking beyond her captors, as if to deny their existence.

After acknowledging Alexander, Sitalkes addressed himself to me. 'This woman murdered Rhascus. She tricked him into climbing down into a well. Then she threw stones. When we found him, he was dead. I demand vengeance.'

Perhaps it was a measure of where we had got with the Thracians that they had not taken her life there and then. Although it could be they hoped for some exemplary public punishment.

'This is for the King to decide.'

'You lead these men,' Alexander said. 'It is for you to judge.'

'Who are you?'

'My name is Timocleia.' She spoke clearly, looked me in the eye. 'I had the good fortune to have a brother Theagenes, who was a general at Chaeronea, and fell there, fighting against you Macedonians for the freedom of the Hellenes.'

'And did you kill Rhascus.'

'The Thracians broke into my house, looted my property, outraged my maids. Their leader, having treated me shamefully, demanded to know where I had hidden my gold and silver. I told him it was at the bottom of the well. Now I have no wish to escape death, perhaps it is better, rather than live to experience another such night.'

In the sack of a city women could expect to be raped, girls and boys too. It was the nature of the world. Had not old Nestor urged the Achaeans not to return home until they had lain with the wives of the Trojans? But this was a Greek woman of gentle birth who had been forced by a barbarian. Macedonian noblemen are odd creatures. We can be brutal, but respect courage and honour and the taking of revenge in our enemies. I saw Philotas, who no doubt would have forced a woman against her will the previous night, wiping away a tear of compassion.

'Amyntas,' I turned to my nephew, 'detail a squad of your men to escort the Lady Timocleia to safety, wherever she wishes to go, beyond the borders of Thebes. Let her take her possessions that can be recovered and those of her household that have survived and can be found.'

'This is an outrage!' Sitalkes shouted. 'We fight your battles, but you deny us justice!'

'Remember who you are—' Alexander's voice was like a sword sliding out of its scabbard '—and who you are talking to.'

Sitalkes turned on his heel, and stalked out, his men trailing after.

Alexander smiled at me. 'That was the decision I would have made. But now I think Memnon had better remain as *strategos* of Thrace, and you will accompany me to Asia.'

CHAPTER SIXTEEN

Spring 334 BC

'**Y**OU SAID WHAT?'

It was late in the night, and I must leave in the morning. Electra's head was on my shoulder, and I could not see her face, but I knew she was not really angry.

'Alexander asked his companions about our finances before the army departs. To those who were short of money he gave gifts from the royal estates. Some received a farm or a village, others the income from a hamlet or a harbour. Perdiccas asked Alexander what he would have left for himself. He replied his hopes. After that we could not take anything, but said it would be an honour to share his hopes.'

I could tell Electra was smiling. 'Perdiccas is Orestid, you are a Lyncestian. Let me guess it was all uplanders who refused the gifts. You are so touchy about your honour. Perhaps it is all you ever had in your bleak mountain fastnesses.'

'Without honour a man is nothing.' Although heartfelt, it sounded pompous to my own ears.

'You did the right thing. It binds you closer to Alexander.'

Electra raised herself on an elbow. In the soft light of the one lamp she looked into my eyes. 'But I wish you had agreed to be initiated into the mysteries of Dionysus. Should anything happen, we would be together in the afterlife.'

Her words put a chill in my soul. My mind pictured the night in the foothills of Mount Bermion, the terrible curse: *Let justice come for all to see, let her come sword in hand.* The mysteries were not for *the godless, the lawless, the unjust.*

'It is not for me.'

I thought about Neoptolemus, somewhere in Persia, in exile. I wondered if he would stand against us on the field of battle, wondered what I should do if he faced me. My mind wandered to my father – drunken and feckless, even cruel, but Aeropus was still my father. He too was serving the Persian King. What if I should meet him in the front rank? There was no worse crime than patricide. A man who killed his father faced an eternity of torment in Hades.

'Anyway, uplanders are very hard to kill.' I traced her cheekbone with my finger. 'It is you that must take care here in Pella. Olympias hates you because she hates both your father and me.'

Electra kissed me. 'Do not fear for me. Alexander has left Antipater the Great Seal of the kingdom. The Queen will not dare do anything openly against the Regent or his family.'

'Arrhidaeus did not end up with the mind of a child through anything open. Olympias is a witch.'

'All our slaves were bred in the house of my father. They are loyal. No drugs will be slipped into our food.' She took my hand in hers. 'It is you that must be watchful. Distance will not allay her hatred. Olympias will always try to poison Alexander against you. But there will be another threat closer at hand. Olympias fears you because she sees you as a rival for the throne; Hephaestion loathes you as a rival for the affection of Alexander.'

'I love Alexander, but I have no wish to share his bed. Anyway Hephaestion is nothing without Alexander.'

'He knows you all think that – you, Craterus, Perdiccas, all the sons of the great barons – and that is why you must be on your guard against him.'

There was a tap at the door; old Eumaeus telling me it would soon be dawn. I told him I would be ready, and heard him grumbling as he went away.

Electra's hand moved down over my stomach.

'There is no time.'

'You can be quick.'

'You are insatiable.'

She laughed, and straddled me.

Afterwards, she kissed me gently, as if it might be the last time. 'Take good care of yourself. I would not want your child to grow up not knowing its father.'

'You are pregnant?'

'A couple of months now. So make sure you come back to us.'

* * *

Some god had watched over us, or over Alexander. We crossed the Hellespont unhindered by storms or the enemy. Our fleet was weak, that of the Persians strong. We could not have fought them at sea. Our hopes would have drowned in the cold waters before anyone set foot on land. But the Persian warships had not yet even been sighted in the Aegean. Some said they were delayed crushing a native revolt in Egypt, others that the Great King considered us beneath his notice. If the latter, Darius might come to regret his contempt. Those the gods wish to destroy they first drive mad.

At the midpoint between Europe and Asia, Alexander sacrificed a bull to Poseidon, and made libations to the Nereids.

Parmenion oversaw the laborious process of ferrying the army to Abydos. The previous year, after the death of Philip, and while we were fighting against the northern tribes and Thebes, a Persian army had counter-attacked up the coast. Led by a Greek mercenary, Memnon of Rhodes, it had driven our advance force back north. Ephesus and most of the other cities we had gained had been lost. But we still held a bridgehead.

Alexander took the helm of the flagship. Leaving the main fleet, he steered for the Achaean Harbour, where long ago Agamemnon had beached his ships. From the prow, Alexander hurled a spear into the soil of Asia. It was the age old Macedonian custom, announcing this was no mere raid, and appealing to the gods to grant us this land as spear-won territory; ours to hold and to rule. The will of the gods would be revealed in the outcome. Alone, ahead of everyone else, Alexander leapt into the surf, and waded ashore.

This was it, what I had been born for. To follow a great war leader, my friend Alexander, to win honour and wealth, to do some great thing, so that men should remember me when I had gone down to Hades.

We went up to Troy, a small, poky place, quite unworthy of its ancient glory. Alexander sacrificed at the tomb of his ancestor Achilles. The locals produced what they claimed was the armour of the hero. It looked suspiciously new to me, but Alexander was delighted to exchange it for his own equipment. The King also made offerings to the shade of Priam to assuage the blood guilt of Achilles' son killing the old man in a sanctuary. Some of the Companions, like the heroes of Homer, raced naked. I did not join them. My thigh had never been quite the same since the tusk of the boar in the marshes of Lake Loudias had laid it open.

At the end of the race Alexander placed a wreath on the tomb of Achilles, Hephaestion one on that of Patroclus. I caught a significant look from Craterus. If it was needed, this was a reminder of the influence his lover had over Alexander. Electra had been right – Hephaestion had to be watched.

We rejoined the army at Abydos. We needed a victory, and we needed to win it soon. Harpalus calculated that, although we had supplies for thirty days, there was only money to pay the troops for just fourteen. The spies of Eumenes, the Greek secretary Alexander had inherited from his father, reported the deliberations of the Persian counsel of war. They had the ring of truth. The Greek mercenary Memnon of Rhodes had urged what we most feared: defend the walled cities, torch the countryside, avoid open battle, and let hunger drive us to retreat back over the Hellespont. But fortunately for us neither Memnon nor anyone else had overall command. Instead, Memnon was faced by a cabal of the Persian satraps. These proud noblemen put little trust in the Greek, who apparently had once, before I arrived in Pella, been an exile in Macedonia. Arsites, the governor of Hellespontine Phrygia, the province we had invaded, announced he would not allow a single home to be burnt. No doubt the Persian noblemen were puffed up by the successes they had had against our advance force last year. They had overruled Memnon, and decided that their forces would stand their ground, and wait for us somewhere on the road east.

We marched fast, but circumspectly, ready for battle. The infantry advanced in two parallel columns, flanked by the cavalry. My nephew Amyntas went ahead with the mounted scouts and the light horsemen from Paeonia. Not all the towns welcomed us as liberators. Most closed their gates. It was hard to blame them after our setbacks the previous year, and while the issue was in doubt. Should we lose, those who had joined us would suffer cruel retribution from the Persians. We bypassed those that stood out against us, lacking the time or the materiel for a siege. Everything depended on a victory.

The countryside through which we marched was verdant with spring; the fruit trees clouded with blossom, the fields enamelled with bright flowers. Early in the afternoon of the third day Amyntas came galloping back. Even my dour nephew was glowing with excitement. The Persians had formed up on the far bank of a small river ahead. The locals called it the Granicus.

While the army manoeuvred from column of march to battle line with the smoothness of long practice, Amyntas led Alexander, with his Companions and senior officers, to a point of vantage on a low rise.

The first view was not encouraging. We had always been told that Persians fought well on horseback, but were nothing on foot. Their only infantry worth anything were those Greek mercenaries they could hire. There were just a handful of pickets along the river, but beyond them, about a hundred paces from the bank, were squadron after squadron of Persian cavalry. They filled the plain; perhaps twenty thousand of them, certainly outnumbering our horsemen. Some three hundred paces behind them, arrayed on the forward slope of a low range of hills, we could make out the distinctive round shields of Greek hoplites. Assuming they were eight deep as usual, that was a phalanx of another twenty thousand. This was no levy of unwilling subjects. We faced the best troops the Persian Empire could put in the field.

A further scrutiny did not improve things. The bed of the river was broad, but, although it was spring, its waters did not appear deep. The problem was the depth of the banks. Here and there they had collapsed into washes of gravel, but along most of its length they were taller than a man and precipitous. If anything the further bank was steeper than that on our side.

'They are in a strong position,' Parmenion said, 'and it is getting late in the day. We should camp, then under cover of darkness find another crossing, turn their flank, and fight them on the open plain tomorrow.'

'Yes,' Alexander said, 'but I should be ashamed of myself if a little trickle of water like this were too much to cross after having no trouble crossing the Hellespont.'

'For the gods' sake,' Parmenion snapped, 'this is no time for heroic posturing. You are not Achilles fighting the river Scamander. A setback at the outset could be fatal.'

Alexander's face and neck flushed; a sign of temper. 'As you say, Parmenion, a setback now could be fatal.' His voice always became high and harsh when angered. He had never been one to cross. 'That is why we must beat the Persians in such a way that they can find no excuse for their defeat. They must be made to believe they are inferior to us.'

The old general grudgingly accepted this.

Alexander turned to Amyntas, his tone more normal. 'Did you check the bottom of the river?'

'Not much mud, mainly compact gravel and sand; good going.' My nephew had always been thorough.

Alexander studied the enemy lines for a time. 'They have made a mistake leaving the hoplites too far back. The main fight will be over before they can intervene. But their cavalry is well placed to charge and catch us as we are disordered from crossing the river. We need to draw them to the riverbank, better still down into the water. Amyntas that will be your task.'

My nephew had done well with the scouts, and before that defending the Cadmea, but I was the head of the Bacchiad House of Lyncestis, and the honour should have been mine.

The sun was getting close to the horizon when our men were in position just short of the river. Its light was at our backs, and in the faces of the enemy. The army was drawn up in its customary array. The Thessalian cavalry on the left, six battalions of the phalanx and the *hypaspists* in the centre, the Companion Cavalry on the right. With the latter were Amyntas' scouts and Paeonian horse, as well as the Agrianian javelin men and the archers. The mercenaries and contingents from the Greek allies that had not been left at Abydos and the bridgehead remained in our marching camp. This battle would not be decided by sheer numbers, but by fighting spirit. All our best troops were in the line.

In the slanting light the Persian horsemen made a splendid sight, clad in blues and yellows and greens, the points of their javelins shining. Among the riders were a few in Greek armour. Although I peered I could not see the scarlet sword-belt of Neoptolemus, nor recognise my father. I made an earnest prayer to Heracles the Ancestor that my eyes did not deceive me.

Alexander was at the apex of a wedge formed by the three hundred troopers of the royal squadron of Companions. I was just behind him, with Cleitus the Black, the commander of the unit, on one shoulder, and Leonnatus on the other. We faced one of the natural ramps down to the water. It was noticeable that where the action of the stream had undermined the bank on one side of the river it had done the same on the other. It was the sort of thing that Aristotle could have explained.

There was a profound hush, as if everyone was in awe of what was about to unfold.

Alexander signalled to the trumpeter, who blew one clear note.

Amyntas and his scouts and Paeonians were waiting in front of the next wash to our left. He raised his spear in acknowledgment, and led the riders down into the bed of the river.

As soon as Amyntas moved, in response to wild waving by their pickets on the far bank, the Persian squadron opposite began to pace forward.

Amyntas led his men, not to the wash directly across from them, but angled into the stream towards the one opposite us. As soon as the last of his men were clear, Socrates, son of Sathon, led his squadron of Companions down and straight across. To their left the first unit of the *hypaspists* began to clamber down the sheer bank. As more Persian squadrons advanced to counter these threats the rest of our army waited motionless and quiet.

Watching the men splash across, my anxiety transferred itself to my mount. Borysthenes started to fidget and shift under me. I leant forward and fussed his ears, talking low and soothingly. The mundane action somehow calmed me as well as the stallion.

Amyntas was wearing a helmet with a tall yellow crest. I saw it swaying and bobbing as his charger scrambled up the loose gravel incline. The Persians had timed their charge to perfection. As Amyntas and the leading scouts emerged in ones and twos at the top of the bank, the easterners hit them in one compact mass. Macedonians were pitched to the ground, some of their mounts were bowled over. I lost sight of the yellow crest.

The scouts had long *sarissas*, but the Persians were in close, jabbing with short spears. Dropping the unwieldy two-handed *sarissas*, the scouts drew their swords, and hacked and slashed. They fought valiantly, but they were at a disadvantage. Numbers began to tell. Soon the scouts were back in the bed of the river, mingled in confusion with the supporting Paeonians. Some of the Persians, elated at their success, pressed their horses down so they too were in the water.

A glance to my left told me the same story was playing out with Socrates and the Companions at the next ramp: a confusion of men and horses, fighting and dying in the stream.

Then, in the time it takes to click your fingers, everything changed. All our men were hauling their horses round, booting them to get away. There was Amyntas. Thank Heracles, he was alive. Tall plume streaming, he led his men diagonally back across the river, back the way they had come.

Now to the front of us in the royal squadron the riverbed was empty, except for a scatter of dead or injured men and horses, and a handful of the most foolhardy Persians. The rest of the easterners milled or stood at a standstill, scattered up the opposite slope and along the edge of the bank.

'Now is our time,' Alexander said.

All apprehension forgotten, I booted Borysthenes forward.

The ramp was steeper than it looked. Leaning right back, my head almost on Borysthenes' rump, I managed to keep my seat. Then we were spurring through the river; the spray cold on our thighs. The foremost Persians were fleeing. One or two were too slow, and long spears plucked them from the backs of their mounts.

We surged on up the other slope. Churned and pockmarked by hundreds of horses, this was much harder to negotiate. Now

I had to crane forward, and cling to Borysthenes' mane; all the time praying that he did not stumble, and pitch me to the ground to be pounded by the clattering hooves.

The Persians were stationary, in no order. They were spent. When you think you have already won it is hard to fight again. With Alexander at our head, we went through them like a meteor. As one the easterners turned and fled. Those too slow died.

'Rally on me!' Alexander's voice rang above the din.

It is difficult to smother the urge to chase and to kill.

'To me! To me!' A high, wild cry.

Long days of training told. The Companions reined in, and formed up again.

Another squadron of Persian horse was coming. At its head was a group magnificently armed and attired, riding huge Nisean horses. This was the high command, the satraps. These kinsmen and friends of the King of Kings would fight. This, as Alexander had hoped, would decide the whole day.

'*Al-al-al-al-ai!*'

We screamed, as we hurled ourselves at them.

Each cavalry melee separates into a thousand duels. Suddenly it is as if you are alone. The nobleman aiming for me had a curled black beard. His mouth was a red hole, as he yelled some barbaric war cry. The long cornel-wood shaft of my *xyston* outreached his spear. My thrust caught him square in the chest. The impact shivered through my arm. He went down, but his corselet was well wrought. It turned and snapped the point of my *xyston*.

'Lyncestes, give me your spear!' Alexander was just ahead. His weapon was shivered too.

I flourished my own broken *xyston*, reversing it to use the spike at the foot.

In the confusion someone tossed a fresh weapon to Alexander. As soon as it was in his hand, he drove Bucephalus deeper into the mass of the enemy. A Persian jabbed at me. I parried, but before I could strike back, his horse crashed forward, a javelin protruding from its neck. A man on foot finished him off. As ordered, the Agrianians had joined the melee. Up ahead I saw the three white plumes of Alexander's helmet. He was alone in the midst of the enemy.

Another Persian got in my way. I battered him aside by using my broken *xyston* as a staff.

I saw Alexander drive his spearpoint into a man's face. Concentrated on his kill, he did not see the other two closing from each side. A scimitar glittered in an arc that ended at Alexander's head. One of the plumes was sheered from his helm. He reeled, looked as if he would fall, but turned and jabbed his *xyston* through his assailant's armour deep into his chest.

'Alexander, behind you!' He could not hear my shout, and Black Cleitus was between me and him.

The Persian had his sword raised for the killing blow. It never landed. He stared stupidly, eyes wide with shock. Black Cleitus had sheared off his arm at the shoulder.

Every battle has a tipping point. Later we discovered the names and rank of these Persians: Mithridates, the son-in-law of Darius, and the noble brothers Spithridates and Rhoesaces. Their deaths broke the enemy horsemen. Panic spreads through an army like a wildfire on a summer hillside. The plain was covered in Persians galloping for their lives.

'Rally on me!'

But it was not all over. There were still the Greek mercenaries.

Alexander led the Companions to cut off the retreat of the hoplites. Some of the mercenaries had slipped away, Memnon the Rhodian among them, but most remained. They asked for terms. Alexander shouted they were traitors, fighting for the Persian King against the Greeks. Their surrender must be unconditional.

In the twilight the archers and the Agrianians showered them with missiles. Then Alexander sent in the phalanx. The hoplites were professionals, but they were not the Sacred Band at Chaeronea. When the Companions charged their rear they broke. Then it was just killing.

When the moon was high, the final two thousand were spared. Alexander had them chained. They would be sent to Macedon to labour as slaves in the mines. In time they might wish they had died at the Granicus.

CHAPTER SEVENTEEN

Spring to Autumn 334 BC

THE DAY AFTER THE battle Alexander visited our wounded. He took his time, examining their injuries, encouraging them to boast about their exploits. Listening with compassion, and saying words of praise, he heard much the same stories over and over again. For hours his interest did not flag. No wonder all the men were coming to love him.

The dead of both sides were treated with respect. The Greek mercenaries might have been traitors to our cause, but they had been brave. They were each given a coin to pay the ferryman, and the Persian noblemen were also buried. At the time we had no idea that the latter was sacrilege in their eastern religion, and that the relatives of the deceased might take it as an insult. Our own dead were cremated, and their ashes interred with due ceremony. Their families were declared exempt from military service and all taxes. Alexander commissioned a sculpture group of the twenty-five Companion cavalrymen who had fallen at the outset. It was to be made by the famous sculptor Lysippus, and would be set up at Dium, the Macedonian city of the Muses along with one of Alexander himself. My nephew Amyntas was less than pleased. He complained – thankfully only to me – that his scouts were Macedonians too, and had led the way across the Granicus; they were just as worthy of honour. Perhaps I was unsympathetic. Calas had just been appointed satrap of the province. Although I did not approve of Alexander's decision to keep the Persian title, I was delighted to accept his commission to replace Calas as commander of the Thessalian cavalry. When Amyntas, ever mindful of the gods, muttered that Alexander leading the dead could be taken as a bad omen, I brusquely told him to keep such superstitious nonsense to himself.

We had taken the enemy camp. Harpalus said the plunder would allow us to pay the troops for another month or so, but the need for more funds remained urgent. Despite his treasurer's abacus counting note of caution, Alexander distributed gifts to those who had fought with distinction; a captured horse or an item of fine weaponry. A selection of gaudy luxuries – embroidered robes and golden drinking cups and the like – were set aside to be sent home to Olympias. This consideration to his mother nettled Hephaestion, ever jealous of Alexander's affections, and that appeared to please Craterus and some of the other Companions. In all honesty, it pleased me too. Alexander also arranged for three hundred sets of Persian armour to be shipped to Athens to be dedicated to the goddess Athena with the carefully worded inscription:

'Alexander son of Philip and all the Hellenes, except the Spartans, won these spoils from the barbarians in Asia'.

The enemy could not be allowed to rally. Within a couple of days, Alexander took the main army south. Parmenion was left with some of the mercenaries, along with Calas, who had been assigned most of the contingents supplied by the Greek allies, and me with the Thessalians. Apart from my horsemen, these were all second-rate troops, but we faced no serious opposition. A march of two days to the east brought us to Dascylium, the capital of Hellespontine Phrygia. Its defenders had fled, and the town opened its gates.

Parmenion and the mercenaries now set off after Alexander. My orders were to use my Thessalians to help Calas establish control of his province. There was no fighting. Mainly it consisted of persuading the natives to come down from where they had been hiding in the hills and resuming their normal lives. The task was made easier by our treatment of the settlements. The few that had come over before the battle were rewarded, the rest pardoned on the grounds that they had been constrained by fear of the enemy. The great landed estates of Persian grandees were assigned to various Macedonian noblemen. It made no difference to the peasants or serfs; they exchanged one foreign absentee landlord for another. Rent and taxes still had to be paid. The holdings of Memnon were the only exception. Leaving them untouched, Alexander had shrewdly thought, might make the other Persian commanders, perhaps Darius himself, mistrust the Rhodian mercenary.

For the first two months of the summer we marched by easy stages through green plains, where the fields were lined by tall poplars, and across rounded hills pungent with sage, frequently fording cool streams which ran north to the Propontis. It would have been idyllic had Calas been better company. The newly appointed satrap was a member of the old royal house of Elimea. There was no denying he was brave. The Thessalians said he had charged at their head at the Granicus, laid into the enemy manfully. But the quick wits of Harpalus and his father Machatas had passed by Calas. The previous year, when he had taken over the command of part of the advance force from the executed Attalus, he had been driven back by Memnon. In his cups Calas exulted at his role as the first governor appointed to rule the new

Spear-won Land. Yet it was evident that part of him thought he had been sidelined, left behind in an unimportant province with the constant reminders of his own defeats.

It was better to spend time with Medius of Larissa. The Thessalian had been with us at Mieza. He was also a foster-brother of Alexander, and together we had shared the prince's exile in Illyria. Medius was my second-in-command. The nobles of Thessaly are much like us Macedonians. They are almost born on horseback, and enjoy nothing more than hunting and fighting and drinking. By any standards, Medius was a prodigious drinker. As the fields turned from green to gold, we caroused our way across Hellespontine Phrygia.

The news from the south was all good. The Persian commander of Sardis had surrendered at the approach of the army. The treasury of the wealthy province of Lydia had fallen untouched into Alexander's lap. Surely now Harpalus must stop moaning about economising. The great city of Ephesus had welcomed Alexander, its ordinary citizens ecstatic when it was decreed that henceforth it would be a democracy. Miletus had fallen after a brief siege. It too was made a democracy. It was not that we Macedonians favour such irresponsible government, but it pleased the Greeks we had come to liberate. The gods approved. At Didyma the sacred spring had started to run again, and, after a long silence, Apollo spoke through the oracle.

Once it was known we had secured Hellespontine Phrygia, frequent messengers came from Macedon. My mother wrote with parochial news from Lyncestis. From Pella, Electra wrote that she was the size of a whale – it was bound to be a boy – but the pregnancy was going well. Looking back those summer months are still tinged with a haze of happiness. The runt of the litter was dead. Bards would sing for ever of Alexander of Lyncestis, who had fought at the side of Alexander of Macedon, and routed the barbarians on the banks of the Granicus. Then the order arrived to march the Thessalians to rendezvous with Alexander at Halicarnassus.

* * *

Although he greeted me fondly, Alexander was in a foul mood when we reached Halicarnassus. The siege was not going well. The city was built at the tip of a peninsula. It was defended by high, well-founded walls with a ditch in front that was at least forty feet across and twenty deep. Catapults were situated along the curtain walls, and inside were no fewer than three fortified citadels. Halicarnassus was well provided with supplies and troops. There was a garrison of several thousand Greek mercenaries led by an Athenian exile called Ephialtes, and a greater number of Persians under the Satrap of Caria, Orontobates. In overall command was Memnon of Rhodes. Alexander's scheme to sow mistrust had failed. Memnon had sent his wife and children to the Persian King as proof of his loyalty. This time, unlike at the Granicus, the enemy would not be hampered by a squabbling war council of equals.

Alexander's first attempt to storm the walls had incurred casualties and achieved nothing. At Miletus, Alexander had disbanded all the allied fleet, except for some transports and twenty Athenian warships, retaining the latter as hostages for the good behaviour of their city. He had grandly announced that he would defeat the Persian navy from the land by taking their bases. The fleet had been ruinously costly to maintain, and inferior in both numbers and quality to that of the enemy, but it had been a mistake. Now it was dispersed there was no question of starving Halicarnassus into surrender. Nothing could be done to prevent the defenders bringing in reinforcements or further supplies. Persian control of the sea also created a danger shipping Alexander's heavy siege train south from Miletus. A night attack to secure a nearby port at Myndus had failed. Eventually, the supply ships had evaded the enemy squadrons, and unloaded the equipment at a deserted cove. No sooner had it been assembled before Halicarnassus than the defenders sallied out and burnt several of the machines. When, with enormous labour and the loss of more men, part of the ditch had been filled, and the towers and rams had thrown down a section of the defences, it was revealed that Memnon had built another semicircular wall inside the breach. This new wall was topped by a tall wooden tower, equipped with artillery.

Things had got worse. Two soldiers from Perdiccas' battalion of the phalanx had got drunk, and, boasting of their courage, had launched an impromptu attack on the newly built wall. It had drawn many others into the rubble, where they were shot down from three sides and from above. The next morning, Alexander had been forced to endure the humiliation of asking for a truce to recover the bodies of his dead. Much encouraged, a few days later the defenders had again emerged from the town and set fire to yet more siege engines.

Alexander was not the only one suffering. The whole army was on edge, frustrated and angry. A siege frays the nerves more than any other type of warfare. A raid is over in a few days. A battle is finished by nightfall; survive a few hours and all is well. But a siege drags on for ever. For almost two months the army had sat before Halicarnassus. All that time exposed to the constant fear of the enemy suddenly issuing forth. It is hard to sleep.

Darkness brings not rest, but added anxiety. And the longer an army remains in one place the greater the risk of disease. The peninsula of Halicarnassus is a barren, waterless place; uncomfortable in any conditions.

Cavalry are no use in a siege. My Thessalians set up their horse lines in a camp well back from the Mylasa Gate. The breach was on the other side of the city. I kept them busy with inspections and manoeuvres. Having nothing to contribute, I stayed away from Alexander's tense headquarters. Most evenings I drank with Medius.

Perhaps it was the excess of wine that brought the nightmares. It was still dark one morning when Eumaeus shook me awake.

'You were shouting in your sleep.'

The horrible image faded away: the tall mound of red earth, the stark crosses outlined against the scudding clouds, the certainty that I would be nailed to one of them.

'The same dream?'

I pulled the blanket round me like a child.

Eumaeus patted me on the shoulder. 'A dream of crucifixion can be good. It is auspicious for a seafarer, for the cross is made of wood and nails. For a bachelor it means marriage, because the bond between victim and the cross is not an easy one.'

As he often said, his mother had been a dream diviner.

'I am not a sailor, and I am already married.'

Eumaeus was undeterred. 'Such dreams signify honour and wealth for anyone. Honour because the crucified man is in a high position, and wealth because he provides food for many birds of prey.'

'What time is it?'

'The last watch; be light in a hour or so.'

'Then let's have a drink to set us up for the day. The strong Lesbian will do well.'

Eumaeus stomped out of the tent. I knew there were other ways of interpreting the dream. For the rich – and the Bacchiads are not poor – it signified harm, since the crucified are stripped naked, and lose their flesh. It also meant the betrayal of secrets, as on the cross the victim is seen by all.

Eumaeus was back. There were no cups in his hand, and he looked as if he had encountered a ghost.

'Someone to see you,' the old man croaked.

A tall figure muffled in a hooded cloak entered.

Automatically, my hand started to reach for where my sword hung next to the camp bed. But Eumaeus was shocked, not frightened.

The visitor pulled back his hood. 'Health and great joy, Xander.'

'Neoptolemus! How did you get here?'

My nephew made a self-deprecating gesture, to indicate it had been easy. 'A postern gate, a few words with a Lyncestian file-leader in Perdiccas' battalion, and a small gift.'

What was he doing here? His expression was grim. Had he come to blame me for encouraging him to go over to the Persians? Even worse, did he intend to try to persuade me to join him?

Neoptolemus stepped forward, arms wide to hug me. He was wearing his scarlet sword-belt and sash. I was unarmed. Surely his Persian paymasters had not sent him to kill the leader of the Thessalians?

We embraced. I felt ashamed of my thoughts. Yet he was not himself.

'Xander, I bring bad news. Your father is dead.'

I understood his words, but they seemed to have no meaning. All I could think to say was 'How?'

'A fever in the summer. Aeropus was recovering, but then went on a drinking spree with Damasippus. I am sorry.'

'May the earth lie lightly on him.' Despite the ritual words, I was not sorry. In truth I felt nothing. Except that made me feel guilty. At least I did not want the dogs to dig him up.

'Any chance of a drink?' The message delivered, Neoptolemus was more like his old self.

'Eumaeus was just getting one.'

'Good, I cannot stay long. I have to get back before the guard changes.'

Eumaeus went out.

'Do you have to go at all?' Now I was reunited with Neoptolemus, I knew how much I had missed him. If only I had not listened to Electra's advice. I did not want to let Neoptolemus go again. 'I am sure I can reconcile you with Alexander. Your brother is high in his affections, me too.'

'Too late, I am afraid.' Neoptolemus smiled in a way that tugged at my emotions. 'The gold of Darius is very persuasive. And I have acquired a Persian wife, and a daughter.'

'My congratulations.'

'And mine to you. I hear Electra is expecting.'

'How did you know?'

'Our intelligence is good. As I said, Darius' gold is very persuasive.'

An awful thought struck me. 'They are not here in Halicarnassus?'

'No.' He shook his head. 'If they were I could get them out. Like Memnon's family, they are in Persepolis at the Persian court.'

I must have looked horrified.

'Besides, this war is not decided. As you said, the Bacchiad House needs a man on either side.'

Eumaeus returned, and we all drank.

All too soon, Neoptolemus said he must go. Once more wrapped in the voluminous cloak, he walked out into what was left of the night.

* * *

Eumaeus had taken me to dine with a Lyncestian veteran called Atarrhias. They had both served my grandfather, both had survived his defeat at the Hyacinth Meadow. Afterwards, Atarrhias was one of those drafted into the phalanx by Philip. He had risen to be a file-leader in the battalion raised from Lyncestis and Orestis. Now he was commander of the time-expired soldiers and youths that were the camp servants. His tent was in the main encampment on the other side of Halicarnassus, near the siege works, and opposite the bricked-up Triple Gate.

We ate lamb and onions and fresh bread, and drank local wine flavoured with honey. They talked about the old days. Although I drank my share, it was a sobering experience. Their understanding of the past was different from mine.

'It's like this, Lord,' Atarrhias said, 'your family never had enough men to protect Lyncestis. The Illyrians and Paeonians were always coming over the border. All too often we ended up fighting the other upland houses of Pelagonia or Orestis. Philip gave us security, brought us down from the hilltop refuges, made Macedonians something in the world. That is why we ordinary men love the Argeads.'

Free speech was the right of every Macedonian, even if it was unwelcome to their betters.

We had reached the apples and nuts when there was a commotion down at the siege lines: torches flaring, many men shouting.

'Another sortie over the breach,' Atarrhias said, without undue concern. 'Greeks by the shape of their shields, but Craterus' battalion will throw them back.'

'Maybe not,' Eumaeus said, 'look!'

Another phalanx of Hellenes was streaming out of the Triple Gate.

'Cunning old Memnon,' Atarrhias said, 'he must have had only a single skin of bricks blocking the gate, ready to be demolished. The cunning old Rhodian.'

This was bad. Craterus' men, already fighting the defenders from the breach, would be taken in the flank by those from the gate. Atarrhias summoned a youth, and told him to run and warn Perdiccas and Meleager; their battalions were needed at the front. The boy shifted uneasily, and said both officers were away dining with Alexander. Atarrhias snapped that he should tell their deputies to bring up the men as fast as possible. The youth sprinted away.

The hoplites from the Triple Gate had run a boarding bridge out over the ditch. You had to admire whoever was in command.

Atarrhias stood, tugging at his beard. 'It will take too long,' he muttered. 'Craterus will be overwhelmed before the other battalions get here; all the siege machines will be alight.'

As if to confirm his words, there was a huge outcry as the hoplites from the gate crashed into the unshielded right of the Macedonians defending the siege lines.

'Fuck it,' Atarrhias said, 'it's down to us.' He roared for the veterans to arm, and form phalanx on him, then stomped into his tent. Eumaeus and I followed.

'We will fight with you,' I said.

Atarrhias nodded to me. 'You can use my spare *sarissa* and shield. Eumaeus go and borrow each from the next door tent.'

These old warriors knew their trade. In no time at all, without any fuss, a phalanx of at least two thousand strong was formed in the darkness. I took my place at the head of the file alongside Atarrhias.

'You have no panoply, my Lord—' Atarrhias was polite but firm '—go to the rear ranks.'

'No.' I was equally insistent. 'The Bacchiads may no longer be Kings of Lyncestis, but our place is among the forefighters. Why else are we paid honour in the Land of the Lynx?'

'And paid rents,' he laughed, and singled out a very elderly veteran. 'Damon, you are about the same build, give the Lord your armour and helmet, then go and act as file-closer.'

It was nicely done, not demeaning the dignity of the old warrior Damon. In battle the file-closer is the next most important place after the leader.

'The youths get some torches behind us, so we can see what the fuck we are doing.' Atarrhias had a clear head, was thinking of everything.

The helmet was too small, so I gave it back. I would have to rely on my hat – a *kausia* is made of thick felt, it might turn a weak blow. The linen armour did not fit all that well, but was a lot better than nothing.

'*Sarissas* vertical! Phalanx advance at a walk!'

Already some soldiers from Craterus' battalion were leaving the fight, trying to melt into the night. The veterans mocked them as they ran: *Wait a little, see how real men fight!*

Ahead there was a spurt of flame as the first siege tower was fired.

'Easy boys,' Atarrhias shouted. 'As the old bull said to the young one, let's just walk down to the meadow, and fuck them all.'

The hoplites had seen us coming. By the lurid light of the burning tower, I could see Greek officers in bright sashes and with elaborate plumes on their helmets shoving men into line to face this unexpected attack.

'Level *sarissas*!'

Those of us in the first four ranks brought our pikes to horizontal. We were in assault order, three feet for each rank. On either side of me, at waist level, three shafts of ash wood swung into place. Now projecting out in front of us was a layered hedge of deadly iron points.

It had all happened so fast, I had had no time to be scared. Until this moment I had not realised Eumaeus was leading the file on my right. The old bastard had no armour or helmet. I should have given him my borrowed panoply, or sent him to the rear. Too late now.

Advancing inexorably, backlit by torches, we must have looked a hideous sight to the ragged line of mercenaries. To their credit they stood and fought. As we came together, there was a deafening clatter of iron on wood and metal. Our *sarissas* outreached their spears. They tried to use their shields to push the points of our pikes aside, and get in close. I concentrated on keeping the head of my pike in line. Once a hoplite got past. A *sarissa* from behind me took him in the groin. On either side of me, Atarrhias and Eumaeus were jabbing and thrusting with the skill of long experience. Greeks were falling. The old Macedonians went through the enemy like peasants harvesting grain; steady and methodical, with no wasted effort.

As we ground forward, I had to somehow watch my footing, as well as keep my *sarissa* in place. There were dead and injured men under my boots. Desperate pleas and screams sounded from behind as the wounded were finished off by our rear ranks with downward thrusts of the *lizard-killers* on the butts of their pikes.

Then the mercenaries broke. In a mob, they dashed back towards the Triple Gate.

'Hold the line!' Atarrhias bellowed. 'Don't chase them!'

The discipline of our geriatric phalanx held. We dressed our ranks, then plodded after the rout.

The mercenaries were fighting each other to get across the boarding bridge. It was overladen. With a sharp retort it gave way, hurling men down into the ditch. Those trapped on this side threw away shields and weapons, and scrambled down the slope. And then someone in the city lost their nerve. The great wooden doors of the Triple Gate were closed.

There were hundreds trapped outside the walls, unarmed and panic stricken. It was a massacre. Our long *sarissas* probing down into the ditch, cruel steel punching down into the huddled masses.

Time loses all meaning at such moments. My shoulders and arms ached with killing. No compunction or sympathy. They would have done the same to us.

'Fall back!'

Groggily, like men waking from some sanguine reverie, we shuffled away. Eumaeus was still beside me, so too Atarrhias. Suddenly I was very tired.

We halted out of range of javelin throw, hunkered down in close order behind our shields. No bowmen or catapults shot at us from the battlements. The defeat had been too total.

'Now we wait for orders,' Atarrhias said.

As the night wore on, the wind rose. It carried the moans of the wounded. Someone passed me a wine skin. I drank greedily.

About midnight we saw the flames. The defenders had fired the tower on the wall beyond the breach. Then more flames from the citadel to our right within the town.

'They are abandoning the city,' I said.

'Perhaps they are withdrawing to the citadels by the harbour,' Atarrhias replied.

'We should force the gate. We can take the city.'

'We wait for orders.' Atarrhias pointed into the town. 'Anyway, we would be burnt alive.'

The veteran was right. The strengthening breeze had whirled burning embers into the sky. Whole blocks of the city were beginning to burn.

We stood to all night, watching Halicarnassus burn.

At some point, I must have fallen asleep standing up. Eumaeus nudged me as the sun rose. It cast its rays on a carpet of the dead. Everywhere men sprawled in unnatural stillness, some were piled on each other. Off to my left, on the lip of the ditch, my eyes were caught by a bright scarlet sword-belt and sash. At that instant I knew that my world would never be the same.

CHAPTER EIGHTEEN

Autumn to Winter 334 BC

WE CREMATED NEOPTOLEMUS THAT morning: me, Amyntas, Leonnatus, Eumaeus, and Atarrhias. We made suitable offerings to his shade, although I took his scarlet sword-belt and sash for the sake of his memory. Neoptolemus may have fought on the other side, but no one objected to our act of familial piety and affection. As the flames began to crackle, others joined us; Lyncestians who remembered him as a child at Lebaea, or the high-spirited youth in Pella. When the smoke billowed, bringing the horrible smell of burning flesh, I thought of his wife and daughter that I would never meet; anything rather than dwell on the physical reality of the pyre.

Or would I meet them? In camp the ultimate goal of our expedition was often discussed. Its stated aims were to liberate the Greeks of Asia, and to gain revenge for the Persian burning of Athens. The former was largely accomplished already, although there were cities that claimed to be Greek on the southern coast of Anatolia and on Cyprus. The latter aim might imply something altogether larger. Some considered it would not be achieved until we had torched the Persian capitals of Susa, Ecbatana, and Persepolis. Whenever one of the Companions raised it with Alexander, he just laughed, and said it was too soon to say, after all we had yet to meet the Great King on the battlefield.

Atarrhias was proved right. The garrison of Halicarnassus had withdrawn to the two seaward citadels of Salmacis and the Isle of Arconnesus. Memnon and the Persian fleet had sailed, it was guessed to the island of Cos. Alexander sent men into the city. Once the fires were extinguished, they pulled down the buildings facing the two citadels, and began to erect fortifications to seal the citadels off from the land. There was nothing we could do to prevent Memnon bringing in fresh troops and supplies by sea. The troops had suffered prosecuting the siege. Our own provisions were running short. There was little to be gained in prolonging the suffering. Alexander decided to leave Ptolemy with three thousand mercenary infantry and two hundred cavalry to contain the garrisons of the citadels, and, if he could, take any other neighbouring places that had not come over. I did not envy Alexander's illegitimate brother. The force left with Ptolemy seemed barely adequate for the task.

Alexander's decision about the governance of the province caused much comment in our ranks. Caria had long been ruled by a local dynasty. Before he reached Halicarnassus Alexander had been approached by an elderly lady called Ada. She had once governed Caria, before being ousted by a male relative. Ada had retained one strong fortress. This she had handed over to Alexander. The two had got on well. She sent him sweetmeats and delicacies. More importantly she had adopted him as her son and heir. Alexander referred to her as 'Mother'. Certainly, many of the troops joked, she would be less trouble than Olympias. Now Alexander appointed her Satrap of Caria. Such an arrangement was nothing unusual for the locals. It is a measure of the servility of these easterners that they can stomach being the subjects of a woman. We Macedonians thought it as well that Ptolemy would be on hand to watch what she did.

The siege had caused many casualties, and the morale of the army had suffered. Alexander ordered that all those who had been newlywed before we had embarked should return to Macedon for the winter. I wished I was going with them. Electra must be near her time. Every day I hoped for a letter. Frequently I prayed. Childbirth was more dangerous than battle.

Two of the Companions, Meleager and Coenus – the latter a son-in-law of Parmenion – were to lead those returning to Macedon. While there, they were to raise fresh levies. Similarly, Cleander – the brother of Coenus – was to go to the Peloponnese to hire more Greek mercenaries.

Meanwhile the army was to divide. Alexander was to head south with the main force to take the coasts of Lycia and Pamphylia, establishing his winter quarters in the region. Parmenion, with just Socrates' squadron of the Companions and my Thessalians of the frontline troops, along with all the allies, for what they were worth, was to march inland to Phrygia. We were saddled with the baggage train. After ousting the Persian satrap, we were to winter at Gordion, the old capital of the province. There, both Alexander and those returning from marital leave as well as the new troops from Macedon and Greece would rendezvous with us next spring.

It made strategic sense. The Great King had no army in the field in Asia Minor, and it would ease our supply problems. But it took me away from all my friends, except Medius, and even further from news of Electra.

We marched north back up the coast, via Miletus and Ephesus, before turning away from the sea and east to the city of Sardis. From there we went up the Haemus valley. Here, the trees were red and gold, their leaves edged with fire in the sun. The tannic smell of autumn was in the air. After a few days' march, we left the valley, and turned north-east into the high country. It was fortunate that there was a good Persian road. Not all the plunder of the campaign so far had found its way into the royal coffers. The ordinance of Philip against wagons had gone by the board. Every officer in the army, and many tent-groups of soldiers, had acquired at least one, heavily laden with whatever had taken their eye.

The road ran along an upland river called the Sindros, then went due east across a remote region to pick up the headwaters of another called the Kaystros. The terrain in places here was rugged, well suited to defence. Yet there was no fighting to speak of, nothing but a few skirmishes, where bandits tried to raid the baggage. None of the high towers set on crags attempted resistance.

When the wind had shifted to the north, and carried the bite of the coming winter, we reached Gordion. Here at last we understood our largely undisturbed progress. The Satrap Atizyes had been one of those who had escaped the slaughter at the Granicus. Soundly defeated when fighting alongside other satraps, he did not believe he could do any better alone. It was said that he had levied all the troops he could from Phrygia, and retired south-east in the direction of Cilicia. The only fortress still prepared to fight was Celaenae, the new capital of the province, which lay south of our route, and was garrisoned by mercenaries from Caria.

In a sense we were not the first Macedonians in Gordion. Long ago, Midas had been King here after being driven from Emathia in Macedon, the original Gardens of Midas, by our ancestors. The guides at every temple in the town enthusiastically pointed out endless heirlooms of the King. The most interesting was an ancient wagon kept on the acropolis. Its yoke and shaft were joined by an elaborate knot. Legend said that whoever could undo the knot would become King of Asia. It was the sort of thing that Amyntas would have approached with reverence, and Neoptolemus tried to untangle. I examined it closely – it appeared to be made of strips of cornel wood bark – but could find no ends to the cords.

Midas had been a man of poor judgement. Offered any gift by Dionysus, he asked that everything he touched turned to gold. When he discovered that he could neither eat nor drink, he was forced to beg the god to take away the deadly benefaction. The story was enough to induce our soldiers to start digging up the many burial mounds outside the town. Parmenion soon put a stop to this as harmful both to discipline and our relations with the natives. A regime of strict training marches was introduced instead. In the territory of the town was an enormous hunting park of the Great King; one of those the Persians call a Paradise. Darius had never been there, nor had his immediate predecessors. No one except the King could touch its inhabitants, so within its walls was a multitude of all sorts of game: rabbit, hares, deer, boars, even panthers. To show who was now master here, and to demonstrate that as a Macedonian king Alexander was no oriental despot, we organised a mass hunt for the troops. It added much meat to our provisions for the winter, and for the soldiers made a happy change from marching through the rain.

Towards the middle of *Peritios*, the second month of winter, when the cold rain was turning to sleet, miraculously a courier arrived from Macedon. He would not have been more welcome if he had been Dionysus descended from Olympus to revel among us. There were many letters in his satchel. Two were for me. One was from my mother, giving the doings of Lyncestis: harvests, weddings, deaths; nothing to cause concern. The other was from Electra. I read it second, and had to steel myself to open it at all, in case it contained the news I dreaded. As I broke the seal, I consoled myself with the thought that at least she had not died in childbirth. She was well, and delivered of a healthy boy. As I had instructed, she had named him Arrhabaeus.

I was so excited I picked up Eumaeus and carried him round the room.

He did not seem at all pleased. 'Put me down, you young fool.'

Having done as he asked, I drew my blade, and danced with that instead; a traditional wild sword dance from a Macedonian feast.

'You sure Arrhabaeus was a good choice?' Eumaeus said.

'A time-honoured name in the Bacchiad House,' I replied.

'And the name of an executed traitor.'

I concentrated on a few complicated steps before answering. 'A child can hardly be implicated in the crimes of his long-dead uncle.'

Eumaeus looked unconvinced. 'You remember the swallow in Halicarnassus?'

During the siege, while Alexander was taking a siesta, a swallow had landed on his head, twittering with alarm, and not flown away until he was fully awake.

'Of course I remember: the seer Aristander told Alexander it portended that the treachery of a friend would be unmasked, for swallows are friendly to good men, and exceedingly talkative.'

'So Alexander will be alive to any hint of disloyalty among his Companions.' Eumaeus spat on his chest to avert bad luck.

'Your grandfather, Arrhabaeus III, killed Alexander's uncle with his own hand.'

'Yes, years before Alexander or I were born.'

'Three years before, and kings have long memories.'

'Alexander is not suspicious.'

Eumaeus snorted. 'Amyntas, son of Perdiccas, might disagree, if he was still alive.'

I stopped dancing, went and held the old man's shoulders in my hands, looked into his eyes. 'Alexander will not see treachery in the choice of my son's name.'

'No, but others will drip that poison in his ear: Hephaestion in his pillow talk, Olympias in every letter.'

'You worry too much.'

'And you,' he said, 'do not think enough.'

Parmenion ordered a dinner to celebrate my news. It was a small party: Parmenion as host, me as chief guest, with Socrates, Medius, Antigonus, the one-eyed Macedonian commander of the Greek allies, and his deputy young Peucestas of Mieza. Our number was completed by Atarrhias, as leader of the baggage train. Four had served under Philip. Medius, Peucestas, and I had been promoted by Alexander.

We ate well – goose, roast boar, and venison – and toasted my son in large bumpers of strong wine. Yet, beneath a veneer of conviviality, Parmenion was out of sorts.

'I told Alexander not to disband the fleet at Miletus,' he said. 'Look at the difficulties it caused at Halicarnassus, and it leaves the Aegean free for Memnon to cause havoc come next spring.'

'The Greeks are restless,' Antigonus agreed. 'It is not a risk Philip would have run.'

'The fleet was a liability,' Peucestas said. 'We could not afford to pay the crews, and it was outmatched by the Persians.'

Antigonus, nettled by the contradiction, turned his one baleful eye on his second-in-command. Evidently, there was no love lost there.

Parmenion continued as if neither had spoken. 'And we have shed our blood to conquer these barbarians, not to make them our equals. Mithrines, the Persian traitor who surrendered Sardis, is now treated almost as if he were one of the Companions, and my brother Asander has been left in Lydia to train local youths in Macedonian tactics. Now Alexander has appointed this barbarian woman Ada as Satrap of Caria.'

After taking a long pull on his wine, Parmenion continued. 'For once that ghastly, posturing know-it-all Aristotle was right – we should treat these barbarians like plants or animals.'

Interestingly, although they did not speak, neither Antigonus nor Peucestas appeared to agree.

The reference to his brother betrayed the real cause of Parmenion's resentment. Although his sons, Philotas and Nicanor, commanded the Companion cavalry and the *hypaspists*, the old general felt he was being pushed aside. His brother Asander had been left as Satrap of Lydia, his son-in-law Coenus sent back to Greece, Parmenion himself delegated this task far from the main army. Along with his friend Antipater, no one had been closer to King Philip than Parmenion. Now others, youngsters like Hephaestion and Perdiccas, had the ear of Alexander.

Medius tactfully suggested a drinking game, and soon the faint whiff of dissent was lost in the renewed jollity. Some hours later, the feast ended with the floor covered in debris, and the guests reeling to their quarters.

As Eumaeus supported me down the deserted midnight corridor to my room a figure was waiting in the gloom. The light Eumaeus carried showed a tall man with heavy dark ringlets and curled dark beard wearing eastern costume. Hand on hilt, Eumaeus stepped in front of me.

'Do not be alarmed, Alexander of Lyncestis, I am an old acquaintance.'

He spoke not Greek, but Macedonian with a pronounced Persian accent.

'We spoke some years ago at Aegae, when you arrived with your kinsman Leonnatus, son of Anteas. There is no reason that you should remember me, but I am Sisines, son of Ochus.'

I remembered him, outside the palace, but he had spoken to Leonnatus, not me. 'Health and great joy.'

'And to you. I have a message to deliver to you alone.'

'Anything you can say to me can be said in front of Eumaeus.'

'To you alone! If you wish, I can give your man my sword.'

'Tomorrow would be better, tonight I am drunk.'

Sisines laughed. His teeth were very even and white. 'We Persians have a custom of discussing important matters drunk, then making a decision when sober.'

'You had better come to my room.'

We walked side by side down the corridor. I opened the door, and went inside. A nightlight was burning on the table. Sisines followed me in, and shut the door. Belatedly, I realised that he had not handed Eumaeus his weapon. Such carelessness might bring my death.

Sisines came very close. His eyes were black and fathomless. I watched him carefully, ready to react.

'Darius, the beloved of Ahura Mazda, does not want this war.' He pitched his voice so that he could not be heard if Eumaeus was listening at the door. 'Were you to take the throne, and sign a peace treaty, the Great King would reward your alliance with a thousand talents of gold. Darius believes it is time the true King Alexander emerged from the shadows.'

There, the thing that had always haunted my life was out in the open. Alexander would not be the first Argead to meet a violent death at the hands of a Bacchiad – Orestes, Amyntas the Little, Perdiccas III had all been struck down by men of my House. I would not be the first from Lyncestis to rule Macedon: Aeropus, and his son Pausanias, had been acclaimed in Aegae. Despite my love for Alexander, I felt a deep ancestral ambition stirring. The Bacchiads were a race of kings.

'As you say, it is best decided sober. Return here tomorrow at dusk for my answer.'

Sisines bowed, and blew me a kiss from his fingertips, as you would the effigy of a god, or a Persian would a king. 'Until tomorrow.'

For a man alone in an enemy camp, who had just suggested treason and regicide, Sisines seemed oddly calm. He turned and went and opened the door. Eumaeus was standing outside. My decision was made.

'Arrest this man.'

CHAPTER NINETEEN

Winter 334 BC to Spring 333 BC

WE WERE IN PARMENION'S rooms at dawn. Braziers were lit, and the wind was rattling the shutters on the windows. The same seven men were gathered as at the feast. Each one of us nursing a hangover.

'Sisines is well known,' Parmenion said. 'From a noble family, he fled into exile after a conspiracy against the Persian King Artaxerxes III, and found refuge with Nectanebo the last Egyptian Pharaoh. Nectanebo sent him to Macedon to try to negotiate an alliance with Philip. After the Persians reconquered Egypt, and Artaxerxes had died, Sisines returned to Persia.'

Parmenion took a sip of very watered wine.

'Sisines is a remarkable man: charming, cunning, and brave, also deeply avaricious. It could be he was working for the Persians all along. Although Philip was an old fox. Even Antipater and I did not share all his secrets. We wondered at the time if he had suborned Sisines with gold, and sent him back to Persia as his spy.' Parmenion sighed, and rubbed his forehead. 'Perhaps after a time an intriguer like Sisines becomes unsure himself in whose interest he is acting.'

'What do we do with him?' I said. At the moment the Persian was chained in a dungeon.

'Torture the truth out of him,' Antigonus said.

'No, we send him to Alexander.'

Parmenion's words took us all by surprise. It was midwinter, the mountains were still in Persian hands, quite likely all the passes would be blocked by snow, and we did not know where Alexander and the main army was quartered.

'Can it wait until the spring?' Antigonus asked.

'No, he must be taken to Alexander now.'

I must have looked dubious.

Parmenion turned to me. 'A delay in reporting sedition is as bad as joining its ranks. You will not be the only one Darius has approached.'

Another heavy sigh from Parmenion. After last night's excess, he looked old and drawn. 'I know you are Alexander's foster-brother, but trust me, I have spent my life at court. Kingship changes a man. For your safety, for the safety of all of us, you must take him to Alexander without delay.'

'How many squadrons of the Thessalians will I take?'

'None. You would never fight your way through, and it would leave our forces here in Gordion exposed. You must go in disguise, slip through the enemy unnoticed. As he speaks Persian, Peucestas will go with you. Both take one servant. I will find you a native guide.'

As we left the next day, the sleet turned to snow. The last we had heard Alexander was making for Phaselis, a town at the eastern end of the coast of Lycia. That was far to the south-west, and for the first six days we went back down the Persian road by which the army had approached Gordion. The snow did not settle, and we each had a spare horse, so made good time. At a place called Prymnessos, we bought fresh provisions. Then the guide took us off onto another road heading due south, and into enemy territory.

All six of us were clad in Persian clothes: trousers and a thick, hooded cloak. Our story was that we were Macedonians who had been persuaded to desert by Sisines. If pressed we would say that we had been sent by Atizyes from Phrygia to reconnoitre Alexander's winter quarters. Peucestas and the others would use their real names. I would claim to be Neoptolemus. To further the pretence, I wore his distinctive scarlet sword-belt and sash. Peucestas would do the talking. Sisines was told that if he betrayed us he would be dead before we could be taken. Strangely, he received this news with apparent equanimity. Even so, I took the precaution of sealing his sword in its scabbard, and tying him up at night.

The weather was getting worse; the gusting wind brought flurries of snow, which began to lie in the hollows along the road. When we could not find an isolated farm, or some shed in which to shelter, it was cold and hard camping. The conditions were not good for the horses, but it meant there were no other travellers, and the locals did not stray far from their homes.

Even in the relative safety of our isolation Peucestas was unhappy. He rode alongside me, full of complaints.

'Do you not see what is happening? Antigonus has got rid of me, and Parmenion has replaced you as commander of the Thessalians with Philip, the son of Menelaus, one of his own followers. Neither of them expect us to come out of these mountains. Then they can say that Sisines persuaded us both to turn traitor, or that we were in league with him all along. Under Macedonian law our families can be executed.'

'So far more a high plateau than a mountain.'

'This is no joke.'

'What else could we have done – refused a direct order?'

Peucestas had no answer to that.

'If you are right, we have to disappoint them by getting through alive.'

On the third day out from Prymnessos, we left the road altogether, and followed a sheep track up to a pass. It was, the guide explained, the only way to avoid the garrison at Celaenae. The snow had drifted here, and the horses struggled. Before we reached the crest one foundered, and had to be killed.

From the top, between limestone cliffs too steep to hold the snow, we saw a lake. The crests on the far shore were reflected in its smooth surface. The sky, which had been lowering with storm clouds, cleared and became a hard, ceramic blue. We went down through rounded hills, white with snow in the sunshine, and where the thin and bare branches of black shrubs shivered in the breeze.

A smudge of smoke showed a settlement at the water's edge. The peasants here spoke a local language with which even our guide had difficulty. They were poor and mistrustful, but gold coins and sign language induced them to part with some twice-baked bread and hard cheese, and a little fodder for our mounts.

At the southern end of the lake we came to a plain, no more than a mile wide, and flanked by towering crags. We were now, our guide told us, in the Taurus Mountains. The plain led south to another smaller lake. To get around this, we had to take to a goat track clinging to the western slopes. Two more horses went lame, and had to be left. Like the passage of a miniature army, we were leaving a trail of dung and broken animals.

After picking our way down south of the lake, we entered a broad saddle of land. Clouds rolled in from the north, and the daylight took on the pink tinge of coming snow. In places here, the horses sank to their bellies. Progress was slow, men and beasts cold, soaked, hungry, and exhausted. The days and nights of our journeying were running into one another, merging into a long and repetitive dull pain. Like Peucestas, I started to wonder if we would ever leave these mountains.

The slopes crowded in from either side, leaving just a twisting trail, barely wide enough for two horses abreast. We turned a corner, and the horsemen were in front of us. There was no point in running. Their horses were moving well, far fresher than ours. We stopped and waited. They were twenty to our four; neither the guide nor Sisines were going to fight. We would have to brazen it out. Beside me, Peucestas drew himself up ready. His Persian had improved on the journey.

Their leader signalled a halt. Although, like us, swaddled in layers of local cloaks, these were no bandits. Each carried a long cavalry spear.

'Identify yourselves!'

Peucestas took a breath to reply. With a hand on his arm, I stopped him. The leader had spoken in Macedonian.

The scouts, part of the *prodromoi* commanded by Amyntas, gave us food and wine, and what forage they could spare. Escorting us south, they were alert, and pushed us as fast as our worn mounts could go. All the Pisidians in these mountains were brigands, and a settlement of them in the next valley had refused to submit to Alexander. When we had descended below the snow line, the scouts relaxed, and set a gentler pace. After what we had endured, the coastal plain seemed almost balmy. The army was billeted in a town called Selge in the next valley to the east. A messenger had been sent ahead, and Alexander was waiting for us on foot at the gates.

'You look terrible.'

'Thank you.' I dismounted, and Alexander kissed me.

I pointed to the prisoner. 'This Persian brought me an offer from Darius – a thousand talents of gold to kill you.'

'I know.'

'You know?'

'He wrote me a letter.'

'Darius?'

'No, Sisines.'

I spread my hands wide, palms open, in a probably universal gesture of bafflement.

Alexander smiled. 'Sisines was a friend of my father. For many years, at great personal risk, he has informed us of events at the Persian court. When Darius gave him his orders, he wrote to tell me.'

I felt my anger rising – what we had suffered in the mountains, before that my fear, and the awful glimmer of ambition, it had all been for a sham. 'So you let him test my loyalty?'

'No, I did not know anything about it until the letter arrived; probably about the time you were approached. After all Sisines had to carry out his orders. And you did absolutely the right thing.'

That all made sense. Now I was left with the guilt of that tiny moment of temptation.

Alexander greeted the others. 'There are hot baths ready. After that we will eat and drink, and I can tell you what has happened. Come along, Lyncestes; you too, old Eumaeus.'

The army had had a busy autumn and winter. Not all the towns in Lycia and Pamphylia had submitted peacefully. One called Aspendus had agreed terms, then reneged on them, and had had to be attacked. Nearchus had been appointed satrap, with orders to take those places that remained defiant. To the north, in Pisidia, some of the hillmen likewise had proved obdurate. An attempt to open a way north had been thwarted at a place called Termessus because the siege train was with Parmenion. The situation had been saved by the people of Selge, where we were quartered. They had both offered to deal with Termessus in the coming campaigning season, and told of an easier route north through the Taurus Mountains. The only problem was that this road was blocked by hostile Pisidians at a place called Sagalassus and the Persian garrison of mercenaries at Celaenae. As soon as the weather improved, we would set off to deal with them.

Peucestas and I told Alexander about our largely uneventful march with Parmenion to Gordion.

'There is something there that might interest you,' I said to Alexander. 'It is an old cart in the Temple of Zeus on the acropolis. The locals say that it is the one in which Gordion and his son Midas travelled from Macedon. They had had an oracle to acclaim King the next man to arrive in a cart.'

'You want me to enter the town in a cart?'

'Not exactly. The yoke and shaft are tied together with a complicated knot. It is said whoever can loose the knot is destined to rule all Asia.'

Alexander always loved a challenge. That look of longing, that I knew so well, lit his face. But then his eyes were veiled, as if he suspected a trap. 'And what if I fail?'

'You won't. You always find a way.'

About a month later – rested and restored – we set out for Sagalassus.

Some barbarians never learn. Like the Triballi in Thrace, the tribesmen, vaunting in their reputation as the fiercest of all the Pisidians, had drawn up in the open at the top of a slope. The incline was too steep for our cavalry. All six battalions of the phalanx drew up at the foot of the hill. Alexander entrusted them to my nephew Amyntas. I suspected it was his way of showing that the offer of Darius had not shaken his faith in us Lyncestians. Leonnatus and I were with the Companions attending Alexander, who took personal command of the *hypaspists* on the right. Out in front of us he stationed the archers and the Agrianes.

When we reached the steepest part of the hill we were attacked by small parties of Pisidians, who took advantage of the rough ground to fall on both our flanks. Unequipped for close combat, the archers broke and ran. Although javelin men, the Agrianes yielded nothing. When the *hypaspists* came up, after a brief and vicious melee, the unarmoured Pisidians turned tail. Knowing the country, most got away. But, pressing in the footsteps of some of the fugitives, we took Sagalassus.

Our route lay by a salt lake, bordered by wide salt flats. Five days later, we reached Celaenae in the south of Phrygia. This was a very strong place, its central citadel surrounded by sheer drops on all sides. Before retreating from his satrapy, Atizyes had garrisoned it with mercenaries: one thousand Carians, and a hundred Greeks. There could be no question of attempting a storm, and our siege equipment was with Parmenion. The mercenaries had stockpiled all the provisions in the area into the citadel. As it was early spring, and there were no ripe crops for us to gather, we could not starve them out. For ten days we sat impotently before the defences – men, horses and mules eating our dwindling reserves. When the garrison offered terms – that they would surrender if no relief appeared within sixty days – Alexander accepted with alacrity. He left 1,500 of our mercenaries to watch the garrison, summoning Antigonus the one-eyed to command them, giving him the title of Satrap of Phrygia. Another of Philip's old generals, Belacrus, was sent ahead to take over the allied troops from Antigonus.

It took almost a month – quite a hungry month – to cross the Anatolian uplands to Gordion. Medius celebrated our arrival with a feast which lasted until dawn.

It was good to be back in charge of the Thessalian cavalry. On the second day, I was about to carry out an inspection when Alexander summoned me. We went up to the acropolis in a crowd of Companions and many hangers-on. Everyone surmised our goal.

In the cavernous gloom of the Temple of Zeus, Alexander studied the knot on the cart of Gordion. Rather than attempt to untie the cornel wood cords, he tried to draw out the pin that ran through the knot. It is a typically clever device. Yet no matter how hard he pulled, it would not budge. You could sense those at the rear of the crowd – mainly locals and Greeks – starting to look at each other. News of the King's failure would reach the ends of the world.

Alexander – red in the face, furious as ever when frustrated – stood back. Now people were whispering. In distant Persepolis Darius would be delighted, so too the democratic rabble in Athens. Zeus decreed the Macedonian would not be Lord of Asia.

With a flourish, Alexander drew his sword, and slashed it down into the tight-packed knot. It took several blows, then the last strands parted. Alexander held the severed knot aloft.

'It is loosed!' As he spoke, he gazed into my eyes with an expression that I had never seen before.

CHAPTER TWENTY

Spring 333 BC

I N THE AFTERNOON GREAT purple-grey thunderclouds rolled down from the north, trailing curtains of rain. Darkness came early, and the air was full of water; gushing from gutters, and running in streams down the streets. The old buildings of the citadel shook with the thunder. Zeus was showing his approval of the cutting of the Gordion knot, so said Aristander the seer. But I was still preoccupied with the look Alexander had given me.

'It was not just an expression of triumph,' I said to Eumaeus, 'more as if he had defeated me in something important.'

We were sitting by the open window of my quarters. The blackness between the lightning was absolute.

'Thunder without lightning signifies plots and treachery because it comes unexpectedly, whereas lightning without thunder means groundless fears. If they come together, it has no meaning; this is just a storm, that was just a look.'

'Eumaeus, it had a meaning.'

A flash of lightning showed his face for a moment. He looked old and careworn.

'There is another story about Midas,' Eumaeus said. Usually there was some thread linking the seemingly unconnected elements of his conversation. 'When he gave the prize for music not to Apollo, but to Pan, the archer god cursed him to grow the ears of an ass. Midas hid his shame under a turban. But his barber knew the truth. Eventually the barber could not keep it to himself any longer. He dug a hole and into it he spoke the secret. The barber filled in the hole, but a bed of reeds grew up there, and when the wind blew they rustled together saying, "Midas has ass' ears".'

In the darkness, I put my hand on Eumaeus' shoulder. 'Don't worry, I have not told anyone else.'

Another bolt of lightning revealed Eumaeus did not look any less concerned.

Perhaps Parmenion was right; perhaps kingship changed a man. I found it hard to believe about Alexander. But there had always been a part of him that I could not reach. Still, what had things come to if a Macedonian could not speak what was on his mind.

The following night, Alexander invited me to dinner. Of course I accepted, although still troubled. Alexander was back to his usual self; easy and charming to me and the other guests. As often, the problems started in the endless rivalries among the Companions. Alexander invited old Demeratus to share his couch. The Corinthian had brought Alexander back from Illyria, and the King never forgot a service. Unfortunately, I shared a couch with Hephaestion. Banished from his accustomed proximity to his lover, Hephaestion seemed on edge. Yet, loathe each other as we did, the trouble did not start with us.

We were eating and drinking from gold and silver vessels, all plunder taken from the Persians. Likewise the walls were hung with eastern tapestries. They were purple and gold, embroidered with images of griffons. We had come a long way from home, but our nature remained unchanged.

'A few cubs is nothing,' Ptolemy said.

'Nothing?' Perdiccas leapt to his feet. 'You call these nothing?' He yanked his tunic down to his waist. There were livid gashes across his arms and chest.

Ptolemy, who had recently rejoined us from Halicarnassus, looked unimpressed. Drink taken, Perdiccas had been boasting hard about his hunting exploit. In the competitive world of the Companions someone had been bound to take offence.

'Those cubs were well grown,' Perdiccas said. 'I went into that cave alone, and I thought the lioness was there.'

Ptolemy muttered something inaudible.

'What?' Perdiccas shouted. 'Have the courage to speak so I can hear!'

'I said your father was a better man than you.'

'You bastard!' Perdiccas hauled his tunic up. 'At least my father acknowledged me.'

Ptolemy, broad fleshy face white with anger, jumped up, reaching for his sword.

'Stop!' Alexander's high voice cut through the hubbub.

The other two, breathing hard, stared at the King.

'We are all brothers here, no matter who sired us.' Alexander got down from his couch. 'No one doubts the courage of any one of us.' He went and embraced and kissed first Ptolemy then Perdiccas. He brought them together, made them clasp hands.

We banged our cups on the tables in approval.

'This is a night for friendship and celebration – Zeus has given us a sign that we will rule all Asia.' Alexander picked up a flagon. 'He that drinks most will have least sorrow.'

We took Alexander at his word. It was as if the argument – the immanence of violence and its aversion – had cleared the air. The Companions roared with good humour. After a time some got up to dance. In the raucous goodwill even Hephaestion thawed. He poured me wine, and we talked of hunting dogs. Not once did he mention my ancestors' pack tearing Euripides apart.

In the early hours of the morning, no chink of light yet showing through the shutters, I got out of bed to relieve myself. Although still drunk, immediately I knew something was wrong. My chest was tight, heart thumping, hard to draw breath. I staggered when I tried to return, my legs slow to obey. Then a sharp excruciating pain sliced into my liver like a spear. I cried out and collapsed.

I was back on the plains outside Aegae. The sky was black with storm clouds, but somehow the three stark crosses on top of the mound were bathed in light. A gold crown hung askew on the brow of Pausanias. He watched me through sightless eyes long since torn out by crows. I tried to keep my gaze on his putrid flesh, not look at the other two.

'This is your fault,' Heromenes said.

'The treachery was your idea.' It was hard to force the words out. My chest felt constricted, banded with iron. 'I warned you.'

'What about me?' Arrhabaeus said. 'Am I not your brother?'

'You are my brothers, but fools.'

'Do I deserve such a fate?'

'It was never going to work. Oath-breakers are hated by men and gods.'

Nailed to the cross, Heromenes laughed, showing his long, white animal teeth. 'Our father was right: the runt of the litter is a coward.'

'Justice comes . . . sword in hand . . . stabbing the throat . . . the lawless, the unjust.'

I was in my bed, bathed in sweat, a blinding agony in my head. Dimly, I was aware of others around me. A cool, damp cloth was pressed to my forehead. A scent of myrrh. Odd, hyacinth eyes gazing into mine. Someone cradled my head. A drink was brought to my lips. It caught in my throat, then I swallowed. It left a strange aftertaste. The hushed voices receded, and again I sank into a world of nightmare.

Perdiccas was half-naked, covered in wounds. Ptolemy was danc-ing. We were all laughing. Hephaestion handed me another goblet. I tried to push it away, but he was insistent. Then I was running, through the woods, down the slope of Mount Bermion, the pursuit hard on my heels. Something huge above the treetops. A gryphon, its coat shimmering purple, its terrible talons and claws gold. It swooped down on me. I thrashed to escape. Strong hands held me down.

'You are not dead then?'

'How long?' My throat rough and parched, my voice no more than a whisper.

'Three days,' Eumaeus said.

He helped me sit up. The room was shuttered, stank of sickness. We were alone.

Eumaeus gave me a cup of goat's milk. 'Alexander brought his doctor Philip. But he wanted to bleed you. Alexander thought you were so weak it would kill you, so he sent him away. Helped me nurse you himself for the first two days until you were out of danger.'

I remembered the concern in the hyacinth eyes.

'Knows the qualities of plants does, Alexander.'

'He learnt from Aristotle . . . and his mother.'

Eumaeus sat on the bed, and felt my pulse. 'He made up an infusion of ash bark, wormwood and vervain to bring down your fever.'

'It was not a fever,' I said. 'Hephaestion poisoned me.'

'No, I put a whetstone under your pillow.'

'What?'

'Something my mother taught me. A whetstone detects poison. The victim calls out the name of the poison, when and where it was given.' Eumaeus shook his head. 'But he never says the name of the poisoner.'

'What did I say?'

'Nothing. You just raved about your brothers.'

The terrible figures on the crosses came back into my mind, along with a feeling of dread. 'What about them?'

'Nothing that matters. You were delirious.' Eumaeus looked away, disconcerted. 'Mind you, the deepest rivers flow with the least noise.'

CHAPTER TWENTY-ONE

Spring to Autumn 333 BC

ALEXANDER CAME TO SEE me later in the day. Thank the gods, he did not bring Hephaestion. He brought me some figs and dates, but, not wanting to tire me, did not stay long. There was no mention of whatever I had said in my fever.

With the vigour of youth, I was back on my feet within a few days.

'Eat this,' Eumaeus said, as I was about to leave for Alexander's council. He passed me a small pellet, about the size of a hazelnut.

'What is it?'

'To help you regain your strength.'

'What is it made of?'

'Ground-up figs, nuts, dried rue, and a juniper berry.' Eumaeus looked shifty.

'And?'

'And some Lemnian earth.'

'I thought your whetstone proved I had not been poisoned?'

'Better safe than sorry,' the old man muttered.

I was welcomed by the Companions with rough humour, jokes about my return from Hades. I could barely bring myself to reply to the formal greeting of Hephaestion. One day, I thought, one of us will kill the other.

Although Zeus may have approved of the cutting of the Gordion knot, the council revealed that while I had been ill the news of men was all bad. Back in the Aegean the Persian fleet under Memnon had taken the island of Chios, and all the cities on Lesbos, except Mytilene, and that was under siege. Once Mytilene fell, Memnon could either sail north to Abydos and the Hellespont, and cut us off from Macedon, or cross to the Greek mainland and use Persian gold to stir up revolt. Memnon was a commander to be feared. Quite possibly he could accomplish both. If his warships patrolled the Hellespont, he could seize the grain fleet from the Black Sea, and threaten the Athenians with famine, if they did not join an insurrection. Clandestine despatches from the east – evidently Alexander had informants at the Persian court other than Sisines – contained little to celebrate. Darius had left Susa, and was gathering an enormous army at Babylon. Whichever way you looked at it, we were caught between two fires.

None of us thought Alexander would turn back. Not unless Macedon itself was threatened, and then the men would insist. The first duty of a Macedonian king was to protect his people. Our custom fitted with the teaching of Aristotle: a king did not rule for himself, but for his subjects; if he ruled for himself, he was not a king at all, but a tyrant.

Alexander sent Amphoterus, the brother of Craterus, and Hegelochus, a relative of the executed Attalus, with five hundred talents to rebuild the fleet. Parmenion managed not to point out that he had advised against it being disbanded in the first place back in Miletus. Another six hundred talents were despatched to Antipater to bolster the army in Macedon. Alexander himself, as we had known all along, would continue east to meet Darius.

Towards the end of spring, midway through the month of *Daisios*, Coenus and Meleager returned from Macedon bringing both the men who had spent the winter with their wives and the new recruits: three thousand reinforcements for the phalanx, and three hundred for the Companion cavalry, along with two hundred more horsemen to replace casualties among my Thessalians. The mission of Cleander to the Peloponnese had not gone so well, so far he had sent only one hundred and fifty volunteers from the city of Elis. Either the Greeks were reluctant to serve Macedon, or the limitless coffers of the Persian King paid better.

Even after the arrival of the additional troops, eager as Alexander was to bring Darius to battle, we had to wait. Cappadocia, the country through which we would march, was a high and mainly bare plateau. For two months we kicked our heels until the harvest was ripe and we could gather supplies along our route. By day, I drilled and trained the Thessalians – the wheeling squadrons raising clouds of red-grey dust across the plain – and at night, drank with Medius. Sometimes Alexander joined us. Tactfully, he never brought Hephaestion. The shadow that had fallen on our friendship seemed gone.

Eventually, we got the order to move out. The first town we came to was Ancyra. While we were there, two parties of shaggy horsemen arrived. The first, from the north, was an embassy of Paphlagonian tribesmen. They brought earth and water, but, before offering their submission, asked that Alexander impose no tribute, as had been the immemorial practice of the Persian kings. This they were granted, although they were told that from now on they should obey Calas, our Satrap of Hellespontine Phrygia. The Paphlagonians handed over some hostages, who they swore were important men and close relatives, but, from the villainous look of the speakers, they were lying. Once we had left, the odds that they would take any notice of Calas were minimal. The second embassy comprised various chieftains of the Cappadocians through some of whose territory we would march. They too offered a submission in which only a fool would put any faith. But we were in a hurry, and had no time to fight to impose our authority. Even so, many of the Macedonians did not take it well when Alexander appointed as satrap a local baron called Sabictas. It was a practical measure, but we had not come east to elevate the natives.

At Ancyra, a courier from the west brought more welcome news. Our great adversary Memnon of Rhodes had sickened and died during the siege of Miletus. There was also a rumour that Darius had recalled many of Memnon's Greek mercenaries to Babylon. It was too early to celebrate, but perhaps the threat in the Aegean was receding.

From Ancyra our route turned south. Although the surface of the old Persian Royal Road was good, it took us through a rocky and desolate landscape under a burning sun. To our right glimmered a vast salt lake. The march was hard on men and beasts, but our greatest concern was what lay ahead. There was only one pass through the Taurus Mountains down to the sea. The Cilician Gates were said to be impregnable and garrisoned by Arsames, the Satrap of Cilicia to the south. Alexander went ahead with the *hypaspists* and the Agrianes. The next day, as we trudged up into the mountains, walking beside our horses, a messenger came back. The pass was ours. Surprised by the sudden appearance of Alexander, the defenders had fled. The messenger brought an order for me to bring up the Thessalians as fast as possible.

The Gates were worthy of their reputation: a long defile, at times so narrow we could only ride two abreast, the surface cut by gullies and dry storm channels, both sides dominated by towering cliffs. Alexander was waiting with some of the Companions a few miles to the south, where the path was wider.

'What did you think?' Alexander asked.

'A hundred good men with food and water and I could have held them against you forever.'

Alexander gave me a sharp look, then smiled. 'You are right. This was the greatest stroke of luck so far.' As he spoke, his eyes seemed to become focused on something only he could see. 'Or perhaps not luck, but something more.'

No one spoke until Hephaestion touched his arm and brought him back.

'We caught a few stragglers.' Alexander was normal and brisk again. 'They say Arsames intends to burn everything in our path. Lyncestes, take the Thessalians straight down the road to Tarsus, the capital of the satrapy. Stop for nothing. Try to prevent Arsames removing the treasury and torching the place. Parmenion will follow you with the Greek allies and mercenaries and Sitalkes' Thracians. As soon as he reaches Tarsus, requisition any horses you need, round up some local guides, and ride ahead and seize the pass on the coast road south to Syria. When I arrive with the main army, Parmenion will follow to reinforce you.'

The Cilician plain was broad and flat, so well watered that even in the height of summer it was still green. An early morning mist hung low in the orchards and fields. There was a tang of woodsmoke in the air. On either side of the Royal Road, smoke coiled into the still air from burning farms. But there were not many alight, and those that were lay close to the road. Arsames' Persians were not spreading destruction across the plain, but obviously retreating fast.

We went at a fast canter that ate up the miles. Even though Alexander had stressed the need for speed, I called a halt every hour to pick stones out of the horses' feet, rub their backs, smooth their saddlecloths, let them have a little water. We might be able to find new mounts in Tarsus, but they would not be trained warhorses, and our task would not be done. I did not intend to leave us unable to fight.

It was good to have an independent command. The Bacchiads are born to lead, not to follow. And it was good to be away from the court, away from Hephaestion. Not content with the daily pellet of antidote, Eumaeus had taken to surreptitiously tasting my food. One day I would settle with Hephaestion, not with poison, that was the way of women and easterners, the way of a coward.

When the sun burnt off the mist it was hot – hotter than anything I had known in Macedon or Greece. The very air seemed to scorch your lungs. The flanks of Borysthenes, who I was riding, were strung with white ropes of sweat. My own sweat was slick under my linen armour, which began to rub and chafe my shoulders. All I could smell was hot horse, leather, and my own stink. Things would be worse for those at the rear of the column, breathing the thick dust kicked up by eighteen hundred horses. At every halt, I altered the order of march. One of the benefits of command was that I remained at the front.

At the end of a long day, Tarsus came in sight. A dark line of mounted troops were leaving the eastern gate. They were moving fast, heading for the Amanus Mountains and the safety of Syria. Shading my eyes against the low sun, I saw the first tendrils of smoke rising from the heart of the city. Now we kicked on into a full gallop.

Some local worthies came out to surrender the city. As Tarsus claimed to be Greek, the notables wanted to make long formal speeches about their origins, mentions in Homer, and mythical links to Heracles and thus the Argead House of Macedon. I cut their oratory off, thanked them briefly, told them they were liberated, and set about securing the town, leaving them standing disconsolate in their best clothes by the side of the road. Medius took the troop from Larissa to follow and watch the retreating Persians. One half of the rest of the Thessalians were detailed to occupy the walls and gates, the other to put out the fire in the palace of the satrap.

The fire had not really caught, and by nightfall was extinguished. Although the building was somewhat damaged, the treasury was intact and unplundered. That, I thought, would please Harpalus – his abacus would click with pleasure. Finally we could see to the horses, post guards, commandeer billets, and last of all demand food and drink from our somewhat reluctant hosts. My orders for the night were draconian – there was to be no looting, rape, or excessive drunkenness on pain of death. Tomorrow we had more ahead of us.

The ill-assorted allied troops under Parmenion plodded into Tarsus, bone-weary, late the next afternoon: Greeks and Thracians can't march like Macedonians. By the time I had handed the town over to the old general, the evening was too far advanced for us to leave; a night march often leads to confusion, troops going astray, getting lost. Another night of rest would help restore the Thessalians. We could make up the time on the march.

We left at sunrise. Despite my best intentions, I had had too much to drink. Sitalkes had invited me to dinner. Our relations had been cool ever since Thebes. He had quartered himself in a house of one of the town councillors. Perhaps he wanted to demonstrate that not all Thracian nobles behaved like Rhascus had with Timocleia in Thebes. The homeowner joined us, along with Parmenion. It was a pleasant, civilised evening. We kept our hands off the flute-girl and those serving the food, and there were no fights. Parmenion was on good form, telling stories about when the philosopher Euphraeus had tried to insist that only Macedonian noblemen who knew philosophy and geometry were allowed at the table of Perdiccas III. It was a reminder that Parmenion had served kings before Philip. It struck me that his spirits always rose when he was away from Alexander.

Although jaded, it was good to ride while the day still held the cool of the night. The Thessalians strung out behind me were in good voice, singing obscene songs about the men of Tarsus snorting as they were buggered. It was best not to enquire how they had discovered that. Twelve hours later – hot, bedraggled, and silent – we clattered into a place called Adana. Medius had left word that he and the troop from Larissa were waiting for us at the end of the next day's march at Mopsouestia.

Medius told us that the Persians had divided at Mopsouestia. Most had continued south-east towards the Syrian Gates, which we had been ordered to take, but a considerable number had ridden north-east. Medius had questioned the inhabitants. Apparently there was another pass through the Amanus Mountains. Over dinner we discussed what to do. Alexander's orders were clear, but when he had given them he had not known of this alternative route into Syria. In the end I thought it best to send Medius with the three hundred horsemen from Larissa to the north-east, while I continued to our original destination with the main body of fifteen hundred.

It took two long days to reach the southern pass. The first day, the road ran down to the coast, and we stayed the night at an insignificant town called Issus. At sundown on the second day, having forded several small rivers, we came to the pass. It was a formidable obstacle. The road switch backed up a high spur of the mountains that ran right down to the sea. Through the gloom, tiny figures of Persian troops could just be seen at the top. Although it was late in the day, and both men and horses were tired, I decided to try and emulate Alexander. We ascended at a walk, leading our horses, until we were almost at the summit. Then we mounted and formed up to charge uphill. Some of Alexander's good fortune had rubbed off. By the time we got to the crest the Persians had gone. I posted pickets to the south, and made camp.

There are many problems campaigning in unknown country: you get lost, can't find fodder or water or grain, run the risk of ambush, and sometimes the land itself springs unfortunate surprises. The next morning a Greek-speaking local told us that ahead the Amanus Mountains again curved round to the sea. To cross into Syria it was necessary to take another pass, running to the east. From the heights, you could actually see the range meeting the pale blue waters. Nevertheless, I sent just one troop – although the second best, that recruited in Pherae – to reconnoitre and, if possible, take the next pass. The gathering army of Darius was far away in Babylon, and the Persian troops in the vicinity seemed to have lost all desire to fight, yet I was wary of moving all the Thessalians forward and possibly getting trapped between the two passes.

Three days later, Parmenion arrived with the reinforcements. The old general was not in the mood for small talk. As soon as the formalities were over, he said he needed to speak to me alone. I took him to my tent, and told Eumaeus to keep everyone out of earshot.

'A messenger overtook me yesterday.' Parmenion's beard was matted with dust. There were lines on his face where the sweat had run through the grime of the road. 'Alexander is ill. The doctors think he may die.'

My ears heard his words, but my mind struggled to understand or believe. 'What?'

'He bathed in the Cydnus River that runs through Tarsus; it gave him a fever.'

'A fever?' I said stupidly. It had never crossed my mind that something so mundane might kill Alexander.

'If he dies,' Parmenion continued patiently, as if talking to the very stupid, 'what do we do?'

'The Macedonians assembled in arms acclaim a new king.'

'Arrhidaeus?'

'Alexander's half-brother has the mind of a child. We are hundreds of miles from home, surrounded by enemies.'

Parmenion nodded. 'Then who?'

One winter, when I was young, Neoptolemus had dared me to walk out onto the ice on Lake Lyke. It felt like that now. 'You and Antipater are the most experienced generals.'

'With not a drop of Argead blood between us.'

The ice was getting thin. 'The House of Elimea is closest in blood to that of Alexander.'

'Harpalus has already fled.'

'Where?' I did not ask why. The troops would not follow a disabled man. Harpalus could never be king, but he had royal blood. The accession of a new king was a dangerous time. Those close to the dynasty, as well as personal enemies, tended to die – as the shades of Amyntas and Attalus might testify.

'Commandeered a ship, sailed west. His brothers are too young to be considered.'

I stood very still, as if literally unsure of my footing, spoke carefully. 'Then the House of Orestis: both Perdiccas or Craterus command a battalion of the phalanx.'

Parmenion combed his fingers through his beard. 'My son Philotas and Craterus loathe each other. Things would not go well for Philotas if Craterus was hailed King. They would not go well for me, or the rest of my family.'

'Craterus is from the cadet branch of Orestis', I said, eager to reassure, eager to prevent the conversation going where I feared. 'Perdiccas is the more likely choice.'

'But not the only choice.'

The ice was groaning, a spider web of cracks spreading.

'There is the House of Lyncestis.'

I reached for a jug of wine, poured cups for both of us, added no water. 'Alexander entrusted the left wing of the army to my nephew Amyntas at Sagalassus.'

Parmenion took the offered cup. 'Whoever the army in Asia chooses has to be acceptable to that in Macedon under Antipater. You are married to Antipater's daughter.'

The deep black waters of Lake Lyke were closing over my head. There was nothing I could say.

'My sons, Philotas and Nicanor, command the Companion Cavalry and the *hypaspists*. The men of the phalanx have to be won over.' Parmenion took a drink. 'We will pray Alexander recovers, but if not I think we understand one another.'

I understood only too well.

Parmenion finished his drink, held the cup out for more. 'The messenger also brought an order – Alexander has summoned you to his sickbed.'

CHAPTER TWENTY-TWO

Autumn 333 BC

I RODE BACK TO TARSUS with Eumaeus and six Thessalians. If Alexander was close to death – and the flight of Harpalus suggested as much – it was the King's duty to the Macedonians to appoint a successor. My journey might end in two ways. Either Alexander would name me, or I would be put out of the way to smooth the accession of the chosen man. Of course, if Alexander was already dead, I knew what Parmenion expected of me. All the way – down from the Amanus Mountains and across the Cilician plain – the taste of fear was in my mouth like a copper coin.

There were no evident signs of mourning as we went through the town.

Hephaestion was standing with the guards outside the royal quarters. No one would take more pleasure in my arrest and execution.

'Alexander said I was to take you straight to him,' Hephaestion said.

Alexander was alone. He was sitting up in bed, very pale and with blue veins shadowing his eyes, but very much alive.

'You don't have one foot in Hades then?'

Alexander smiled. 'Philip and the other doctors like to exaggerate. It gives them a sense of importance.'

He held out his arms. I leant over, and we kissed.

'Sit.' He gestured at the bed. 'Hephaestion, pass him the letter, then you had better go and find out what Craterus wants.'

The broken seal on the letter was that of Olympias.

'Read it.'

I read out loud, as I knew that was what Alexander wanted. After enquiring after her son's health, Olympias launched into a lengthy and bitter denunciation of Antipater: the Regent was overstepping his authority, spying on her household, humiliating her in public. Then I stopped speaking. 'Antipater is encouraged by his daughter, Electra.' I remembered the fate of Attalus' niece and her two children. My stomach was hollow with fear, but I forced my mouth to frame the words. 'She writes in code to her husband, urging the Lyncestian to avenge his brothers, kill you, and take the throne.'

'It is not true. I have all her letters. You can read them.'

'There is no need.' Alexander's odd-coloured eyes, so hard to fathom, regarded me. 'My mother charges a high rent for nine months lodging. Now, get us both a drink, and then you can tell me about the Syrian Gates – apparently there are two passes, not one.'

As I poured the wine, I realised Alexander had stage-managed the entire scene. He was alone, ill, and unarmed. I wore my sword. With typical courage, he had not said anything, but had demonstrated that he trusted me by putting himself in my power. I had never loved him more than at that moment.

When Alexander was recovered enough to ride, we cross quartered Cilicia. Some cities were rewarded, others were fined for insufficient zeal or alacrity in coming over. The army went into the foothills of the Taurus to overawe the tribesmen. We were holding a festival and athletic competitions when Parmenion's messenger arrived: scouts had spotted the army of Darius out on the plain about two days' march to the east of the Syrian Gates at a place called Sochi.

The news spread like wildfire through the camp. The men cheered and laughed. This was what we had come for – to overthrow the Great King. One battle and the wealth of Asia would be ours. We broke camp the next day, and marched round the head of the gulf. Parmenion was waiting for us at Issus. To increase our mobility, Alexander left our heavy baggage in the town, along with those soldiers who were too injured or ill to keep up. As they were frontline troops, he also recalled Medius and the Larissa squadron of Thessalians from where I had stationed them at the pass to the north-east. I suggested that some of the allies or mercenaries be sent to replace them, but Alexander said there was no need; we would be upon Darius at Sochi before he knew we were coming. As so often, Parmenion proposed a more cautious strategy. We should cross the first pass to the south, then wait in the small plain between it and the Syrian Gates. There we could be supplied by sea – having acquired a number of merchantmen and a handful of warships from the seaports of Cilicia – while sooner rather than later lack of provisions would force Darius to come and seek us out in terrain where the huge numbers of his army would count for nothing. Alexander was having none of it. The next day we set off south.

The sky was lowering with a storm building out over the sea to the west as the army syphoned over the narrow saddle of the first pass. As night fell the second day out from Issus, thunderheads, pulsing with lightning, rolled ashore, and the heavens opened. Soldiers were washed out of their tents, and the rain threatened to beat down the roof of the royal pavilion. The Companions were with Alexander when the apparition appeared.

A Royal Page, too shocked to speak, ushered in the terrible figure. A Macedonian by the *kausia* on his head, soaked to the skin, and plastered in mud. Both his arms ended in cauterised stumps. The smell of tar was strong. The amputations recent.

'They are all dead or mutilated.' His voice was surprisingly strong, but his eyes held the blankness of those who have looked on horror.

'Who?' Even Alexander was unnerved.

'They came down from the north-east, Persians, thousands of them.'

'Where?'

'Issus.'

None of us spoke.

'They led me round before they cut off my hands. Led me round, then released me to tell you.'

'Was Darius there?'

'Thousands and thousands of them.' His task accomplished, he was gone into a place where our further words meant nothing, into a solitary world of pain.

Alexander always recovered quickly. 'Summon Philip the doctor, and have two of the Pages tend this man.'

They took the broken man away.

Alexander started pacing, as if the anger and the energy inside him had to find an outlet. 'We need to find out if this is a diversionary force, or if Darius has got behind us.'

'I will go,' Craterus said. 'One man riding hard can be there and back by tomorrow.'

'It will be quicker by boat,' Alexander said.

'But the storm?'

'The wind is dropping. Take one of the galleys. Lyncestes, go with him.'

The wind had eased, but it had left a swell. The black waters were cresting white. The small galley pitched and wallowed. Waves broke over the sides. From the start, the sailors were bailing, the rowers fighting to manage their oars. Out to sea, lightning danced across the darkness.

Craterus and I clung to the sternpost behind the steersman. As the galley climbed the leading edge of the waves, we were plunged down, the sea rearing high all around, above our heads. Then, when the vessel slid down the far side, we were thrust up high, like Ixion bound to his wheel.

A war galley is not designed for rough weather. But Alexander was right. We could be there and back before any horseman. We might drown, but we would not be captured. After the apparition that was a comfort.

In a flash of lightning, I saw Craterus grin at me. No more a seaman than me, there was no denying his courage. I was glad Alexander had not died of the fever; glad that I had not had to carry out Parmenion's instructions, and try to kill the Orestid clinging on for dear life next to me.

Ixion's punishment was eternal. The hours passed, and ours felt the same. But repetition deadens fear. At some point, unnoticed, the motion of the ship became almost reassuring. The night was dark, but the storm had almost blown itself out.

A tardy squall of rain lifted, and we saw the shore. A low black line fringed with the white of the surf, while beyond twinkled a myriad of lights, as if the storm had washed all the stars from the heavens.

'There is our answer,' Craterus shouted, 'Darius has come. Steersman, take us back.'

We arrived about mid-morning. Alexander addressed the troops. Our enemies were Medes and Persians, men who for centuries had lived soft and luxurious lives. We were Macedonians, men from a hard land, trained for generations in danger and war. The gods themselves had brought the hordes of Darius into the narrow confines between the mountains and the sea. Their numbers would breed confusion. They had no means of escape. Alexander always had a gift for finding the right words for the troops. Yet that day he could have said anything. The men were burning to avenge the dead and mutilated of Issus. They pressed forward, clasped his hand. As one they shouted: 'No Delay! No Delay!'

We ate a hot meal, and prepared cold rations for the next morning, then set out to retrace our steps northward. At midnight, we camped at the pass. Alexander went up into the mountains with some of the Companions to offer sacrifices to the local gods. Eumaeus said I should have accompanied him; I was getting a reputation as a man who neglected the gods. But Eumaeus knew nothing about the curse of Olympias. Better I kept my distance from the divine.

The storm had gone, but it was *Apellaios*, the last month of autumn, and a cold wind blew through the heights. Wrapped in my thickest cloak beside a guttering campfire, it was hard to sleep on the stony ground. In the third watch of the night, I was awake when Alexander sought me out. He was alone except for Hephaestion. As if at an unspoken command, Eumaeus and those around me drew back.

For a time Alexander sat in silence, his eyes veiled in thought. When he spoke his voice was pitched low.

'You were right, and I was wrong. A guard should have been left at the pass to the north-east.'

Alexander's confession did not please Hephaestion. He had a face like a starving cat forced to eat a cucumber.

Alexander was not finished. 'What happened at Issus will remain on my conscience. Did you know the messenger died? But a man must learn from his mistakes. This time I have sent some of the mercenaries to hold the Syrian Gates behind us.'

'I thought they might raid Cilicia once we had left,' I said, 'but I did not expect Darius to come with his whole army from the north-east. As you told the men, the Great King has made a mistake negating his numbers in the narrows.'

'Perhaps a god put it in his mind.' Alexander had a faraway look. 'Sometimes I feel the gods very close to me.'

I said nothing. Olympias was in my mind.

'You are also descended from Herakles. Do you sense their presence?'

'Once, a long time ago, in a skirmish against the Illyrians, up near Lake Lyke, when I was very young. But not since then, not for years.'

Alexander nodded, wearily, as if accepting a burden he must bear alone. Then he put his hand on my thigh. 'I know you want to lead the Thessalians. But tomorrow it will be the Royal Squadron of the Companions that decides the day, and I want you by my side. Tomorrow you and I hunt the greatest quarry of all – the Persian King. We have to kill Darius. If the gods do not grant I strike him down, it would be good if it was you.'

Hephaestion gave me a look of pure hatred. Riding among the Companions tomorrow, the Persians would not be the only danger we both faced.

At first light we started to filter down from the pass. The Persians were waiting: a mass of cavalry drawn up a couple of miles ahead in front of one of the small rivers that cut the plain. There were more, many more, horse and foot on the far bank.

Our heavy infantry went first. Nicanor, son of Parmenion, led the *hypaspists* out onto the plain. The six battalions of the phalanx followed. They marched thirty-two deep until the ground widened, and they redeployed into files of sixteen. As if on parade outside Pella, each unit took its place in the battle line: Nicanor on the right, the battalion of Amyntas, son of Andromenes, held the left. Our allied cavalry rode down to the sea on the extreme left, and Alexander led the Companions and Thessalians to the right wing. Persian infantry could be seen in the foothills that curved round inland. Alexander sent the Agrianes and some other light troops to keep them from our flank and rear.

The whole manoeuvre took time, and it was well gone midday before everyone was in position. All this time the Persians had made no move. But, as we began to advance, their cavalry splashed back across the stream. They angled down to the shore. Now we could see their whole array. Almost all their horsemen were on our left; inland of them, along the riverbank, was a block of Persian infantry, then a phalanx of Greek hoplites, and finally another body of Persian foot. Behind the latter, where they joined the Greeks, tall standards revealed the presence of the Great King. Further back was a great body of tribal levies that extended from the sea to the hills. At the sight of Darius, the Companions round me stiffened, like gaze hounds spotting their prey.

Alexander called a halt, and sent the Thessalians to reinforce our left. Philip, son of Menelaus, led them behind our phalanx. The tall *sarissas* of the infantry might prevent the Persians noting the rearrangement. Despite Alexander's words the night before, watching Medius ride past at the head of the squadron from Larissa hurt my pride, and gave me a stab of regret. My place was with my Thessalian friend and the horsemen I had trained. The head of the Bacchiad House should lead not follow. He should, like Achilles, always strive to be the best. My nephew also was no longer in charge of the Scouts. Amyntas now rode at my side in the Royal Squadron, along with our kinsman Leonnatus. None of us Lyncestians had an independent command. Had Alexander's near fatal illness made him see us as potential rivals? But the Orestids also had royal blood, and Perdiccas and Craterus still commanded their battalions of the phalanx. Perhaps it was the offer of Darius brought by Sisines, or the steady drip of poison in the letters of Olympias, and the pillow talk of Hephaestion, but I could not get the old saying out of my head: you keep your friends close, but your enemies closer.

We advanced slowly, often stopping to dress our lines. At our final halt, just out of arrow shot, about two hundred paces from the river, Alexander again rode down the line. He went alone, mounted on Bucephalus. Both horse and rider looked magnificent. This time, from the snatches I heard, Alexander appealed to baser instincts. Look at the gold and silver ornaments of the Persians. Dressed like women, they would fight like women. They were not enemies, but so much walking plunder. The wealth of their camp would make every Macedonian rich for life. Apart from the tent of Darius – custom reserved the possessions of the enemy leader for the King of Macedon – everything would fall into the hands of our men.

I fidgeted with my helmet and equipment, fussed the ears of Borysthenes, spoke fondly to the charger. My chest was tight, but for once I was unafraid. The apparition with no hands was in my mind. Today, in the few hours before nightfall, I intended to avenge that mutilation; show Alexander that I was to be trusted; demonstrate to all the Macedonians that I could do great things amid the din of battle. Should Alexander fall, the Macedonians under arms must acclaim me their King. And if they did, my first act would be to kill Hephaestion.

The enemy did not frighten me. The Persians opposite us carried large round hoplite shields and Greek spears. But they wore eastern costume, not helmets and body armour. Leonnatus said they were Cardaces, young men being trained for war. Better that than veterans. It takes time to train a man for war. Living in a soft land, the Persians were cowards. They would never stand close to the steel.

Alexander returned. His words to the Companions were brief: we break these infantry, then we kill Darius.

The river was shallow. Its banks opposite our phalanx were almost the height of a man. But down by the shore and here near the foothills they were less of an obstacle. Alexander had already chosen our crossing. The Royal Squadron would charge slightly to the left, where the banks were lowest. The Persians had erected an abatis of thorn bushes on the far bank. It was low, easy to jump. The other squadrons of Companions would follow us.

A final look round, and Alexander drew his sword. He raised it high, then brought it down. Trumpets rang out. The whole army set off.

We went straight into a fast canter. Arrows arced up from behind the enemy frontline. They seemed to hang suspended, then sliced down among us as hissing black lines. We pushed on into a gallop to get through the storm as quickly as possible.

Tucking my chin into my chest, my world shrank to my immediate surroundings: the triple crest of Alexander's helmet just ahead, the thighs and arms of Amyntas and Leonnatus on either side. The earth quivered under the hooves of our horses, the air seemed to shake. A falling arrow whipped by Borysthenes' head. As if in the far distance someone screamed in pain.

We were plunging down the riverbank, water fountaining up from our crossing. A line of overlapping shields crowning the far bank. If they held firm, our mounts would refuse. Leaning forward we went up towards the glittering spearheads.

Bucephalus leapt the abatis. The enemy opened before Alexander. We were among them. They had not held their line. I stabbed overarm down into the face of a Persian. One moment it was young, full of beauty, then it was a ruin of blood and bone.

The Cardaces were running, fighting each other to get away. We speared them like fishermen among a school of tuna. The Companions were slipping into a killing frenzy, as if into some terrible religious ritual. Nothing mattered but blood.

'To me! Follow me!'

Alexander's voice was high and harsh, but it carried over the clamour. That was when we showed why we were the best cavalry in the world. Any other troop would have carried on the slaughter. Deaf to all commands or reason, they would have chased the Cardaces until the horses could go no further. But we came to heel like hunting dogs.

The tall standards were off to our left. Alexander – one of the crests of his helmet was gone – was driving straight at them. I closed up on his left, urging Borysthenes to get in front.

There was Darius. A tall man standing in a chariot. His mouth was open, and he made a curious open-handed gesture. Between him and us was the pride of the Persian nobility. They were gorgeously accoutred, mounted on magnificent Nisean stallions. Unlike the Cardaces these men fought. Our momentum was gone, our close order too. Each step was contested. A dismounted Persian slashed at Alexander's thigh with a dagger. Leonnatus stabbed him between the shoulder blades.

A gap appeared in front of me. Only one rider separated me from the Great King. I drew back my arm, and hurled my spear. The cast missed. The steel cut into the shoulder of one of the chariot horses. It reared and plunged. The charioteer fought with the reins. For a moment I thought the whole team would bolt, bringing Darius into our midst. Then I saw a horse led up, and the Great King jumped onto its back. As his nobles died to protect him, Darius fled.

'After him!' someone yelled.

We hacked our way through the remaining Persians. Darius only had a brief start. We could overhaul him.

'Rally on me!' Alexander's voice again. 'On me!'

Some cavalry can be called back from a pursuit once, only the Companions twice.

The battle was not won. The phalanx was struggling, pinned in the bed of the stream by the Greek mercenaries. We jostled our tired and bleeding mounts into a rough wedge.

'Charge!'

The Greeks were professionals. But when they saw us bearing down on their flank they knew it was over. A few knots of brave men withdrew in close order. Most cast aside their heavy shields and ran. And with that the whole right wing of the Persian army turned tail.

'Now after Darius!'

As the sun's fires lit the horizon far out to sea, we turned again to the pursuit.

CHAPTER TWENTY-THREE

Autumn 333 BC to Summer 332 BC

LOOKING BACK PERHAPS THAT was when it all started to go wrong – in the hours after our greatest triumph.

Once we were sure the Persians were defeated, we turned to the pursuit of Darius. By now the sun was almost below the western horizon. The shadowed plain was full of fleeing men. The majority were from the tens of thousands of tribal infantry, who had played no part in the fighting, and now were being ridden down by their own horsemen. Most of the fugitives tried to scramble out of our way. Those that were too slow we killed. But their sheer numbers delayed us.

Eventually, we had outpaced the men on foot. We assumed Darius would be heading north towards Issus, but could not be certain. There might be other trails a few men, but not an army, could take eastwards over the mountains. We pushed our tired horses on into the darkness, fording one small river after another. Like Tantalus reaching for the fruit, time after time we thought we had Darius, but always he eluded our grasp. None of the groups of riders we overhauled contained the Great King. We lacked the numbers to take them prisoner, or the time to kill them. After about three hours, Alexander called a halt. Our mounts were spent. We had to walk, leading them, much of the way back. The sky was spangled with stars. Borysthenes was slightly lame.

It must have been close to midnight when we got back to the battlefield. We were challenged immediately by a picket of *hypaspists*. Nicanor, Parmenion's son, was a conscientious officer. A detachment of his foot guards escorted us to the tent of the Great King. The Persian camp was in expected uproar – Macedonian, Greek, and Thracian voices shouting and singing with triumph, laughing with drink and pleasure; Persian women screaming and weeping, as they were stripped of their valuables and their clothes, then driven naked, with slaps and spear-butts, through the lines from one degradation to the next – only the scale of the revelry and rape marked this from the aftermath of any other victory.

The tent of the Great King was a series of enormous connected pavilions. It was an oasis of calm in the Bacchanalian chaos, guarded by the Macedonian Royal Pages. Some of them took our horses, and one – Iolaus, the youngest son of Antipater, still a child – presented Alexander with Darius' bow and shield and cloak taken from the chariot the Great King had abandoned.

Alexander thanked the boy. 'Now I need Darius' bath to wash off the dirt.'

'No, not Darius' bath,' Hephaestion said. 'Now it is yours.'

Inside, we stood transfixed. The light was muted and soft, like in the women's quarters of a Greek house. Everywhere you looked – in the huge main room, and the spacious bedchamber – were gold, silver, and silk hangings; cups, bowls, and lamps; the air scented with the costliest perfumes; engraved braziers to keep out the autumnal chill, embroidered fans against the heat of the day; fine delicacies on inlaid tables; eunuch servants bowing and scraping. It made the palace at Aegae resemble a Spartan barracks, or a shepherd's hut. No Macedonian had ever experienced such luxury.

At length Alexander spoke. 'So, this it seems is what it is to be a king.'

Afterwards, Callisthenes, the court historian, presented it as irony. Callisthenes, like many Greeks, never let his own touchy self-regard stand in the way of sycophancy.

There was nothing ironic in Alexander's words. They struck a chill in my heart. That short sentence was a sign. Alexander was setting his feet on a path that would take him away from us Macedonians; a path that would lead inexorably to him adopting the role of Darius, and so to our servitude.

That was the first sign. There was another. That night, before we ate a late dinner that had been prepared for Darius, the sound of wailing came from another part of the pavilions. Alexander was told that the women of the Persian royal house, having been informed Darius' weapons had been presented to his conqueror, had assumed they had been stripped from his body, and were mourning his death. Alexander had sent Leonnatus to tell them to be quiet: Darius was alive, and they would be well treated.

In the morning, Alexander went to their quarters. A flabby eunuch, sweating with fear, drew back the hangings. The room was full of women, all modestly veiled, silent now, and hugging themselves with apprehension. An elderly woman tugged the covering off her face, and threw herself full-length on the floor at Hephaestion's feet. She clasped his ankles, grovelling and jabbering in her barbaric tongue.

I managed not to laugh, although behind me someone sniggered. What else would you expect from an eastern woman?

Even their men were cowards. And Hephaestion was taller than Alexander.

The eunuchs simpered in alarm, pointing to Alexander.

The old woman, unashamed in her abasement, crawled across, and grabbed at Alexander's legs.

'Never mind, Mother, for he is Alexander too.' He raised her to her feet, promised all sorts of things: none of the women would be molested, dowries would be given for her granddaughters, and continued royal dignity enjoyed by them all. No doubt someone translated it for her later.

That was the second sign that we were losing Alexander. This was no Timocleia at Thebes. This was not a Greek woman, horribly abused, but standing straight, showing courage before her captors. This woman had been born and bred and thrived in a cruel despotism. This was the mother of Darius, the man who had mutilated and killed our defenceless wounded at Issus. She showed no more courage than her son. We Macedonians had not marched for months, fought and bled and died to raise up and exalt the Persians, to pamper their women. We had come for revenge and conquest. Alexander liked to see himself as Achilles. But this was not the action of the heroes at the fall of Troy.

Callisthenes, of course, would write it up in another way.

As he would another of the Persian women. Apparently Darius' wife, the most beautiful woman in Asia, stood there unveiled. According to the Greek flatterer, Alexander ordered her from his sight, calling her an irritation to his eyes. Of course it was all lies. We had no idea which she was among the muffled figures. Although Alexander said nothing of the sort, the words came to be widely believed.

Looking back it all started to go wrong in those few hours. Of course hindsight can invest an event with a significance it did not hold at the time. Memories are rebuilt each time you bring them to mind. They are like Heraclitus' river – each time you step into them they are different. Yet I knew that night and that morning that everything had changed.

* * *

It was carnage. Men blundered through the thick smoke, stumbling over charred corpses, as they tried to help the burnt and screaming wounded. At the end of the long mole jutting out into the sea the two collapsed siege towers were wreathed in flames. The stern of the fire-boat that had wrought their destruction was still in the water. Four months of back-breaking labour, constant danger, and mounting casualties had been largely undone in half an hour. A couple of hundred paces beyond the mole the defences of the island city of Tyre remained unbreached. The siege had been unnecessary, brought about by Alexander's arrogance and temper. It was hard to believe that in just seven months he had led us from the triumph of Issus to this reeking failure.

After Issus, we had discovered that Darius had ordered the majority of his baggage train some two hundred miles south-east to Damascus. Alexander had sent Parmenion with a flying column. With typical efficiency the old general had seized it all – wealth beyond imagining. Harpalus – returned from the west and reinstated as treasurer by Alexander – was delighted. Philotas was delighted too. Among the captives was an enslaved Macedonian girl called Antigone, who Philotas took as a mistress. Alexander himself also took a woman: Barsine, the beautiful widow of Memnon of Rhodes. At this point Alexander was not totally lost to the traditions of Macedon.

Darius was reported to have retired east to Babylon, where he was thought to be summoning levies from distant provinces to build a new army. Alexander decided not to pursue him. The final reckoning would come later. Instead, while Parmenion was still away, we marched south with the main army, through the Syrian Gates, and down the coast of Phoenicia. The first cities – Aradus, Marathus, Byblos, and Sidon – opened their gates, and came over without a fight. At Marathus, Alexander received an envoy from the Great King hoping to ransom his captured family, and offering to recognise Alexander as a friend and ally. Alexander wrote back telling Darius to come in person as a suppliant. It was rumoured in the camp that Darius had offered more, to cede all the lands west of the Halys River. In the old days I would not have believed that Alexander would have suppressed the truth, but now I was not so sure. Only Hephaestion had been present when Alexander saw the envoy. If true, the offer would have fulfilled our aim to free the Greeks of Asia. Now it began to seem that Alexander had set his mind on much more, not just freedom for the Greeks and revenge, but taking for his own all the Persian Empire.

Tyre also offered to submit. Its King was still away with the Persian fleet in the Aegean, but the crown prince came out to meet us bringing Alexander a gold crown and pledges of allegiance. Alexander took it into his head that he wanted to sacrifice to his ancestor Heracles, the patron god of Tyre, in his temple on the island. The inhabitants said it was prohibited by their religion, but there was another temple in the old city on the shore. Alexander flew into a rage, uttering any number of threats.

The siege went badly from the start. The Tyrians abandoned the old settlement on the coast. The new city on the island was heavily fortified, and lay about half a mile offshore. The people of Tyre had many warships, we had very few. The only way to approach was to build a mole from the land. At first, where the channel was shallow, it went easily. We demolished old Tyre for material. Then the water was deep, and the currents strong. A storm destroyed much of what we had done. One night a huge sea monster beached itself on the mole. Aristander, of course, interpreted it as a favourable omen. I was not so sure. The Tyrians came out in boats and continually harassed and raided our working parties. Progress was slow and costly. Now it had all been nullified by the fire-ship.

We walked through the smoke to the end of the mole. Men with grappling hooks and chains were pulling down the remains of the siege towers. They collapsed in gouts of flame and showers of sparks.

'We will build new ones,' Alexander said, 'and guard them better.'

The announcement was greeted with silence. But Alexander was right. Once undertaken, we had to see the siege through. To abandon it would be a defeat. Darius would take heart, and his former subjects be encouraged to throw off our rule. Besides we had all seen the Tyrians up on the walls torturing to death those Macedonians they had captured in their raids. We had a debt of blood.

Alexander turned to one of his siege engineers. 'Diades, you will need to fell fresh timber in the mountains.' Then he turned to me. 'Lyncestes, take Sitalkes and the Thracians to protect the working parties.'

Despite my gathering doubts, not all trust was lost between us. Perhaps my friend was not completely corrupted by the wealth and power of his conquests. Part of him must realise that he needed the Macedonians as much as we needed him. It was the duty of us Companions to guide him back to the ways of our ancestors.

* * *

Virtue lives on a mountain top, so say some philosophers. Heracles was in the foothills when he encountered two women. One was seductive and alluring. The path to her was soft and easy. Of course, she was Vice. The other was stern and forbidding. The road to her was rocky and full of pitfalls. She was Virtue. Few men reached her remote abode.

In reality, the inhabitants of mountains are shepherds and brigands. The two are the same. Moving with their flocks, always armed and ready for violence, shepherds live beyond the laws of cities and kingdoms. Like Autolycus, the thief among the Argonauts, they are always ready to snap up anything they can carry away.

The Arabs of the Libanus Mountains gave us much trouble. I doubt they were fighting either for Darius or against Alexander. Quite possibly they had heard of neither. They were poor, and brigandage a way of life. To them our provisions and the few coins in our belts, let alone our weapons, were wealth. Fortunately, Sitalkes' Thracians were also hillmen. After the first raid on our camp I burnt the nearest two villages. Then the local headmen came to us, giving great oaths of submission, asking for handouts and work for their men. Of course the raids did not stop. Each swore they were the doing of a neighbouring tribe; they would show us the trails to their settlements; the timber there was far more suitable for our needs.

I had returned from a hard day in the hills. A logging party had been attacked. One was dead, three more seriously hurt. By the time we arrived the tribesmen had gone. They had taken three mules, the dead man's sword, and five sacks of grain. I washed in a cold mountain stream; one of those we would use to float the tree trunks down to the plain. I ate bacon and flatbread and an onion, drank a couple of cups of wine, and went to sleep in my tent. The pickets were posted, and there was no reason to worry.

I dreamt of a lynx padding through the glens of my homeland. Its amber eyes shone in the moonlight. The wind brought the baying of hounds, and the sounds of men.

'Wake up!'

By the light of the night lamp, I could see old Eumaeus had stuck his head through the flap.

'A native wants to talk to you.'

Not another headman ready to perjure himself about the innocence of his clan, offering to guide me to the lair of the true killers of the logger, men who happened to be ancestral enemies with whom he was at blood feud.

'Tell him to wait until morning.'

'He says he has important information.'

'Don't they all.'

Eumaeus did not move. 'There is something different about this one.'

Half asleep, I did not reply.

'He is not a local. He speaks Greek.'

Instantly, I was awake. 'Search him and bring him in.'

I swung my legs off my camp bed, splashed cold water from a bowl into my face, and reached for the scarlet sword-belt that had once been worn by Neoptolemus. This was trouble.

The man was wrapped in an eastern sleeved cloak, and the lappets of his cap were tied under his chin. Sensible attire, it was chilly in the mountains at night, but also suitably nondescript. Eumaeus stood behind him, wary, and on edge.

'King Alexander,' the man said.

'No, I am Alexander of Lyncestis.'

The visitor bowed from the waist, and blew me a kiss from his fingertips.

'Do not perform adoration, I am neither a god nor an oriental despot.'

'As you will, my Lord.' He straightened up. 'I have a message for your ears only.'

That was what I had feared. Like Heracles, I was to be presented with a choice that would define my life.

'Anything you can say to me, you can in front of Eumaeus. I have no secrets from my friend.'

Behind him, Eumaeus looked thoroughly alarmed. I hoped the same did not show on my face.

'The Great King Darius, beloved of Ahura Mazda, Lord of Iran and non-Iran, recognises you as King of Macedon. Out of the greatness of his soul, he grants you one thousand talents of gold, all the lands west of the River Halys, and his eternal friendship, if you remove the tyrant who occupies the throne of your ancestors, take your rightful place, and return to Darius his family held prisoner by that tyrant.'

He produced a sealed papyrus scroll from his cloak. 'As proof my Lord also sends you this in writing.'

I took the scroll. The seal depicted the Persian King wielding a spear and a bow.

It was so quiet I could hear the flame of the lamp hissing.

'Am I right,' I said, 'that you Persians are taught three things: to ride, to shoot a bow, and to avoid a lie?'

He bowed in acknowledgment.

'I took an oath to Alexander, as I took an oath to his father. Were I to break them, I would have lied to the gods. Take that as your answer.'

'Arrest him!' Eumaeus had drawn his sword. 'You can't let him go. Under torture he may tell Alexander many things – if other men have been approached.'

'Men say anything under torture.'

The Persian bowed yet again. 'You are gracious, my Lord. In his infinite wisdom Darius made certain I knew no more than the contents of his letter to you.' This man had more courage than his master.

'Let him leave, Eumaeus.'

Afterwards, I broke the seal, and read the letter. It contained nothing that the messenger had not said. I went to the lamp.

'Are you mad?' Eumaeus grabbed my wrist. 'That is your proof when you tell Alexander.'

'I am not going to tell Alexander.'

'You told him about Sisines.'

'Alexander then is not Alexander now. Our King has changed. I am not sure he would believe me again.'

'But he will find out!'

'Not unless this Persian, like Sisines, is already in his pay. No one here knows but the two of us.'

Eumaeus looked stricken.

I took his fingers from my wrist, and held the papyrus to the flame.

* * *

When we got back to Tyre the siege had changed. The Phoenician fleets had returned from the Aegean. All, apart from the Tyrians, had come over to Alexander. Soon afterwards, the Kings of Cyprus declared for Macedon, and sent many more galleys. There had been two naval battles off Tyre. Both had ended in a minor victory for our allied fleet. The war galleys of Tyre were bottled up in her two harbours. On land also things had improved. Cleander had finally returned from the Peloponnese, bringing four thousand mercenary Greek hoplites. More importantly, the mole had been widened, and extended to within less than a hundred paces from the island.

With the timber we had brought down from Mount Libanus, Diades and the other engineers set about constructing two new siege towers. Torsion artillery, throwing both bolts and stones, was fitted on our ships. The sturdiest were even equipped with rams. Some were lashed together to provide a steadier platform. As we had control of the sea, our fleet started probing for weak spots along the whole circuit of the defences of the island.

While the work went ahead – the artillery battered the walls, and the mole nudged forward – the season turned to high summer. I tried not to think about the Persian in the mountains. I had not betrayed Alexander, but nor had I told him. Had I done the right thing? Had my foster-brother changed to such a degree that he would have suspected me? What did it say of our friendship that I had feared to tell him? And what had happened to a Macedonian's right to speak his mind to the King or anyone else?

With the siege there were many demands on Alexander's time. As one of his Companions I was kept fully occupied. There were always troops to inspect, provisions to distribute, disciplinary cases to be heard. Alexander and I were seldom alone. When we were, I thought I detected a reserve. Yet perhaps I was seeing, not reality, but what I expected to see. Although we never spoke of the nocturnal visitor, I could tell it preyed on Eumaeus' mind. The old man's conversation retreated more and more into gnomic and gloomy utterances about the interpretation of dreams and arcane pieces of folk wisdom.

Towards the end of the month of *Loos*, when the heat and flies were becoming unbearable, the mole was so close to the defences that a boarding bridge could have been run out from our siege towers to the battlements. No assault was ordered. The mole was no more than two hundred feet wide. The wall here was sturdy and very high. To attack only here would end in a bloody repulse. If the other Phoenician cities, and the Kings of Cyprus, had not come over, we now knew we would never have taken Tyre. Veterans began to grumble that Alexander's father would have found another way to get inside: traitors and a sack of gold opened any gate.

We waited and fretted while the fleet continued to batter the rest of the perimeter. Finally the rams on the ships brought down a short section of wall at the south-east of the island, just beyond the harbour known as the Egyptian. Alexander ordered an immediate assault.

Perdiccas' battalion was sent into the breach. The order of precedence of the phalanx battalions – which led the march or held the right in battle – changed each day. But the King chose the day of battle. The uplanders, especially those from Lyncestis and Orestis, often grumbled that it was always them in the van. Yet it was also a source of pride: we were the best fighters, and the King knew that.

The breach was too narrow, no more than twenty paces. The rubble of the fallen wall was too steep and jumbled. No diversionary attacks had been organised to draw off the defenders. Perdiccas wisely withdrew his men before they had suffered many casualties.

The breach had to be widened. But that evening a wind got up from the south-west. For three days the sea was too rough. We watched impotently from the shore as the Tyrians laboured to build new makeshift defences.

This morning dawned fine. The wind had dropped, and the sea was calm. For hours, the artillery on our ships battered the damaged section of the defences. At midday, the assault parties filed onto the ships.

Two galleys had been modified for the attack. Both had an unwieldy boarding bridge cantilevered upright on its bows. Alexander was in one with a detachment of the *hypaspists*. One of their officers, Admetus, would lead the first wave; Alexander the second. The men on the other vessel were from Coenus' battalion recruited in Elimea. I would go at their head; Coenus would follow.

Leading a storming party was close to suicide. Alexander had announced a sliding scale of rewards for those who reached the walls. Should they fall, the huge sums of money would go to their families. At least Electra would be rich if I died. It was a small comfort; Antipater's daughter was wealthy anyway. I did not want to die. Waiting under a hard blue sky, sweat running under my linen armour, I just wanted it to be over. Waiting is always the hardest part. There is too much time to imagine what is to come: the agony of the wounds, the dark embrace of death; the terrible fear that the coward that lives inside all of us will emerge, and you will be disgraced for life.

A cheer from the ships with the artillery. They began to back-water to clear our approach. Through the dust raised by the endless projectiles I could see more of the wall – at least fifty paces – had toppled down into the water.

Our rowing master blew a note on his pipes. Like the wings of a bird the oars rose and dipped and bit into the sea. The galley, cumbersome with its unusual burden in its bows, groaned and shivered, then reluctantly began to wallow forward.

This time we would not go in alone. The Cypriot fleet would attempt to force its way over the boom into the northern har-bour; the Phoenician would do the same at the southern. The battalion of Craterus would cross the boarding bridges from the siege towers on the mole. From all round the island galleys would come close and release a hail of missiles. Their crews had grapnels and ropes should any stretch of battlements appear deserted, axes in case a postern was unmanned in the confusion.

The gap between our prow and the foot of the slope of rub-ble closed. The shooting from our other ships was keeping the heads of the Tyrian archers down. But some of their catapults were protected by hoardings. A bolt sliced just over the bow where I stood. We all ducked, then grinned at each other, laughing guiltily. Artillery was unfair – it killed brave men as easily as the craven.

The galley nosed in slowly; the rowing master leaning out over the ram. The jagged boulders could tear out its keel.

'Back-water!'

The other galley had drawn ahead of us. I saw its boarding bridge swing down and crash onto the incline. Admetus, a tall scarlet plume nodding above his helmet, led his men up the bridge.

'Bridge away!'

With pulleys and blocks squealing, our bridge tipped forward. It unbalanced the entire ship. The vessel bucked like a horse, and its planks shifted alarmingly under our feet, as if they might come apart.

Admetus was already at the top. I saw him leap out onto the defences. He had won the greatest prize. One defender, then another, went down under his spear. He turned to encourage his men, and a spearhead took him in the chest. As he fell, another Tyrian brought an axe chopping onto the tall red plume and his head.

Our bridge thumped down onto the rubble.

Al-al-al-al-ai! The cry rose the hairs on the back of my neck.

No time to think, nothing to do but advance, I edged up the ramp. The arrows and slingshots that now filled the air rattled into the wicker sides of the bridge. Crouched behind a big hoplite shield – my eyes peering out between its rim and the brim of my helmet – I went up half-turned to the right, the cavalry spear I had selected underarm, tucked close to my side; making myself as small a target as possible. The bridge was only wide enough for two men. At my side was a grizzled Elimiot called Peucolaus.

Tyrians appeared at the top, as if they had sprung from the boulders themselves. These warriors wore full hoplite equipment, and had wicked long spears. They were several ranks deep. Fighting for their homes and families, the sanctuaries of their gods, their lives, they would stand fast in the storm of terrors.

'Let us be men!' I shouted to Peucolaus.

The hoplite facing me stabbed down overhand. I brought up my shield, felt the impact as his spearhead gauged into my shield, then skid off. I thrust blindly, missed. The shield of the man behind me smacked into my back, forced me shield to shield with my opponent. A spear came from the rear ranks of the Tyrians, over the shoulder of the one I faced. I jerked my face out of the way. It caught the side of my helmet. The blow and the clanging of metal on metal made my head ring.

A spray of hot blood on my right arm. Peucolaus reeled away, his throat torn open. Another Elimiot took his place.

If we did not get off this bridge, we would be slaughtered here, like sheep in a pen.

I tucked my left shoulder into my shield, braced my legs, and using all my weight and strength drove against the man fighting me. He gave back a step. The man behind me had his shield in my shoulder blades pushing. I dropped my spear – too crushed to use it – and gripped the rim of my shield. We were moving, slowly, a pace or two. Our momentum built inexorably.

The man I was wedged against lost his footing. Falling, he knocked those behind him off balance. Somehow I trampled over him. I drew my sword, thrust at another man. He stepped back. Coenus' men were pushing past me. The dam was broken.

I looked over at the other bridge. Alexander stood there. His white armour was spattered with gore. His face was serene and triumphant, like some *daemon* of war. And I knew what we had done was irreversible. Tyre had fallen.

CHAPTER TWENTY-FOUR

Summer to Autumn 332 BC

'WALK WITH ME.'

We were on the shore opposite Tyre. Above our heads, along the beach, were two thousand crucified men. In the sack another eight thousand had been killed. The rest of the population, some thirty thousand women and children, had been sold into slavery. I had bought a Tyrian boy, who spoke a little Greek, to help Eumaeus. He had an unpronounceable name, so I had called him Agathion, *Good Fellow*. I had bought a girl too. I loved Electra, but sexual abstinence is bad for a man. I had called her Leucippe, which sounded a bit like her Tyrian name.

Alexander stopped, and looked up at one of the crosses. 'It was hard for you to watch your brothers crucified.'

'Yes.'

He looked into my eyes. 'In Gordion, when you were ill, you talked about them.'

'I do not remember.'

'You were arguing with them about the assassination of my father.'

I kept my eyes fixed on his. 'I remember there was a gryphon with huge claws. It was chasing me.'

Alexander looked away, and smiled. 'You are right. After my fever in Tarsus, people said I had talked nonsense.'

We walked on.

I knew with complete certainty that Hephaestion had twisted my words into an admission of complicity in the killing. There had to be a reckoning.

Abruptly, Alexander changed subject. 'Parmenion would have accepted the offer.'

After the fall of Tyre envoys had come from Darius. They had offered Alexander the hand of one of the King's daughters in marriage, a ransom of twenty thousand talents for the rest of his family, and all the territories west of the River Halys.

'Would you have rejected it?' Alexander asked.

'Yes.' Again I looked into Alexander's eyes, keeping my face very calm, and not breaking stride. There was no way he would have been alone with me if he had known of my encounter on Mount Libanus. 'We already hold many cities this side of the Halys. If we had accepted it, we would have had to hand back Tyre, and our men would have died for nothing.'

Alexander nodded. 'And we have not yet got what we came for. We have liberated the Greeks, but have not exacted revenge.'

'Then we must go on to put Susa and Persepolis to the torch, before we can return to Macedon.'

'Not all of us will go home.'

I stopped walking, and looked at Alexander.

'The Persian domains are vast,' Alexander said. 'We can kill Darius, but if we do not hold their heartlands they will acclaim another King in the east, then another. If we do not make ourselves masters of Susa and Persepolis, we condemn ourselves to generations of warfare.'

I took his point, but, on that logic, we would have to march to the furthest recesses of their empire, all the way to India. The Macedonians would never contemplate that.

Alexander gazed out to sea. The sunlight playing on the surface glittered like diamonds. You could taste the salt of the spray on your lips.

'I know many of you do not approve of the way I treat the Persians; Cleitus mutters into his great black beard, Philotas looks like I have thrust a rotting fish under his nose.' Alexander smiled. 'But we need their nobles if we are to rule this empire. Aristotle was wrong. We can't treat them like plants or animals.'

Once again I felt like Heracles confronted with his choice. Virtue demanded that I speak words that might be unwelcome to Alexander. If I did not, I would forever think less of myself.

'Treat the Persians how you wish, but you are King of the Macedonians. We have given you our oath. We will fight and die for you. Yet you are one of us, and have to remember our customs. All Macedonians are free men.'

Alexander continued to look not at me but at the sea. 'And, if I do not remember, just as you acclaimed me, so you will depose me?'

That was our right, but I did not say so. This was very dangerous ground. 'Macedon has never had a king like you; not even your father. No one could replace you.'

Alexander laughed. 'If a stray arrow catches me in the neck, someone will have to.' He turned and embraced me. 'When I thought I was dying in Tarsus, I was going to give the seal of the kingdom to you.'

I nearly blurted out what had happened in the mountains – nearly, but I did not. 'I thought you said the doctors exaggerated.'

'Sometimes a king has to dissemble.'

'Not Perdiccas?'

'Too headstrong.'

'Craterus?'

'He was my other choice.' Alexander pulled away, looking very serious. 'You should always tell me the truth. Most men are afraid. It is the loneliness of the throne.'

* * *

If we thought Tyre would be a warning – submit or suffer the same fate – we were wrong. The last Persian satrapy in the west was Egypt. The city of Gaza barred our route to Egypt. Gaza did not surrender.

Gaza was situated on a high hill, on the edge of the desert, a couple of miles from the sea. Its walls were massive. The seven months we had sat before Tyre had given Batis, the Babylonian eunuch who held the place for Darius, ample time to stockpile provisions, build catapults, and recruit mercenaries. We had stumbled into another difficult siege.

The terrain itself was against us. We had to transport all our water, food, fodder, and siege equipment from Tyre. To make things yet more testing, off the shore nearest to Gaza there were shoals which prevented our ships beaching, and the sand close to the city was deep and soft. Alexander assigned Hephaestion to oversee our supplies; his first independent command of any importance. Detest Hephaestion as I did – and the emotion was more than mutual – it had to be admitted he had a natural bent for the mundane task, and, at least, I could eat meals without worry while he was away.

We did not run short of anything, but the siege did not start well. Diades and the other engineers shook their heads: the hill was too high to bring up rams and towers. Alexander ordered a ramp heaped up against the southern wall. The wheels of the siege towers sank into the soft sand and it broke their axles and bases. Alexander had the ramp surfaced with timbers laid on stones. When the repaired towers were moved forward, Batis' Arab mercenaries sallied out with pitch and torches. They would have burnt the machines if Alexander had not led a counter-attack. A catapult bolt hit Alexander. It penetrated his shield and armour, lodging in his right shoulder. The wound was serious. He lost a lot of blood, but it did not become infected. This time in my hearing there was no speculation about the succession.

Soon back on his feet, Alexander doubled the guard on the ramp, and had a ditch and palisade constructed completely round the town, to prevent further sorties. Learning the lesson from Tyre – never attack a fortified position from just one place – work began digging mines on the other three sides of the defences.

For the two months since we had invested Gaza I had fulfilled my duties as a Companion of the King, but in the last few days my mind was elsewhere. Old Eumaeus had taken a fever. Coming back from a war council, I found Agathion and Leucippe nursing him.

'What news?'

Eumaeus seemed more himself. When I had left, he had been delirious.

Before answering, I sent the two slaves out of the tent. 'The western tunnel is under the walls. Tonight the miners will hollow out a chamber. It will be fired in the morning. Alexander has given the task to me. The assault goes in when the wall comes down.'

'Let's hope the enemy have not dug a countermine. Bad business fighting in tunnels. When Philip first came to the throne we dug under the walls of a settlement in Thrace. They knew we were down there; broke through the side of our mine; threw in pots full of bees. We all ran. Bad business.'

I went to get him a drink. By the time I got back his eyes were far away. The fever had him again, and he had retreated into memories from his youth.

'Bees mean good luck for farmers and beekeepers, but for other men they signify confusion because of their hum, wounds because of their sting, and sickness because of their honey and wax. They are bad luck. They mean death because they settle on lifeless corpses. To dream of them indicates you will be destroyed by a mob or soldiers.'

I passed a damp cloth over his brows, and he stopped talking. He was very hot.

Suddenly, his bony old fingers gripped my wrist. 'You should have told Alexander about the Persian.'

'Too late now.'

He let go, sank back within himself. 'Yes, too late now.'

Then he slept.

I sat with him for a time. His breathing was fast and shallow. Under my hand he seemed to have no more life than a frail bird.

When the shadows began to lengthen, I called in the boy and girl, and went to my own tent. I ate some bread and cheese, and took a long drink to bolster my courage. By the time I was armed, Sitalkes came to collect me.

A man should not go underground. It is too close to the underworld. Mining is best left to barbarians. Sitalkes had selected Thracians from tribes accustomed to such work. Although most of the endless baskets of soil had been removed at night, there had been no way to hide the entrances of the mines from the defenders up on their eminence. To make countermining more difficult our tunnels did not run straight towards the defences, but went at an angle, before turning towards their goal.

Sitlakes led me down into the mine. Once away from the entrance it was dark, but not as cool as I had expected. Torches in sconces spluttered every few paces. When we had walked some way the air became very close. Shafts had been dug to the surface, but they were widely spaced. If there had been more, it would have given away the route of the mine. To make detection harder, fake air holes had been dug, and the real ones camouflaged.

The floor was level until we reached the turning. Then it began to slope upwards inside the hill towards the defences. Sitalkes told me that the digging had been easy; soft, sandy soil, with the picks striking very few rocks. The main danger was a cave-in. The roof and sides were braced with many close set beams and props. Even so, the almost continuous trickles of fine sand sifting down worried me.

We passed a stream of men hauling baskets of soil back to the mouth of the tunnel. By the time we reached the head of the mine, I was drenched in sweat, and finding it hard to breathe.

The men were naked, glistening and panting. They worked hard with picks and shovels, but went at it as quietly as they could. Their swords were piled next to the big water butts from which they often drank. Frequently all work halted, and everyone strained their ears to listen for sounds of the enemy. I held my breath the better to hear. So far, thank the gods, there was nothing. Eumaeus was right – fighting down here would be a bad business.

The gallery was directly under the walls. Some of their foundations were exposed above our heads. As the men laboured, the shifts changed and the hours passed and the space expanded, I thought of all the ways the defenders might detect our location. A shield laid on the ground amplified sound from below. If it was filled with water, the vibrations of our digging would ripple its surface. Or, of course, a deserter could have pointed out the place. When not thinking about that, I worried that the Thracians were not using enough props to hold up the cavern.

Finally – the darkness and the men's repetitious work made the passing of time uncertain – Sitalkes sent for an engineer called Charias. The latter pronounced himself satisfied. He also told me that above ground it was the beginning of the fourth watch of the night. The miners left, and for a time Sitalkes and myself were left alone. It was very quiet. Once, I heard a sharp cracking sound from behind us in the mine. I grabbed Sitalkes' arm, but he shook his head, and mouthed that was just the earth settling.

Two Thracians came down the tunnel and extinguished all the torches. They each carried a carefully shuttered lantern. One they handed to Sitalkes, the other they placed in a niche hacked out of the wall. Fire would be our enemy until we had left the head of the mine and it would become our ally.

We heard the new shift coming, horribly noisy after the silence. The bright, moving light of another lantern, casting unearthly shadows, preceded their arrival. They dragged with them all manner of combustibles – pitch, tar, pig fat, even a little naphtha – and the straw and dry wood they would burn. A stray spark now and we would all die a horrible death.

As the Thracians set about building the fire, I kept my eyes on the lanterns. My mind kept seeing sparks, and hearing the whoosh as the incendiaries ignited and the first screams of horror and pain. When I looked at the workers in the lamp-light the tattoos on their bare flesh moved, the animals and geometric patterns took on a life of their own. My head was swimming, the thin air clouding my thinking. Then I heard something I was sure was not conjured up by my imagination – a ringing sound of metal on metal. It came from in the tunnel. I glanced at Sitalkes. He was engrossed in the work.

I held out my hand, Sitalkes gave me his lantern, and I went back into the mine. Holding up the light revealed nothing except thin trickles of sand falling from the roof. After about twenty paces, I stopped and listened. There was no sound. I put my ear to the wall on my left. There it was – a rhythmic noise, like a gardener digging with a spade.

I did not run back – still fearing tripping, and dropping the lantern, and immolating all of us – but I walked fast.

'A countermine!'

Sitalkes and the dozen Thracians all goggled at me.

'Half of you get your swords, and come with me. The rest finish the fire.'

Now they all gazed at Sitalkes. I had spoken in Macedonian. Sitalkes spoke in Thracian. I caught some names – presumably he was detailing the best fighters – but I was already returning to the tunnel.

The head and shoulders of a man emerged from a hole in the wall. He squinted into the light I held. Deliberately, I put down the lantern, and drew my sword. By now the man was through, he rolled to his feet, drew his own blade. I lunged at his chest. As he blocked the blow with the edge of his blade there was a flash of sparks. My heart quailed. He feinted a cut at my head, dropped his shoulder, and drove it into my chest. I staggered across the tunnel, my back thumped into the opposite wall.

The breath was knocked out of my body. More figures were crawling through the opening like cockroaches. Hades knew how many they were. Sitalkes and a handful of Thracians were coming. We had to hold the enemy long enough to light the fire. If they overwhelmed us, they would bring down our tunnel away from the foundations, and all our efforts would have been in vain.

The man jabbed at my chest, but I turned the strike. His momentum carried him into me. Too close to use our weapons. I stamped the heel of a boot down onto his instep. His mouth opened in a grunt of surprise and pain. But he did not flinch. The fingers of his left hand were clawing at my throat, clenching, trying to crush my windpipe. I raised my boot again. He shifted his feet out of the way. Bracing my boot against the wall, I shoved him backwards. He stumbled, off balance, into two men behind him. All three went sprawling.

There was fighting everywhere: at brutal, close quarters, without shields.

Someone came at me from my left. I spun and cut in one motion. My blade opened up his chest. For a moment I thought I had killed one of the Thracians, but the mortally injured man wore a tunic.

Another was coming from the right. But then the dark tunnel was flooded in yellow-red light. Everyone – friend and foe – stood frozen, like sculptures on a frieze. A great gust of wind roared down the subterranean passage, as the fire sucked in the air. I turned my face. Sharp grains of sand stung my exposed flesh. It was impossible to breathe.

Someone pushed me aside, and ran off into the blackness. Another bumped into my back, drove me to my knees.

'Get out of here! Go!' Sitalkes was yelling, perhaps to me, his men, or himself.

Fighting to get air into my lungs, I used the wall to lever myself upright. Sitalkes seized my arm, began dragging me with him.

We ran from the terrible conflagration. Soon its light was gone, and we plunged through inky darkness. We knew we had reached where the mine turned when we ran full tilt into the wall. No sooner were we back on our feet, bruised and smarting, than there was a thunderous din far behind us. A few paces later, our backs were buffeted by dust and small debris as the foundations of the wall collapsed into the cavern.

Sunlight, fresh air. Escaped from the realm of Hades, we threw ourselves down full length, coughing and spitting. Someone was throwing up; another praising an outlandish god. I raised myself on an elbow next to Sitalkes, and counted. Ten dust-covered figures. We had only left two dead down there. No, three. One of the figures wore a torn tunic. There were no tattoos on his skin. Two men, naked and inked, dragged him to his knees. One pulled his head back by the hair, the other forced the tip of a sword down inside his collarbone. It is said to be an agonising way to die.

Al-al-al-al-ai!

Where there had been a wall was a jumble of fallen masonry. The battalion of Craterus had already laid planks across. They were over the tumbled defences.

Al-al-al-al-ai!

Gaza was about to experience the suffering that had been the fate of Tyre. I felt nothing but savage pleasure.

* * *

Alexander was in a dangerous mood. Although his shoulder was not healed, he had led the way into the breach, and there he had taken another wound to the leg.

Batis stood before Alexander. Philotas and Leonnatus guarded the prisoner. Batis had been ill treated. One of his eyes was swollen shut, and there was a gash across his forehead.

'Has he knelt to me?' Alexander's voice was high and harsh. When very angry his hair stood up like the mane of a lion.

Batis gave Alexander a look that was not only fearless, but defiant.

'Do you see his obstinate silence?'

Batis had not uttered a word.

'If you won't talk, I will make you groan.'

Alexander gave the orders. A chariot was brought up. Philotas and Leonnatus wrestled Batis to the ground. They tied a rope round his ankles, and fastened the other end to the chariot.

'You will not have the death you wanted.'

Alexander gave the signal, and the charioteer lashed the horses into a gallop. Then Batis screamed as he was dragged around the walls of Gaza.

The eunuch was alive after the first circuit; his arms still flailing desperately. After the second he was dead. His head lolled at an impossible angle.

Batis had been a corpulent man. Now his body was a mangled, hideous sight. Later flatterers, like Callisthenes, called him a Babylonian slug. They compared his treatment by Alexander to that of Hector by Achilles.

This was not Homeric revenge, but wanton cruelty. Hector had killed Achilles' lover Patroclus. Batis had not killed Hephaestion. Hector had been dead, Batis bound to the chariot alive. Homer himself had called the treatment of Hector shameful. Macedonians are raised to emulate Achilles – *always strive to be the best* – but we often forget the great harm that Achilles brought on the Achaeans. Achilles cared for his own honour, not his people. He was not a good king.

Agathion was tugging at my arm. 'Eumaeus . . .' Words failed the boy. He spread his hands wide in a gesture of despair.

CHAPTER TWENTY-FIVE

Autumn 332 BC to Spring 331 BC

EUMAEUS WAS DEAD WHEN I reached his tent.

The next day I cremated him. Leonnatus and Amyntas were there, along with his friend old Atarrhias and many of the other Lyncestians in the army. There were less of them than at Halicarnassus for Neoptolemus. Since then the shades of all too many had gone down to Hades. Issus and Tyre and Gaza, disease and accidents, all had taken their toll. As I put the torch to the pyre, Alexander came, using a spear as a crutch. I was grateful, but wished he had not brought Hephaestion.

The intensity of my grief took me by surprise. Eumaeus had always been there – dependable and trustworthy, talking old wives' tales of dreams, but someone to whom I could unburden my cares, speak my mind openly; the only one in the whole expedition to whom I could talk without reservation – and now he was not there. You can never know how much you rely on someone until they are gone.

Grief is a simple word in any language, but it covers a multitude of emotions. At first there is disbelief. You wake and for a blissful moment you have forgotten the loved one is dead. There are times when you hear or see something during the day, and you think, *I must tell them that*, or *What will old Eumaeus say?* before the crushing realisation that you will never talk to them again. Or, at least, they will never talk to you.

Regret follows for all the things you never said. *Too late now*, would remain the last words we spoke to each other. With regret comes guilt; unwanted memories of all the times one could have shown more consideration, or just greater kindness.

At night, alone in my tent, I found I frequently spoke to the shade of Eumaeus. Belief in an afterlife might have brought some comfort. The hope we would be reunited in the Isles of the Blessed, and walk together in the Elysian Fields. That path was closed to me after Olympias' curse. Although I had never really thought sentience beyond the grave feasible.

Aspects of grief are unworthy of a man. There is the irrational anger – *How could you desert me? How could you leave me alone?* And there is something like envy. Long ago in Argos the oxen did not arrive to pull the wagon of a priestess of Hera from the city to a rural shrine. Her two pious sons put themselves in the harnesses and hauled the heavy thing in their place. Their mother prayed to the gods to give them the greatest blessings of mankind. They lay down and died in their sleep. If death is a return to quiet and rest, perhaps we are better off out of this world of cares and tribulations, of doubts and pain. At times, like Achilles, I thought of lying in the dirt and taking a knife to my throat. Only if I could kill Hephaestion first. The hope of one day returning to Electra and Arrhabaeus, the son I had never seen, stayed my hand from both killings.

Like an automaton – riding, shitting, eating the food my slaves prepared, sitting silent and disconsolate in councils, failing to sleep at nights – I accompanied the army as it marched through the desert to Egypt. The first four days we hugged the coast, where the sand was smooth and compacted by the sea. The fleet shadowed us offshore, unloading water and provisions. On the fifth day, the fleet sailed ahead to the fortress of Pelusium, and we struck inland to avoid the Serbonian Marshland. Even my dulled senses knew it was a gamble. We carried supplies for three days, the length of our march. If Pelusium had not opened its gates to the fleet when we arrived, we would be in a parlous position.

The concern was not the Persians – Mazaces, the Satrap of Egypt, had already written to Alexander offering his submission – but the natives. The Egyptians had always detested Persian rule. They had risen against it many times, and maintained their independence for long stretches. Optimists among the Companions argued the Egyptians would welcome anyone as liberators from Darius. The more sceptical pointed out that the Egyptians had no reason to love the Macedonians. At the start of Alexander's reign, when Amyntas, son of Perdiccas, had been killed, one of that rival's foster-brothers, also called Amyntas, had fled to the Persians. Darius had given Amyntas command of many Greek mercenaries. Amyntas had escaped from Issus with four thousand hoplites. Seizing ships, he had made his way initially to Cyprus, where he gathered more men, then invaded Egypt. Amyntas claimed to be acting for Darius. At first his campaign went well, but then his troops turned to rape and plunder. When they were scattered, the natives massacred every one of them, Amyntas included. That was the Egyptians experience of Macedonians.

As so often, Alexander's gamble paid off. He, of course, put it down to divine providence. More and more, his conversation turned to the favour of the gods. When we came in sight of Pelusium, we were met by thousands of Egyptians, not carrying weapons, but offerings. They hailed Alexander as their Pharaoh.

Alexander sent Hephaestion with the fleet up the Nile to the ancient capital Memphis. I prayed he might drown. The army went by an inland route so that Alexander could sacrifice in some of the native temples. My prayers were not answered. Once army and fleet were reunited at Memphis, Alexander announced athletic and musical competitions. Performers braved the winter seas to come from all over the Greek world. It was splendid, but designed to ameliorate the outrage most in the army would feel about the ceremonies enacted today.

In the mild winter sunshine we processed around the white walls of Memphis by the Nile; Macedonians and Egyptians alike. I had no desire to be any part of it, or the barbaric rites to follow, but it was my duty to attend as a Companion of Alexander. Disillusioned and distraught, duty was the only thing I had left. Yet in the confusion of my thoughts that duty was becoming ever less straightforward. Who did I owe that duty to – Alexander, or my family and the traditions of Macedon?

Alexander emerged from a temple, and the natives sang hymns. Alexander was bare-chested, wearing a linen skirt. Around his neck was a blue and gold necklace that would have suited a rich man's concubine. A herd of priests, wearing the ludicrous animal masks of their bestial gods, escorted him to a throne. One of them placed an elaborate red and white crown on his head. Others handed him a sceptre in the shape of a shepherd's crook and a whip. He held them crossed across his body. Then they hailed him, first in their own tongue, then in badly pronounced Greek.

Pharaoh of Upper Egypt, Pharaoh of Lower Egypt, Son of the god Ra, Beloved of Ammon, the god Horus on earth.

To the Companions, Alexander had argued the necessity for these alien rituals. Egypt was rich. We needed their grain and money. There were four million Egyptians. We could not leave a large enough garrison to hold them down when we marched east against Darius. We needed their acquiescence. Their priests were powerful. The populace obeyed the priesthood. If it took an outlandish ceremony, Egypt was worth the price.

It reeked of sophistry. Cleitus the Black and Philotas argued against such a degrading foreign spectacle. Alexander over-ruled the opposition. He was within his rights. A King of the Macedonians has to listen to his subjects, but he does not have to follow their advice. But, of course, if he ignores it, or if he fails on the battlefield, or if he goes against their ancestral customs, they do not have to follow him anymore. The Macedonians under arms acclaim their King, but they can also depose him. There are always others waiting in the shadows.

* * *

There was a breeze from the north-west, cool from the sea. It was a fine place to found a city. Alexander was full of enthusiasm. He was striding along marking out the walls. Architects and builders, Companions and Royal Pages, foreign envoys and Egyptian priests trailed in his wake. They had run out of chalk, so someone had suggested using flour from the ration bags of the escort. Alexander was scattering handfuls of the stuff.

I went and sat in the shade of a palm tree. Even in early spring it was warm in the Nile Delta. I reread the letter from Electra. The news it contained was unexceptional. Arrhabaeus was healthy and growing fast. His hair was fair like mine, and he had an amiable disposition. Our house and estates were flourishing. My mother in Lebaea was well. The presents I had sent from

Tyre had been received with pleasure. She loved me and missed me. She prayed for my health and safety.

There was nothing the malice of Olympias, or my own highly strung nerves, could construe into a coded incitement to treason. Yet somehow its open affection further depressed my spirits. Obviously it was written before word of the death of Eumaeus had reached Pella. Rereading it merely increased my loneliness. Agathion and Leucippe were obedient servants, but I could not talk to them. My nephew Amyntas was too upright, my kinsman Leonnatus too devoted to Alexander. The rest of the Companions I could not altogether trust. My isolation was near complete. I longed for nothing except to leave this endless campaign and return home to my wife and son. Self-pity is a dangerous emotion. Like all strong emotions it can drive a man to desperate actions.

'Lyncestes!'

Medius the Thessalian was walking over with Antipater's youngest son Iolaus. They were lovers. It was open and respectable: the older man, the *erastes*, and the younger *eromenos*, the object of his desire. Few families like mine had a hereditary reason to avoid such affairs. Medius and Iolaus were happy in each other's company. I envied them their close companionship, their happiness.

'May we join you?' Iolaus was a polite, well-brought-up Macedonian boy. As he spoke, I abruptly saw myself through his eyes. My beard unshaven and my hair hacked short in mourning; a silent figure who sat alone. I realised he pitied me.

'It would be my pleasure.'

They sat and Medius produced a jar. We drank the cool, sweet wine, and talked about nothing in particular. When it was finished, he produced another.

'So why are we bound for an oasis in the middle of the Libyan desert?' My tone sounded querulous, although that was not my intention.

'To secure the western frontier,' Medius said. 'Ambassadors from the city of Cyrene will meet us on route to exchange oaths of alliance.'

'They will be waiting on the coast, not five days journey to the south at this place called Siwa.'

'Alexander wants to consult the oracle of Ammon,' Medius said.

Ammon had long been known to the Greeks. It was the name of Zeus in Africa. At the siege of Thebes, Zeus Ammon had prophesied our victory.

After a good-mannered glance at both of us, Iolaus spoke. 'Some of the other Royal Pages overheard Alexander tell Hephaestion that his ancestors Herakles and Perseus both travelled there.'

'They were both the sons of a Greek god,' I said, 'just as Alexander is now the son of an Egyptian one called Ra.' The habit of bitterness was not easily cast off.

Iolaus laughed. The wine had flushed his cheeks. 'It is whispered that Olympias claims he was fathered by a god in the form of a snake.'

'The Egyptians have another story,' Medius said. 'Olympias was seduced in secret by their last Pharaoh Nectanebo.'

We were all quite drunk now.

'Olympias put a crown on the head of Philip's murderer,' I said. 'She hated Philip, but Alexander would be nothing without him; just as he would be nothing without the Macedonians.' I nodded to Medius. 'And, of course, the Thessalians.'

Neither said anything, but they did not remonstrate.

'If Alexander thinks he is the son of a god, let him go and fight his battles with his new father.'

'Look!' Iolaus jumped up, pointing.

Great flocks of birds were descending on the lines of flour that marked the walls: gulls from the sea, waders from the marshes. They squawked and flapped, fighting over the feast. Soon all the food would be gone, and it would be as if Alexander's plans had never existed.

A youthful figure was bounding towards us; Hector, one of Parmenion's sons, another Royal Page.

'Guess what?' he said. 'Aristander has saved the day again. Our venerable seer told Alexander that it is a sign from the gods that his new city will flourish.'

'How did the old charlatan reach that interpretation?' Medius said.

'Like the birds, immigrants will come from every side.'

With advice like that no wonder Alexander was losing his way.

* * *

The expedition to Siwa started badly and got worse. The local guides said there were two routes. One was shorter, but harder through open desert to the west. The other eastern path was longer, but easier, running mainly over ridges of rock and through other oases to reach Siwa. Characteristically, Alexander chose the quickest.

As well as some of the Companions and the Royal Pages, Alexander took a detachment of a hundred soldiers; just enough to deter any nomads or bandits. Half the troops were

Companion Cavalry, half Agrianes. The latter were given horses for speed of march. As there was said to be no water or forage on the way, we had to carry all our provisions on a long train of camels. They were driven by the locals. Camels are refractory beasts; large and noisy and foul smelling, with an unpleasant habit of spitting. No wonder they scare horses that are unused to them. Given the predicted hardships of the march, I was not going to risk Borysthenes or any of my string of warhorses, so bought a couple of hardy-looking local African nags.

Although it was springtime, we travelled by night. The moon was near full, and it cast a blue-white light that made the endless sand dunes sparkle like ice. The only sound was the plod of our animals' feet and the creak of their tack. Once I saw the pointed ears of a desert fox. Otherwise the emptiness was complete. Ominously, the path was marked by the skeletons of camels. In the day, we erected shelters, and rested shaded from the glare of the sun. The guides warned us about snakes; there were many of them, all poisonous. Iolaus said he had heard they could take the form of beautiful women. When you approached them, they reverted to serpentine shape and dragged you down into their lairs. Medius laughed, and said it was a parable about the dangers of consorting with women. I no longer felt quite so envious of their happiness. Before we left our servants at the coast, Agathion had shaved me, and Leucippe trimmed my hair to look more respectable. Outwardly, and to an extent inwardly, I was more myself. Time dulls even the sharpest pain, or perhaps we become inured to suffering.

At dawn on the fourth day, we were setting up our tents when I saw a low line of black hills on the southern horizon. I thought the guides' claim that the journey would take five days was borne out. Not far now. Then there was a commotion. The guides were pointing and jabbering, the camel drivers rushing to tether the beasts in a circle, their heads facing north.

'Take down the tents.' Alexander was striding through the camp. 'There is a storm coming. Lash everything down. Hobble the horses inside the ring of camels. Get their backs to the south.'

The line to the south was taller and already appreciably closer. Now it was revealed as a high mass of dark clouds. They were purple-black, roiling, pulsing with lightning. Around us the air was oddly still, but seemed to crackle with tension. In my head was a dull, throbbing ache.

'Cover your faces. This will soon blow over.' Alexander was at his best in a crisis.

The storm seemed to gather speed as it approached. A great cliff rearing up to the heavens. Lightning stalked at its base. The ground shook. The noise was as if every mill in the world was grinding towards us. Then it was upon us. The force was like a door slamming in your back. I staggered a pace or two forward, grimly hanging on to the bridles of my mounts. The local nags were head down, hunched, infinitely patient and enduring. Out in the swirling gloom other horses were screaming and plunging; Macedonian voices yelling as they fought to control them.

I had wrapped a scarf over my face, pulled up the hood of my cloak, but the flying sand was in my eyes, mouth and ears. It was hard to draw breath, almost as if drowning. There was a story that Cambyses, the Persian King, had sent an army of fifty thousand into this desert. A storm got up, and buried them all. *Don't panic, be a man. This cannot last. Just close your mind, just endure like the ponies.*

A short figure, leaning at an improbable angle into the wind, fought his way to my side. Only his eyes were visible. A bolt of lightning showed their different shades of hyacinth. Alexander put his arm round my shoulders. We supported each other against the fury of the storm.

'Courage, Lyncestes.' His mouth was next to my ear. His breath was sweet, as if perfumed.

'Why are we here?'

For a moment I thought he had not heard above the howling cacophony, but then he gripped me tighter, almost as a lover would.

'My mother told me things before we left Pella. Ammon will tell me if they are true.'

Of course they are not true, I wanted to shout. *Your mother is a lying Epirote witch. You were not sired by a snake or a god. Your father was Philip. The Macedonians chose you as King, not some deity or providence.*

'And I need to know if all my father's murderers were punished.'

His words planted a pain in my chest as if I had swallowed a shard of glass. I knew then that Olympias had told him about the night on the slopes of Mount Bermion, about my sacrilege, and her curse. I thought of my brothers, broken and hanging on their crosses. I thought about the other lies she would have whispered in his ear. If Ammon said I was guilty, I would be killed as a traitor. Electra and our son would be exposed to the vengeance of Olympias. Her cruelty was infinite. And I thought anything could happen in the heart of this storm. A silent thrust of a knife, the next morning a body half buried in the sand, his killer unknown.

Alexander squeezed me tight. 'I must tour the men.' And he went, staggering off through the storm.

At dawn, the sky was clear except for a few high clouds to the south. Several of the horses had broken free. Their flight had panicked and scattered some of the camels. Their drivers had not run after them, but six of the Agrianes had chased into the storm after them. We found one of their bodies. The rest were lost, but we did not look hard. There were more pressing worries. The camels had been carrying skins of water. There was next to none left. And we were lost. The path was buried, the whole landscape made anew. Not a tree or a hill or an outcrop of rock. No landmark, just endless new rolling dunes of sand.

'Siwa lies south-south-east,' Alexander said. 'We can navigate as sailors do by the sun and the stars.'

Except none of us were sailors.

We drank the last of the water, and set off under the hot African sun. There was no time to waste. Without water we would not last long. In a day, perhaps two, we would be too weak to carry on.

The newly piled sand was powdery and yielding. With every step, man and beast sank and slipped. After only a couple of hours, the first soldier collapsed. I went with Alexander to force him back to his feet, between us we half carried him, and put him on one of my ponies.

After a time your mind closes down. You just put one foot in front of the other, leading the animals up and down one slope after another. You think about nothing, especially not your thirst.

The excited shouts were an irritating intrusion. If I let them distract me, started to think, I knew I would stop, and never resume this agonising march.

'Lyncestes!' It was Hector, Parmenion's son. He had me by the arm. 'Stop and look!'

Like an animal emerging from a painful hibernation, I gazed round. There was no sun. Clouds rolled overhead. The first drops of rain spattered into my face.

We gathered the rain in anything we could: tents, shields. Some ran round with their heads tipped back, trying to drink it as it fell. We scooped it out of hollows with our helmets, filled every skin we still had. We were still lost, but now we had hope.

The rain had dampened the sand, made it a firmer footing. The rest of the day the walking was easier. As the sun went down, I saw some tiny black specks in the sky to our left. Just as in my childhood in the woods of Lyncestis, the rooks were going home to roost. And so I knew the direction we had to follow.

We marched all night and reached the oasis of Siwa not long after dawn. A long green line in the desert, thousands and thousands of trees surrounding a rocky citadel on which was the temple of Zeus Ammon.

The inhabitants saw us coming. They streamed out in welcome, singing and bringing cool drinks and morsels of food. Alexander sent Hephaestion and the Royal Pages to see to the animals and our quarters. Hephaestion looked hurt. Somehow I knew Alexander wanted to be alone. His audience with the god meant everything to him. Whatever he was told would define his existence, and he did not want to share that with anyone. Yet he let the rest of the Companions accompany him through the delicious shade of the trees. Swallows flitted and banked above the date palms, and doves cooed in their branches. Everywhere was the sound of water running from innumerable springs. The

Elysian Fields could not be more beautiful. In such a place, after our ordeal, anything was possible.

The chief priest met Alexander at the steps of the temple. A thin, wiry man with the physique of an ascetic, he raised a hand in greeting.

'*O pai Dios*,' the priest said in heavily accented Greek; O Son of Zeus.

Only Alexander was allowed inside to consult the oracle. We waited, sitting in the shade outside.

Eventually, Alexander returned. Everyone crowded round him, asking questions. He looked straight at me. 'All the murderers of *Philip* have been punished.'

Relief, not for myself, but for my family, coursed through my veins, but I noticed the odd stress on *Philip*. He had not said *my father*. Something fundamental had changed.

'But what else did Zeus Ammon say?' Philotas asked sharply. We were all exhausted and dirty; not in the mood for games.

Alexander smiled. 'What my heart desired.'

CHAPTER TWENTY-SIX

Spring 331 BC

OUR RETURN FROM SIWA was uneventful. On the way, Alexander formally laid the first stone and founded his new city in the Nile Delta. By the time we reached Memphis, rumours abounded about the trip to the oasis of Zeus Ammon. In the desert, when we lagged behind, the rooks had waited, chattering until we caught up. Some versions held the birds – often ravens or crows – spoke in human voices. Others said we had been guided there and back by snakes. These too were credited with speaking like men. Presumably these African creatures were fluent in Macedonian or Greek.

Every idler in the marketplace could tell you what the god had vouchsafed to Alexander in his solitary consultation. Zeus Ammon had promised the King, not just victory over Darius, but dominion over the whole world. The deity had warned Alexander against blasphemy: the murderers of Philip had all been punished, but it was sacrilege to suggest that the King's father could ever be killed, for he was immortal; none other than Zeus Ammon himself.

For those of us who had been there, patiently waiting outside, it was easy enough to believe these indeed accurately reflected the words spoken. In our hearing the chief priest had greeted Alexander on the steps of the temple with *O pai Dios*, O Son of Zeus. That fateful saying was much on my mind.

As far as we knew, Darius remained in Babylon gathering levies from across the breadth of the eastern provinces of the Persian Empire. It made little odds. Wherever he was we would have to seek him out, defeat his army in one more great battle, and this time make sure Darius died. After that, we would burn Persepolis and Susa, retain what was worth keeping of the Persian Empire, presumably as far as the Tigris, so we ruled the wealthiest province of Babylonia, then we could return home. Another year of campaigning, two at most. To me, returning home was everything.

The army was rested after a peaceful winter in Egypt. Alexander had decided to leave a garrison of four thousand, mostly mercenaries. We had hoped to receive significant reinforcements from Macedon. Antipater had sent only nine hundred; four hundred mercenaries, and five hundred Thracians. The Regent wrote that Olympias was hindering his efforts at recruitment in Macedon by sheltering her clients from the draft. Olympias aside, there was trouble in Greece, and more troops could not be spared. The Spartans, obstinately clinging to long vanished glories, had refused to join the League of Corinth. Now, one of their kings, Agis, was campaigning against those on Crete who supported Macedon. Antipater was concerned the fighting might spread to the mainland. Alexander sent orders for Craterus' brother Amphoterus to take our Aegean fleet to the island.

Another problem would have to be settled before we could march east against Darius. The Samarians, a people of southern Syria, had risen against Andromachus, the Macedonian officer left to oversee them. They had captured Andromachus and burnt him alive. The savagery and stupidity of these eastern races beggars belief. Did they imagine Alexander would ignore their perfidy, or were they so inflated with arrogance that they thought they could defy the Macedonians in arms?

After a great military parade in Memphis, with sacrifices to Zeus Ammon, the army departed. Hephaestion had been sent ahead to build pontoon bridges over the branches of the Nile and the various canals that had to be crossed. The cavalry marched last. After the men had set off, Philotas gave a dinner for some of the officers and other friends. As we would follow the army by boat the next day, we drank until late in the night.

* * *

Iolaus was shaking me. Our baggage and servants had gone ahead.

'Wake up, Lyncestes. The last boat is leaving now.'

Opening my eyes brought a sharp pain in my head. 'Water.'

He held out a jug. Lifting my head brought a wave of nausea. Last night was a blur. I remembered being in deep discussion with Philotas. His mistress Antigone had been there; his brother Hector too. Iolaus had been serving the drinks. I hoped I had not been too indiscreet, not said anything that could be construed as treasonous.

I drained the jug; felt sick, but kept it down.

Iolaus laughed. 'The others are in no better condition than you.' He gave me a hunk of bread and cheese. 'Here, eat this as we walk. We need to get on that boat.'

It was one of those native vessels, built out of reeds, that looked like a long, thin basket for holding bread. Low in the water, it was crammed with people.

'Over here.' Hector helped me aboard. The slight sway of the boat increased my queasiness. At least I could always throw up over the side.

'That is everyone,' Philotas said. 'Cast off.'

The Egyptian boatmen jabbered in their incomprehensible tongue and looked mutinous.

Philotas stood up, and clouted two of them round the ears. 'I said, *Cast off*, you crocodile-worshipping barbarians.'

The boatmen looked at each other unhappily.

Philotas raised his fist.

The Egyptians pushed us out from the dock.

Once we were in midstream the current took us and bore us smoothly to the north.

Egypt would be nothing without the Nile. The land is best imagined as a narrow strip of greenery running south to north through arid desert. When the river rises, the peasants irrigate the fields. When it falls, they plant in the fertile mud. The yields are greater than anywhere else in the world. The Egyptians themselves are an ancient race, mired in superstition, addicted to magic. They worship cats and dogs and other animals. Although always ready to murder each other, they are cowards and make terrible soldiers. That they defied the Persians for decades proves nothing. The Persians are even bigger cowards.

Closing my eyes, I retreated into my hangover.

What had happened to my foster-brother Alexander? Some Greek sophists argue that the isolation of power corrupts. Of course they are wrong. It is the people around the ruler that undermine his character. Olympias had started the rot with her hatred of his father, and her dark hints of snakes and divine parentage. Nothing might have come of it if we had remained in

Macedon. But in the east, Alexander had Persians grovelling to him, performing adoration as if he were a god; Egyptian priests crowning him as the son of Ra; the oracle at Siwa hailing him as the son of Zeus Ammon. This spring even some embassies from the Greeks had gone as far as to recognise him as divine. For all their talk of freedom, the Greeks are habitual sycophants. They are like Macedonians gone soft and rotten. If only I had spoken to him on the way to Siwa. But how can you talk in the howling jaws of a sandstorm? Nowadays, hemmed round with courtiers and ceremonies, it was almost impossible to be alone with Alexander.

'Lyncestes, wake up!' It was Hector. The motion of the boat had changed. It seemed slower, if not stationary in the water. Men started shouting, their voices high with alarm. There was a loud splash, as if someone had fallen overboard.

'Wake up! The boat is sinking!'

A series of splashes as bodies hit the river. Through the lingering wine fumes, I realised the youth was right. There was water coming up round my boots. The overladen boat was not so much sinking as coming apart. The boatmen had already abandoned the doomed vessel. They were swimming to the eastern shore. I looked out over the brown waters. The river must be over a mile wide. We were in midstream, but slightly nearer the eastern bank.

'Fuck!' Swearing repetitively, I tugged off my boots.

Philotas dived, almost gracefully from the bow. Iolaus jumped after him.

I knew I would not be able to swim wearing my sword-belt; its ungainly weight would drag me down. But the sword was the eagle-headed one I had taken from the Illyrian, and the belt was the scarlet one, my last link to Neoptolemus. I slipped it over my head, and held it irresolute in my hands. It felt like casting off a part of my personality.

Hector was standing next to me.

'Swim,' I said.

'There are crocodiles in the Nile.'

'Swim fast.'

'I can't swim faster than a crocodile.'

'No, but you might swim faster than me.'

I got to my feet, dropped my sword-belt, and took him by the shoulders, then pushed him over the side. The boat was settling so fast I could almost step into the river. Pushing off, I was about to swim after the rest when something made me look back at the boat.

Only the stem and stern were above the surface. Someone was on the other side, swimming towards the more distant shore. It was Hector. I called, but he did not hear.

As I set off after him, the force of the current gripped me. The Nile does not flow very fast, but it is strong beyond measuring. I resigned myself to its hold, and shaped a course after the youth. The water was warm, nothing like the cold lakes in Lyncestis. The alarm and exercise had dispelled my hangover.

Hector had a head start, but I was a strong swimmer. I had to negotiate a trunk of a tree carried down by the river, then judged where the river was taking him, and set off after. When I paused to look, the bank was still far off, but Hector was closer, although beginning to flounder. I ploughed through the water in his direction.

When I had nearly closed the distance, he began thrashing desperately, and went under. Taking a breath, I dived. The water was brown, full of silt, impossible to see through. I surfaced, treading water, and looking round wildly. No sign of him. I shouted his name, although I knew it could not help.

Hector came up behind me, then sank again. I turned and dived. My hands groping blindly closed on his sodden tunic. Getting a grip, I hauled him to the surface. His eyes were open. They stared through me with a look I had seen on wounded men on the battlefield. Keeping his face just above the water with my left arm, I swam with my right and my legs. Hector was a dead weight, but at least he was beyond struggling.

All the false well-being drained out of me; the after-effects of the wine returning. My limbs felt heavy, my whole body exhausted. Doggedly, I ploughed on through the river.

Near the riverbank the current seemed stronger. It swept us downstream. Our progress towards the shore was terribly slow. A low dark object was coming downstream towards us. I had never experienced such abject terror. If it was a crocodile, I knew my cowardice would make me sacrifice Hector in an overwhelming desire to try to save myself. I could let go of him now. The insidious thought was hard to dispel. Like a man possessed, I clawed our way towards the bank.

My hand touched the bottom. We had reached a mudbank. My feet sinking into the slime, I got him under the shoulders and dragged him out of the water. No sign of any crocodiles in the river. I remembered they were also at home on land. With vigour renewed by fear, I hauled him to the top of the levee. None of the monstrous creatures were in sight.

As I lay Hector on his back, his eyes gazed into mine. He gave a great sigh. Thank the gods he would be all right. Then I saw he had stopped breathing.

Kneeling astride him, I pushed down on his chest. I had to force the water out of his lungs, get him to breathe. I don't know how long I continued. It seemed like eternity. Eventually, I accepted it was hopeless, and I collapsed beside him.

That was how they found us – side by side, the living and the dead.

* * *

Alexander gave Hector a magnificent funeral, but said there was to be no further public mourning, the army had to march. Agathion told me some of the camp followers thought Alexander secretly was not unhappy. The King wanted to be free of the influence of Parmenion, and this was one less of the old general's sons for whom a high command would have to be found.

Hector's death taught me another lesson about grief. It is contagious, and spreads like a fever. One case leads to another. The new loss reopens the wounds of the old. Awake in the dogwatches of the night I thought about Neoptolemus and Eumaeus. In snatches of troubled sleep, sometimes I dreamt of alternative worlds where my brothers had not conspired to kill Philip, and ended up hanging from crosses. More often I dreamt that Black Cleitus had not saved Alexander at the Granicus, or that Alexander had succumbed to the fever in Tarsus. In all these dreams I was led out of the shadows to face the Macedonians assembled under arms. Sometimes they acclaimed me King, sometimes they hefted javelins or picked up stones to put me to death.

On the fourth night after Hector's funeral, Parmenion summoned me to dinner in his quarters. It was a small and unhappy group: the old general and me, Philotas and his mistress Antigone, with Iolaus serving. None of us had much appetite, and we quickly turned to drinking. Parmenion and Philotas were unshaven in mourning.

'I should have saved him,' I said.

'You did everything you could,' Parmenion said. 'It was an accident.'

'It is my fault,' Philotas said. 'If I had not insisted the boat cast off when overladen, he would be alive.' In his suffering, Philotas had put aside his arrogance, and was far more human.

'It was an accident,' Parmenion repeated. 'It could not have been foreseen.'

Our talk was fractured and disjointed with unhappiness and alcohol.

'*O pai Dios*,' Parmenion mused, as if thinking aloud, 'O Son of Zeus. Some say the native priest at Siwa mispronounced *O paidion*. He meant to call Alexander *My boy*.'

Philotas shook his head. 'Greeks have been going to the oracle of Zeus Ammon for centuries. The priests there speak good Greek. Lyncestes and I were there. There was no mistake. The priest said what Alexander wanted to hear.'

'Even if it was a mistake, it makes no odds,' I said. 'Alexander now believes the nonsense of Olympias that Zeus was his father, not Philip. All his victories were won by him with the help of his divine sire.'

Philotas snorted with derision. 'All his victories were won with Macedonian blood. It was not a god that held the left at Granicus and Issus, but Parmenion; not Zeus that led the *hypaspists*, but my brother Nicanor; not Ammon that charged at the head of the Companions, but me. All his victories were won by us and Macedonian courage. We have won his victories for him.'

It was all true, but I tried to turn our thoughts to better things. 'One last campaign against Darius, and we can return to our estates. You can take the bones of Hector home.' Returning home was my obsession. 'If not later this year, then next.'

'If the *Son of Zeus* decides to ever return to Macedon.' Philotas said the epithet with contempt.

'The Royal Pages overhear Alexander and Hephaestion at night.' I had forgotten young Iolaus was there. The boldness with which Antipater's son spoke reminded me of Neoptolemus when we were young. 'Alexander has been talking of Parthia and Bactria and Sogdiana, even India. He intends to march to the encircling ocean. I heard him say that myself.'

Somehow it was what I had feared – being led ever further from home by a man in the grip of a divine mania. 'He must be stopped.'

'How?' Parmenion asked.

'We must make him see reason.'

Parmenion shrugged. 'He does not listen to me; does nothing but belittle my advice.'

'He will not listen to me,' Philotas said. 'We have never been close, unlike some of the foster-brothers.'

They were all looking at me.

'It is impossible to be alone with him,' I said.

'One night when he is on duty, Iolaus can get you into his tent,' Philotas said.

'I will talk to him,' I said.

'And if you cannot make him see reason?' Philotas asked.

I said nothing.

'Then he must be stopped,' Parmenion said. 'After that, it will be as you and I discussed at the Syrian Gates.'

And so, with no explicit statement, the fateful decision was made.

CHAPTER TWENTY-SEVEN

Spring 331 BC

WAITING IS ALWAYS THE hardest part. Every fibre in your being screams just get this over. Your breathing is shallow, you fidget with barely suppressed anxiety, your mind finds it difficult to hold any thought except for better or worse just let this happen.

Tonight it was worse than before battle. Then you have your comrades around you. A sympathetic look, a pat on the shoulder, a few words of encouragement; they help you get through. You know that every one of them, like you, is praying that they do not reveal their fear, and that when the dread moment comes that they do not let the others down.

I was alone in the middle of the night. Agathion and Leucippe I had sent away. It would have been impossible to appear normal in front of them.

The army had crossed the desert from Pelusium and had made camp near Gaza. We had had to wait for a night when Iolaus' squad of Royal Pages were on duty. As a Companion, my tent was pitched close to the King's pavilion. When all was ready, Iolaus would fetch me.

Philotas had visited me the morning after the dinner with his father. The Persians were right – something decided when drunk was best reviewed later sober. I had told Philotas that I stood by my decision. Something had to be done. To avoid suspicion, or retaliation should anything go wrong, there had been no more meetings. Iolaus would send word the day before he was on duty.

The night was quiet. There were no clouds and no moon. The stars enamelled the blue vault of the heavens. The air smelt of woodsmoke and horses with a faint tang from the latrines. In my mind I went over again and again the justifications for what I was about.

The Macedonians elect our king. We swear an oath to fight for him, to protect him: *no man, so long as I am alive, and see the light of day, shall lay the weight of his hands on you or your descendants.* But the oath is contingent and the bond reciprocal. The king has a duty to his subjects – to consult them, to listen to their concerns, to lead them to victory, to give them justice, above all to serve their interests. A king is not free to pursue his own course. Kingship is a noble servitude. If the king betrays their trust the Macedonians can leave his service, depose him, and acclaim another.

Our customs meshed with what I could remember of Greek philosophy from the time at Mieza with Aristotle. There are three kinds of polities: rule by one man, the few, or the many. Each has two opposed sides – the good and the bad. If the poor majority rule for the benefit of all it is a democracy, but if they rule in their own interests it is nothing but ochlocracy, mob rule. Likewise, if a few rich men govern for everyone it is an aris-tocracy, literally the rule of the best, but if they look to their own concerns it degenerates into an oligarchy. The contrast is even more striking in an autocracy. If the ruler chooses Virtue, like Heracles, he is a king, and his subjects should love him. If, however, he indulges his own desires, and turns to Vice, he is a tyrant, and it becomes the duty of his subjects to reform him. If that fails, they must cast him down.

A Macedonian king is not elected by god but by the people. He is a first among equals. Alexander, the self-proclaimed Son of Zeus, surrounded by fawning Persians and Egyptians, led astray by sycophants, had forgotten the ways of our ancestors. It was my duty to bring my friend and foster-brother back to the path of Macedon.

From somewhere out in the desert a fox barked. For old Eumaeus a fox had signified a violent enemy, rapacious and wicked. An enemy that will not attack openly, but plots in a sly, underhand way.

What if Alexander did not listen, remained deaf to our customs, refused to return to the ways of Macedon? *If I must die, let me first do some great thing, that men thereafter shall remember me.* Not all tyrannicides were well remembered. Archelaus had been a typical Argead tyrant, capricious and cruel. He had broken his word to Crataeas and Hellanocrates, the Royal Pages he had used his position to seduce, and had handed over another, Decamnichus, against Macedonian law, to be flogged by Euripides. Yet when the young men had justly punished Archelaus' *hubris* with death they were condemned as traitors.

If it came to such a desperate act, the future would make its own judgement. Perhaps I would be remembered like Crataeas as a treacherous man, avid with ambition, in love with monarchy, and grasping at power. There was a better possibility. Long ago, Harmodius and Aristogiton had personal motives for plotting the death of Hippias the tyrant of Athens. They failed, only killing the tyrant's brother Hipparchus. Yet they were immortalised in statues and literature as patriots who risked everything for freedom. Of course, like Crataeas and his friends, they were executed. Few tyrannicides survived.

'Lyncestes.'

Iolaus was here. It was the beginning of the third watch of the night, gone midnight. Half of me had hoped he would not come.

I put on the white sword-belt my father had awarded me for killing the Illyrian, slid my new blade into the scabbard, slung my cloak round my shoulders, and reached for my hat.

'There is not much time.' Understandably, Iolaus sounded scared. There was plenty of time. The next group of Royal Pages would take over at dawn.

I jammed the *kausia* down on my head, and followed him out into the night.

The guards would be awake on the palisades, but the rest of the camp was sleeping. If anyone was about they would not question a man in the distinctive yellow-bordered purple cloak of a Companion of the King walking with a youth wearing the cloak of a Royal Page.

From my days as a Page I knew the dynamics within a squad. Irrespective of seniority, some boys had influence because of their own personalities or the status of their fathers. Iolaus, the confident son of the Regent Antipater, had both. There should be no problems gaining admittance.

Iolaus took me to the rear entrance of the great pavilion Alexander had captured from Darius at Issus. It was the way Macedonian kings other than Alexander would have had girls or boys discreetly brought to their beds. Every night the King was guarded by a squad of nine Royal Pages. Only if an enemy were close at hand, or there was some other clear danger, would one or more of the seven Companions with the title of

Bodyguard be in attendance. In Egypt, one of the Bodyguards had died. Leonnatus had been appointed in his place. I was glad there was no likelihood of running into my kinsman.

The entrance was unguarded. I paused in front of its threshold.

Iolaus was impatient. 'We cannot delay.'

'You are sure Hephaestion is not with him?'

'Yes.'

'Or the Persian girl Barsine?'

'He is alone.'

'And you removed the dagger he keeps under his pillow?'

Iolaus just nodded. His eyes were wide with fear.

One more step and there was no way back. Actually, there was already no way back. Parmenion and Philotas knew what I intended. If I did not go through with it, they would assume I had lost my nerve, and would tell Alexander of their incitement to treason. To save their lives they would have to denounce me first. Antigone, Philotas' mistress, would be their witness.

I did not want to die here, but live to return to Electra and our son. Apart from Iolaus, there would be eight Pages in the pavilion. Some would be sleeping. As the entrance was unguarded, some must have been suborned by Iolaus. If the worst happened, I should be able to fight my way out and reach Parmenion. Then the old general would have to play the role taken by Antipater after the death of Philip. Philotas commanded the Companion Cavalry, his brother Nicanor the *hypaspists*. The phalanx would have to be won over. Craterus was a problem. Philotas would insist on his death. Half the battalion of Perdiccas were Lyncestians. Most of the battalions with the field army were recruited from the uplands. I would not be the first king of Macedon to be acclaimed after killing his predecessor. Hephaestion, of course, would not long outlive his lover.

But I did not want to kill Alexander. I wanted to save him; to make everything as it had been before we came here. As they say, it is a fine line between love and hate.

There was no point in further hesitation. It would happen as the Fates decreed.

Through the entrance was a vestibule. It was empty. Iolaus pointed out the hanging over the door to the bedchamber, and stood back. I slipped through the curtain.

The room was smaller than I remembered from Issus. The same gold and bronze ornaments, the same rich tapestries, but somehow closer together.

'Lyncestes.'

Alexander was wide awake, sitting on his bed, propped up with pillows. He was wearing a plain tunic, and had no weapons. Strangely, he appeared unsurprised to find an armed man in his bedroom.

'The Macedonians are unhappy.' All my carefully prepared words had crumbled to dust.

'Why?'

'You surround yourself with barbarians.'

'They are necessary to rule the empire.' Alexander spoke as if we were debating in a gymnasium.

'Aristotle taught us to treat them like animals or plants.'

'Aristotle was wrong.'

'It is revolting to see them prostrating themselves before you.'

'Everywhere custom is king. It is their way. I do not demand it from Macedonians.'

This was getting nowhere. The demand had to be made.

'When we have defeated Darius, and taken our revenge by burning the Persian capitals, you must swear an oath before the Macedonians that you will lead us home.'

Alexander actually smiled, as if totally at ease. 'That is impossible. I explained at Tyre. We have to hold the heartlands of the Persian Empire, or we expose Macedon to generations of warfare.'

'You are lying!' My temper was rising. 'You and Hephaestion have been heard plotting to lead us to Sogdiana and India, and beyond to the ends of the earth.'

'You understand nothing!' Alexander's odd-coloured eyes flashed with anger in the torchlight. 'It is my destiny!'

'As the *Son of Zeus*?' My tone was sneering. 'A man who demands to be believed a god shows contempt for the gods as well as men.'

'Careful what you say.'

'You cannot believe the lies of your mother and some Egyptian priests. Your father was Philip, not some god.'

Alexander rolled off the bed, pulled a sword from under the pillows.

Damn Iolaus. He had lied.

'Never call that man my father!' Alexander's voice was high and harsh with anger.

Instinctively, my own sword was in my hand.

We both dropped into a fighting crouch.

'You would draw a blade on the man you swore to protect?'

'If he is no longer the same man.'

As I spoke, the hangings were hauled back on either side. Armed men bundled into the room.

I still had a chance, if I struck immediately. In their haste they were getting in each other's way.

But I dropped my sword. Whatever he had become, I could not kill my friend.

Philotas and Leonnatus seized my arms.

'I am sorry you chose this path,' Alexander said.

'Let me put him to the torture.' Hephaestion was beside Alexander; his face glowing like a malicious child promised a cruel treat.

'There is no point.' Alexander gazed into my eyes. 'I know all your secrets. Your slave Agathion reports to me, as before him did old Eumaeus.'

And then I knew there was no loyalty to be had on this earth.

CHAPTER TWENTY-EIGHT

Spring to Summer 331 BC

THE CART HAD FOUR wheels, and was pulled by two draught horses. A leather canopy like a tent fitted over the top. There was a straw mattress at each end of its interior, a chamber pot, and a steel ring screwed into the centre of the floor. At night, the manacles on my wrists were chained to the ring. The cart was my prison.

My jailor was a large, brutal man called Copreus, *Dungman*. The name was fitting as he emptied the chamber pot; not just the night soil, during the day I was not allowed to visit the camp latrines. Copreus seldom spoke, except to issue curt orders: *Eat*; *Close the canopy, keep out of sight*; *Don't go any further from the cart*; *No talking*; *Sleep*. His accent was from the Macedonian lowlands, but a tattoo on his arm suggested Thracian ancestry.

I was alive, had not been tortured, and was fed army rations. There had been no trial or condemnation. That was because of Electra. Under Macedonian law the family of a traitor was liable to be executed. Executing Antipater's son-in-law might push the Regent into revolt. Half the army had been left in Macedon with Antipater. The Regent loathed Olympias, and his eldest son, Cassander, hated Alexander.

As the cart lumbered north through Syria in the baggage train no one visited me. In my solitude, the depth of betrayal weighed on me. Thinking back on the dinner, Parmenion and Philotas had led me, step by step, to treason. Either they had got cold feet, or it had all been a calculated plot to remove a potential rival at court. Parmenion had survived and prospered through several reigns. To do that in Macedon, you had to be a fox. Iolaus I could forgive. My brother-in-law was little more than a child. Most likely Parmenion had deceived him too.

None of this duplicity weighed on me like that of Eumaeus. How long had he been reporting my every action and thought to Alexander? I had trusted the old man with my life. That trust had been betrayed.

When the army was quartered at Tyre, I received my first visitor. Leonnatus looked very splendid in the cloak of one of the seven Royal Bodyguards. His beard was trimmed, and he smelt of perfume. Unshaven, my long hair unwashed, probably I looked like a vagrant or some philosopher who had renounced worldly possessions.

Leonnatus had brought some wine and dates. We sat in the shade of the cart.

'Alexander held a great festival for Herakles. The Kings of Cyprus funded the choruses. Actors came from all over the world. The judges awarded the first prize in the tragedies to Athenodorus. Afterwards, Alexander said he would have given up part of his kingdom to see his friend Thessalus win, but he did not intervene. The Athenians fined Athenodorus for breaking a contract with them to appear. Alexander paid the fine himself.'

Leonnatus, who had always shown more interest in hunting and wrestling than the theatre, seemed happy to prattle on forever about the safe topic of the festival.

'In one of the comedies, the actor Lycon of Scarpheia inserted some lines asking for a gift of ten talents. Alexander laughed and gave them to him.'

Finally, Leonnatus ran out of things to say.

'You have not suffered because of my arrest?'

'No.' Leonnatus looked uncomfortable. Copreus was within earshot.

'And Amyntas?'

'He has no command, but still enjoys the favour of the King.'

We relapsed into silence.

Leonnatus shifted uneasily. 'Before I go, you have a letter from your wife.'

He drew it out from under his cloak, and handed it to me. The seal was broken.

'She wrote it before the news had reached Macedon,' he said.

'You read it?'

'No, Eumenes the secretary told me the contents.'

'So Alexander has read it?'

Leonnatus looked away. 'Eumaeus passed all your letters to them after Sisines approached you at Gordion and you took him to Pamphylia.'

'Why?'

Leonnatus leant close, so Copreus could not hear. 'Eumaeus had family settled on royal land in the lowlands.'

Before I could ask if Eumaeus had been bribed or threatened, Leonnatus stood up, muttered a farewell, and walked away.

Electra's letter almost broke my heart. Of course it contained nothing overt about politics. Instead, it talked of comfortable domestic affairs: our son, our home and estate. To me it read like a missive from an ancient happier time, as a memory of a blissful and innocent childhood suddenly will come to a man beset by troubles.

We left Tyre at the height of summer. At Berytus, the army left the coast and turned inland between two mountain ranges to reach the Orontes River and follow it north. Copreus had mellowed since the visit of Leonnatus. Occasional delicacies were produced, and at times he was talkative, almost affable. Leonnatus might have given him money, or perhaps enforced intimacy tends to foster a certain affinity, even between jailor and prisoner. Or there again it could have been that he thought it wise not to be on bad terms with a kinsman of one of the Royal Bodyguards. Just conceivably such a prisoner might be pardoned, even returned to favour.

At the end of a long, jolting day on the road, as we sat eating our evening meal, Copreus mused on our route.

'It would have been easier to march up the coast, but the Arabs round here needed to be reminded of our forces. Not all of them heeded what happened to the ones in Samaria who roasted Andromachus alive.'

'What happened to them?'

'While we were marching up to Tyre, Alexander took a flying column, massacred the treacherous Arab bastards.'

In my close confinement, I had known nothing of this. Gambling on his benign mood, I asked if he might be able to get me writing materials and papyrus.

'What for?' Instantly, he was suspicious.

'To write to my wife. I miss her.'

'We will see. Now, time to fix your chains for the night.'

We reached the Euphrates at a place called Thapsacus. Hephaestion had been sent ahead to build two pontoon bridges. There were Persian cavalry on the far bank, so the last few boats had not been floated into place. When our army appeared, the horsemen vanished, and work resumed on the bridges.

Copreus gave me the writing materials. I wrote to Electra. Knowing the letter would be read by Eumenes and Alexander, I phrased it with care: begging her forgiveness, it had been an act of temporary madness – one she would have prevented – some god, or malign *daemon*, must have possessed me, the insanity had passed, I prayed for the chance to prove my loyalty to Alexander in the heat of battle.

I doubted the letter would do much good, but I had to try. With the remainder of the papyrus, I started writing this memoir.

One morning, there was a great stirring in the camp. Copreus did not come to unshackle me or bring my breakfast. Mealtimes become an obsession to men in solitary confinement. When he did eventually arrive, Leonnatus also appeared. My kinsman was in high spirits.

'Darius has sent another embassy.'

Leonnatus took some of my bread and started to eat. My kinsman was never the most thoughtful of men.

'This time he offered all his empire up to the Euphrates, thirty thousand talents to ransom his family, the hand of one of his daughters in marriage, and his son to remain as a hostage.'

Rather more than he offered me, I thought sourly.

'Parmenion said, "If I were Alexander, I would accept."' Leonnatus picked up a hunk of my cheese. 'Can you guess what Alexander said?'

'No.'

Leonnatus was laughing so much he had trouble getting the words out. 'So would I, if I were Parmenion; but I am Alexander.'

Then he ordered the Persians to go and tell Darius that the universe cannot be guided by two suns, nor the world be ruled by two kings. If Darius submitted, Alexander would let him rule the rest of Asia as his vassal.'

Leonnatus slapped his thigh with amusement. 'Wonderful, eh?'

'Wonderful.'

Leonnatus got up. 'Thought you would like to know. By the way, you need anything?'

I did not say freedom and a fast horse. At times my bluff kinsman could be a trial. 'Some books.'

'Why?'

'To read.'

Leonnatus looked puzzled.

'I am bored. Try to get me something long, to while away the time.'

'The *Iliad*?'

'Not Homer; everyone knows it off by heart. Try to find Herodotus' *Histories*, or the *Anabasis* of Xenophon. Something about Persia.'

'Where am I going to find them in an army camp?'

'A bookseller? There will be some among the traders.'

'As you wish.' Leonnatus went off, shaking his head at the eccentricity of his relative.

When he was gone, Copreus brought some more food. Relations were much better between us.

'Not everyone in the council was as pleased as your kinsman,' he said, as we sat munching.

Through a mouthful of bread, I made a nondescript noise. Although we were getting on well, he remained my jailor.

Alexander, or someone close to him, may well employ him to lure me into some treasonous statement.

Copreus looked round in such a furtive way that it would have drawn attention if there had been any observer. He would have made a very bad conspirator.

'A lot of the men in the camp think that was a fair offer,' he spoke in an exaggerated whisper. 'We are needed at home. Memnon, our *strategos* in Thrace, has risen in revolt. Agis the Spartan has seized the chance to bring his forces from Crete to the Peloponnese, and is calling on all the Greeks to join him against us. They say the Achaeans have already joined him, and the Athenians might throw in their lot with the rebellion. Antipater needs our help. The army of your father-in-law has been stripped to the bone. Over the winter, Alexander demanded more reinforcements from Macedon. Burning Persepolis is all very well, but our families are at risk.'

Although my heart sang, I kept my tone neutral. 'There is nothing I can do.'

'No, not as things stand.' Copreus got up, and stomped off to see to the horses.

Copreus was right. There would be Companions who shared the views of the ordinary soldiers. If Alexander would not lead them home, they knew that I would.

When Pandora opened the jar, and released all the evils into the world, hope had remained.

CHAPTER TWENTY-NINE

Summer to Autumn 331 BC

After we crossed the Euphrates, I expected us to follow the route of Xenophon and the ten thousand, and march south, along the left bank of the river, to Babylon. Instead, Alexander led us north then east, across the plains of northern Mesopotamia. I wanted to know why. Never had I so much missed being a Companion of the King, knowing what was happening. Eventually, Leonnatus came and explained. There was better forage, and the climate was not quite so hot. We would march down the Tigris. It made no odds which route we took – either way Darius must stand and fight for Babylon.

At least Leonnatus had brought me some books at Thapsacus. Among them were the first chapters of Callisthenes' account of our expedition. I scrolled through the beginning, but it was just the nauseating sycophancy anyone could have expected. Seemingly all the battles had been won by Alexander alone, with only the aid of the gods. The Macedonians hardly got a mention. Xenophon's story of the mercenaries he had led fighting their way out of the heart of the Persian Empire was far better. The *Anabasis* had convinced the Greek world of its martial superiority over the innumerable eastern subjects of the great King: no matter their numbers, Greeks, let alone Macedonians, would always beat them. Admittedly the Persians had failed to stand up to the ten thousand at the battle of Cunaxa, but after that

Xenophon's men had been retreating, only seeking to escape. It could be that the Persians would have fought rather harder if their enemy had been advancing, and attempting to overthrow their empire and seize their homelands, as we were now. It also struck me that Xenophon unfailingly portrayed himself in the most positive light. Perhaps that was inherent in every auto-biography. Was I doing the same in this account? Every author writing about himself wants to be sympathetic, wants to be liked and admired. I was trying to tell the truth – about myself and others – but I could not be sure.

We journeyed in a leisurely fashion until we reached the town of Carrhae. Then the pace increased – long, bone-jarring days as the horses hauled the wagon. This time Copreus told me the reason. Some captured Persian scouts had revealed that Darius had set out north from Babylon, and intended to contest our crossing of the Tigris. Thinking about the distances involved, from my reading of the *Anabasis*, I suspected that could not be true. Sure enough, when we came in sight of the river, the far bank was empty.

The Tigris is one of the great rivers of the world. But in early autumn, after the long, dry season, this far upstream it was shallow, no more than a couple of feet of water at its deepest. No doubt Callisthenes would conjure up a raging torrent, complete with whirlpools and tumbling boulders, men and animals swept away, baggage dashed to pieces or lost forever. For Callisthenes the army would only manage to struggle through by some brilliant stratagem of Alexander.

The night after we splashed across, about the beginning of the second watch, I was woken by a loud commotion outside. The night-chain was long enough for me to reach the front of the wagon and peer out through the opening of the cover. Camp followers were rushing about. The women were banging pots and pans together, and keening. The men beat their weapons on their shields, calling out invocations to the gods.

'Bad omen.' Copreus was beside me. He pointed to the heavens.

Slowly but steadily, in a cloudless sky, the moon was disappearing.

The Thessalians would be especially alarmed. They believe in witches that can draw down the moon.

'A natural phenomenon,' I said.

Copreus looked at me as if he had no idea what I had said. Although that might have been because his vocabulary did not stretch to *phenomenon*.

'When the earth passes between the sun and the moon, its shadow falls on the moon.'

Copreus looked frankly disbelieving.

'Aristotle taught us the explanation.'

That seemed to carry no weight with Copreus.

'Silence! Silence in the camp!' A herald with a voice of brass was making his way through the lines. 'The omen is propitious. So the Egyptian priests have told the King. The sun is the symbol of Macedon. Look at your standards and your shields. The moon represents Persia. The gods vouchsafe our victory. Aristander the seer says the eclipse proves our victory will be ours within a month.'

Soldiers are superstitious and changeable. At one moment they fight like lions, the next they are disturbed by any sound or sight, and take flight like antelopes. In the wake of the herald, the lamentations turned to a buzz of excited chatter.

Of course the Egyptian priests had given a positive interpretation. They hated the Persians, and were prepared to say anything to please Alexander. His delusion that he was the son of Zeus was largely their fault. Aristander had taken a gamble. Perhaps he feared the Egyptians might replace him in Alexander's favour. Still, if there was no victory within a month, Aristander was nimble enough to find an explanation.

Our rest was disturbed again the next night by the high-pitched wailing of women. The wagon was parked in the guarded section of the camp with the other prisoners and hostages. The wailing came from the big pavilion housing the family of Darius. Copreus went off to find the cause from the soldiers on duty outside.

'Darius' wife is dead.' Puzzlingly, he looked as if it was amusing. 'Died in childbirth. Which is odd when you think how long it has been since she saw her husband. Maybe Alexander found her an *irritation* to more than his *eyes*.'

He wheezed with laughter. 'Although the smart money is on Philotas. Always been a terrible one for the women. Needed a replacement after he got rid of Antigone.'

This was news to me. 'Antigone is no longer his mistress?'

'No, not since . . . ' Copreus looked embarrassed. 'Not since Egypt, just after you . . . '

Alexander gave Darius' wife a stately funeral. Maybe it was intended to dispel the gossip. What became of the child, if it lived, no one knew.

A couple of days later, the camp was in ferment. There had been a cavalry skirmish. Prisoners had been taken. Darius and all his forces were twenty miles away to the south. That night, at the start of the second watch, Alexander led out our army.

A swift night march would be followed by an assault at dawn. Persian discipline was lax. They were slow standing to in the morning. With luck they would be caught unprepared.

That night and the early hours of the next day dragged in our camp. The veterans under Atarrhias manning the rampart could not tear their gaze from the hills to the south. Through them would come either the first fugitives streaming from a lost battle, or messengers bringing the best of tidings.

At long last a horseman was spotted. The news he brought was an anticlimax. There had been no assault. Locals claimed that pits had been dug, and caltrops laid, in front of the Persian line. Alexander had stopped to reconnoitre. The baggage was to be brought up to the army.

We made excellent time, arriving in the afternoon. The new camp was on a hill. From it you could see the whole plain. The locals knew it as Gaugamela, the House of the Camel. The Persians were drawn up across the plain. They were close enough to distinguish blocks of horsemen from foot soldiers. Their first line was almost entirely composed of cavalry, the second of infantry. In front of the cavalry you could just make out three lines of chariots: one on each flank, and one in the centre. The scouts had reported the chariots had scythes attached to their wheels, jutting out from the poles.

The scythed chariots were nothing to fear. I knew from Xenophon they had failed at Cunaxa, and they would fail again here. They posed no threat to disciplined troops. Likewise the second line of Persian infantry were of no account. They were levies of peasants who would run as they had at Issus. The horsemen were the danger. These would be proper warriors, born to ride and handle weapons. Their numbers were impossible to judge. But there were many thousands of them. They must outnumber our cavalry by four or five to one.

The plain itself favoured the enemy. It was smooth and open. In places the earth was a different colour, where it had been disturbed to flatten the surface. That might have sparked the false rumour of pits and caltrops. The going would be as good for our cavalry as that of the Persians. It was the width of the clear ground that was the problem. At Issus our flanks rested on the sea and the hills. Here there was nothing to prevent the vastly superior numbers of the enemy outflanking us.

As evening drew in, we posted pickets and settled in to get whatever rest each man could find. The Persians remained under arms. As darkness fell, torches moved along their lines, as officers checked the men remained ready. Presumably, Darius feared we might attempt another night march.

I had hoped that Leonnatus might come. He did not. Copreus fixed the chain from the dangling loop of my manacles to the ring in the bed of the wagon. I asked if he would go to Alexander with a message: let me ride with the cavalry as a common trooper; this was my chance to prove my renewed loyalty; whatever my failings, let me fight. Copreus flatly refused.

In the morning the Persians were still there. After a day and a night standing in formation, holding their fretful mounts, they would be tired and anxious, the ground round them mired and stinking with their own waste.

Our men were late having breakfast. Copreus said that in the end Parmenion had to give the order, as Alexander was still asleep. Eventually, the Companions had to wake Alexander. The rank and file took this as evidence of his confidence.

They drew up in front of the camp, and Alexander made the rounds alone, speaking to each body of men. I climbed up onto the roof of the wagon to see better. Something inside me ached at the sight of the white plumes and the flash of silver of Alexander's helmet. He was not yet mounted on Bucephalus, saving the old charger for the final clash.

The allied Greek hoplites were at the rear, close enough for those in the baggage train to catch some of Alexander's words. It was much what I would have said: 'They are Persians, you are Greeks, they ran from you at Marathon and Plataea, they will run from you today; by this evening, you will be the lords of Asia, and you can take your revenge.' But he ended with an appeal to the gods, that revealed his mind, and offered a hostage to fortune: 'If I am sprung from Zeus, give us victory.'

The sun was almost directly overhead when the trumpets sounded the advance. The army moved off in silence. The troops were arrayed as always: the six battalions of the phal-anx in the centre, the *hypaspists* and Companion Cavalry to their right, the Thessalians their left. Both flanks were screened with allied horse and light infantry. The line went in echelon, the left wing under Parmenion held back. On that side the Persians would have further to go to get round our flank. The allied hoplites formed a second phalanx about a hundred paces behind the Macedonian. Should the Persian horse get behind our front, the Greeks could face about, and hold them off, while the Macedonians drove the main body of the enemy from the field.

The Persian horde remained stationary. In the bright sunlight I could see a cluster of huge purple banners shimmering to the right of the centre of their frontline. As at Issus that was where the King of Kings had taken station, and, as at Issus, that was where the day would be decided.

About half a mile from the enemy the Macedonians began to advance at an angle to the right. The manoeuvre would prevent the Companion Cavalry being outflanked, but it would leave the Thessalians more exposed. Not long afterwards, bodies of Persian horsemen spurred across to counter the move of the Companions. The hooves of their mounts raised a haze of dust.

Trumpets rang out across the plain from the enemy line. The chariots, little bigger than beetles at this distance, gathered momentum, trailing plumes of dust. On the right, the tiny figures of our light infantry swarmed. The chariots veered and swerved, then went crashing as a hail of missiles killed their teams of horses in their traces. In the centre, the chariots had a longer run to the echeloned battalions of the phalanx. When they were about to smash home into the solid blocks of men a great noise rolled over the field. *Al-al-al-al-ai!* The pikemen roared, beating their weapons on their shields. The sudden pandemonium terrified the chariot horses, many refused, turning away, some so sharply they overturned. As if at the hand of a god, lanes opened in the phalanx battalions. Instinctively, the chariot horses still charging ran into these gaps. As they passed, the pikemen stabbed the crews. By the time I looked to our left all the chariots there were ruined.

More trumpets signalled the Persians' next throw of the dice. On both wings their cavalry charged. They came on like a dark shadow moving across the land. Thousands of pounding hooves raised great billows of dust. There was no wind, and in moments the thick clouds obscured the scene. Just before everything was blotted out, I glimpsed a gap opening in the battalions of our phalanx. The two on the left had halted to keep in contact with the Thessalians, while the rest continued to follow the Companion Cavalry.

'What is happening?' Copreus called up from the bed of the wagon.

'Anyone's guess. No way to see.'

A local gust of wind must have got up down on the plain. It opened a curtain in the swirling gloom. Through it I saw the Companion Cavalry. An arrowhead of armoured horsemen following a glinting silver helmet with white plumes charging at an angle back towards the tall purple standards. Then the curtain fell again.

'Alexander is heading for Darius. It will be decided now.'

'What is that?' Copreus was pointing at something closer.

Out of the murk came a column of riders heading straight at us. Turbans, trousers, dark faces – Persians and Indians from the easternmost provinces – they must have spurred through the gap in the phalanx. The camp was only defended by Atarrhias and the veterans with a few Thracians. There was a palisade, but there had been no time to dig a trench yesterday.

'Take off the manacles!' I jumped down next to Copreus.

'Give me a sword!'

Copreus shook his head.

'They are going to kill us.'

Already there was the sound of fighting in the camp.

Copreus backed into the shelter of the covering. I followed him.

'We can't hide in here. They will find us, and kill us. Give me the key to these manacles!'

It was too late. A fierce bearded face appeared in the entrance. There were two more behind him. These men were Persians.

'Name?' He spoke Greek.

I announced myself, like a doomed minor hero in the *Iliad*. 'Alexander, son of Aeropus.'

'Lyncestis?'

'Alexander, Lord of Lebaea in Lyncestis.'

The warrior pushed into the tent. The others followed. He beckoned me. 'You come.'

'Where?'

'To Great King. Darius want you.'

I stood still, rooted to the spot with indecision: escape into exile or remain a prisoner?

The Persian leader gestured to one of the warriors behind him. The man moved toward Copreus, sword raised. Without thought I stepped sideways, and swung the chain of my manacles at his head. The heavy links caught him a glancing blow to the ear. Not enough to knock him down, but it sent him staggering into the side of the tent.

With a growl, the other warrior jumped at me, ignoring the shout of his officer. He thrust at my chest. More by luck than skill, I turned the blow with the chains. He thumped into me, chest to chest. I used an old wrestling move to whip his leg from under him. As he fell, I dropped on top of him, my knees coming down in the small of his back.

Rolling off the fallen man, my fingers scrabbled for the hilt of his blade. The manacles impeded me, but once I had a grip, in a moment I was back on my feet. Facing the leader, I got in front of Copreus.

The two Persians were up again. The one whose sword I had taken drew a long knife. They moved to take me from either side.

From outside came the din of fighting, and the high-pitched screams of women.

The leader yelled a string of orders. With the utmost reluctance, his two men backed away, and out of the tent. The leader waited, looking into my eyes. 'You are fool,' he said, then he too was gone.

Panting, still in a fighting crouch, I waited. Outside was madness. No one else entered the covering of the wagon.

'Come on.'

Glancing over my shoulder, I saw that Copreus was going nowhere. He was curled into a ball, like a frightened child.

There were men fighting in the alleyways. From the elevated bed of the wagon, I had a good view. Persians were rushing into the pavilion that held Darius' mother and family. Off to my right, Atarrhias and a bunch of veterans were facing off against some now dismounted Indians. The latter had their backs to me.

Al-al-al-al-ai! With the war cry ringing out, I jumped down, and leapt at the unsuspecting enemy. All troops run when unexpectedly attacked from behind.

'Atarrhias, your men with me. We have to stop them rescuing the hostages.'

Atarrhias grabbed my arm. 'Not that way. There is a nearer entrance.'

We burst into the huge tent, through a deserted antechamber, then out into the main room. Darius' mother was sitting on a high throne. Behind her cowered younger women, a child, and some eunuchs. A Persian noble, resplendent with gold, stood respectfully in front of the old woman. He held out a hand, beckoning her to go with him.

'Don't move!'

The Queen Mother looked back at me. Her face was blank with shock, but her eyes revealed a world of uncertainty.

With Atarrhias and his men, I edged towards the throne. There were more of us than there were Persians. Outside, I could hear trumpets blaring, foreign voices shouting.

For an eternity the two lines of armed men watched each other, the women and eunuchs in between. Then a Persian burst into the chamber, and gabbled a few words to the leader. Without ado, the nobleman turned, and stalked from the tent.

'Atarrhias, guard the hostages.'

The old veteran again grabbed my arm. 'Where do you think you are going?'

'Outside to see if we have won.'

Atarrhias grunted, rapped out a string of commands, and followed me.

The alleyway was empty. From close by the sounds of running horses.

We climbed up onto my wagon. The Persian and Indian riders were streaming out of the camp. Greek hoplites from our rear phalanx were inside.

Further off, the dust clouds hung and shifted over the plain of Gaugamela. Understanding the battle was like interpreting a damaged painting, where only smudges and shadows revealed the figures. To our left, the dust billowed straight up into the sky in thick, unmoving swags. Outflanked, and against the odds, Parmenion and the Thessalians had held the onslaught. Everywhere else across the House of the Camel all the curtains of dust were heading south, away from our camp.

Alexander had won.

CHAPTER THIRTY

Autumn 331 BC to Spring 330 BC

A T THE HOUSE OF the Camel, as at Issus, Darius had abandoned the fight. When he fled, his men had streamed after him, and again the battle was lost. Alexander went in pursuit, as he had after Issus, but again failed to catch the Great King. Long after sunset, when the horses were spent, Alexander finally accepted that he would not overhaul Darius that night. Returning to Gaugamela in darkness, there was a brutal encounter with retreating Persian horsemen. Unfortunately, Hephaestion was among the wounded, not the sixty Companion Cavalrymen who died.

The next day, well before dawn, Alexander set out again with fresh mounts. About forty miles south, at the town of Arbela, he captured the empty chariot of Darius. Yet again Gaugamela paralleled Issus. In the future writers and artists surely will conflate the two battles. Even the memories of those of us who were there get confused. The locals told Alexander that the Great King had ridden east into the Taurus Mountains. Darius was accompanied by cavalry from the distant satrapies commanded by a kinsman of his called Bessus, and the last couple of thousand Greek mercenaries still loyal to the King. Alexander called off the hunt, and rode back to the army.

Our dead were cremated and buried with all due honour. The stripped corpses of the Persians were left to rot where they had fallen. Before the stench became overpowering, and men started to sicken, we headed south towards Babylon.

The plunder taken was enormous. It included fifteen Indian elephants. Luckily, their handlers were also captured. Alexander, still playing the role of the general of the League of Corinth, sent some of the more conventional spoils back to the Greeks. A portion was even sent to the obscure Greek city of Croton in Italy in honour of an athlete from there who had fitted out a warship at his own expense all those years ago when Xerxes invaded Greece. Most, however, Alexander divided among his Companions. Me, I was still a prisoner in the wagon.

Should I have gone with the Persians? Little doubt I would have got away. The Persians had had horses, the Greek allies who retook the camp were on foot. Almost all the raiders had escaped. My father had enjoyed a comfortable exile with the Great King. I had urged Neoptolemus to the same. Like them, I would have been welcomed as a useful diplomatic tool. Twice before Darius had tried to recruit me. I would have been given some military command. Quite probably Darius would have granted me the rents from a village or two for my maintenance.

But circumstances had changed. When I wrote to Neoptolemus advising him to go to Persia there was no intention he remain there forever. Everything had hung in the balance. Whoever was victorious – Alexander or Darius – Neoptolemus and I would have secured the pardon and safe return of the other. Now Darius had been irrevocably defeated. For the present the eastern satrapies still owed him allegiance, but would their men continue to answer the call of a discredited king who had twice run from battle, leaving his troops to their fate? If I had gone with the Persians, I would have joined a fugitive court, and, in the eyes of all Macedonians, become a marked man, to be hunted down to the ends of the earth, and killed on sight.

My only chance of returning to Electra, of one day riding in the hills of Lyncestis, was Alexander granting a pardon. Initially, as the wagon lumbered south, I was hopeful. Had I not prevented the rescue of Darius' family? Old Atarrhias would bear witness to what I had done. But, instead of a pardon, an order came that from now on I was to be chained to the wagon in the day as well as the night.

I composed a letter to Electra. Knowing full well it would be opened by Eumenes, and that the secretary would pass it on to Alexander, I recounted with truth the fight in the camp, and facing down the Persians in the pavilion to stop the flight of the royal hostages; only omitting my own thoughts of joining them.

We crossed back over the Tigris, following the Royal Road down through Mesopotamia. The land here was flat, cut with irrigation ditches, well supplied from the river. The soil was dark and fertile, the yields would be immense. Overhead the fronds of palms clattered in the breeze, and white clouds tracked across a huge sky.

My letter provoked no reaction. Leonnatus did not come. My only conversation was with Copreus, and he was more reserved, perhaps ashamed of his cowardice at Gaugamela. Alone and bored, I read and reread Xenophon and Herodotus, and wrote this journal or confession.

The journey to Babylon was enlivened by setting fire to a boy. We had reached a lake of bitumen. The properties of its fire are mysterious. It could spontaneously combust, but did it burn human flesh? Some Athenian hanger-on, with typical misplaced ingenuity, suggested Alexander conduct a test. There was a bath attendant, an ugly slave boy, but with a pleasant singing voice. Inexplicably, the boy agreed to the suggestion of the Athenian. I watched from the wagon as they smeared him with the bitumen. When he was alight the onlookers had trouble putting him out as he struggled and thrashed in agony. The boy survived, but I never heard him sing again.

We entered Babylon through the Ishtar Gate along with the baggage. The road was covered in crushed and broken flower petals. They had been trodden under by thousands of boots and hooves, and were soiled with congealing blood and the droppings of innumerable animals. Some smoke from the sacrifices still hung across the street. Its lingering scent of incense was overlaid by horse piss and dung, and the pungent reek of close-packed humanity and the hot entrails that had been pulled from eviscerated beasts. The crowds had gone, apart from a few slaves desultorily packing up the altars. The parade was over. Alexander had entered Babylon in triumph some hours earlier.

Mazaeus, the Satrap of Babylon, had commanded the right wing of Darius' cavalry at Gaugamela, and had fought hard against the Thessalians. Deserted by his King, he had extricated his men, and force-marched to Babylon. Seeing full well which way the wind was set, Mazaeus had sent messengers to Alexander offering the surrender of the city. In return, Alexander had reappointed him as satrap. Similarly, Mithrenes, the Persian nobleman who had surrendered Sardis, now was made Satrap of Armenia. Although Alexander put Macedonians in charge of both the garrison and the collection of taxes in Babylonia, and Armenia was unconquered territory, the Macedonians had not crossed the Hellespont, marched so many miles, and fought so many battles, to exalt such easterners.

Alexander took up residence in the palace by the Euphrates. The wagon was tucked away out of sight in the sprawling compound. I did not see the famous hanging gardens, or the ziggurat the Jews called the Tower of Babel. I saw nothing and no one except Copreus, had nothing to do except reread Herodotus and Xenophon, and continue this manuscript.

Copreus, belatedly remembering that I had saved his life, clumsily put himself out to raise my spirits. The soldiers were having the time of their lives in Babylon. Even the recruits newly arrived from Macedon had been given large sums from plunder. Women were available everywhere; not just prostitutes, but the wives and daughters of respectable Babylonians. When they invited you to dinner, the women gradually removed their clothes, without you having to ask. When they were naked – presumably when you got to the dessert – they were happy to let you fuck them. Their husbands and fathers did not object; they termed it being *sociable*. As I could not imagine any respectable family ever inviting Copreus to dinner, I was inclined to doubt the story.

Copreus asked if I would like him to bring me a woman. Frequently at night my imagination curled a woman beneath me. Most often it was Electra, and we were in the room in Pella with the sunlight reflected from the water casting patterns on the ceiling. Somehow copulating with a whore, while I was chained in the bed of a prison wagon, was less appealing.

'You heard about . . . ' It was one of Copreus' most infuriating conversational opening gambits. *Of course I have not heard, no one speaks to me except you*, I wanted to shout.

I held my tongue, precisely because no one spoke to me except him.

'. . . the Queen Mother?'

'She has gone Babylonian, and removes all her clothes at dinner?'

Copreus gave me a look that suggested he thought I was becoming unhinged. 'No.'

'What then?'

'Alexander sent her some purple cloth, and women to instruct her how to weave some clothes.'

'So?'

'The old girl was furious, never been so insulted in her life. Persian ladies don't weave. Alexander had to go and apologise; virtually grovelled.'

To please Copreus, I laughed immoderately. It was like rewarding a dog that had come when you whistled.

Perhaps I overdid the amusement. Copreus gave me another look that doubted I was entirely sane.

After about a month, we departed for Susa. I say *about* a month. I had taken to scratching a line with my nails on a plank under my mattress each day. But I had become confused, missing some days, doing others twice.

On the way out of the city, I glimpsed the Hanging Gardens – many trees – and the Tower of Babel; lofty, but in need of repair.

It took twenty days to reach Susa. Now I always scratched the day after my morning meal. Like Mazaeus at Babylon, Abulites opened the city to Alexander, and remained satrap.

On the second night in Susa I had a visitor. Leonnatus smelt of myrrh, and the studs on the soles of his boots appeared to be solid silver. Not mentioning that he had not come for some three months, he was more bluff and genial than ever.

'When Alexander sat on Darius' throne his feet did not reach the footstool. Iolaus replaced it with a table. Two people burst into tears. Old Demaratus wept with joy, said those Greeks who had not lived to see that moment would be unhappy! The other was some Persian eunuch. Through an interpreter, he wailed that Darius used to eat off the table. Alexander was going to have it removed, but Philotas persuaded him it should stay. You should have been there!'

Leonnatus laughed, the implication of his words not registering.

'Can you get me some more books?' Solitary confinement had eroded my social skills.

'Err, of course.' Leonnatus looked slightly thrown. 'What books?'

'More Xenophon. What has happened to my horses, and to Agathion and Leucippe?'

'Taken them into my household. More Xenophon; must remember.' Leonnatus flicked a mote of dust off his yellow-bordered purple cloak of a Royal Companion. 'Been wrestling. Have sand brought from Egypt; very fine, but gets everywhere.'

I could really think of no comment.

'Came to tell you some good news. Alexander assembled the men, and had them vote prizes for valour. Amyntas came sixth, and was given command of a thousand of the *hypaspists*.'

That was a lowly command for a man who had commanded a wing of the army in Pamphylia. 'You told me he had not fallen from favour.'

Leonnatus shrugged. 'You know how it is.'

'Who won first prize?'

'Old Atarrhias for what he did at Halicarnassus. He was promoted to lead another thousand of the *hypaspists* for what he did at Halicarnassus.'

'Did Alexander not believe him about the camp at Gaugamela?'

Leonnatus shifted uncomfortably.

'About my stopping the rescue of Darius' family?'

Now Leonnatus looked thoroughly unhappy. 'His story was not the same as yours.'

'What?'

'He said he caught hold of you when you were running off with the Persians.'

The rest of his attempts at conversation passed me by. Quite soon he left.

First Eumaeus, now Atarrhias. Betrayal by every hand, from those I trusted. I gave up marking the days; there seemed no point. Copreus watched me night and day. The gods knew how he thought I might manage to do away with myself. Strangling myself with the chain that ran from my manacles to the ring seemed the only way.

One morning, Copreus came back to the wagon beaming, bearing a letter from Electra.

The seal, of course, was broken. It started with domestic affairs. Then, for the first time in her correspondence, she moved to politics. Antipater had settled affairs in Thrace. Memnon had submitted. The Regent had appointed Zopyrion as *strategos* in Thrace. Having gathered an army of more than forty thousand, Macedonians and Greeks, Antipater was marching south. By the time this letter reached the east, he would have defeated the twenty thousand or so rebels with Agis of Sparta. Her father was glad I was in good health, and prayed that I remain so.

It was neatly done. There were no threats, but Alexander was reminded that Macedon, Thrace, and Greece obeyed Antipater, that the Regent commanded a significant army, and that he wanted no harm to come to his son-in-law. I had to remind myself that the gods had placed Hope in the jar with the other evils that afflict mankind.

We left Susa in midwinter. Outside the gates I caught a glimpse of Alexander as he rode down the column. He was wearing a Macedonian *kausia* and cloak. But underneath he was dressed in a white and purple striped Persian tunic, and had one of their eastern girdles round his waist. Several Persians, with their carefully curled black beards and exotic decorated costume, rode in his entourage. When Leonnatus had brought me the rolls of Xenophon, he told me that Alexander had sent the statues of the tyrannicides Harmodius and Aristogeiton back to Athens. Would the irony be as lost on the other Companions, as it was on Leonnatus?

Some Persians made a stand on the road to Persepolis. They were brushed aside by a frontal charge from the phalanx, while the Agrianes took them in the flank. After that the army divided. Parmenion was to take the allies and mercenaries, along with the baggage, by a longer and easier route looping south, while Alexander with the best troops struck straight through the mountains.

Loneliness is like a chronic illness. It drags you down, never leaves you. Weary, empty days, bumping along in the wagon. My wrists were calloused from the manacles. The Hope brought by Electra's letter had slipped out of the jar. I was alive. You could say little more than that. I slept, ate, eased my bladder and moved my bowels, and read Xenophon, *The Education of Cyrus*. Like me, Cyrus had been a king in waiting. Like me, he had won victories for others. He had had an easier path to the throne than me, but his story and mine began to merge in my mind. I dreamt of training armies for great battles. Like Cyrus, I would bring justice, and free my people from foreign tyranny.

The palace at Persepolis was enormous, some distance from the town. It was set on a high platform in a wide plain ringed by distant mountains. The wagon was parked close against a rear wall. Alexander had arrived before us. The Satrap Tiridates had surrendered. The palace, and the fabulous wealth of its treasury, was spared, but Alexander had given the town over to the soldiers. They had killed the men, and raped the women, enslaved them and the children. Discipline had broken down. Comrades had fought each other over their prizes. Copreus told me that the men were angry; there had been many casualties storming a pass in the mountains. I did not care.

One night, I was woken by the sounds of drunken revelry. It had happened before, but this time it was louder. Copreus was nowhere to be seen. Crawling to the head of the wagon, I peered out from the canopy. Soldiers were rushing through the darkness towards the palace. They carried buckets of water. Then I smelt the smoke. Looking up, I saw the first tongues of flame flickering high above on the roof.

The soldiers stopped, put down the buckets, made no attempt to fight the fire. Instead, from somewhere out of sight, torches were passed from hand to hand. Yelling encouragement to one another, the men ran forward, and hurled the burning brands into the building. I saw a figure in the cloak of a Royal Companion staggering along the line with a girl supporting him. He was laughing, clapping the men on the back.

Here was the revenge for which we had come. Alexander was burning Persepolis, the most hated city in the world. When it was ashes, perhaps he would lead us home.

With a roar, the whole roof caught. The flames leapt into the night sky. The nocturnal breeze dragged burning embers far and wide. Like fireflies they eddied down all around the wagon. And then I was afraid.

Where in Hades was Copreus?

'Help!' My voice was lost in the pandemonium.

With a great crash the roof of the palace collapsed. A pillar of flame lifted above the walls. The soldiers fell back before the conflagration.

'Get me out of here!'

No one heard. Sparks were landing on the canopy. Patches of the leather began to smoulder.

'Help!'

The soldiers were moving away. I pulled at the chain. The ring was screwed into a plank of oak. I braced my feet, tugged with the strength of fear and desperation. My wrists were torn by the manacles. The blood made my hands slippery, hard to grip the chain. The heat was like an oven.

Of all the ways to die being burnt alive must be the worst. Like a holocaust to some savage deity, I was left to immolation. The smoke was thick. I began to choke. It would be a mercy if the smoke killed me before the fire. I wondered if I could loop the chain round my throat and throttle myself.

In one place the leather of the tent was beginning to burn. The chain was round my neck. If I hurled myself hard enough, I might break my neck.

A squat figure – coughing and bent double – was in the wagon. Copreus fumbled with the key. Then I was free.

'This way!'

I ignored Copreus. On my hands and knees – the air was purer down there – I scrambled to the rear of the tent to get my only possession. The papyrus rolls that captured my life in my hands, I followed Copreus out of my burning jail.

CHAPTER THIRTY-ONE

Spring to Autumn 330 BC

Persepolis had gone up in flames at the drunken whim of a courtesan, so people said. At the feast Thais, an Athenian *hetaira* and the mistress of Ptolemy, had said what better revenge for Persian *men* having burnt Athens than an Athenian *woman* should burn Persepolis. Flown with wine, the company had thought it a fine notion, and had formed a procession. Alexander had thrown the first torch, Thais the second.

There were other stories. Before the fatal night all the treasure had been removed from the palace. The conflagration had been planned. Parmenion was said to have argued against the idea: *Why burn your own property?* The old general had been over-ruled for reasons of policy. What Greeks would rally to Agis the Spartan in the name of Greek freedom against the Macedonians who had taken such decisive action against Persepolis, the capital of the true oppressors?

Whatever the truth, everyone had overlooked the prisoner chained in the cart. Alexander had forgotten his foster-brother, and once dear friend, and left me to be burnt to death. Only the actions of my jailor had saved me. Or had the forgetfulness of the King been purposeful? If the son-in-law of Antipater died in an accident there would be little to strain the loyalty of the Regent of Macedon.

Darius was at Ecbatana in Media gathering another army. We left Persepolis in late spring, as soon as the passes over the mountains were free of snow. Eleven days out, deserters brought news that the Great King was retreating to the Caspian Gates and the satrapies beyond in the north-east. Alexander divided the army. Parmenion was sent to Ecbatana with the Thessalians and the other Greek allies, the mercenaries, and the Thracians of Sitalkes. He was to wait there for the royal treasury escorted by Cleitus the Black and four battalions of the phalanx. Then, when he had pacified Media, he was to dismiss the allies, pay them a bonus, and see them off on their long march home. Those who wanted to re-enlist as mercenaries, with an even larger cash payment, were to be forwarded to the main army, along with Cleitus and the Macedonians. Parmenion was to hand control of the treasury to Harpalus, but remain in Ecbatana. Media was an important satrapy, vital to our communications with the west, but the general who had won so many victories for Alexander and his father was being left behind. Alexander force-marched the rest of the men north after Darius.

We went through a monotonous landscape, enveloped in thick palls of dust. The new prison wagon seemed even more uncomfortable than the last. Leonnatus had not come to see me after the fire. Copreus claimed it was impossible to obtain any books or new writing materials on the march. Unable to write or read, mainly I brooded if Alexander had really intended that I should have died in the flames of Persepolis. The youth I had met at Mieza would not have contemplated anything of the sort, nor the King who had summoned me to his sickbed at Tarsus, but the Son of Zeus, the new Lord of Asia, was capable of anything.

Copreus told me we were still a couple of days' march from the Caspian Gates when the column halted. Darius was already through the pass. For five days the army recovered from the rigours of the road. Obsessively, I read and reread my own words, struggling against the constraints of memory. Herodotus wrote the stories he had been told, but did not vouchsafe the truth of any of them. Xenophon claimed to tell the truth. My aim was to outdo the honesty of Xenophon in the *Anabasis*. Yet every time you revisit a memory it seems slightly different. I resisted the temptation to alter what I had already written. If anyone reads this, they will be in a better position than me to judge what sort of man was Alexander of Lyncestis.

Coenus was given some cavalry and sent with his battalion of the phalanx to gather provisions, and the march resumed. It was fortunate that the Caspian Gates – a long, forbidding series of gorges – were not defended. No sooner were we through than another batch of Persian deserters brought fresh news. It ran through the camp like wildfire. Darius had been overthrown, betrayed by those closest to him. His kinsman Bessus had proclaimed himself the new Great King. Darius was a prisoner, bound by golden chains in a cart. Of any Macedonian probably I felt the most sympathy.

Alexander pressed ahead, not waiting for Coenus to return, and leaving the slower elements to follow. With the baggage my wagon plodded along. The days grew hotter – the air under the coverings was stifling – but the routine never changed: wake, relieve myself, eat, brood on fate and the decisions I had made, eat, sleep, and dream. At night, my unfettered thoughts took two courses, either idyllic reminiscences of home, or wild fantasies of revenge. Alarmingly, sometimes the two converged, and I would wake with a cry, my heart pounding.

When Alexander caught sight of the column of the Great King it was no more than some dusty wagons and a trailing bunch of horsemen. Spotting the riders coming from the west, the Persians scattered and fled. Eagerly, the Macedonians searched the wagons. There was no sign of their quarry. An officer, tormented by thirst, left the road, and went to a spring shaded by trees. Under the boughs was a cart. He thought it odd that its oxen were wounded. Climbing up, he pulled back the hangings. There on the floor, still bound in golden chains, was the Great King. The sometime Beloved of Mazda lay in a pool of blood, pierced with javelins. Darius was dead.

Later people told of last words, freighted with poignancy and significance. Darius had asked the officer for a drink of water. When it was brought in a helmet, he thanked the officer; he was glad not to die alone, and praised Alexander for the treatment of his family. In other tellings, the last words were spoken directly to Alexander, and Darius named the Macedonian his successor, and entreated him to take vengeance on his killers. In one version Darius was not completely abandoned; his pet dog remained faithful to the end.

The messenger whose arrival started the stories also brought orders to rendezvous with Alexander at a city called Hecatompylus. Despite its name, it did not have a hundred gates, but after the long march it was an oasis of comfort. Copreus even managed to find new writing things. Perhaps he even paid for them himself. I did not ask.

I was woken by singing; men lifting up their voices in joy. Pulling back the hangings, I saw soldiers and camp followers taking down tents, and packing wagons. Everyone was laughing, calling out words of good omen.

'It is over!' Copreus came up beaming. 'At least you have nothing to pack.'

'What is over?'

'The campaign!' Copreus was grinning like an idiot. 'Darius is dead, and we are going home!'

If it was true, it was all I wanted. But Hope had played me false before. 'Are you sure?'

'The Greeks are well on their way from Ecbatana, and now it is our turn.'

'How do you know?'

'Someone in the commissariat told me; he heard it from one of the Royal Pages.'

From out of sight came cheering. It swelled as Alexander appeared. For once, he was dressed wholly in Macedonian clothes. He was backed by my former companions; among the foremost Philotas, Craterus, Perdiccas, my kinsman Leonnatus, and, of course, Hephaestion.

Alexander jumped up onto a nearby wagon. The onlookers roared their pleasure, called out blessings on his name. He held out his hands to be heard. Gradually, a happy and expectant silence fell over the crowd.

'Men such as us – men who have marched so many miles, forded so many rivers, crossed so many mountain ranges, trodden so many snows, won so many victories – naturally long for peace, long for their wives and children, their aged parents, long for home.'

They cheered so loud, he had to pause.

'If I believed our grip on the lands we have conquered was secure, I would be the first to break loose from here, even if you tried to detain me, back to my home, to my mother and sisters, to the rest of our countrymen. There, we could enjoy the reputation and glory and riches we have won together.'

The mood had changed. They were quiet, but looking at each other.

'Our empire is new, and the necks of the barbarians are stiff beneath our yoke. They fear us while we are here, if we left they would become our enemies again. What we are dealing with is a pack of wild animals; even captured they will only be tamed by the passage of time. Bessus has declared himself Great King. If we leave him unconquered, he will take back all the territories that are ours as spear-won land. What will we feel when his hordes are devastating Greek cities, are poised at the Hellespont to invade Macedon itself? Let us deal with Bessus now, before he can gather his strength. Only a march of four days remains. We stand on the threshold of victory. Then the Persians will be reduced to obedience, and we can think of returning home.'

Although his voice was not melodious, Alexander had every other gift as an orator. He had won them over. They chanted – *Lead us, lead us, wherever you wish!*

As he basked in their reaffirmed affection, Alexander caught my eye. It was the first time since the night in his tent in Egypt. His face betrayed no emotion, but he leant down and whispered something in Hephaestion's ear. And then I was quite sure that he did not intend me to be among those who made the journey home.

* * *

The four days was a barefaced lie. Alexander did not lead us east against Bessus. Split into three columns, the army went north through the mountains to the shores of the Caspian Sea. That summer, at a place called Zadracata, Alexander's identification with the army – his Macedonian costume; his use of 'we' and 'our' – were exposed as far more insidious falsehoods.

Alexander again appeared clad in a purple and white Persian tunic. Now, around his brows he added the diadem of eastern royalty. He gave presents of Persian attire to his Companions. Some – chief among them Hephaestion and Peucestas – even wore them in public. The Companion Cavalry were issued with Persian bridles and horse furniture. The correspondence of Alexander was sealed with the ring of Darius. Persian nobles who came in from the hills, having deserted their own kind, were elevated to the rank of Royal Companions. At court, access to Alexander was controlled by Persian ushers, many of them eunuchs. One of this sinister tribe, a youth called Bagoas, who had been the catamite of Darius, was taken to the bed of Alexander. So much for treating them as a pack of wild animals. It was evident, for those with eyes to see, that Alexander was the heir of Darius, and no longer the King of the Macedonians.

Eventually – after many more days than four – we moved east after Bessus. The first satrap we encountered, Satibarzanes of Areia, surrendered, and was promptly reinstated. Alexander left only a garrison of forty Macedonians; not to watch Satibarzanes, but to prevent any of our troops harming the tribesmen.

We were on the borders of Areia when Copreus brought me sad news. Nicanor, the commander of the *hypaspists*, had died of a fever. We had never been close, but Nicanor had been a brave officer, and it brought back memories of the death of his younger brother Hector. Now Parmenion only had one surviving son. Philotas was said to be devastated. Alexander said there was no time to halt the army for a dignified funeral.

No sooner had we left Areia than Alexander's mendacious words about Persian unfaithfulness came back to haunt him. Satibarzanes had massacred the isolated and defenceless Macedonian garrison, and proclaimed his allegiance to Artaxerxes IV, as Bessus now styled himself. Taking a flying column, Alexander retraced his steps, and exacted a sanguinary retribution. Many tribesmen were burnt to death, but Satibarzanes eluded him. Learning little from his misplaced trust, Alexander appointed another Persian as the new satrap; although this time he did found a colony of veterans to make treachery more dangerous.

When the army reunited, Alexander again postponed seeking a reckoning with Bessus. Instead of taking the direct route east to Bactria, we went south into the satrapy of Drangiana. The satrap here also fled east to Bessus.

Even in the autumn, Drangiana was a hot, dry land. A persistent wind from the north-west brought little relief. We were resting at a place called Phrada. Copreus had gone off, excited to be asked to a drinking session with some grooms from the Companion Cavalry. It was a stifling night, impossible to sleep. I had drawn back the hangings of the wagon, and sat naked in my chains. The stars studding the skies were remote. Only fools would see the future in their constellations.

It was late, perhaps the third watch, and the other carts and tents were quiet. The campfires were deserted. My more fortunate neighbours were sleeping. A tall figure, wrapped in a nondescript cloak, broad-brimmed hat pulled down low, came towards the wagon.

When you are starved of conversation, you watch people closely. The way they move reveals much of their character and emotions. Every gesture is a form of communication. There was an assurance, even arrogance, in the man's gait. Yet he was anxious, walking fast, trying not to look around, failing to appear nonchalant.

Under his cloak was the outline of a sword on his left hip. An unknown assassin in the dead of night would succeed where the fire at Persepolis had failed. Even now, when Hope had long flown, some foolish instinct for survival made me afraid. Be a man, I told myself. A coward dies a thousand times, a brave man once.

At least Electra and our son were safe with Antipater.

The figure climbed up onto the wagon. I knew him now, but did not say his name.

Philotas let down the coverings. When we were hidden from view, he sat next to me. Despite his rough cloak, like Leonnatus, he smelt of myrrh.

'How are you?' Philotas whispered.

After all this time a prisoner, I could think of no response.

'Some say captivity has turned your mind.'

'Some men say all sorts of things.'

Philotas grinned. His teeth were very white in the darkness. 'You are yourself.'

'I was sorry to hear about your brother. May the earth lie lightly on Nicanor.'

'Thank you.'

Philotas took a deep breath, like a man steeling himself against a trial.

I waited. As he had not come to kill me, there could be only one other reason.

'The men are unhappy. They want to go home.' Once he started talking, the words tumbled out. 'Alexander lied to them. He has no intention of returning home. After Bessus, he wants to march east until he reaches the ocean. Even that will not satisfy him. We will never get home. Alexander does not listen to the Macedonians anymore. You have to pity men subject to anyone who believes he is the Son of Zeus.'

'Why are you telling me this?'

'You already know.' Philotas ran a hand over his cloak, as if surprised by the coarse material of his disguise.

'Why now?'

'By chance, or maybe providence. As Persian eunuchs stop ordinary Macedonians from seeing Alexander these days, a soldier called Cebalinus could not get near the King. So Cebalinus came and told me of a plot. He wanted me to warn Alexander, hoping to save his brother, who is the lover of one of the conspirators.'

'And you have not told Alexander?'

'No.'

'That is a risk.'

'Not if the plot succeeds. And if it fails—' Philotas shrugged '—then I will say I thought the whole thing ludicrous, and not worth reporting. I might get away with pleading negligence.'

'Will it succeed?'

'One of the seven Royal Bodyguards, Demetrius, has access to Alexander. He will strike the blow.'

'When?'

'Tomorrow night.' Philotas put his hand on mine. 'The Macedonians will acclaim a king who promises to lead them home.'

'And that king will be me?'

'Who else? You have Argead blood. With my backing, and that of my father, no one is better placed. I command the Companion Cavalry here; Parmenion has the treasury at Ecbatana, guarded by the Thracians of your friend Sitalkes; and your father-in-law Antipater holds Macedon and its army as Regent. Everything is in place.'

He paused, squeezed my hand. 'Olympias and Darius were not mistaken. Since Philip was murdered by your brothers, you have been the Shadow King.'

'You, and your father, betrayed me in Egypt.'

'We had no choice. That bitch Antigone had told Craterus. To save ourselves we had to tell Alexander before he did. There was no time to warn you. I am sorry.'

Philotas stood up. 'I will not ask for any oaths. You know everything. I have put my life in your hands.'

CHAPTER THIRTY-TWO

Autumn 330 BC

THE CHOICE OF HERACLES was straightforward. Vice was dressed like a whore. It was easy to see through her tawdry charms. Virtue was stern and austere, but obviously made a better companion for life. Choices in reality were more complex.

After Philotas left, the night passed slowly. I was still turning over my choices when dawn first touched the eastern sky. At some point, Copreus reeled back, collapsed on his mattress, and started to snore.

Philotas was right. His life was in my hands. If I informed against him, Alexander might grant me a pardon. But it was not simple. There was no way a chained prisoner could get to Alexander. As the King now was surrounded by Persian ushers and court protocol, an ordinary Macedonian like Copreus had no opportunity to talk to him either. That was why Cebalinus had been forced to approach Philotas. Yet there was a way. I could kick Copreus awake, and send him to Leonnatus. My kinsman, one of the seven Royal Bodyguards, still had access to the royal pavilion.

Could I trust Copreus? When Philotas came, Copreus was away, invited to drink with the grooms of the Companion Cavalry. That had never happened before. Philotas commanded the Companion Cavalry. The coincidence was suspicious. If Copreus was in the pay of Philotas, my message would never reach Leonnatus and, no doubt, I would be found dead in the wagon. Maybe they could even make it look like suicide. After all these months in the wagon, isolated and ignored, not many people would be surprised that I had given way to despair.

Even if my suspicions were unfounded, who would Alexander believe? He had never been close with Philotas, but the word of one of his Companions might carry more weight than the wild accusations of a disgraced traitor, desperate to regain his freedom.

I could do nothing, and let events run their course. If the plot failed, Philotas would say he thought it no more than a fantasy. It would undermine his own defence to name me. But if Philotas was implicated by Demetrius and Cebalinus and the nameless others, Alexander could entertain doubts, and act decisively. Philotas might be put on the rack. Under torture names tumble out. A man will say anything to stop the agony.

If Alexander was killed, they would come for me, strike off my chains, lead me through the camp to the royal pavilion, and acclaim me king. Was it my destiny to be king? For twelve generations the Bacchiads had been the Lords of Lyncestis. Two of the House had ruled all Macedon. Yet I was a third son, not born even to rule the Lyncestians, let alone all the Macedonians. Now, however, was it my duty to take the throne? Kingship was a noble servitude. A King of Macedon owed his position to his subjects. No one had ever refused their call. When on the throne he must rule in their interests. Alexander no longer listened to the Macedonians. Hedged round with Persian ceremonies, he ruled for himself, for his own glory. Alexander, my once dearest foster-brother, had become a tyrant.

Why had Philotas chosen me? He had given the same reason as had Parmenion at the Syrian Gates, when Alexander had been near death in Tarsus: Argead blood. I was not the only man in the camp with that bloodline. None of the others were suitable. Craterus detested Philotas, and the feeling was mutual. Leonnatus was far too dutiful to be willing to accede over the body of Alexander; so too my nephew Amyntas. As for Perdiccas, courageous and stubborn, he was too much his own man. Philotas and his father, unable to seize the throne themselves, wanted to elevate a puppet ruler. Broken by confinement, I fitted their requirement.

Things would not play out as they hoped. After Philip was assassinated, Parmenion and Antipater might have expected a malleable young king. They had got Alexander. If acclaimed, I would not follow the whims of Philotas and Parmenion, but do what I thought right, what the Macedonians wanted. Although, of course, my first act would be to kill Hephaestion.

Philotas and *Parmenion* – if Cebalinus only revealed the conspiracy two days ago, Parmenion in distant Ecbatana knew nothing. Philotas was playing a dangerous solo game. I wondered if the deaths of his two brothers – Hector drowned in the Nile, and Nicanor succumbing to fever in Ariea – had affected his judgement.

If I became king, I knew the path I must follow. First, make peace with Bessus. That he had murdered Darius was nothing to me. Then, draw our borders back to the Tigris, or even the Euphrates. These bleak eastern satrapies held nothing for us except savage tribesmen and constant insurrection. Like Philip, I would secure a frontier with a diplomatic marriage. Bessus must have an eligible daughter or sister. Electra would not be pleased, but the Kings of Macedon had always been polygamous, and she was a sensible woman. Our son, Arrhabaeus, would be heir to the throne, not any son born from a dutiful coupling with some barbarian woman.

Mercenaries and volunteers could garrison the east. As soon as the frontier was secure, I would lead our men back to Macedon. There was much to be done at home. That was where our interests lay. It was madness to campaign in Bactria, while the Illyrians, Epirotes, Getae, and other tribes remained unconquered, and able to threaten our homes and families. The treasures won from Persia would last for generations. Our armies must march north and west. For the safety of Macedon our empire must reach to the Danube and the Adriatic.

The sun had risen, and Copreus still slumbered drunkenly. After a time, I rummaged through the stores in the wagon, and found some bread and cheese.

In the light of day, a hideous thought wormed its way into my mind. What if Alexander had sent Philotas? There was no plot to kill the King, but one to rid him of a troublesome rival? If I were lured into an overt act of treason, Antipater could have no grounds for objection when news arrived of my execution.

About midday, Copreus woke, and went to get us some food. When he returned, we ate, but did not speak. Watching him closely, I could not work out if his ill-favoured face showed guilt, or just a hangover.

The afternoon wore on, and I reached no decision. All I wanted was to return to Electra and our son. I did not care how. Except to take no action was a decision in itself.

At dusk, we ate again. Afterwards, Copreus stomped off without any explanation. For a moment, I almost called out and begged him to stay. With him gone, I had no options. But, as he vanished into the gloom, I realised it was probably too late already.

Early in the evening, a squadron of cavalry passed heading out of camp on a night manoeuvre. The Mounted Scouts might not have the status of the Companion Cavalry, but they were equally well trained.

Much later, about the end of the third watch, they came for me. I must have fallen asleep. I heard the tread of their boots before I saw them: a file of *hypaspists*. The junior officer who climbed up into the wagon was unknown to me; the soldiers likewise. Until his death Philotas' brother Nicanor had commanded the *hypaspists*. Perhaps this file belonged to the thousand men commanded by my nephew Amyntas. The officer had keys, and unlocked both chain and manacles.

I pulled on a clean tunic and my boots. Inconsequentially, I wondered if Leonnatus or anyone had kept my white sword-belt after my arrest.

'Quickly,' the officer said. 'They are waiting.'

It felt strange to move unfettered after so long. My arms were unnaturally light. The manacles had left callouses on my wrists.

The *hypaspists* formed up on either side, and we marched through the dark camp to the royal pavilion. The wind had finally dropped, and the air had the first chill of autumn. The night was still and quiet. Somewhere a dog barked, and a woman hushed a crying infant.

More *hypaspists* were on guard in front of the tent. The officer led me inside.

The antechamber was not empty. Alexander was waiting; Leonnatus with him.

My first thought was not *this is the end*, but how short Alexander was next to my kinsman.

'Why?' Alexander said.

'Because you have changed.'

'The world has changed.' Alexander sounded sad. 'Unfortunately, you have not.'

In the main chamber, behind the hangings, a man shouted in satisfaction.

'Does Antipater know?' Alexander asked.

'No.'

Craterus stuck his head through the curtain. 'He has confessed.'

Alexander signed for the officer to bring me.

Inside, three men stood around a table. Their arms and chests were spattered with gore, as if they had been working in an abattoir. There was a nauseating stench of blood and burnt flesh. A figure was tied to the table. Philotas was barely recognisable; swollen with bruises, seamed with cuts, his flesh singed.

Craterus, Hephaestion, and Coenus had tortured Philotas with their own hands. They still held the knives and heated irons. Coenus was Philotas' brother-in-law.

'Has the Lyncestian confessed?' Hephaestion asked Alexander.

'Yes.'

'Did he name others?'

'No.'

'Antipater?'

'No.'

'He will under torture.' Hephaestion evidently relished the prospect of inflicting further pain on a defenceless victim.

Alexander shook his head. 'There is no need. He has no secrets. We have read all his correspondence. Copreus swears no one has visited him in the cart, except Leonnatus here. Let him stand trial before the army.'

CHAPTER THIRTY-THREE

Autumn 330 BC

THE NEXT DAY, BACK in the wagon, nothing had changed: the same manacles and chain, the same food, still Copreus the jailor. But, of course, everything had changed. The trial would be tomorrow at dawn.

I wrote Electra a letter. Knowing it would be read by Alexander, I confessed my guilt. Philotas had divulged his odious plot to kill the King and, my thoughts confused by long imprisonment, I had treacherously kept quiet. I knew that this would come as a terrible shock to both her and her father. They would find it hard to believe, as their loyalty to Alexander was unshakable. If Antipater were with the army the next day, he would vote for condemnation. I had no defence. No god had put this in my mind. Either it had been the work of some evil *daemon*, or suffering had left me deranged. My only consolations were that Alexander had survived, and that in my insanity I had not attempted to involve anyone else in my ruin.

Rereading the letter, I was uncertain if it was enough to ensure her safety, and that of our son, and her father. In a postscript, now I was restored to my senses, I urged her to forget me, and to bring up young Arrhabaeus to faithfully serve Alexander and his successors. The days of an independent Lyncestis were over. The world had changed.

I could not bring myself to write to my mother in distant Lebaea.

The day dragged slowly. Copreus was silent. I tried not to dwell on the choice I had made, tried not to think about tomorrow. But I was unsuccessful. Invidious Hope kept creeping back. A nobleman accused of treason is entitled to an open trial before the Macedonians under arms. His fetters are struck off, his arms and uniform returned. After the King has read out the indictment, the nobleman can make a speech in his defence. It was not unknown for the assembly to go against the wishes of the King, and to clash their spears on their shields to acquit the accused, and find him not guilty. I could dwell on the battles and sieges in which I had fought with distinction: Chaeronea, Thebes, the Granicus, Halicarnassus, Issus. My silence about Philotas was a temporary insanity caused by my brutal confinement. In the long months since my arrest I had longed for nothing other than a trial to prove my innocence. I could appeal to the emotions of my fellow Macedonians, my comrades in arms. In Egypt, far from trying to kill Alexander, I had tried to reason with him. Like all true Macedonians, I had wanted him to cast out his servile barbarian courtiers, his foreign habits, to remain one of us, and to lead us home to our families.

In the evening, Leonnatus came. He brought a flask of wine, and for a time we drank in silence.

Eventually, I spoke. 'Will Philotas get a trial?'

'That is his right.'

'He can't walk.'

'He will be carried there.'

'The Macedonians will know he has been tortured.'

'It will make no difference.'

I took a swig of wine. 'Philotas has friends, if he is executed, they will fear for their own lives. Some will flee to his father. Parmenion has an army and the treasury.'

'They will not get there,' Leonnatus said. 'The Mounted Scouts put a cordon round the camp yesterday evening.'

'Sooner or later, Parmenion will hear of the death of his last son.'

Leonnatus reached for the wine. He looked old and careworn. 'Orders have already been sent by racing camel. They will be in Ecbatana in eleven days. Sitalkes and the other generals will deal with Parmenion.'

'*Deal with?*'

'Their orders are to kill him.'

'Will they obey?'

'The messengers have the confession of Philotas.'

'Alexander will stoop to the assassination of his father's oldest friend, the general who commanded the left in all his own victories?'

'It is necessary. Otherwise there will be civil war.' Leonnatus gazed off into the distance. 'That is the great fear.'

Something very cold lodged in my heart.

'If the Macedonians turn on each other, all our subjects will rise against us,' Leonnatus said.

'Just tell me what you have come to say.'

Leonnatus took a deep breath, unhappy at his own role in this. 'In the morning, if you say nothing in your defence, assassins will not be sent to Macedon to Antipater and your family.'

And that was when Hope finally escaped from Pandora's jar, and flew off after all the other evils in the world.

EPILOGUE

Summer 323 BC

ALEXANDER IS ON HIS deathbed. Already the whole of Babylon is full of the sounds of mourning. The place reeks of incense. Today the soldiers filed through his bedroom to say a final farewell. Perhaps my kinsman Alexander of Lyncestis is taking his revenge.

Eavesdroppers hear no good of themselves, so my old nurse used to say. Reading this manuscript has proved her right. Not one word of thanks for all the times I risked myself visiting him in the wagon. Instead complaints: Leonnatus has not come; Leonnatus has not brought more books or papyri. Apparently, I am slow and uncultured and thoughtless, my lifestyle is ostentatious, and my bluff demeanour is irritating. He even drags up a mistake I made as a youth in a long forgotten skirmish in Lyncestis. Yet I have always loved Xander.

After the trial of Philotas, and the execution of Parmenion, we had two years hard campaigning in Bactria and the eastern satrapies. Of course we won in the end. The Macedonians are invincible, when we are united. And that is what worries me now that Alexander will soon be dead.

Alexander got worse in those two years. There was a drinking party in some dusty place. Flatterers, mainly Greeks, sought to praise Alexander by belittling Philip. Cleitus the Black would not sit silent: Alexander owed everything to Philip. Alexander was drunk and furious. They yelled insults at each other. I was one of those who bundled Cleitus out of the room. We left him outside to sober up, but he burst back into the room, shouted some more about Alexander's real father, about Zeus not being his sire, about his victories being won by the Macedonians. This time Alexander snatched a *sarissa* from one of the guards, and ran it through the old Companion, who had saved his life at the Granicus. As soon as it was done, it was regretted. We had to get the *sarissa* off Alexander before he turned it on himself. For days Alexander tried to starve himself alone in his tent. The army was thousands of miles from home, surrounded by enemies. In the end the Macedonians declared Cleitus had been a traitor, and Alexander was persuaded to eat.

Another drinking party in another remote place that has slipped my memory. Alexander wanted us all to perform *proskynesis*, to grovel in adoration before him as if we were Persians. Some, Hephaestion to the fore, debased themselves. Callisthenes the Greek was the first who was seen to refuse. Like my kinsman, I had never had any time for the historian; not until then. Alexander abandoned the attempt, but never forgave Callisthenes. Some time later, a squad of Royal Pages entered into a conspiracy to kill the King. To me, their motives were obscure. Callisthenes was their tutor, and took the blame. Alexander never forgave being crossed. Callisthenes was arrested and, like my kinsman, was kept chained in a cart. The Greek died in the cart; of illness or starvation or poison, no one was sure.

Before we left the eastern satrapies Alexander married the daughter of a local chieftain. Nothing wrong in that; Philip had taken several barbarian wives to secure the allegiance of their fathers. But Philip had bred acceptable heirs: first Arrhidaeus, until Olympias' poison robbed him of his mind, then Alexander. None of us were happy that some child of Roxane might one day become our king.

Two years in the eastern satrapies was succeeded by two years campaigning in India. Yes, we won the great battle of the Hydaspes, defeated Porus and all his elephants. But what ground us down was the endless marching in the continual rain, our uniforms rotting, our weapons rusting, poisonous snakes everywhere, men dying from disease, always heading further east. Finally, at the Hyphasis River the men had had enough. Coenus was their spokesman. They would go no further, demanded that Alexander led them home. Again Alexander sulked in his tent. This time the Macedonians were inflexible. Alexander announced we would return.

Coenus died shortly afterwards. Almost certainly from the unhealthy climate, but there were sinister rumours.

To get home Alexander, of course, insisted we had to travel south down the great river to the ocean. That involved more hard fighting. At the storm of a town the men hung back. Alexander mounted a siege ladder himself. I was one of those at his heels. That shamed the men into action. But, when they all tried to climb at once, the ladders broke. Four of us were stranded on the battlements: Alexander, me, Abreas, and Peucestas. Silhouetted there, we were a target for every missile. We jumped down into the town. Abreas was killed. An arrow hit Alexander. It went through his armour, deep into his chest. Somehow Peucestas and I covered him with our shields until the rest of the army broke through the defences. The soldiers killed every living thing in the town. Alexander survived, but was never quite the same. His breath had bubbled up through the open wound.

Alexander left me with the Agrianes, some archers and cavalry, as well as some mercenaries, to assist Apollophanes, his satrap, to settle affairs of a tribe called the Oreitae. As soon as the main army left, they rose in revolt. Apollophanes was killed, but we slaughtered some six thousand of them. Our own losses were trifling. Later, Alexander awarded me a gold crown for my campaign. The problem with the Indians, like the Bactrians, no matter how many times you defeat them in battle, they never know when they are beaten. Xander was right, we should never have tried to conquer them.

For the homeward journey, Craterus took several battalions of the phalanx, all the elephants we had acquired, and the heavy baggage back on an inland route that to some extent retraced our steps. Inspired by rivalry with the god Dionysus, who was said to have gone that way, Alexander went via the coastal route, across the Gedrosian Desert. It was a terrible mistake. Unable to find food or water, under a relentless sun, wading through soft sand, then hit by flash floods, the men died in droves. None of the pack animals, and next to none of the camp followers made it out alive. Fortunately, when the Oreitae were crushed, I was ordered to follow a gentler, inland road.

Many of Alexander's satraps and generals never expected him to return alive from India. They had been ruling, not like independent kings, but as lawless tyrants. Sitalkes, Xander's friend, was among them. He had reverted to his Thracian origins, and had devoted himself to theft and raping freeborn virgins. Sitalkes was summoned to court, and executed. He was just one among many. Alexander's childhood friend Harpalus, who had treated the treasury as if it were his own, once again fled west. This time he took several thousand talents and a troop of mercenaries. It did him no good. Having failed to find sanctuary in Athens, Harpalus sailed to Crete, where he was murdered.

At Susa, Alexander ordered ninety-one of his Companions to marry eastern noble women. I was given a docile enough Persian. When Alexander is dead, I will send her away. Very few, if any, of these marriages will outlive the King. Macedonians like to marry their own sort.

At Ecbatana, after prolonged drinking, Hephaestion contracted a fever. His doctor put him on a strict diet. As soon as the doctor had left to go to the theatre, Hephaestion ate a boiled fowl, washed down with a great quantity of wine. His closest friend and lover was dead by the time Alexander reached his bedside. Alexander's grief was immoderate. Everyone had to offer sacrifices to Hephaestion as if he were a divine hero; even those like Craterus who had hated him. A massive tomb was decreed for the new semi-divine being. The unfortunate doctor was crucified.

There were many portents and omens warning Alexander against entering Babylon – Chaldean ravings, and ravens dropping dead at his feet. He tried sacrifices to appease the gods, and went in anyway. Huge dockyards were being constructed in the city. Babylon was to be the base for his next expedition to conquer Arabia. Even now many of us were not destined for home. Some thought Alexander intended to make Babylon the capital of his new empire.

Inside the city there were more dire forebodings of death. A passing lunatic wandered into the palace, and seated himself on the empty throne. It was a sign howled the sobbing eunuchs.

One day, when Alexander was boating, a gust of wind blew off his Persian diadem. It snagged on some reeds. A sailor dived into the river. To keep the thing dry as he swam back, he tied it round his head. Alexander had him flogged, some say executed. It was not the behaviour of a Macedonian king, but nor was wearing a diadem.

In the spring the Thessalians hold a festival for the death of Heracles. Of course Heracles did not die like a mortal man, but ascended to Olympus. Medius held a drinking party. I was not invited. There were twenty guests. Alexander toasted each, drinking from the Cup of Heracles, an Argead heirloom that held a vast quantity of wine. That night he felt a fever coming on, and slept by the bath in the palace. The following day, although still unwell, he was able to carry out his duties. But the next day he had to be carried out to perform the morning sacrifices. Today, when the soldiers filed through, he was unable to speak or move. Only his eyes showed he was still alive.

All the great men with the army are here: Perdiccas, Meleager, Ptolemy, Menander, Peucestas, me. We are all waiting, and watching each other. It will not be long now. When the news of Alexander's death reaches them, other eyes will turn to Babylon and the empty throne: Antipater and Olympias in Macedon, Craterus somewhere in Cilicia, Antigonus the one-eyed in Paphlagonia. Alexander gave his signet ring to Perdiccas, but when we asked him to whom he left the empire, he whispered, 'To the strongest.'

There is another story. Alexander sent Craterus to replace Antipater as Regent of Macedon. Antipater was summoned to Babylon. Fearing the fate of Sitlakes and the others, the old general sent his son Cassander with the excuse that it was too dangerous for the Regent to leave Macedon until Craterus arrived with the ten thousand veterans he was leading home. Antipater had a point. Zopyrion, the *strategos* of Thrace, had lost an army of thirty thousand, and his own life, beyond the Danube at the hands of the Getae. The defeat had encouraged Seuthes, the brother of Sitalkes, to lead the Thracians into revolt. Yet Cassander was a bad choice. Antipater's son and Alexander had always hated each other. A bad choice, unless the other story is true.

Antipater gave Cassander a poison. It was so strong it would eat through any container except the hoof of a mule. In Babylon, Cassander gave it to his brother Iolaus. At Medius' feast, Iolaus put it in the Cup of Heracles. The first guest Alexander toasted was the nephew of Cleitus the Black. As soon as he drank, Alexander cried out as if he had been struck in the liver by an arrow. Perhaps Alexander of Lyncestis finally had his revenge.

My kinsman died like a man. At his trial, as is our custom, he appeared before the army unshackled, wearing his uniform, the cloak of a Companion round his shoulders, and with a spear in his hand. I had given him back the white sword-belt he won all those years ago in Lyncestis. After the King had denounced him, he had the right to speak in his own defence. For a moment I thought he would betray his word of the night before. He mumbled something like, *These are no ignoble men, these kings of ours*, then he drew himself up and was silent. The first javelin hit him in the chest. My hand threw it. I owed him that – a quick death.

Now I will keep my side of our pact.

My kinsman was wrong. He was not entirely betrayed. I paid Copreus well. The jailor handed over Xander's letters to Alexander, but never revealed the existence of this manuscript.

For a large sum of money a Chaldean priest will seal these rolls of papyri in a waterproof lead chest. They will be placed in a chasm under one of the temples here in Babylon. A curse protects the place. Should anyone disturb its sanctity, a terrible plague will be released over the earth. The eastern magic may be enough to preserve the memory of my kinsman and friend – Alexander of Lyncestis, the Shadow King.

HISTORICAL AFTERWORD

The Shadow King is a novel, and should be read as such. However I have tried to stick as far as possible to what seems to me the most likely and plausible reconstruction of the history. Except, as detailed below, I have deliberately played with the life of Alexander of Lyncestis.

Macedonia

The excavation of the tomb of Philip II by Manolis Andronicos in the 1970s sparked a renaissance of Macedonian studies: M. Andronicos, *Vergina: The Royal Tombs* (Athens, 1984).

The most comprehensive overview is *A History of Macedonia* in three volumes: volume I (*Historical Geography and Prehistory*) by N. G. L. Hammond (Oxford, 1972); volume II (550–336 BC) by N. G. L. Hammond, and G. T. Griffith (Oxford, 1979); volume III (336–167 BC) by N. G. L. Hammond, and F. W. Walbank (Oxford, 1988). More concise are Eugene N. Borza, *In the Shadow of Olympus: The Emergence of Macedon* (Princeton, 1990); and R. Malcolm Errington, *A History of Macedonia* (Berkeley, Los Angeles, and Oxford, 1990).

The many entries in four recent collections are invaluable: J. Roisman (ed.), *Brill's Companion to Alexander the Great* (Leiden, and Boston, 2003); Joseph Roisman, and Ian Worthington (eds.), *A Companion to Ancient Macedonia* (Malden, 2010);

Robin Lane Fox (ed.), *Brill's Companion to Ancient Macedon* (Leiden, 2011); and W. Heckel, J. Heinrichs, S. Müller, and F. Pownall (eds.), *Lexicon of Argead Makedonia* (Berlin, 2020). Also indispensable for sorting out individuals is W. Heckel, *Who's Who in the Age of Alexander the Great* (Malden, 2006).

Heracles to Alexander the Great: Treasures from the Royal Capital of Macedon, a Hellenic Kingdom in the Age of Democracy, edited by Angeliki Kottradini and Susan Walker (Oxford, 2011), a catalogue of an exhibition held in the Ashmolean Museum, 7 April – 29 August 2011, makes an excellent introduction to visual culture.

The modern scholarship is surveyed by M. B. Hatzopoulos, *Ancient Macedonia* (Berlin and Boston, 2020).

Philip of Macedon

The two main sources for Philip II are Diodorus Siculus, book 16 (translated by Charles L. Sherman, Cambridge, Mass., 1952, and C. Bradford Welles, Cambridge, Mass., 1963); and Justin, books 7–8 (translated by J. C. Yardley, Atlanta, 1994).

Two enjoyable modern biographies are N. G. L. Hammond, *Philip of Macedon* (London, 1994); and I. Worthington, *Philip II of Macedonia* (New Haven, 2008). Another excellent place to start is Adrian Goldsworthy, *Philip & Alexander: Kings and Conquerors* (London, 2020).

Alexander the Great

For Alexander, Diodorus Siculus (book 17), and Justin (books 11–12 are joined by Arrian, *Anabasis* (translated by A. de Selincourt, Harmondsworth, rev. ed., 1971); Quintus Curtius Rufus, *The History of Alexander* (translated by J. Yardley, Harmondsworth, 1984); and Plutarch's *Life of Alexander* (translated by Ian

Scott-Kilvert, Harmondsworth, 1973), and *On the Fortune or the Virtue of Alexander* (translated by F. C. Babbitt, Cambridge, Mass., 1936).

Robin Lane Fox's enthralling and digressive biography *Alexander the Great* (London, 1973), a Christmas gift from my godfather, first kindled my interest in ancient history as a schoolboy. There are endless retellings of the life of Alexander. Among the most pleasurable are Paul Cartledge, *Alexander the Great: The Truth behind the Man* (London, 2004); Ian Worthington, *Alexander the Great: Man and God* (Harlow, 2004); and, for the first part of his life, Alex Rowson, *The Young Alexander: The Making of Alexander the Great* (London, 2022). The clearest, and most compelling recreation of his campaigns is A. B. Bosworth, *Conquest and Empire: The Reign of Alexander the Great* (Cambridge, 1988). Illuminating thematic studies are Claude Mossé, *Alexander: Destiny and Myth* (Eng. tr., Baltimore, 2004); and Edward M. Anson, *Alexander the Great: Themes and Issues* (London, 2013).

The Macedonian Army

Introductions are provided by G. T. Griffith in Hammond and Griffith, *op. cit.*, pp.405–411; and N. V. Sekunda in Roisman and Worthington, *op. cit.*, pp.446–71. Although perhaps the best place to start is Duncan Head, *Armies of the Macedonian and Punic Wars, 359 BC to 146 BC* (Goring-by-Sea, 1982) with superb line drawings by Ian Heath. Specific aspects are investigated by J. F. C. Fuller, *The Generalship of Alexander the Great* (London, 1958); and Donald W. Engels, *Alexander the Great and the Logistics of the Macedonian Army* (Berkeley, and Los Angeles, 1978). For specialists, there is much to think about in David Karunanithy, *The Macedonian War Machine: Neglected*

Aspects of the Armies of Philip, Alexander and the Successors, 359–281 BC (Barnsley, 2013); and Christopher Matthew, *An Invincible Beast: Understanding the Hellenistic Pike-Phalanx at War* (Barnsley, 2015).

Macedonian Women

Understanding in this area is shaped by the many works of Elizabeth Donnelly Carney, who gives a lucid introduction in Roisman and Worthington, *op. cit.*, pp.409–27. Particularly useful for this novel was her book *Eurydice and the Birth of Macedonian Power* (New York, 2019).

Alexander of Lyncestis

The only study that I know devoted to him is E. D. Carney, 'Alexander the Lyncestian: the Disloyal Opposition', *GRBS* 21.1 (1980), 23–33. Useful for Upper Macedonia and the Bacchiad dynasty are Hammond, *A History of Macedonia I*, pp.102–105; Hammond and Griffith, *A History of Macedonia II*, pp.14–22; and A. B. Bosworth, 'Philip II and Upper Macedonia', *CQ* 65.1 (1971), 93–105.

In *The Shadow King*, to place Alexander of Lyncestis with Alexander the Great at Mieza, I have made the former probably rather younger than he was in reality. In antiquity there were two (Arrian, 1.25.1–10; Diodorus Siculus, 17.32.1–2), perhaps three (Plutarch, *Life of Alexander* 12; Polyaenus, *Stratagems* 8.40), different versions of the fate of Alexander of Lyncestis (my vagueness here is for those readers who, like me, often turn to the endnotes first!). I have drawn on all of them to create my own.

Other Peoples: Illyrians, Thracians, Persians, and Greeks

Illyrians – A good first port of call is John Wilkes, *The Illyrians* (Oxford, 1992).

Thracians – R. F. Hoddinott, *The Thracians* (London, 1987) offers a general overview, and Chris Webber, *The Gods of Battle: The Thracians at War, 1500 BC–AD 150* (Barnsley, 2011) looks at their armies.

Persians – There are several good recent introductions, including Amélie Kuhrt, *The Ancient Near East, c.3000–330 BC*, volume II (London, and New York, 1995), 647–701; Josef Wiesehöfer, *Ancient Persia* (New York, 1996), pp. 5–101; and Maria Brosius, *The Persians: An Introduction* (London, and New York, 2006), pp. 6–78. A well-illustrated study of their forces is Duncan Head, *The Achaemenid Persian Army* (Stockport, 1992).

Greeks – The Greeks are always a special case – we know far more about them, and there are many more modern studies. A splendid, and wide-ranging, place to start is Paul Cartledge, *Ancient Greece: A Very Short Introduction* (Oxford, and New York, 2011). Simon Hornblower, *The Greek World, 479–323 BC* (4th ed., London, and New York) covers the relevant period.

The armies of all these peoples are included in Duncan Head, *Armies of the Macedonian and Punic Wars, 359 BC to 146 BC* (Goring-by-Sea, 1982).

Quotes

It is impossible to overestimate the importance of Homer in the thought world of the Macedonians. All the citations of the *Iliad* are from the translation of Richmond Lattimore (Chicago, 1951), sometimes slightly adapted.

Alexander the Great was not the only Macedonian influenced by Euripides. In Chapter Three when characters quote *The Bacchae* it is in the translation of John Davie (London, 2005).

If you enjoyed *The Shadow King,* why not join the
HARRY SIDEBOTTOM READERS' CLUB?

When you sign up you'll receive an exclusive short story,
THE MARK OF DEATH, plus news about upcoming books and
exclusive behind-the-scenes material. To join, simply visit
bit.ly/HarrySidebottom

Keep reading for a letter from the author . . .

Hello!

Thank you very much for picking up *The Shadow King*.

In a sense, it is a return to my roots in the Classical world. When I was a child I was lucky that one of my godfathers was the manager of a bookshop in Cambridge. Every Christmas and birthday he gave me hardback books. When I was sixteen I received Robin Lane Fox's biography of Alexander the Great. It is a big book, with many pages of scholarly endnotes; rather daunting to me as a teenager. After a few months, I thought I would pretend to be grown up (a game I am still playing all these years later), and started reading. Up until then my interests in history revolved round the Napoleonic Wars and World War Two. Robin's book inspired a new interest: ancient Macedon, Greece and Persia. It made me want to spend my life reading and writing similar books. Studying Ancient History and Archaeology at Lancaster University, one of my tutors, David Shotter, converted me to ancient Rome. My Master's and Doctoral theses were on Rome, as has been the majority of my publications, both the novels and the non-fiction. But for years I taught Alexander at various universities, and the lure of Macedon always remained. Finally, a few years ago, I knew it was time to return.

There have been many fictional retellings of the story of Alexander, the charismatic young king who, against the odds, conquered the mighty Persian empire, and led an army to India. It is the greatest ever tale of military adventure. One trilogy stands head and shoulders above the others – those by Mary Renault. In *The Persian Boy*, perhaps her finest novel, she recreated not one but two lost worlds, as Alexander and the Macedonians are observed through the eyes of Bagoas, the Persian eunuch. In *The Shadow King* I take a different approach. I have long been fascinated by the dynasties of the great barons of upland Macedonia, such as Lyncestis, Orestis, and Elimeia. Until the reign of Philip II, the father of Alexander, these were independent rulers, who only occasionally acknowledged allegiance to the Argead kings, the royal house of the lowlands. Yet members of these dynasties formed the core of Alexander's friends and generals. In *The Shadow King* I explore the tensions of their position – torn between adherence to the old customs to Macedon, where the king was a first among equals, and the riches and glory of the new empire created by Alexander, where the king was becoming a divine monarch. Alexander's companions were riven with murderous rivalries, their loyalty contingent. The threat of treason, inspired by ambition and Persian gold, or honour and principle, was ever present. As they conquered the world, disaster was never more than a sword stroke away.

Alexander of Lyncestis, the protagonist of *The Shadow King*, was the first to acclaim his namesake king, but he was never safe. Others – Persians and Greeks, as well as Macedonians – saw him as a rival for the throne. For six years, as the Macedonians fought their way East, his life hung by a thread. Alexander of Lyncestis was *The Shadow King*.

If you would like to hear about my books, you can visit **bit.ly/HarrySidebottom**, where you can become part of the my Readers' Club. It takes only a few moments to sign up, there are no catches or costs, and you will receive a free Ballista short story, a prequel to the *Warrior of Rome* series, not available anywhere else.

Bonnier Zaffre will keep your data private and confidential, and it will never be passed to a third party. We won't spam you with lots of emails, just get in touch now and then with news about my books, and you can unsubscribe any time you want.

If you would like to get involved in the wider conversation about my books, please do review *The Shadow King* on Amazon, or Goodreads, or any other e-store, on your own blog or social media, or talk about it with friends, family, or book groups! Sharing your thoughts helps other readers, and I always enjoy hearing what people experience from my writing.

If you have any questions, or would just like to get in touch, please contact me via my Facebook page – www.facebook.com/Harry.Sidebottom-608697059226497

Thank you again for reading this story, and I very much hope you share my excitement with *The Shadow King*.

All the best,

Harry Sidebottom

ACKNOWLEDGMENTS

I N EVERY BOOK I thank the same people, but it is no less heartfelt.

Family: my wife, Lisa, my sons Tom and Jack, my mother Frances, and my aunt Terry.

Friends: my agent Jim Gill, my editor Ben Willis, Peter and Rachel Cosgrove, Jeremy and Katie Habberley, Jeremy Tinton, Jack Ringer and Sanda Haines, Ben Kane, Peter Hill and Sara Fox, Donna Leon, and Lynne and Ernie Moss.